"Stephen Russell Payne has emerged as a new voice in Vermont's impressive pantheon of creative writers, and a powerful one. His novel, *Cliff Walking*, is a dramatic story of suspense, love, and redemption, written with clarity, passion, and great sympathy for, and understanding of, all aspects of human nature.

"*Ties That Bind Us*, his collection of stories, takes us far off the interstates, ski slopes, and upscale bed-and-breakfasts and microbreweries to the backroads, backwoods, and half-abandoned former mill towns of a Vermont most visitors to the Green Mountain State don't know exists. His wonderfully independent-minded characters are the very last of a breed, whose like will not be seen again. These stories, written with clear-eyed affection, gentle humor, and great expertise, remind me of *Country of the Pointed Firs*."

— HOWARD FRANK MOSHER

"In *Cliff Walking*, what Payne gives us isn't a plotless 'literary' novel, but a warm and touching love story full of suspense and conflict, likely to have wide popular appeal. Payne is in top form."

— X. J. KENNEDY

"Peopled with characters that openly disdain the postcard Vermont, the stories of Stephen Russell Payne plumb the depths of rural hardship, farm life, and small dreams. Thanks to Payne's unerring eye for detail and ear for voice, these stories turn modest lives into treasure, by revealing the tenderness that makes them possible."

— STEPHEN KIERNAN

"Stephen Russell Payne's short story collection, *Ties That Bind Us*, is a spectacular debut by a writer who knows his characters, and the frailties of human beings caught up in the mortal coil; he does it all with grace, depth, intimacy, and at times a sly sense of humor. I love these stories."

— ERNEST HEBERT

"No one writes with as much passion and insight about northern Vermont as Stephen Russell Payne. With the meticulousness of a surgeon, and the lyricism of a poet, Payne captures the tenacity and honesty of the denizens of the Green Mountain State's small towns and villages. Reading Payne is like a visit from a good old friend. His tales are always infused with equal measure of humor, wisdom, and love."

— JENNIFER FINNEY BOYLAN

"Stephen Russell Payne's short story collection, *Ties That Bind Us*, is a terrific piece of work. His stories bring to life—not in the voice of an omniscient narrator—but in the voices of those living them, Vermont's hardscrabble past. Payne leads us into an earlier Vermont, replete with durable characters, both in their own lives and in our memory."

— BILL SCHUBART

YOU WERE ALWAYS THERE

ALSO BY STEPHEN RUSSELL PAYNE

Cliff Walking — A Novel

Life on a Cliff — A Novel

Riding My Guitar — The Rick Norcross Story

Ties That Bind Us — A Collection of Vermont Short Stories

Boston, Vermont — First Poems of Stephen Russell Payne

YOU WERE ALWAYS THERE

A NOVEL

STEPHEN RUSSELL PAYNE

CEDAR LEDGE PUBLISHING

You Were Always There
First Edition August 2022

Author photo by Natalie Stultz
Cover and interior design by Carrie Cook
Cover background photo: Connie Fotakis Meeker

The text of this book was set in Adobe Caslon.

Published in the United States of America by Cedar Ledge Publishing
St. Albans, Vermont 05478

ISBN: 978-1-7322599-4-2
LCCN: 2022911902

Printed in the United States of America

For information, permissions, and appearances, please visit
www.StephenRussellPayne.com,
or Facebook at: Stephen Russell Payne, Vermont Author | Facebook

Somewhere in time, I knew you well
But I can't remember when
We shared a secret, I'll never tell
Can you believe that this is happening again?

Familiar voice, familiar eyes
You're a part of this heart of mine
And as sure as I'm fallin' in love with you now
I have loved you somewhere in time

Somewhere in time
When the world stood still
I said I'd always love you
Now I believe I will

From "Somewhere in Time"
by David Mallett

Dedicated to
Marietta, with love—'Soulmates forever'
and to
America's great folksingers
whose spirits, words, and music
have always entertained and enlightened,
cajoled and comforted us
on our collective journeys

CHAPTER ONE
GREENSBORO, VERMONT - MAY 1970

L UKE TIGHTLY GRIPPED THE STEERING WHEEL AS HIS delivery truck rumbled off the pavement onto the dirt road leading to Caspian Lake. The heavily laden flatbed bounced hard over mud-filled potholes, the road pocked as if a bomber had strafed it. Wired to the dash, Luke's 8-track swung back and forth as "Proud Mary" played over the scratchy speaker. He was hurrying, because his boss, Trace Miller, owner of the local sawmill, insisted the custom-cut posts and beams be delivered by Saturday noon, and it was already after eleven. At nineteen, Luke was Trace's most reliable driver, and he wanted to keep it that way.

Luke glanced at the order sheet clipped to the dash. The delivery was going to John Clements, a federal judge from downcountry, and from the plans Luke had seen, this new cabin looked more suited to an upscale ski area than the shore of a quiet Vermont lake. There was considerable controversy surrounding Clements building a fancy summer place on the eastern shoreline, a favorite fishing spot for Native Americans and generations of locals. Some folks had railed against a city slicker buying up another unspoiled piece of Vermont, while others were all for it, knowing the construction would bring good-paying work to the area. Luke figured it was a blessing his hot-headed father, Elijah, was no longer around to witness what was happening.

The concern that weighed heaviest on Luke's mind, however, was when his draft notice would arrive. With his low lottery number, and with so many soldiers coming home from Vietnam in flag-draped caskets, the war was a constant worry. Even though he and his mother didn't have a television, Luke had seen film clips from the war in the display window of the local RCA Victor store. He and his buddies would congregate on the sidewalk and watch images of sweat-soaked men fighting and dying in the jungle, the injured carried on litters to waiting helicopters. Despite his family's tradition of serving in the military, Luke struggled to accept what he assumed was his approaching fate.

It was the middle of May during an unusually cold, wet spring, and Luke felt his front tires pop through thin plates of ice on the road. Trying to push the war out of his mind, Luke hit a deep pothole, causing a couple of paperbacks to slide across the dash. He kicked a bottle of cola from under his foot, double-clutched, and downshifted into second gear. The truck's engine strained to hold back the load as he descended toward the shimmering lake, the scent of pine coming through his open window.

Luke squinted at the directions on the delivery sheet. "Left past McCaffery's barn, quarter mile toward the lake, bear right along the shore, and go to the end."

Despite the rough road leading past Jed McCaffery's dilapidated dairy barn, Luke kept his speed up. The chains holding the wood squeaked as they rubbed against the shifting load of hemlock. The corner at McCaffery's had turned into a mud bog, and as Luke laid into it, the truck slid sideways. Cranking hard on the wheel, he just made the corner onto Tetreault's logging road where he followed a fresh set of car tracks past an old horse barn, its hayloft door hanging on a rusty hinge. Soon he arrived at a clearing beside the lake.

Luke remembered fishing in that spot as a young boy, with his father. Hot July afternoons in a leaky rowboat with a wiry man who drank longneck Narragansets as he pulled in yellow-striped perch. When he tired of fishing, Elijah would pull out a harmonica and play old military tunes as Luke rowed them home. As much as Luke enjoyed those times, the specter of his dad's tainted World War II military service was ever-present.

His father had fought valiantly and suffered grave injuries in the Battle of the Bulge, but was later caught trading in contraband, and came home with a dishonorable discharge. Luke's family thought his father had been taken advantage of by upper ranks involved with the illegal ring. Nonetheless, after the war he was spurned by many townsfolk, which was painful and embarrassing for Luke and his mother. Luke was motivated to make up for his father's failings by serving his country honorably. Even though Elijah was gone, Luke wanted to make him proud.

As Luke approached the clearing, soft gravel gave way under the weight of the truck. Catching a glimpse of something shiny, he glanced over and saw a bright red Mustang convertible parked at the edge of the clearing, top down, a blond-haired girl sitting cross-legged on the hood. Even through his mud-splattered window, Luke appreciated a brightness in her eyes, a mischievousness in her smile.

"Over there!" the girl yelled, pointing to a clear-cut area beyond the Mustang.

Distracted, Luke felt the truck's rear wheels skid sideways, the deep-lugged tires churning hard through the mud. Knowing the girl was watching him, he pushed the accelerator to the floor, straining to control the steering wheel. The motor roared as the load shifted, and the truck lurched into the ditch.

Luke jammed on the brakes and the engine stalled. "Shit!" He hit the steering wheel, rolled down his window, and looked over at the girl, who had slid off the hood of the Mustang. Sunbeams streaming through cedars illuminated her hair with a soft, radiant light. Neil Diamond sang "Sweet Caroline" on her car radio.

Luke hopped out of the cab and looked the situation over. It was worse than he had thought. The rear end was marooned, the right front wheel up to its axle in mud.

"Need some help?" the girl called over to him.

He looked at her a bit sheepishly. "Doesn't look too good, does it?"

She walked toward him, carefully stepping over the ruts. It was hard not to stare.

"So, this is my dad's fancy post-and-beam cabin?"

"Part of it," Luke replied. "And it's about to fall off the truck."

"I see that."

Amazing eyes, perfect posture. Her long blond hair fell over the collar of an expensive-looking vest, open in the front, revealing a Georgetown sweatshirt, under which he saw the smooth curve of her breasts. She had perfectly formed lips that lifted into a smile. When she looked at Luke, her blue-green eyes seemed to draw him toward her.

"Your dad's the judge, right?" Luke asked, trying to keep his cool.

"The Honorable John Clements himself."

"Are your parents here?"

"No. Mother's home hosting a fundraiser for one of her obscure charities. My father's picking up some things at a hardware store in town."

"He's gone down to Willey's?"

"I guess. I don't know which store."

Luke chuckled. "There's only one."

"Oh."

"When's he coming back?"

"Soon."

She curled a length of hair behind an ear and stood next to Luke. They looked at the stranded load.

"I guess the only question is, who's going to kill me—my boss or your father?" He turned to the girl. "What do you think your father will do to me?"

"He has quite a lot of British in him. They like to behead people."

"Nice. Then I hope my boss gets here first. He'll just shoot me."

She laughed.

They stood quietly for a few moments. Spring songbirds flitted about in the tree branches, the moist fragrance of evergreens permeating the air.

"Name's Luke."

"I'm Sarah."

Luke extended his hand.

"Hey." They shook hands. "Glad to meet you," she said.

"Did you just drive up from Washington?"

"Father did. I drove over from upstate New York. We met up yesterday, stayed at the Greensboro Inn last night."

Luke listened to her smooth, confident voice. He had been in the inn just once for a church function with his mother. Vicky, the owner, had given them a little tour and he'd admired the large fireplaces, flowers in tall brass vases, and hallways covered with elegant, embossed wallpaper. For a couple of moments, he imagined Sarah sleeping in one of their four-poster beds, a quilt tucked under her arm, a breeze from the lake billowing lace curtains in the window.

"Pretty muddy this time of year," Luke said, feeling uncomfortable about the truck situation.

"I see that. The builder said it's too early to start, but my father insisted."

"Why's he want to build way up here?"

"He can't wait to get as far out of DC as possible. The violent war protests and race riots have gotten crazy. He's worried they'll burn down the Capitol." Her voice was self-assured, different than most of the girls he knew. And way sexier. "My father says even the police are scared, just like the judges."

"We worry about the war, but don't see much for protests up here, just on the news. We do have a few hippies that carry signs in front of the post office in town, but the sheriff usually runs them off."

"How quaint," Sarah said, sarcastically. "You're lucky, there were over half a million protesters on the National Mall a couple weeks ago, and the FBI says those Black Panthers are actually killing people."

"I've heard of them, but what *are* they?"

"Some violent, communist group from California. They scare me. Have you had any around here?"

"Black people?" Luke scoffed. "None around here."

Sarah looked at him quizzically. "What do you mean? You have no black people in town?"

"Nope. Seen a couple of Fresh Air Kids that came up from New York one summer. They looked pretty strange up here. Kind of felt bad for them."

"Wow, this really is a different planet."

Luke nodded. "I guess." He kicked a stone into a mud puddle. "Anyway, the war scares the hell out of me, too. I even saw a clip on the news of a bunch of innocent Vietnamese villagers that were murdered by rogue soldiers. Made me sick."

A chilling wind gusted across the lake.

Sarah pulled her hands inside the sleeves of her sweatshirt. "I know, but most of our soldiers are good, fighting to stop the communists from the north. Usually, the country supports the military but my father says he's never seen people so riled up, protesting all over the place. He's been involved in some draft dodger cases, so they really hate him."

Looking at Sarah, Luke wanted to get off the subject of the war. "Weatherman said we might get some snow flurries today. You look cold. Don't you want to put your coat on?"

"I left it at the inn. I'm okay."

A lick of wind went through a hole in Luke's dungarees forming goosebumps on the back of his leg. "I'll get you mine."

"You don't need to."

"No problem." Luke retrieved his canvas field coat from behind the seat in his truck. It was soiled and worn, but he brushed it off and held it out to her anyway.

Sarah looked at the coat for a moment. Luke continued to hold it for her. "Try it on. It's old but real warm."

She slipped her arms slowly into sleeves far too long for her.

"It's soft."

"Lined with lamb's wool. It was my father's."

"Cool. Does he live around here?"

"No. He died in a logging accident over in Maine when I was eleven."

"I'm sorry."

The load creaked as the truck settled further into the mud. "Listen, I gotta' get this rig out of here and unloaded." He looked at Sarah. "There's a farmhouse up the hill that's got a phone. Can we take your car? I could hike up, but your dad'll be back before I can get my buddy down here with his wrecker."

Sarah frowned. "I don't know. My father just gave it to me for my birthday."

"This pony is *yours*?" Luke said, admiring the air scoop on the convertible's hood.

"Cool, huh? It's a '67, but in great shape."

"I'll say. Your old man must be cool, too."

"He's alright."

Sarah looked at the road above the marooned truck. "Alright. The Mustang already has some mud on it."

"Great." Luke walked toward the driver's side.

"What are you doing?" Sarah stepped in front of Luke and opened the driver's door.

"I thought I'd drive, knowing the area better and all."

Sarah climbed in behind the wheel and shut the door. "Get in." She smiled at him and started the engine.

Luke hesitated, then climbed into the passenger's seat. The white leather was soft, the dashboard classy and polished. On the hump sat a paperback copy of *Love Story*. He resisted picking it up and feeling pages she had touched.

"Hang on." Sarah shifted into first.

"You may need to gun it through the deep stuff."

She shot him a knowing grin, slid on her sunglasses, and floored it. Luke's head arched back as they tore off the gravel into the mud. Sarah passed the marooned truck and slalomed her way back along the lake. Shifting again, she raced up the hill, her hair blowing back over the leather seat. They approached the corner at McCaffery's with frightening speed.

"Slow down!" Luke yelled as she hit the mud, the Mustang sliding sideways on all fours. Sarah let out a yelp and floored it again, flying out of the mud in front of a graying farmhouse like an airboat landing in the Everglades.

She turned to Luke. "This the place?"

He nodded.

She wheeled into the driveway and pulled to a stop next to a rusted pickup, its battered license plate wired to the rear bumper at an odd angle. Luke released his grip on the dash and looked at her. "You sure you aren't a native?"

Sarah smiled. "Not yet."

"That was some piece of spring drivin', young lady." An old man in blue overalls and green, duct-taped barn boots stood in the doorway of a sagging porch attached to the house by a couple lengths of logging chain.

"Hey, Jed," Luke called over the windshield.

Holding a corncob pipe in one hand, Jed McCaffery limped down a couple of rickety stairs. Squinting with one eye, he looked Sarah over. "Who you got there?"

"This is Sarah," Luke hopped out of the car. "She's up visiting."

"Hell of a time to visit the Kingdom. Christly spring runoff's pretty near taken out my foundation. You could drown in a mud bog like the one you just come through."

Luke observed Sarah keeping watch of this strange man, whose left eye opened and closed as if run by a puppeteer, and whose right eye was fixed in an outward stare.

"Jed, I need to use your telephone."

"Truck's stuck, ain't it?"

Luke nodded.

"Too damn early to be deliverin' lumber lakeside. Still frost in the ground."

"Trace wanted it down there today."

"Trace just wants to make money." Jed took hold of the pipe railing and climbed back up the stairs, his left leg dragging behind the right. "Who you goinna' call?"

Luke motioned for Sarah to stay with the car then followed after Jed. "I'll try to get Dexter."

"Yep." Jed reached through a tear in the screen door and unlatched it. "He's got the only hook big enough to get you out of wherever you're stuck."

"Hope he can get Nellie started." Luke stepped across the gap between the porch and the doorway leading into the house.

"I hope he's sobered enough to drive." Jed motioned toward the kitchen. "You know where the phone is."

Luke crossed the chipped linoleum floor to a black wall phone. A cat with a patch of missing fur the shape of England snarled and jumped off the counter. Jed sat on a red, threadbare blanket covering a window seat. Sarah came up behind Luke hesitantly, her arms drawn up, seeming to take care not to touch anything.

"Sarah," Luke said, "you should wait in your car."

Sarah shook her head defiantly. "No way. There's a really big dog out there."

"Ah, that's old Taffy," Jed said, waving off with his hand. He looked at Sarah with one eye while the other one stared blankly out the front door. "He's just a blind old sheep dog, wouldn't hurt a flea. Can't see or smell no more. Old boy don't even know when he's taken a shit."

Sarah recoiled. Luke picked up the phone.

Jed pointed at the cat that was back on the counter licking goo out of a metal bowl in the sink. "Dog won't hurt you, but don't let old Claws get ahold'a you. She'll give you lockjaw surer 'n hell."

"Luke," Sarah said half under her breath, "get me out of here."

"Hang on." Luke turned to Jed, covering the receiver with his hand. "There's some lady on the line—not sure who."

"Must be Doris," Jed said. "Spends half Saturday morning bellyaching with her daughter over to Hardwick. Just tell her to get off."

Sarah frowned at Jed. "How can two women be talking on *your* phone?"

"Party line. Got four of us on it. Keeps my rates down so I can afford it. And I mean just barely." He glanced around the kitchen. "This ain't exactly the Taj Mahal."

Something startled Claws, who jumped up and tore across the counter, knocking an open can of baked beans into the sink. Wild eyed, she flew through the air, skidded over an empty TV dinner tray on the table, and landed on the floor. Snarling, she disappeared into the next room from whence a small cloud of smoke emanated.

"Ah, shit." Jed pushed himself up off the window seat. "Forgot I was fillin' the woodstove when you showed up. Musta' left the door open."

He limped out of the kitchen. A few seconds later, Luke heard the squeak of the stove door closing, and then the clomp-clomp of Jed stomping out burning ashes on the wooden floor.

Sarah became angry. "I can't believe you brought me in here!"

"I told you to stay outside." Luke tried not to laugh. She looked even sexier mad.

"This place is disgusting. And he's crazy."

"Odd is all. And wicked smart."

"He's way beyond 'odd.' And what's the matter with his right eye?"

"Hunting accident. Bow and arrow."

Sarah winced. "You mean he got shot with—"

Luke held up his hand. "Hang on, I gotta' get through to Dexter." As Sarah backed into a corner, Luke put the receiver back to his ear. "Doris, could you please get off the line? I've got to make an important call."

Doris continued to talk a blue streak. Luke knew Filly, her questionably disabled daughter who lived in a partially boarded-up trailer at the entrance to Rex Parson's junkyard on the east edge of town. Rex, Filly's occasional lover, had salvaged a damaged McDonald's drive-up window, cut a hole through the side of Filly's trailer with his chain saw, and installed it so she could sit there in her American Legion wheelchair and check trash trucks in as they arrived with their loads. Word had it, Rex would raise his eyebrows to the boys around the table at Thursday night poker and proudly imply Filly's physical disabilities weren't near what she professed them to be to the state welfare office.

"Doris—"

Jed limped back into the kitchen, his dead foot tripping in the loose threads of a braided rug nailed to the floor. "Give me that thing." He grabbed the phone away from Luke and sat down. "For Christ's sake, Doris, get off the damn phone. We've got an emergency here!"

He listened for a moment then handed the receiver to Luke. "There, make your call before another wheeze bag gets on the line."

Luke dialed the number and waited while it rang. "Dex? Dex! Yeah, it's me. Can you get Nellie down to the lake? I got Trace's flatbed stuck below Jed's. Muddier 'n hell."

Luke listened for a few moments. "So what if you're hungover. Take some aspirin or something. Trace is goinna' kill me."

He waited.

"Great. Meet me at McCaffery's. I'm in a red Mustang." Luke lifted his eyebrows at Sarah.

"Never mind, I'll explain later. And don't be your usual gross self. Got a pretty girl with me."

Jed grinned and sat down. Claws jumped up into his lap and started kneading his overalls.

"You two want some viddles whilst you wait? May take Dex a while to get himself and old Nellie started."

Luke nodded. "Sure, I'm starved."

Sarah cringed.

Jed pushed Claws off his lap and limped over to the yellowed Frigidaire. He released the hook and eye and the door swung open. A pungent smell spilled into the room. "Got a bucket of venison stew I can heat up for you."

"Sounds good," Luke said.

Squinting, Sarah shook her head and put her hand over her nose.

Jed pulled a dented aluminum pot from a shelf over the sink. Holding it against his hip with his elbow, he stepped to the stove.

Luke smiled at Sarah. "Aren't you hungry?"

"Oh, god," Sarah murmured as she watched stew slop over the side of the pot onto Jed's overalls. She turned and fled onto the porch, catching her white tennis shoe in the gap. She righted herself as the door slammed behind her. Taffy was anxiously waiting at the bottom of the stairs, so Sarah hurried to the other end of the porch where she squeezed past an old Skidoo piled high with junk. Luke watched her lean over the railing and thought for sure she'd heave, but she managed to settle herself after taking in a few deep breaths.

Jed turned to the stove, struck a wooden match on the stubble under his chin, and lit a burner. Thin jets of blue flame whooshed to life.

Luke picked up a couple of reasonably clean bowls from the drainboard by the sink. "I hope Dex gets up here before her father gets back. It isn't going to be easy to pull that truck out."

Jed shooed Claws off the counter. "You just get down there with Dex. I'll take care of the judge."

"You will?"

Jed stirred the stew with a cracked wooden spoon. "You just worry about the wrecker is all."

The door opened and Sarah stepped back into the kitchen.

"Mr. McCaffery, are those your orchids in the porch window?"

"Yep." He placed a tin lid on the stew.

Luke followed Sarah into the adjacent room.

An old McCulloch chainsaw sat half-taken apart in the middle of the dining room table, surrounded by socket wrenches, a thin-spouted oilcan, and a rag made from a T-shirt that held a blackened sparkplug. In front of the windows, a Texaco oilcan rack held small clay pots of orchids tied to skinny bamboo stakes.

Sarah's delicate hands cupped a blossom at the top of a slender plant. "These are lovely." She leaned close to the flowers. "They smell like jasmine and lemon."

"They're pretty," Luke said, stepping behind her. He enjoyed the smell of Sarah's hair mixed with the fragrance from the orchid blossoms. He spoke in a low voice. "Jed's wife, Mabel, raised them for years before she died. He's taken care of them ever since."

Sarah leaned forward, inhaled the fragrance from a pure white, heart-shaped blossom. "I've never seen this one before, and my grandmother in New York had dozens of orchids."

"The Lady of the Night," Jed said, leaning against the doorframe.

Luke watched Sarah turn to Jed. His right pant leg was pushed up, revealing a rather crude metal leg. His good eye seemed brighter, though his face looked sad.

"They're so beautiful," Sarah said.

"That white one was Mabel's favorite—called it 'Ophelia.' Persnickety to grow up here in the north, though they like being in the south windows." He looked at the orchids lovingly. "I try to keep the house warm enough for them—only reason the woodstove's going."

Sarah smiled, apparently having forgotten about the dreadful kitchen.

"Babe's garden, I call it. Reverend Cummings told me if I keep tending 'em, it pleases her even though she's up there now." Jed pointed heavenward with a crooked index finger. "I think she can still smell the orchids, especially in the morning when she used to tend them."

"I'm sure she can," Sarah said, a new softness in her voice. As she turned away, Sarah noticed a violin on the table next to the chainsaw.

"C'mon, now," Jed said, pivoting on his good leg and limping back into the kitchen. "Get some stew into you. Dex'll be along shortly."

Sarah approached the violin, which rested in a plush, deep purple velour case. "Mr. McCaffery, could I look at your violin?"

"Sure, you can check out my fiddle. Be careful, though, it's very old, a bit delicate."

Sarah reverently lifted the instrument from the case and held it to the light. She looked over the neck and strings then peered into the sound hole. When she read the luthier's label, her eyes opened wide. "My goodness. This is a *real* Jean-Baptiste Vuillaume? An original?"

"Yep," Jed said from the kitchen.

Fearing she might drop it, Sarah held the instrument against her chest. "These are very rare. I can't believe you—"

Jed limped back into the room. "My father bought it in a little shop in Italy after World War I. Someone had covered it with soot to hide it from the Germans. The shopkeeper never cleaned the inside so he didn't know what he had." Jed took the instrument from Sarah and cradled it under his chin. "Could my father ever make this old girl sing. People came from all around when he'd fiddle at a kitchen tunk, said he could make the floorboards themselves dance."

"Can I hear it? Will you play a little?"

Jed seemed pleased. "Sure. Just for a minute." He lifted a rosined bow from the case and drew it across the taught strings. He steadied himself against the table, closed his eyes, and played a brief, spirited tune.

"That's great," Sarah said. "What song is it?"

"A little 'Turkey in the Straw', a great old fiddle tune." Jed looked at her. "You play?"

Sarah nodded. "The violin, yes. Not like that, though."

"You come by our jam session Saturday night at Skinny's and I'll show you how to play that thing proper. We'll be practicing for the summer barn dance."

"Who's Skinny?"

"The Bullpout Café—he owns it."

"Huh?"

Jed shook his head. "Luke'll tell you. He's our best guitar player."

Sarah smiled. "That's cool."

"Glad you young folks are carrying on music traditions. Awful important."

Sarah nodded. "Couldn't agree more." She looked at Luke. "How'd you get into playing?"

"Grew up with it. Everyone played an instrument of some sort. Used to have great kitchen tunks at our house before my dad died."

Sarah frowned. "What's a 'tunk'?"

"You get a bunch of neighbors together in a farmhouse with

their instruments and play together, eat a lot of food, and dance. Jed used to have them here, too. They were fun, seemed everyone would forget their troubles for a little while."

Jed took a step toward the kitchen. "Got us through a lot of tough times."

"At least we keep it all going at the Bullpout, where we have our jam sessions. You'll see."

Sarah shook her head. "You guys are full of surprises."

"Actually, this area is full of top-notch musicians." Luke glanced at Jed. "Most of whom wouldn't be caught dead in the Bullpout."

Jed chuckled as he limped into the kitchen. "Enough, now. We gotta' hurry up and finish lunch if you want to get that truck out."

CHAPTER TWO

J ED LOOKED OUT THE KITCHEN WINDOW THEN PUSHED himself up from the table, soupspoon still in hand. "Better get out there, Luke. I can hear Nellie comin'."

"Sarah, let's go." Luke headed for the door. "Thanks for lunch. Good luck with the judge."

Frowning, Sarah followed Luke out the door. "What about *the judge?*"

"Don't worry. Come on." Luke jumped off the porch, patted Taffy on the head, and ran down the driveway to greet Dexter, who pulled up in an enormous black wrecker with two spiral chrome pipes shooting like corkscrews past the roof of the cab. Streams of heavy black diesel smoke followed behind him. The radiator grill was welded into the shape of a sinister smile with so many mismatched warning lights mounted on top it could have been mistaken for a spaceship. The fender was decorated with rows of small, hand-painted cars and trucks, and the hood ornament was a replica of the Statue of Liberty welded out over the radiator like the figurehead of a ship. A pair of gold eagles adorned the spotlights and the bumper sported a metallic Marines sticker. Though twice turned down by the local recruiter, Dexter held the Corps in the highest regard.

Luke jumped onto the running board and grabbed hold of the mirror. "Where've you been, you crazy drunkard?"

"You're lucky I got the old girl running." Dexter's eyes were bloodshot, his face unshaven.

"Thanks for coming. You're saving my ass."

"As usual." Dexter saw Sarah standing, arms crossed, at the end of Jed's driveway. "Whoa! Who's that?"

"That is the beautiful Sarah Clements, from our nation's capital."

"Shit," Dexter said, pushing his cap back on his head. "You got no business even knowing her name."

"True." Luke looked at Sarah, followed the curve of her hair over her shoulder.

Dexter shook his head. "Now don't be gettin' crazy thoughts. You ain't got a chance in hell with a girl like that. She needs a *real* man." Dexter threw his shoulders back.

Luke ignored him.

"Let's get rolling. I ain't got enough diesel left to just set here, even with her to look at."

"We'll be back," Luke yelled to Sarah.

Dexter revved the engine. The heavily ornamented hood rattled against its supports as the black beast lunged forward.

"Don't leave me here!" Sarah yelled from the driveway.

"You'll be safer up here," Luke yelled back.

Sarah glanced at Mr. McCaffery, who was standing on the porch next to Taffy, and immediately headed for the Mustang.

Dexter shifted gears and blew through the mud bog, the weight of the wrecker displacing a wave of murky water onto the thin rim of snow. Luke rode down the hill hanging off the side mirror, his outstretched hand catching the wind.

As Dexter approached the turn onto Tetreault's Road, Sarah

blew her horn and raced around them, the Mustang fishtailing in the mud as she headed along the shore.

Dexter shook his head. "She's crazy."

Luke smiled and nodded. "Yeah, she is."

At the building site, Dexter pulled to a stop next to Luke's truck. "Man, you *are* stuck."

"You didn't think I'd drag you out of bed before noon for nothing."

"Nope."

"Can you get her out of there?"

"Goinna' be tight." Dexter pointed to a stand of young cedars. "I think I can drive up into those trees far enough to get some purchase on the front of your chassis. Let's give it a try."

Luke jumped off the running board as Dexter pulled past the marooned truck, pushing the Statue of Liberty into the cedars along the side of the road.

* * *

Jed jammed a wad of Redman into his cheek and limped to his pickup. The exhaust pipe rattled against the frame as he backed down the driveway onto the road. He focused his good eye on the mud bog up ahead, grinned, and gave it the gas. The engine coughed, then came to life. He hit the bog with an impressive splash, yanking the steering wheel hard to the left so the truck landed crossways, blocking the road. With his real foot, Jed felt cold water seeping in through the rusty seams of the cab. He shut off the engine, popped the top on a Genesee, and enjoyed the first swallows of the season diving acrobatically in and out of spaces between loose boards of the barn built by his grandfather a hundred years ago.

Soon, a long, white Cadillac appeared from the direction of Greensboro Village. As the shiny car approached, Jed restarted his engine and rocked the truck back and forth in the mud to make sure it was good and stuck.

A tall, distinguished-looking man with sunglasses and a green, button-down chamois shirt stepped out of the Caddy. Clearly, he was the judge. "What's going on, here?" he called out.

Jed feigned frustration. "Guess she's stuck."

"I can see that."

"I'll have to go get the tractor to pull her out. Hope I don't hold you up too long."

From down by the lake, Jed heard the familiar roar of Nellie's diesel.

"Sir, I must get to my building site. I'm expecting an important delivery."

Jed pushed his door open. An oilcan floated out of the cab into the muddy water. "Won't take long. Tractor's right there in the barn."

Jed waded through the mud onto the dry bank.

"You must hurry. I'm sure they're waiting for me."

"I doubt it," Jed said under his breath. Grinning, he limped slowly up the driveway toward the tractor ramp.

"Can't you move any faster?" the man called over, hands on his hips.

Jed turned back and looked at the man with his glass eye. "Well, I'll tell you," he said, pulling up his right pant leg, "this metal leg can only follow along as fast as the real one goes, and it doesn't go very fast." Enjoying himself, Jed belched up some beer exhaust then slipped his chaw from one cheek to the other. "What you see is full speed."

The man looked confounded. "I'd appreciate your hurrying as much as you can."

Jed dragged his artificial leg up the plank ramp leading to the barn doors. Lifting a leather cover, he swung open a heavy cast-iron latch. The doors squeaked as he pushed them open along the rusty metal track. Jed stepped into the shadow of the barn where he was met with the familiar smell of old hay. He pulled a stone away from the front wheel of the tractor, pulled himself up onto the metal seat, and watched the judge pace in front of his Caddy.

Jed took hold of a heavy red wire and touched it to one of the battery terminals. The old Massey Fergusson fired to life, blue exhaust streaming up through shards of sunlight slanting between the rafters. He advanced the spark, popped the clutch, and headed down the ramp.

* * *

With his cap on backwards, Dexter squeezed under the front bumper of Luke's truck and attached a heavy tow hook to the frame. "You sure picked a helluva spot this time." He shot a glance toward Sarah. "This ain't the first time he's got stuck."

"Hard to believe..." Sarah said with a smile.

"Just get me out of there," Luke said.

Dexter pulled a lever on the side of the wrecker, taking up slack in the winch cable then swung up into the cab. "Here goes."

Dexter shifted into low range and revved the engine. As the wrecker's huge tires dug into the muddy gravel, the front of Luke's truck started to dislodge causing the load of hemlock to shift into an even more precarious position.

"Dex!" Luke yelled, holding up his hand. "I'm going to lose the load."

Dexter hit the air brake, and the two trucks settled back down on their springs.

"I'll get in and give her some gas. Maybe that'll help." Luke jumped into his cab and motioned to Dex, who floored the black beast. With a good blast of power, Nellie surged forward, the Statue of Liberty pushing through a couple of small cedars, uprooting them. Luke's rear wheels clawed their way onto drier gravel.

"You outta' there?" Dexter called to him.

"Yes, sir!" Luke yelled back.

Sarah gave Luke a thumbs up.

Dexter unhooked the tow cable, and with Luke's help, extricated Nellie from the cedars.

"Hey, what's this?" Luke said, eyeing something lying beneath the uprooted trees.

"What's what?" Dexter said.

Luke stepped into the hole in the earth left from the torn-up root ball. He crouched down and lifted a few pieces of decaying wood, broken pottery, and what looked like faded colored beads.

"What the hell is that?" Dexter asked, standing over him.

"I'll bet they're Indian relics. They must have camped here."

Sarah peered into the hole. "That's cool." She climbed down with Luke and brushed away the rotting wood, revealing a small cache of stone arrowheads as well the remnants of a clay pot.

Luke said. "Be careful, they're delicate."

Sarah carefully brushed away more dirt, revealing what appeared to be a beaded necklace with a deeply patinaed copper emblem in the shape of a sun. "Wow, look at this."

Dexter spit a wad of chaw on the ground. "Careful. Remember them savages killed a couple soldiers at the old blockhouse on the Bayley-Hazen Road."

Luke scoffed. "Don't be crazy. That was during the Revolutionary War."

Dexter vigorously chewed his tobacco. "I don't care. You guys should get out of there. They coulda' put all kind of evil spells on them things."

"Relax, Dex." Luke gently picked up a piece of leather. "This is amazing. I'm holding history in my hand. I knew Indians were in this area but never heard of a find like this."

"Don't matter," Dexter said. "Let's just push the trees back over this stuff and get out of here."

Luke looked around and noticed other artifacts showing in the gravel, disrupted by the recent excavating.

Sarah stood. "Maybe Dexter's right that we shouldn't disturb them. This may be some sort of sacred place."

Luke looked around at the newly cleared land. "It's a little late not to disturb things."

"What's going on here, Sarah?"

They all fell silent and turned toward Judge Clements, who had arrived in his Cadillac.

Sarah nudged Luke and quickly climbed out of the hole. She brushed the dirt from her hands. "We were just looking at—"

"That looks dangerous," the judge interjected. "You all get out of there." He turned to Nellie. "And get this huge wrecker out of here. It's torn the whole place up."

Luke stepped forward. "It's my fault, sir. I got stuck on the soft shoulder."

The judge pointed to the load. "I paid a lot of money for those logs. They'd better not be damaged."

"They'll be okay." Luke brushed his hand on his jeans and held it out. "Luke Simms."

The judge looked him over for a few moments then shook his hand. "John Clements, Sarah's father."

Luke motioned to Dexter. "My friend, Dex."

Dexter and the judge nodded to each other.

"I gotta' go." Dexter climbed up into Nellie, revved the engine, and drove up the hill, cakes of mud flinging off his tires.

Luke and Sarah looked at each other. He decided he shouldn't say anything about the relics. "I'll drop the load over there," Luke said, pointing to a dry area of the clearing.

"Will you be delivering more today?"

"No, sir. Too wet. In a few days, soon as it dries out."

The judge turned to Sarah. "Then we'll finish a few things, pack up, and head out."

Luke watched Sarah, her fine blond hair sliding across her back as she turned her head. The corner of her mouth was softly drawn into her cheek as if by the stroke of an artist's brush. He didn't want her to leave.

"Nice to meet you folks." Luke acted as if he and Sarah had said little other than hello.

"You, too, Luke." Sarah smiled. "Maybe I'll see you again.

We're coming back in two weeks, after music camp. Right, Father?"

"I plan to if court doesn't run over."

Luke nodded. "Okay, see you then." He climbed into his truck and backed up to the building lot. The judge frowned as Luke raised the bed of the truck and slid the posts and beams onto the ground. On his way out, he stopped next to the judge and leaned out the window. "Be careful on the roads. Lotta' deer on the move this time of year."

Luke shifted into gear and drove up the hill, watching Sarah gradually disappear in his review mirror.

CHAPTER THREE

WHEN LUKE GOT BACK TO THE MILL, HE FOUND A NEW load of freshly-cut pine logs that needed to be checked in. Golden sap oozing from the ends lent a sweetness to the air. He grabbed the logbook from the foreman's office, took out his tape measure, and tried to focus on measuring the logs. But he could think only of Sarah. The load could wait; he had to see her again. He threw the book and tape measure onto the seat of his pickup, jumped in, and headed out.

Luke took a backroad shortcut into town, turning north at Willey's Store before slowing as he approached the Greensboro Inn. The judge's mud-speckled Caddy was parked in front, but Sarah's Mustang wasn't there. "Damn." He hit the steering wheel with the palm of his hand. "Too late."

Across the road, he pulled around back of Andy's Boat Shop, where he had a view of the inn's parking lot. He walked along the side of Andy's storage shed, where runabouts were kept for guests to use during the summer. Feeling a bit like a voyeur, Luke peered around the far end of the shed just as the Mustang appeared from behind the inn. Delighted, Luke watched as Sarah parked by the inn's door and got out. She wore a white dress, her blond hair pulled back in a braid. She loaded a travel bag into the back of the Mustang, and when she closed the trunk, Luke thought she might have seen him.

Luke pulled back out of sight. *What the hell was he doing?* Feeling foolish, his courage left him. Sliding inside the door of the shed, he wound his way around a half-dozen wooden boats to a dusty window in the rear corner that faced the inn. He was surrounded by the smells of aging shellac, gasoline, and motor oil, mixed with the mustiness of a wooden shed closed up all winter.

Luke wiped cobwebs from the window so he could see. She was gone. Her car was still there, but she was nowhere in sight. She must have gone back in to get another bag or to say goodbye to her father. Luke pulled away from the window just as the door behind him squeaked open. Sarah stepped through a shard of sunlight into the shed.

"Luke?"

For a few moments he crouched, breathless, behind a mahogany runabout then slowly stood and looked at Sarah, her white dress glowing in the late afternoon sunlight.

"I'm here by the window," Luke said quietly.

Sarah walked between the boats toward him. "It's chilly in here," she said, sliding her hands up and down her arms.

Luke stayed silent. He wasn't sure if he was trembling or not.

"I was hoping I'd see you again."

"You were?"

She stepped closer, curling strands of hair behind her ear. "You understand I had to act like that with my father. I don't think he would have approved of lunch at that old man's house."

"Probably not," Luke replied. There was a palpable attraction, as well as an awkwardness, between them.

Sarah took hold of the gunnel of the runabout. "So, what's with this Jed guy?"

"What about him?"

"You know, his weird eye, his run-down house. He acts like such a hick but raises beautiful orchids and plays a rare, world-class violin worth a small fortune."

Luke smiled. "Oh, he's a hick alright. Generations of McCaffery's worked that farm before Jed gave up about five years ago. He'd lost his leg, and his hired man died. But I told you, he's wicked smart, studied at some famous music school in Boston."

"Not the *Berklee* School?"

"Yeah, that's it."

"Wow, that's amazing."

"And he used to teach guitar and fiddle up here at Johnson State. Something I might like to do some day." Luke rubbed his hand along the smooth mahogany. "Anyway, Jed's changed a lot since his wife died, misses her awful. He's let himself go, except for the orchids and his fiddling." Luke raised his eyebrows. "And his beloved pets."

"Yes, they were charming. I'm not sure which I was most attracted to—the crazy cat or the blind, incontinent sheep dog."

They laughed.

Luke dared to take a long look at Sarah. "Meeting you sure changed my day, made it a lot more fun."

"You *were* in a bit of trouble."

Luke nodded. "Glad Dex got me out of there. Didn't like the idea of your old man beheading me."

"No worries. My father wouldn't have beheaded you, just sentenced you to hard labor."

"How could you tell?"

"Because he actually spoke to you. And you're real."

Luke looked at her inquisitively. "Aren't most people? Real, I mean?"

Sarah frowned. "No, actually. At least not where I live."

Luke nodded. "I've heard Washington's like a different planet."

"It is, full of self-serving aliens."

"Sounds charming, as they say."

"Wiseass." Sarah smiled at him.

After a short, uncomfortable silence, Luke struggled to find something else to say. "You said you'll be coming back up again?"

"Yes. I love it up here. Just to breathe this clean air is worth the trip." She looked at Luke. "As well as other things."

She was so close to him. He watched her lips as she spoke. His heart pounded into his ears. He was nervous he would say or do the wrong thing. In a way, the outboard motor between them was a comfort.

"Why aren't you and your dad in one car?" Luke felt relief in changing the subject.

"He's driving back to DC. I'm going to a music camp at Hunter Mountain in upstate New York."

"You said you play the fiddle?"

"The *violin*, actually."

"I saw you admiring Jed's. He's amazing, won ribbons at the Craftsbury Fiddle Contest many times, and either he or Betty win the annual contest at Rowell's barn after the Fourth of July dance."

"Is that what he was talking about? Skinny, something?"

"Yeah. Skinny's Bullpout Café, where our group practices for the big shindig over the Fourth. After the boat race and the barbeque, there's a huge party at a beautiful old barn in East

Craftsbury. Bunch of bands, lots of dancing, and at the end of the night there's a fiddle-off. Didn't get a champion till after one in the morning last year."

Sarah chuckled. "That must be really late for all you hicks."

"It is. You'd know so if you had to be in the barn milking at four."

"I see."

Luke wiped a layer of dust from the top of a blue Evinrude outboard. "So, are you a good fiddler?"

"I don't fiddle. I'm a violinist, classically trained."

"How long have you been playing?"

"Mother started my lessons when I was four. It came naturally. I love it." She paused and stared out the window. "It's the one genuinely good thing she's done for me."

"Why's that?" Luke was surprised. "Is your mother mean?"

"Let's say, Mother can be extraordinarily difficult, and selfish."

"How so?"

Sarah became uncomfortable. "Like my father and I always wanted a dog, but she forbid it, said it would be too dirty for her house. That sort of thing."

"Bummer."

Sarah turned to the runabout next to her and ran her hand along the smooth wood surface. "Have you ever driven one of these?"

Luke's face lit up. "Sure, lots of times, ever since I was a little kid."

"How old were you?"

"I think my father let me drive in his lap when I was three or four." Luke chuckled. "I could hardly see over the dash. I raced for the first time when I was twelve. I think I lied to Mrs. Peters, the registrar, that I was thirteen." Luke smiled, patted the top of the engine. "Love everything about boats, and this lake. The race is the best part of the summer."

Sarah took hold of the outboard's throttle. "Why do you care so much about a race?"

Luke became pensive, wasn't sure he wanted to talk about it. He wiped a layer of winter dust off the engine shroud. "Seven years ago, my father almost won the race; he was in the lead when he blew a head gasket on the last lap. His motor oil ran low and the Merc overheated." Luke shook his head. "Dad had a rough, complicated life."

"How so?"

"Oh, you don't want to hear about it."

"I would, if you want to tell me."

Luke glanced at Sarah then looked out the window. "When he came back to town after World War II, no one would give him a decent job, so he went back to farming." Feeling uncomfortable, Luke paused.

"Why wouldn't people give a returning veteran a job?"

"They looked down on him because he wasn't given an honorable discharge. He'd gotten into trouble, been a patsy for higher ranks, I think."

"That doesn't sound good."

"It wasn't, and this town reveres its military, but that wasn't the case for him."

"It sounds difficult."

"It was. He and Mom lived awful close to the bone trying to make a go of it on the farm. We could've really used that prize money—it was like $500 back then. That would've bought us enough grain to get the animals through the winter. But when he didn't win, there wasn't any other work around here, so he left Mom and me with the farm and went to New Hampshire on a logging crew. He came home for Christmas Day, even got Mom and me presents. But the next day there were a couple of big logging rigs heading to Maine and they were paying well, so he headed out with them."

"What's that got to do with the boat race?"

"Lots—" Luke felt himself getting agitated.

"Luke," Sarah said, touching his arm, "it's okay, you can tell me."

"He and a friend of his, Henry Vallencourt, were up near Rangeley Lake cutting a huge pine when it snapped on them. My father tried to jump out of the way, but it twisted as it fell, caught him across his midriff." Luke shook his head, wiped a cobweb from the window frame. "Our neighbor got a call from the hospital up there, said Dad was bad off, that we should come right away. We didn't have a car, so we had to hitch rides, mostly with logging trucks. Took all day to get there. I'd never been that far away."

Sarah held Luke's arm.

"Dad looked awful, I hardly recognized him. The doc said they'd done everything they could. I got to sit with him for a while. He was in and out of it, but he told me he felt bad about losing the race, that he wouldn't have been in Maine logging if he'd won that money." Luke wanted to pull away, but the warmth of Sarah's hand held him.

"Underneath it all, I know my dad was a good man. I don't mean any disrespect, but sometimes he just wasn't as smart as he needed to be. Maybe 'cause he quit school before eighth grade,

I don't know." Luke shifted his weight to his other foot. "When he knew he was going to die, he said he felt like a failure for leaving us with so little, that he wanted better for me." Luke pushed down emotions he hadn't felt in a long time. "He wanted me to get an education and do well in the military, not screw things up like he had. And, most of all, he wanted me to win one of the boat races, to beat Freddie McCormick: for him, for my mother, for some family honor sort of thing." Luke nodded to himself and took a deep breath. "I told him I'd do it, and I've been working on putting together a good enough boat ever since. So far, all I've been able to do is cobble together a racer from parts other people don't want."

Sarah gave Luke a hug. "I'm sorry."

He turned away and wiped the corner of his eye on his shoulder. "Worst part was we couldn't afford to bring him home. They buried him in some poor farm cemetery. It's not right."

"That's way tough."

Luke turned back to his boat. "Anyway, I'm going to drive this baby in the big race over the Fourth of July."

"This is your boat?"

"Yes. May not look like much, but when I get her tuned right, she'll run like lightning."

"I bet she will."

"Going to beat McCormick's butt."

Sarah looked puzzled. "What's that guy got to do with it?"

"Never mind. Not important."

Sarah took hold of Luke's hands. "Luke—"

He shook his head. "Boy, are you persistent."

"It's because I care."

"You just met me."

"So? I can tell."

"Tell what?"

"What a good guy you are."

Luke was touched by her warmth. "Thanks." He stepped back, ran his hand over his outboard. "McCormick and my dad never got along 'cause Dad caught him cheating the dairy co-op out of some money. He was always trying to get back at Dad. When his engine failed and he lost the race, Dad went through the motor with a fine-toothed comb. He found a damaged gasket that was torn and loose, something Dad never would've missed. That caused the oil leak that did him in. He and about everybody else figured Freddie did it. Couldn't ever prove it, but someone saw him around the boats the night before the race. Mom and I felt like he ended up getting Dad killed."

Sarah shook her head. "That's terrible. Didn't somebody go after him?"

"The sheriff tried to look into it, but there was no good evidence 'cause Dad had torn the motor apart."

"They didn't find any fingerprints?"

Luke chuckled, shook his head. "They didn't do anything like that."

"I can sure see why you want to beat this guy."

Luke motioned to his boat. "It's been a challenge. He comes from a big farm family, lotta' money, buys the best boats."

Sarah looked Luke in the eye. "You can beat him."

Luke nodded. "If I can get this new carburetor installed and tuned right, I think I can."

"I *know* you can."

"Thanks." Luke smiled. "You may be the best cheerleader I've got." Luke turned to the other boats in the shed. "Anyway, I help Andy get these beauties ready for guests at the inn. Of course, I have to give the boats a good test run on the lake." He grinned at Sarah. "We wouldn't want any flatlanders having engine trouble."

"You'll probably work on my dad's boat. It's like these, but a little bigger. It has leather seats and the engine has a cool roar, sort of like the Mustang but louder."

"Awesome. I'd love to see it."

Sarah looked at him admiringly. "You have a wonderful smile, Luke Simms." She reached up and gently touched his lips. Her fingertips were soft, scented with a lavender lotion. Embarrassed, not used to a girl being so forward, Luke tried but couldn't look her in the eye.

"I didn't expect to find such a handsome country boy up here." Sarah went up on her toes and kissed him on the cheek. "I'll be back, and you can give me a ride in one of these."

Luke caught his breath. "You bet I will."

She walked back between the boats and slipped out through the shed doors.

Partially in shock, Luke stepped to an open window and watched Sarah hurry back to the inn, her dress curling behind her. She turned and yelled to him. "Follow me out of town. I don't want to get lost."

Sarah knelt beside a garden at the side of the inn, picked a handful of flowers, and slid into her convertible. As she drove off, Luke ran out of the shed to his pickup, tore out of Andy's driveway, and followed after her as she headed for the main road. The Mustang was fast. Even with his pedal to the floor, Luke didn't catch up to her until the outskirts of town where she had to stop and wait for a herd of bulging Holsteins heading for the milking parlor.

Luke pulled up close behind her as the last cow made it across the road. Sarah swerved around a couple of manure patties and turned onto the state highway. Luke followed behind her for a short distance, but couldn't keep up. She waved and released a handful of blossoms into the wind. Luke slowed as tulip petals landed on the faded hood of his pickup. He stopped in the middle of the road, got out, and gathered several shiny yellow petals from the warm hood. By the time he looked down the road Sarah was out of sight.

CHAPTER FOUR

L UKE STOOD BY HIS PICKUP FOR A LONG TIME, WATCHING the sun descend behind Madonna Mountain, an orange afterglow lining the underside of thin cirrus clouds in the west. A few cars passed by, but he hardly noticed them.

It was almost dark by the time Luke arrived at the farmhouse he shared with his mother, Mary. The driveway was lit with golden light from the kitchen, where he saw her leaning against the counter peeling potatoes. With worsening fatigue and shortness of breath from her pulmonary fibrosis, it was harder for her to do the things she enjoyed, particularly cooking. Lifting heavy pots and pans on and off the stove was particularly difficult these last few months, though she usually refused his help with them. Hanging on to her independence was important to her. Truth was, however, without Luke's and the church ladies' help, she might have had to give up.

The Simms' farmhouse set back from the edge of what used to be a gently rolling field that climbed north into pastureland on the south slope of Wheelock Mountain. Hard times had forced his family to sell off large chunks of the 150 acres they used to farm. Now, most of their once beautiful field was filled with rows of slouching house trailers, their overgrown yards littered with cannibalized snowmobiles, junked cars, abandoned grills, and broken swing sets. A few scrawny trees and sections of crooked stockade fence separated the trailers' tiny yards.

Luke walked inside, catching the screen door so it wouldn't slam and startle his mother, who stood with a faded floral apron tied about her thin waist.

"Had to work late, dear?" she asked, rinsing out a blackened pot.

"Not really." Luke hung his truck keys on a hook above the phone. "Got stuck down by the lake today. That fancy cabin job I'm delivering for Trace."

"That big wig's place?"

"Yeah. He's an important judge."

"Dex have to pull you out?"

Luke chuckled. "How'd you guess?" He poured himself a glass of cold milk then sat in front of a plate of corned beef hash waiting for him on the linoleum-covered table.

"I can warm that up if it's cold."

Luke stared out the bay window toward the dark green hills. Tiny winged creatures clung to the outside of the screen.

"Luke?"

"Yes, Mother."

"Is your dinner cold?"

"No, it's fine."

"How would you know?" Leaning on a chairback, she stepped awkwardly to the table. "You haven't touched it."

Luke looked at her and smiled.

She watched his face for a few moments then gathered her apron and sat in the chair next to him. "Why, Luke Simms," she said, a smile breaking across her face, "you've met yourself a girl, now haven't you?"

Luke felt himself blush. "Maybe. How can you tell?"

"I'm your mother." She gave his leg a pat. "You tell me about her when you're ready."

"I will." He quickly ate the entire plate of hash then took her hand. "You look tired."

"Yes, I need to rest." He helped her stand. "Help yourself to more. I'm going to lie down."

"That was delicious but I'm full." He gave her a kiss on the cheek.

She stepped to her bedroom door. "A package came for you. It's by the door."

"Okay, thanks." He was surprised, as it was rare to get mail.

Luke put his plate in the sink then found a small package wrapped in brown paper on the hallway bench. The return address was from Sedona, Arizona, but included no name. Back at the kitchen table, he opened the package, revealing a small hardcover book, *Tao de Ching*, by Lao Tzu. "Hensley" was written inside the front cover, where Luke found a handwritten note.

Dear Luke,

The *Tao* holds all the wisdom and guidance you will ever need. Follow your heart and your principles, and you will always advance steadfastly in the direction of your dreams.

The circumstances of my leaving the school did not allow a proper goodbye, and for that I apologize. I thoroughly enjoyed our association. As they say, 'the student becomes the teacher.' Heroes always enlighten those on their path, and the hero in you is emerging.

Peace,

Mr. Hensley

Delighted to hear from his favorite high school teacher, Luke read the note over several times. Mr. Hensley had suddenly left town the spring of Luke's senior year. Earlier, he'd been reluctantly hired as a replacement for an elderly social studies teacher who'd had a stroke. A Native American with long black hair who wore a beaded necklace, he spoke in a soft, strong voice. He was not what the local school board was used to.

Mr. Hensley cared deeply about the plight of downtrodden peoples, and stoked intense controversy when he assigned Luke's class to read Dee Brown's, *Bury My Heart at Wounded Knee*, which helped to rewrite the standard history of the white man's conquering of the American West. Graphically critical of the government's warfare against its own indigenous peoples, the book talked about Army massacres of the Lakota Sioux and the near-extinction of the buffalo, the Indians' primary source of food and clothing. It made an impression on Luke when Mr. Hensley explained the importance of "teaching the truth," even though it was threatening to the status quo.

Several students and their parents complained about the book. The school superintendent made Mr. Hensley stop teaching it; however, he and Luke continued to meet privately to discuss the book. Luke found it to be a life-changing experience, helping him realize all peoples were integral parts of a greater world family that extended way beyond the confines of his beloved Greensboro. In the end, Luke figured the powers that be finally drove Mr. Hensley out of town, which was a shame.

Luke set the letter on the kitchen table and thought of how Mr. Hensley had taken an interest in him, particularly appreciating Luke's family's painful wounds. Luke was honored to receive a book from his personal library. He read a few passages then brought it to his mother's room and gently sat on the edge of her bed. She roused and pulled a quilt down from her chin.

"What is it, dear?"

"The package was from Mr. Hensley. He sent me one of his cool books and a nice letter."

"Really? Pity, those idiots drove him out." She struggled to push herself up on the pillows. "Let's see."

Luke showed her the *Tao*.

"Who wrote it?"

"An ancient Chinese scholar, from like 450 BC. The man was brilliant. Mr. Hensley used to quote him a lot."

"Goodness, it's too much for me." She looked at Luke. "How do you know so much?"

He smiled. "Books."

"You've always been a reader, fascinated by picture books from the time you could crawl. I wish we'd had more of them."

"Ah, Mom, we had plenty of books for me to get the bug."

She nodded. "I understand, even if your father couldn't. His whole life was lived with his hands."

"I know, and I respect that. I love working with my hands, too." Luke opened the book. "Look at this."

"I don't have my glasses, would you read it to me?"

"Of course."

She relaxed back on the bed and listened.

"I like this passage; I remember it from Mr. Hensley's class:

'I have just three things to teach: simplicity, patience, compassion.
These three are your greatest treasures.
When you are content to be simply yourself and don't compare
or compete, everybody will respect you.
At the center of your being you have the answer; you know who
you are and you know what you want.'"

"Oh, that's nice. Can you read it again?"

When Luke had read it another time, his mother put her hand on his forearm. "Like that Chinese scholar, you're a smart young man. You'll do this family proud."

Luke smiled at her.

"I won't be around to see it all, but know I'll be proud of you."

"Don't say that, Mom."

"You'll be alright." She took in a couple of short breaths and winked at him. "Maybe you'll have a special girl to share it all with."

"Ha," Luke replied. "She's a judge's daughter. Don't think she'll be going out with me."

"She'd be lucky to."

Luke made a face and shook his head.

"You never know what two hearts can do."

"We'll see." Luke stood. "You better get some rest."

"Thanks for sharing that with me. You better get some shut-eye, too. I know you've got to work tomorrow."

Luke nodded. "And I'll head over to Skinny's after work." He pulled the quilt back up over her. "Goodnight, Mom."

"Night, Son."

Luke took Mr. Hensley's book and went to bed.

* * *

After making deliveries the next day, Luke grabbed his guitar and drove to the Bullpout. He sat in his truck for a few minutes, taking in the sweet fragrance of purple lilacs. A bright, three-quarter moon reflected off the lazy section of the Lamoille River meandering behind the 1920s watering hole. Through the café's open windows, he heard his friends tuning up for their Saturday night jam session.

Luke didn't see Dexter's truck in the parking lot, which was strange. Skinny's was usually the one thing Dexter was on time for. Luke took his guitar case and stepped onto the porch. He watched and listened as Betty Kittell drew a horsehair bow across her fiddle. In perfect tune. Of course. Inside, the yellow lights from the antler chandeliers were dimmed a bit now that the paying customers were gone. Luke was greeted by the aroma of Skinny's famous sweet pepper chili.

"Hey, Luke," Skinny called from behind the counter.

"Smells good." Luke pushed the ketchup and mustard jars out of the way and set his guitar case on a table.

Skinny pulled a pan of fresh cornbread from the oven. "How's your boat coming along? You get that engine running right?"

Luke shook his head. "Not yet. Carburetor's off."

"You replace the gas line?"

"Yeah. Didn't make a difference. And I cleaned out the tank."

Skinny started cutting the cornbread into perfect squares. "Well, you'll figure it out. Your boat was fast enough last summer, would've won if you hadn't dinged those rocks."

"I know. Just stupid. I should've known those rocks were in the shallows."

Skinny placed a piece of cornbread on a plate. "They're tricky. Every winter, the ice moves them around. Besides, it's easy to lose track of where you are when you're racing hard."

Luke took his Gibson guitar out of its case. "Won't make that mistake this year."

Luke stepped over to Jed. "How you doing?"

"Fair to midlin'." Jed shifted his peg leg over to better support the guitar he was tuning.

"Thanks for helping me out of that jam."

Jed gave him a sideward grin. "Musta' been something awful, stuck down there alone with Sarah."

Luke smiled. "I managed somehow."

As Luke sat on a chair next to Jed, the *Tao* fell out of his pocket. Jed glanced at it. "I see you've got one of them commie books," he said, with a grin.

Luke quickly put the book in his guitar case and closed it. He knew Jed was just jousting with him, but others might be serious.

Filly came tearing around the corner in her red, white, and blue American Legion wheelchair and pulled to a screeching halt next to the piano. "Well, if it isn't old lover boy," she yelled over to Luke. "S'prised you got time to hang with us woodchucks." She licked her lips with her unusually long tongue.

"Hi, Filly," Luke said, matter-of-factly, knowing the dangers of engaging with her when she had gossip on her mind.

Luke looked at Betty, who laid her fiddle in her lap and gave him a longing smile. She had on a blue, summery dress that fell just over her knees. "Wondered if you'd show up tonight, being so busy at the mill and all."

"I wouldn't miss it."

"Heard you been delivering some heavy loads down to the lake," Skinny said, placing another square of cornbread topped with a slab of butter next to the brass cash register.

"Yeah." Luke pulled the plate toward him and devoured the cornbread in two bites.

From one of the window booths, Fred Jettie cleared his throat. "Ain't right buildin' on the northeast shore. Stupid state shoulda' bought that land and preserved it when they had a chance. Kept it for fishin' like it's always been." He slid his chaw from one cheek to the other then spit into a coffee can on the floor next to his small guitar amp. "Woulda' kept them rich flatlanders out. Now that we got some highfalutin judge building a camp down there, it's likely a whole herd of them'll be moving in. Caspian'll go all to hell." Fred vigorously shook his head, setting a Royal Crown Cola light swinging over his head. "Town's too damn crowded as it is."

Filly waved her hand through the air. "Ah, give it a rest, Fred. Christ's sake, you think we can all make a living selling scrap metal? We need more people with money around here. Businesses are barely making ends meet."

"I don't care," Fred retorted. "We don't need 'em if they's going to ruin the lake. She's our crown jewel."

Luke wiped off the body of his guitar with a lemony chamois cloth. "I suppose one fellow's got as much right as another to build around here."

Fred, Betty, and Jed gave Luke dirty looks.

"Traitor," Fred said half under his breath.

"'Course they do," Skinny said, taking off his apron. "Fred's blowin' off steam is all. Still angry the bank took his dad's place in the '50s."

49

"Goddamn government," Fred said, plugging in his Fender. "Banks, too—they's all the same. Do anything they can to screw the little guy." He slung the strap over his head and rested the Stratocaster on his potbelly. "Mark my words, building that judge's cabin's the beginning of the end for Caspian. Next, they'll be puttin' in a coin-op car wash and one of them drive-through burger joints."

Betty shook her head. "You're talking crazy. We barely have enough people with jangle in their pocket to support Willey's."

Filly pulled a pair of silver spoons out of her pocket, rubbed them with a clean napkin and began to warm up, rhythmically snapping them together on her lap then on the arm of her wheelchair, the corner of the piano bench, and back to her lap.

Dexter arrived, dragging his bass through the screen door, which slammed behind him.

Standing on his good leg, Jed took a fresh pinch of Redman from a pouch and pushed it inside his cheek. "You know, Freddy, times is tough around here. We oughtta' be glad Trace has work for the boys. Like Luke, here."

Though some of their provincial attitudes bugged him, Luke hoped they would keep it to politics and that no one would mention Sarah.

Skinny laid his apron on the counter. "Enough already, let's play some music." He pushed the upright piano out of the corner and sat on a wooden stool in front of the yellowed ivory keys.

Luke turned away from the others and leaned his ear down close to his strings. He tightened the G and B strings until they blended harmoniously with the others. He adjusted his guitar on his hip and started picking a little ditty that quickly broke into the "Wabash Cannon Ball." Jed picked up the tune with his fiddle, joined by Dexter's rumbling bass, Fred's Fender, and Lester's mandolin. Betty stood, cradled her fiddle under her chin, and took off with the refrain. Skinny's fingers laid into the keys and Luke began to sing. Soon the café was filled with music, the group harmonizing into stirring renditions of everything from "Okie from Muskogee," to Elvis's "Jailhouse Rock," during which Fred picked such a mean guitar solo, beads of sweat formed on his brow. After an hour of jamming, Luke led them into "Will the Circle Be Unbroken," brought to a close with a stirring fiddle solo by Betty.

Skinny pushed back from the piano and clapped his hands. "That's more like it. Now, let's eat." He put his apron back on, slid behind the lunch counter, and started ladling steaming chili into china bowls. Everyone put on their own cheese, sour cream, and sautéed onions and peppers, which were lined up along the counter.

Fred dunked a piece of cornbread into his chili, ate it, and then drained a longneck. He motioned to Luke. "You know, if we natives don't take control of our forefathers' land, they'll be none left for us. The only place you'll be able to go fishing is your cast-iron bathtub."

"Give it a rest, Fred," Skinny said, setting the chili pot on the back counter. He turned to the rest of the players. "Alright, now that we're warmed up, we've got to get down to business deciding what we're going to play at the barn dance over the Fourth. Rowell's bringing in his own band, Rick and the Ramblers this year, and they're top-notch. Means we gotta' really have our act together so they don't outdo us."

Filly frowned. "Don't seem fair having a professional band play."

"Well, it's Dave Rowell's barn dance and he's their bass player, so he can do whatever he wants."

Luke wiped a few drips of chili from his mouth and strapped on his guitar. "Then let's figure out what we're going to play. We can't have any Ramblers outdo the Bullpout Band."

After another 45 minutes of practicing, Betty and Jed traded fiddle licks, previewing what to expect when they competed in the annual fiddle contest, held after the barn dance. Luke wished Sarah had been there to hear them—no violinist can make an instrument jump off your shoulder like a good fiddler.

When Luke got home, his mother was long asleep, so he sat in the kitchen for a while looking over the tool section of the new Sears & Roebuck catalog. Mostly, though, he was thinking of the beautiful girl from Washington with the hot Mustang. He tossed the catalog on the table, took the *Tao* with him, and went to bed. He opened it to the passage he'd read to his mother:

> *"At the center of your being, you have the answer;*
> *you know who you are, and you know what you want."*

CHAPTER FIVE

_____

S ARAH'S TIME BACK AT THE MUSIC CAMP IN THE ADIRONDACKS had been emotionally tumultuous. Leaving Greensboro, as she'd watched Luke disappear in her rearview, she had felt an unexpected wave of not wanting to leave him. But that was just a silly crush, something she looked down upon in others. Trying to push Luke out of her mind, she'd pulled onto Route 15 and floored the Mustang. She passed a number of slow-moving pickups and old cars as she sped west following the serpentine bends of the Lamoille River. She smiled watching a freight train traverse a wooden covered bridge over the river, something she'd never seen before.

After crossing the Champlain Bridge into New York, Sarah's thoughts turned to Nick, the handsome tennis player working as a junior pro at her music camp. She'd met him the end of the previous summer, and though attracted to each other, they'd only been able to briefly connect. With her back at Georgetown and him at UCLA, they'd only been able to meet up twice during the school year, including two inseparable days over spring break in Fort Lauderdale. She thought they'd fallen in love, and one moonless night she gave up her virginity with Nick in the sand dunes after a keg party. It was carefree and wildly exciting, followed by a new kind of fear because they'd used no protection. She spent the next two weeks worried about being pregnant, not knowing if she'd want to have his baby. Then, to her relief, she got her period, and went on the Pill.

When Sarah arrived at camp, she was delighted to see Nick waiting on the front porch of her cabin wearing a red and white polo shirt, his designer sunglasses pushed up in his hair. He took her in his arms and they kissed, surrounded by the aroma of his English Leather cologne.

Sarah smiled and started to pull Nick toward the cabin door. "Come in, I want to show you something."

He hesitated. "I shouldn't."

"It's okay, I'm on birth control."

Nick looked pleased but still didn't follow her. "I just wanted to say hi. I'm on my way to meet with a tennis rep from a big company. She wants to talk about a possible endorsement deal." Nick checked his hair in the reflection of the cabin window.

"Sure you don't have a little time to get reacquainted?"

Nick turned and trotted down the stairs. "Sorry," he called over his shoulder, "can't waste a chance like this. I'll catch you later."

Feeling frustrated, Sarah watched Nick ride off in a shiny white golf cart. Excited as she'd been to see him, her thoughts soon turned back to Luke. She sat on the top step looking out at dark green mountaintops touching the azure sky. She liked how Luke had been straightforward about getting pulled out when he was so stuck. He seemed authentic, no BS. In contrast, her preppy friends always seemed to be performing, trying to impress.

It was warmer in the southern Adirondacks than it had been in Vermont. Sarah sat for a long time as dusk fell and the mountains gradually transformed from green to pink to purple. She listened to the sound of peepers rising from a nearby wetland

and the screech of a hawk perched atop a dead tree that rose above the pines. She realized how much she appreciated the clean, refreshing air of the Northeast Kingdom, especially the cedar-scented shores of Caspian Lake. Maybe for the first time in her life, she felt something essential shifting inside her.

Sarah felt embarrassed she'd come on so strong with Nick. Especially because, though unexpected, she'd felt something deeper during her short time with Luke. But they came from completely different worlds—it would never work. Her emotions fluctuating wildly, she went inside the cabin and made herself unpack. When finished, she lit a candle near the stone fireplace and lay down on the cot. Staring at the flickering light against the pine ceiling, she let the events of the last few days wash over her. Smiling, she soon closed her eyes and fell asleep dreaming about Vermont.

* * *

Sarah woke the next morning hearing other girls passing by her cabin. Checking her watch, she realized she needed to hurry or she'd be late for registration. She pulled on a sweatshirt and jeans, ran a brush through her hair, and headed for the administration tent. Standing in line with other young musicians, she said hi to a couple of wealthy girls from Montauk she'd met the summer before. Dressed in designer tennis outfits, with too much makeup, they were complaining to each other that the primitive conditions of the camp hadn't improved a bit. They paid almost no attention to Sarah, so she started reading a smattering of announcements pinned to a bulletin board.

At the bottom of the notices was an unusual one that read:

"Try something new—learn to Old-Tyme Fiddle with Sis!" Sarah smiled, thinking of Jed and his beautiful instrument. She was tempted to tear off one of the contacts, but there were too many people around, and she might get a reputation for not being serious enough about her classical studies. Instead, she stayed in line and chatted with a couple of friendly girls from Wellesley.

After registration there was a meet and greet on the porch of the main building, a 19th century Adirondack great camp built for a friend of the Rockefellers. Sarah then spent the day attending sessions on violin method, including one on baroque music, which she found plodding and melodramatic. To her surprise, it was hard to focus on anything besides Luke.

Dinner was served at long tables covered with white linens. Rustic chandeliers hung over rows of gleaming silver serving dishes. Overhead, enormous golden pine rafters soared to the peak of the room. Dark, split-log walls were lined with memorabilia from over a hundred years of camps. Old photographs, colorful college pennants, posters of archery and canoe competitions, and a primitive bear trap were all mounted around the room. Against one wall stood a glass case displaying Native American pottery, several stone arrowheads, and a buckskin headband with a pair of fragile eagle feathers. Over the double doors to the kitchen hung a pair of ancient wooden snowshoes, their rawhide webbings broken and dangling.

After a meal of spicy barbequed chicken, tender roast beef, baked potatoes, and salad, Sarah sat through several brief speeches served up with strawberry-rhubarb pie and fresh-churned ice cream. After dinner, she talked with a few violinists then, feeling tired, headed to her cabin. As she walked by the bulletin board, there was no one around, so she tore off the info for the old-tyme fiddling lessons.

The next afternoon, after a master's instructional session and a couple of hours practicing Mozart's "Concerto No. 3," Sarah decided to seek out Sis, the fiddle lady from North Carolina. Meeting Jed and hearing about Luke's jam sessions had piqued her interest. She followed the tiny map drawn on the piece of paper, through the camp to the back of the property where one of the original log cabins sat on a slight rise overlooking the Schoharie Creek. Up on the porch, a pair of harmonicas and a Jew's harp sat on a log table next to a sweating glass of melting ice cubes. The dark wood ceiling sheltered the porch from the hot sun.

Hearing someone inside, Sarah knocked softly on the screen door. When no one came, she rapped a little harder.

"Y'all come on in," a woman said in a southern drawl.

Sarah pulled the weathered screen door open. Inside, the air was surprisingly cool and scented with a citrus fragrance. "Hello..."

"Back here in the kitchen. You want some lemonade?"

"That would be great." Sarah stepped into the doorway to a small kitchen where an older woman with long gray hair was juicing lemons.

"Darlin', would you pour that cuppa' suga' into this for me?"

"Of course." Sarah picked up a copper cup of white sugar from the wooden counter and poured it into the large glass pitcher the woman was stirring. "Smells good."

The woman whisked several strands of hair out of her face. "My momma's famous recipe." She held up a ginger root. "Her secret ingredient." She grated several swipes of ginger into the mix, stirred again, and poured a small amount into a glass tumbler.

She handed it to Sarah. "Give her a try. No moonshine in it like my grandpappy woulda' had."

Sarah took a sip of the strong, tart mixture, which made her lips curl.

"Might have a little kick to it."

"Might..." Sarah said, swallowing again.

The woman took a long swig. "Ahh, nothing like it on a parched day." She looked at Sarah. "I'm Sis. What can I do for you, darlin'?"

"I'm Sarah. I saw this." Sarah held up the piece of paper for the fiddle lessons.

The woman broke into a smile. "Bless your heart, I finally got a brave one! And you're that talented gal from DC, ain't 'cha?"

Sarah was surprised. "I guess so, but how did you know?"

"Ha, been comin' up here for years, know' bout ever'thin' there is to know." She smiled at Sarah. "I'm tickled to death you want to learn how to fiddle! Most y'all violinists scared to death of real, old-time music."

"This guy over in Vermont got me interested, though I don't think my parents would approve."

Sis laughed. "Approve of the guy or the fiddlin'?"

Sarah smiled. "Probably neither."

"Well, I don't see either one here, so I reckon there's nothin' to fret about." Sis took another good swig of lemonade. "He a fiddler? Some great ones up there."

"No, he plays the guitar, but he's in a group with a couple of good fiddlers. They get together every week for a jam session and practice for a big annual barn dance with a fiddle contest. Something like that."

Sis raised her eyebrows. "You ain't talkin' about up Greensboro way, are ya'?"

"Yes. Do you know it?"

Sis nodded. "'Course. All the fiddlers know about that, have it every year. Helluva good time."

Sarah became excited. "Wow, have you ever played there?"

"Sho-nuff. Almost beat that damn Jed fella' few years back, but he took me on some crazy reel he pulled off."

Sarah's eyes opened wider. "You know Jed McCaffery?"

"Just through fiddling against him. As much as I'd love to beat him, I respect the hell out of him."

"That's amazing! He's in Luke's group."

"Well, I declare. Beautiful up there. God's country. Just like Carolina." She looked at Sarah. "So, you want to learn some fiddle tunes, break that death grip classical violin got on ya'?"

Sarah nodded. "I sure do."

"Good. Fiddlin's a whole lotta' fun. Gets your juices flowing." Sis motioned toward the door. "Run, get your instrument. I'll meet you on the porch."

"Thank you so much." Sarah pushed the screen door open.

"And don't worry about missing supper over at the mess. I'll feed you by and by."

Sarah wasn't sure how she felt about that, but she was psyched to get some fiddle lessons. She grabbed her violin case and was back on the porch in no time. Over the next couple of hours, Sis taught her the basics of fiddling, similar to how Jed played, but with a few southern twists. She showed Sarah how to saw out a reel, tipping the bow sharply over the strings. Off and on Sis would gently shake Sarah's shoulders and tell her to loosen up, and the more she played, the freer she felt.

By the time the sun had set over the creek, Sarah was playing a fairly respectable rendition of "St. Anne's Reel." When they were done, Sis clapped her hands and congratulated her.

Sarah wiped off her instrument and placed it in its case. "That was awesome. I've never felt like that before."

"Somethin', isn't it?" She squinted at Sarah. "But don't you dare blame me if it ruins your fancy violin playing."

"Don't worry, I won't." Sarah stood. "Thank you so much, I loved it."

Sis pointed to the door. "Don't you want some vittles?"

Sarah shook her head and smiled. "No, thank you. I'm too wound up to eat."

Sis nodded. "Yep. Old-time music'll do it to you."

Sarah started down the porch stairs then turned back. "I almost forgot, what do I owe you for the lesson?"

Sis smiled. "Land sakes, you comin' 'round is plenty for me."

"Are you sure?"

"Yep."

"Thanks again. I'll see you later."

As Sarah walked off, Sis called to her. "Hey, darlin', might you and I think about entering that contest over yonder?"

Sarah stopped. "Are you serious?"

"Course. I was thinking of entering this year. Haven't been up there in a long time, and wouldn't old Jed just mess his britches if you and I competed together!"

Sarah thought for a few moments. "So would Luke."

They laughed.

"Well, give it some thought. I'll see you tomorrow."

"You bet!" Sarah called back as she ran down the dirt path.

Back in her cabin, Sarah was so excited she took out her violin and practiced a couple of fiddle techniques Sis had taught her, doing it quietly so the girls in the next cabin wouldn't hear her. Finally exhausted, she got ready for bed. Looking out the window from her cot, she watched clouds pass in front of a chalk-white moon and soon fell asleep. She was dreaming about Luke when she was startled awake by someone knocking on the door. She squinted at her watch on the bedside stand. It was 1:30 in the morning. *What in the world?*

"Who's there?"

"Nick," returned the loud whisper. He sounded like he'd been drinking.

Sarah felt both aroused and annoyed. "I'm coming."

She opened the door wearing just a T-shirt and shorts.

When Nick saw her, his face lit up as he checked her out. "Wow, do you ever look hot."

He took her in his arms and started kissing her. She pushed him away and stepped back.

"Hey—" he said, sounding confused. "It's me." He grabbed her arm and tried to kiss her again, but Sarah pulled away and hurried onto the porch. "What's the matter?" he said, indignantly. "You were all hot and bothered to jump in the sack with me yesterday."

Sarah crossed her arms. "Sorry. I shouldn't have come on to you like that."

Nick sat on the top step. "So, what's the problem?"

Sarah looked at the reflection of the moon on a small beaver pond a short distance away. "I'm not sure. Something shifted in me after I got here."

"Must be that time of the month."

"No, Nick. Not everything is connected to a girl's period."

He chuckled. "Coulda' fooled me." He became more serious. "What's happening to you? We've had a good thing."

Sarah looked at the floor. "Honestly, I'm not sure. I think you need to go."

"I just got here." He laughed.

"I want to be alone, and you're drunk."

"Who, me?" he said sarcastically.

"Yes, you." Sarah pointed to the path. "It's late."

Nick took hold of the railing and pulled himself up. He looked at her. "I still think you're hot as hell."

Sarah shook her head. "Good night." She watched to make sure Nick made it down the path then went back to bed. As tempting as it was to sleep with him, she knew she'd done the right thing. Someone else was taking hold of her heart.

CHAPTER SIX

LUKE PULLED INTO THE MILL YARD BY SUNUP. HE HADN'T been able to sleep much—images and fantasies of Sarah had filled his dreams. He'd also heard Dexter's words over and over again: "You ain't got a chance in hell with a girl like that." Luke figured Dex was right. Still, no harm in dreaming. On the other hand, there was also the ever-present reality of being sent to Vietnam. Even if Sarah was interested in him, who wanted to hear their boyfriend got blown to bits by the 'Cong?

Luke grabbed the logbook and went to work checking in the fresh pine logs. He was relieved the count was correct since they'd recently had logs stolen from the yard at night.

Luke was hesitant to bring another load of lumber down to the lake, but Trace insisted. Luke backed the delivery truck up to the yard's aging diesel crane, fired it up, and loaded on another part of Judge Clements' order. Luke secured the load with extra straps and headed to the building site. He smiled as he passed old Taffy sitting on the scraggly lawn in front of Jed's farmhouse, and he chuckled about Sarah's introduction to the neighborhood.

The mud bog by the barn had dried up quite a bit so Luke was able to easily make the corner and head toward the lake. As he approached the building site, he stayed as far away from the deep mud ruts as he could, then backed up, undid the straps, and slowly raised the truck's bed. With the new posts and beams safely on top of the previous load, he walked over to where Sarah had sat, cross-legged on the hood of her Mustang. With his eyes closed, he tried to feel her presence, smell the fragrance in her hair.

Feeling foolish, he snapped out of it. "Jesus, Simms, you've gone soft. Get your shit together."

Over where the cedars had been toppled by Dex's wrecker, Luke pushed a couple trunks over with his boot and looked in the hole where they'd found the Indian artifacts. Not seeing them, he jumped down and dug around the roots with his hands. He found a piece of rotting wood, but all of the other artifacts were gone. Luke looked around to make sure he was in the right place as a lot of the area had been torn up by the excavation. No question about it.

Luke grabbed a shovel and continued to dig, leveraging up a good-sized rock under which he found a crushed Redman tobacco pouch. "Ritchie's brand—" Ritchie Morrill, the excavator, must have found the artifacts when he did the site work. And Luke guessed Judge Clements had to have known, assuming he was there for at least some of the work. Luke shoveled away more dirt, revealing a Pall Mall cigarette butt. No one smoked those around there. He bet it belonged to the judge.

Luke frowned. Being partly of Abenaki heritage, it angered him that someone would disturb artifacts, conceal them, and then take off with them. He could see Ritchie not caring about the artifacts, but a federal judge certainly should.

Luke was pretty sure there were state laws protecting such historic sites. He now realized why Dex had wanted him and Sarah to leave the artifacts alone. Dex often got extra work from Ritchie, and if the wrong people knew about the artifacts the judge's whole project might get derailed, including developing the other 600 feet of shoreline beyond what he was keeping for himself. Building a line of homes along the shore meant a lot of money would go into the local economy. That was why the argument had broken out at the jam session. Luke understood both sides of the argument, but felt strongly people needed to follow the rules.

Luke looked around at the crudely cleared trees and the piles of logs lying next to the otherwise pristine shore of the lake he had grown up on. Judge Clements must really want to get out of Washington to have done all this damage and maybe broken the law to boot. Because he was Sarah's father, Luke would try to give him the benefit of the doubt—for now.

Back in his truck, Luke headed up the road. He supposed he could refuse to deliver the rest of the cabin, but then Trace would fire him and there was no way Luke could find another job that paid five bucks an hour. He needed the money to help out at home and to pay for parts to rebuild his outboard. And maybe to buy Sarah something nice.

* * *

The next two weeks were a blur. Luke spent most of his time making deliveries for Trace, and helping his mother plant the rest of their vegetable garden, though he wondered how she'd manage to take care of it once he had left. He also nailed up several strands of string along the east side of the house for morning glories to climb because his mother loved to see them out her bedroom window.

As he worked, Luke was troubled by the missing artifacts, but given the intense local politics about development, he wasn't sure there was anyone he could safely talk to. Luke thought of going to the sheriff, but he usually supported developers, and probably had bigger issues to deal with. Conflicted, Luke tried to put the issue out of his mind. Besides, he was wicked excited Sarah was supposed to be back for the weekend.

By the next Friday, the weather had turned unusually hot and humid. During Luke's last delivery, the temperature in his truck felt like it had reached a hundred degrees and he was drenched with sweat. On the way home he took a dip in the brook down the road from his house. It felt good to lay against the smooth rocks in the shallow pool and let the cold water run over his tired muscles.

Back home, he devoured two plates of his mom's mac and cheese, then they crashed on their overstuffed sofa to watch their favorite show, *To Tell the Truth*. Though he enjoyed trying to outguess his mom, Luke barely lasted through the first round before he was so sleepy his head began to nod. He decided to say good night, turned on the squeaky box fan in his room, and went to bed.

The next thing he knew, Luke heard his name being whispered. Moonlight shone through his curtains, which curled back and forth in the breeze from the fan. Figuring he was dreaming, he rolled over and pulled a thin sheet over him.

"Luke...Luke!"

He sat straight up in bed. He'd heard his name, but it wasn't his mother's voice.

"Luke, wake up!"

Luke went to his open window. Sarah stood on the lawn, her golden hair illuminated by the light of the moon.

"Sarah!" Luke whispered back. "You're here—"

"Come out, it's beautiful."

"What time is it?"

"It doesn't matter."

Judging by the moon, it was well after midnight.

He pulled on a pair of shorts and a T-shirt and quietly went out the front door. As he rounded the side of the house, Sarah jumped from behind a lilac bush.

"Shit!" he said, startled.

Sarah looked as psyched to see him as he was to see her. "I did an extra seminar this afternoon so I got a late start. And the traffic was crazy." She smiled. "Well, until I got up here, where there's no lights or cars. It's like being in outer space."

Luke gave her a hug. "I'm so glad to see you. It seems like forever."

Sarah laughed. "It's only been two weeks, silly."

Luke looked into her eyes, bright and alive in the moonlight. "I'm wicked hot."

"I know," Luke said before he could catch himself.

Sarah laughed. "I mean I need to take a swim or something. It's so humid."

Luke smiled. "I know the perfect place." He took her hand. "Come on. I'll get my keys."

Sarah pulled back on his arm. "You don't need them." She nodded at the Mustang, its hot engine making crackling noises under the hood.

"Cool." Luke moved to the passenger's side.

"Here—" Sarah flipped him her keys. "You drive."

Luke snatched the keys out of the air. "Really?"

"Yes, I'm tired, and besides, I might get lost."

"Wouldn't that be too bad," Luke said, feeling surer of himself.

"Let's go." Sarah climbed into the car.

Luke turned the key. He loved the feeling of the powerful engine, but wanted to be careful with her car. He started down the driveway slowly.

"Is this the best you can do?" Sarah asked.

A little embarrassed, Luke shifted gears. "Let's see." He revved the engine, spun through some gravel onto the tree-lined road heading toward town. The wind felt great against his sweaty face and he was amazed how well the Mustang clung to the pavement on the corners. They were flying when they reached the center of tiny Greensboro Village, tires squealing as they rounded the corner by Willey's Store. They sped north on the Craftsbury Road for a mile or so until he slowed and turned sharply onto a small dirt road that led to Black's Point, south of her father's property. They passed a couple of old, moss-covered camps partially hidden in the woods then descended toward the lake. Luke parked the Mustang where the road was overtaken with long, arching blackberry canes. "Can't scratch this beauty."

"You better not."

They got out, and Sarah went to the trunk.

"Come on," Luke said.

"I'm getting my bathing suit and a towel."

Luke smiled at her. "Maybe only the towel. We like to go skinny around here."

Sarah frowned. "*Really?*"

"Really."

She smiled and took his hand. He led her around the blackberries then through a patch of underbrush, which he held back for her. They walked through an aromatic stand of pine trees then descended a rocky incline toward the lake, which shimmered in the moonlight. Ducking under low-hanging cedars, they made their way along the shore to a small opening where a primitive raft of cedar logs was pulled up onto a large flat rock. "Our own private raft," Luke said, motioning.

Sarah smiled. "This is awesome."

"I'll paddle it out for us."

Luke kicked off his sneakers, pulled his T-shirt over his head, and threw it on the raft. "Come on," he said, climbing onto the raft.

At first Sarah hesitated, but when Luke gave her his hand, she stepped gracefully onto the raft. He was amazed to be alone with such a beautiful girl in the middle of a warm summer night. Luke climbed on, untied the raft from a tree, and pushed it away from the shore. He took hold of the oars and began rowing, his strong shoulders arching back and forth as the raft slid through the inky-blue water. Sarah watched the shoreline recede as they made their way to a spot about halfway across the lake. He stopped rowing, and the raft quickly slowed, gently turning on the placid surface. The moon was disappearing below the horizon, allowing constellations to brighten overhead.

"Lay on your back and watch the sky. As the moon goes down, you'll be able to see a gazillion stars."

They lay next to each other, their bodies barely touching. After a while, Sarah turned to Luke. "What do you want to be when you grow up?"

"The classic, loaded question." Luke put his arm behind his head. "It sounds corny, but whatever I end up doing, I want to be honorable, authentic about it. My parents had their issues, but they were grounded in reality. I stay away from people who seem fake."

"Hmm, I like that. Not corny at all."

"Thanks. What about you?"

Sarah smiled. "We're talking about you."

"Oh."

"So, what do you want to do, like for a career?"

"Maybe become a teacher of some sort, though I feel unsettled, like I want to get out of here *and* I want to never leave."

"What do you mean?"

"I love this beautiful place but it's pretty narrow-minded, you know, provincial. I want to experience other places, get exposed to other ways of thinking and living. I don't mean to be disrespectful of people here, it's just…"

Sarah waited a few moments, then spoke. "I get it. You want to explore the rest of the world."

Luke looked at her. "I think so, at least parts of it, without demeaning where I came from."

She smiled. "You don't seem the demeaning type."

"I hope not."

"What a relief—"

Luke looked at her quizzically.

Sarah chuckled. "That you don't want to be president, like every guy I know in Washington."

"Don't worry about that." Luke pointed to the north sky. "See there! A shooting star."

Sarah looked up. "So cool. I've never seen so many stars."

"See over there. The Big Dipper and Cassiopeia."

"Where? There are so many."

Luke took her hand and pointed to a cluster of stars. "Right there." He drew the shape of the constellation with Sarah's finger. "And below it is Pegasus, the wild horse."

STEPHEN RUSSELL PAYNE

Sarah chuckled. "I think the wild horse is on this raft."

"And he's hot." Luke let go of her hand. "Time for a swim." When he started to unbuckle his shorts, Sarah looked apprehensive.

Luke hesitated, held his shorts together. "If it makes you uncomfortable, we won't. Skinny-dip, I mean."

Sarah gave Luke's body a long look then slowly undid her shirt, and then her bra. Luke watched—mesmerized—as she shed her clothes, including her jeans. He quickly dropped his shorts to the raft, realizing there was no hiding his arousal.

Looking up into Luke's eyes, Sarah took a step toward him. As he reached for her, she sprang off the raft, her sleek body arcing through the air as she dove into the dark water. Luke dove after her and came up quickly as the lake was so cold. Treading water, he looked around but couldn't find her. He knew it was too deep for her to have hit a rock, but he became worried when she didn't surface.

"Over here, you hick."

He swung around and saw Sarah twenty feet away. He started swimming toward her but she disappeared under the surface again. A few moments later he felt her come up behind him, her arms sliding around his waist. He turned and their bodies met, her breasts and thighs warm against his skin.

Smiling, Luke shook his head. "Where in the world did you come from?"

Sarah chuckled. "I was just thinking the same thing."

71

CHAPTER SEVEN

WITH LUKE'S STRONG LEGS KEEPING THEM AFLOAT, HE and Sarah stared at each other for a few moments before their lips came together. Hers were soft and warm, and she moaned as they drew each other's tongues into their mouths. As they kissed, Luke stopped treading water and they inadvertently drifted under the cold surface.

With them both coughing, Luke held Sarah with one arm and forced his other arm down through the water, bringing them back up. He took a deep breath. "Might be safer on the raft."

Sarah laughed then coughed again. "Nice kiss, but I'd rather not drown." She started shivering. "Plus, this water is frigid!"

"I knew it'd cool you off."

They swam together to the raft. Luke climbed on then pulled Sarah up. Her skin was silky, like no one he'd touched before. He wrapped a towel around her and they shared a long, lingering kiss in the darkening night. He wanted to run his hands all over her body, but didn't feel sure enough of himself. When Sarah loosened her embrace, Luke helped her dry off, gently passing a towel over her shoulders and down her back. She smiled, kissed him again, and pulled on her clothes.

He was in love.

They quietly watched the sky fill with stars as Luke slowly

rowed them back to shore. He tied up the raft then they walked back up the hill to the Mustang. Sarah sat on the hood and took Luke into her arms. They held each other for what seemed like a long time.

"Thank you for bringing me here."

Luke gently lifted strands of wet hair away from her eyes. "You're welcome. It's a special place. My family's come here for generations."

Sarah looked up the lake toward the property her father had bought. "It's so beautiful. I feel a little bad my father is developing it."

Luke nodded. "I know. Lotta' folks against it, but he's got as much right as anyone." Luke held his tongue about the Indian artifacts.

Sarah looked him in the eye. "You are a fair man, Luke Simms."

"Thanks."

Sarah hopped into the driver's seat and drove them back through town. They held hands, their hair drying in the warm wind.

As they approached the turn to Luke's house, he looked at Sarah. "We're having a jam session at the café tomorrow night, if you want to come."

"I don't know," she said, giving him a sideways grin. "I can't play your kind of mountain music."

Luke chuckled. "I don't know about that, but you'd have fun anyway. My friends are really good musicians. We'll be practicing songs for the barn dance."

"You really have a dance in a barn?"

"'Course, social event of the season."

"I'll bet," Sarah said, sarcastically.

"Seriously. And I think I told you there's a great fiddle contest at the end, sometimes goes half the night."

"That does sound like fun."

Luke grinned, lifted his nose in the air. "Too bad you only play the violin."

"Clearly, a superior instrument," she replied in a faux aristocratic accent.

Luke got out and walked around to Sarah's side. He leaned against the door. "I loved being with you tonight."

"Me, too."

Luke leaned down and kissed her. He noticed she was still shivering. "Hang on," he said, running over to his pickup. He returned with a sweatshirt. "Here."

Sarah smiled and pulled it on. She pushed up the long sleeves and hugged herself. "Thanks. I'm about frozen."

"Can't have that." Luke gently slid the hood up over her tousled hair. "You staying over at the inn?"

Sarah nodded.

"How about I pick you up around 4:30? You can meet my mom and have supper with us. Then we'll go over to Skinny's."

"I don't know, my dad may want to have dinner together."

"Okay."

"Actually," Sarah continued, "I think he's having dinner at the Conovers' tomorrow night. I'd much rather eat with you."

Luke smiled. "Great."

"I'll just drive back over here for dinner."

Luke thought for a moment. "Why don't you let me pick you up? It would be better."

"How so?"

Luke looked at the Mustang. "This beauty might make the neighbors jealous."

"I see." Sarah looked at herself. "What about *this* beauty?"

Luke smiled. "Definitely make them jealous."

Sarah revved the engine. "Pick me up at 4:30. And don't be late."

"You got it."

"I've got to go, or my father will have the feds out looking for me."

"Tell him you just took the long way up here, got lost, or something."

"He's not stupid." Sarah goosed the Mustang and sped off, leaving Luke smiling at the side of the road.

Luke shook his head as he watched her disappear. "You're amazing." He walked down his dark gravel driveway, the familiar sounds of peepers coming from the beaver pond beyond the field. As he approached the house, he noticed an oil drum was still burning down behind one of the trailers. Dale Ketchum probably had the boys over and forgot to put the fire out. It didn't seem to be near anything that might catch fire, so Luke quietly walked inside.

He drank a glass of cold milk, then noticed it was after four in the morning, according to the kitchen clock. Tiptoeing down the hallway to his bedroom, he slid under the sheet and stared up at the ceiling. A slight breeze meandered through the open window, cooling his warm body. All he could think about was Sarah, her spirit, and how beautiful she was in the glow of moonlight.

After a short while, he heard his mother's door open. He listened as she slowly stepped along the wall to the bathroom.

When she came out, she gently nudged Luke's door open. "She must be—something special," his mom said quietly, her speech slow and hesitant from her poor lungs.

"She is, Mom. I've got it bad."

"Good—for you," she said. "Now get some—fast sleep, you've work—in the morning. *This* morning."

"I will. G'night, Mom."

"Good night, Son."

The door closed silently behind her. Luke listened to make sure she got back in bed safely.

Chapter Eight

S ARAH PULLED THE MUSTANG AROUND TO THE BACK OF the inn and parked in a spot farthest from the building next to a bed of hollyhocks. She closed the convertible roof and quietly shut her door. The inn was mostly dark except for a light over the back porch and one in the parlor that shown through a stained glass window. Sarah made her way silently up the stairs and into the foyer covered with dark, flowery wallpaper. Next to a black-and-white photograph of the inn with horse carriages in front of it stood a stately grandfather's clock that read 4:38. As she turned to go up the stairs, she detected a familiar cigarette smell. Her heart jumped; her father *couldn't* have been waiting up for her all night. She backed up and peered around the corner into the parlor. At the far end of a blue and purple braided rug her father sat in an upholstered chair, a folded newspaper across his lap. Looking like he had just awakened, the judge immediately got up and walked toward her. "Sarah, thank god you're alright."

Seeing the concerned and tired look on her father's face, Sarah felt terrible. In all the excitement of seeing Luke, it hadn't occurred to her he would be worried. They hugged each other.

"Has it been raining?" he asked.

Realizing her hair and clothes, including Luke's oversized sweatshirt, were still damp, Sarah took a step back. "No, it was really hot on the long drive, so I took a swim when I got here. The lake is so beautiful."

Judge Clements nodded. "I'm sure it is. I hope you weren't alone swimming at this hour. God only knows who might be roaming around these parts in the middle of the night."

Sarah blushed but didn't respond.

The judge cocked his head a bit. "Well?"

"Not to worry, I was with someone who knows the area."

Still looking concerned, the judge waited.

Sarah stepped toward him. "I'm sorry, Daddy. I was late getting out of Hunter Mountain and the traffic was crazy. I was so hot when I got here..." She looked at him sheepishly. "And I had to stop and see him."

"Luke?"

Sarah nodded. "He took me to swim on this cool wooden raft he built."

The judge put his hand to his chin. "You're soft on this boy?"

"Kind of. He's different than other guys."

"I'll say."

"He's, like, authentic."

Her father pondered for a few moments. "Are you serious about him?"

Sarah frowned. "I hardly know him, really." She shrugged her shoulders. "Maybe a summer romance. He's fun to be with."

"Alright, Sarah, but no more all-night swims. And don't get into any trouble."

"I won't." She gave him a quick hug. "Thanks, Dad."

"Now get some sleep. Your mother would have a fit if she knew you were up this late."

Sarah stifled sarcastic thoughts. She was sure her mother could care less what she was up to. "You, also, had better get some rest. Much too late for a man of your stature to be up."

"Wise cracker." He took hold of the smooth wooden banister and climbed the carpeted stairs.

When she heard her father's door close, Sarah thought of sneaking out and snuggling in with Luke but quickly decided that would be a very bad idea.

* * *

At sunrise, which came awfully quickly, Luke dragged himself out of bed. He didn't want to be late for work. Mostly daydreaming about Sarah, he hauled several truckloads of aromatic spruce and pine shavings to Patenaude's farm up on the Creek Road, loaded a couple hundred hemlock planks into the mill's kiln dryer, then raced home to clean up for Sarah.

"What're you making for supper?" he called out to his mom after a shower. He found her resting under an afghan on the couch in the living room. She looked worn out, too tired to make a meal. Luke sat next to her on a threadbare ottoman, and took her hand. "You okay?"

She looked up at him. "Yes, tired is all."

"I don't need to have Sarah come over if it's too much."

His mom's eyes brightened. "Heaven's no," she said, feigning more energy than he figured she had. "I can't wait to meet her." She pushed the afghan off her legs and sat up.

"You had fun with her last night?"

Luke smiled. "It was awesome. Took her out on my raft. The water was calm and the stars bright after the moon went down."

Mary looked at her son's face. "Never seen you this excited over a girl."

Luke nodded. "Never met anyone like her. She's so beautiful, and smart, and loves music. I'm going to take her to Skinny's after supper."

"That oughtta' be fun."

"Yeah, if they don't scare her off. Jed nearly did till she saw his antique fiddle."

Mary adjusted the pillows supporting her back. "She tough?"

Luke smiled. "Tough enough."

"Good." Mary leaned on Luke to get up. "Let's get supper on. I've got baking powder biscuits ready to go in the oven. Chicken and gravy just needs to be warmed up on the stove."

"My favorite. Thanks, Mom." He gave her a kiss on the cheek. "I think you'll like her."

"Bet I will." Mary straightened her apron and leaned on the wall as she walked to the kitchen.

Luke checked himself in the hall mirror. "Sure I can't help with anything?"

"All set. Just go get your girl."

Luke headed out the front door. "See you soon."

He stopped at the mill on the way and quickly washed off his truck with a high-pressure hose. He drove slowly out of the gravel drive so as not to get it dirty again, and floored it when he hit the pavement. His truck hesitated, then took off, a cloud of smoke visible in his side view mirror. At the inn, Luke parked near Sarah's Mustang, and strode up onto the grand porch. He leaned against the railing and looked out over the lake and the undulating spine of the Green Mountains to the west. He was pretty sure he lived in the most beautiful place in the world.

Luke knocked on the inn's heavy wood and beveled glass door. He waited a minute but no one came, so he walked in and stood in the middle of the foyer. An ornate brass cash register sat on an oak desk that had a hand-carved "Welcome" sign mounted on the front. There was a brass bell on the corner of the desk next to a thick leather book with a gold tassel hanging out of it. "Guest Register" was printed on the cover in fancy letters. The air held a slight mustiness tinged with hints of chocolate.

Luke looked around and saw a side table set up with a polished silver teapot and a small wooden box full of teabags. Next to them sat a plate filled with chocolate chip cookies. Luke stared at them for a few moments then started to reach for a cookie, but figured he'd better not. They weren't for people like him, only for the well-to-do guests. He started to turn away but couldn't resist and snatched two of the warm cookies off the top of the pile. Hearing someone coming down the hall, he stuffed one in his mouth and slipped the other into his jean's pocket.

"Can I help you, sir?" A woman in a plaid flannel shirt and jeans stepped behind the desk. Her graying hair was held down by a brimmed hat. She placed a pair of dirty gloves next to the brass bell. "I'm Victoria, Vicky for short. Excuse my appearance, I've been working in the vegetable garden out back."

Luke forced himself to swallow the last of the cookie. "I, I'm here to pick up Sarah Clements."

"The judge's daughter?" Vicky sounded a bit surprised.

"Yeah. We're friends."

She lifted the receiver from an antique wooden wall phone. The phone's chimes gently rang as she turned the crank three times. She listened then spoke into the small black cone attached to the wooden case. "Miss Clements, you have a visitor…" She turned to Luke. "What was your name?"

"Ah, Luke."

"A Mr. Luke." The woman paused. "Yes, I'll tell him." She hung up and turned back to Luke. "She said they'll be right down."

"*They?*"

"I presume Sarah and her father."

"Alright, then," Luke said in a nervous voice.

He heard a door open above him and within a few moments Sarah and her father were walking along the banister that led to the grand staircase. She looked beautiful as she descended the stairs, carrying her violin case. Trying not to stare at her, Luke shoved his hands in his pockets, his right hand smooshing the melting cookie.

"Oh, god—" He turned away and pulled his chocolate-streaked hand out of his pocket. Knowing he needed to shake the judge's hand, Luke tried to quickly lick it clean. "Hi, Luke," Sarah said in a bit of a formal voice.

"Hey, Sarah," Luke replied, wiping his hand on the butt of his jeans.

Sarah motioned to her father. "You've met my father."

Judge Clements stepped forward and extended his hand, but seeing the chocolate on Luke's fingers, pulled it back.

"I couldn't resist the cookies," Luke said, feeling embarrassed. He wiped his hand on his jeans again.

"I can't resist them, either," the judge said as he took a white linen handkerchief from the pocket of his sport jacket. He handed it to Luke, who wiped off his fingers but then wasn't sure

84

what to do with the handkerchief. The judge took it back and folded it into his pocket.

"So," Luke said, "you ready for some homemade supper?"

Sarah smiled. "Absolutely." She lowered her head and whispered to Luke. "As long as it isn't venison stew." She turned to her father. "Please say hi to the Conovers for me."

"I will."

"Good night, sir." Luke turned and held the door open for Sarah.

"Don't stay out too late," the judge said.

"We won't," Sarah called back to him.

Around back, Luke opened the passenger door of his pickup and an empty soda can rolled out. He quickly pushed a parts catalog and other junk onto the floor and brushed a layer of sawdust off the seat. "Sorry, I didn't want to be late so I didn't get to—"

Sarah put her finger to his lips. "I'm just glad to see you and get out of that stuffy inn."

Luke nodded. "Me, too."

As they drove away, they looked at each other and chuckled.

"That was really smooth with the cookie."

"I thought so. It would've been okay if I hadn't stuffed one in my pocket."

They laughed. Luke shifted gears, and they headed for his house. Sarah stuck her head out the window and let out a yell, the warm wind blowing through her hair. Luke got a thrill out of seeing her feeling free, like she was in a movie.

As they made the turn for his road, Luke pulled off to the side and looked at Sarah. "I just wanted to tell you something. My mother's cool and looking forward to meeting you, but she's not very well. She was injured on her farm as a young girl. Her lungs are bad, and she has heart failure, so she gets really tired easily."

"What happened to her?"

"She's never said much, but Trace told me she was crushed when she and my grandfather were trying to get a huge bull into a pen. It jammed her against a gate post and crushed her chest."

Sarah grimaced as a chill raced up her spine. "That's awful! It's amazing she survived."

"Yeah, and to make matters worse, when she was a teenager, she worked in the asbestos mine over in Eden and ended up with pulmonary fibrosis."

"Poor woman." Sarah put her hand on Luke's forearm. "It means a lot that you're bringing me to meet her."

"I'm glad you could come. My family's owned this farm for four generations. It's too bad they had to sell off some of the fields to make it through the Depression, then most of the rest of it when the price of milk bottomed out about ten years ago. A sleezy developer bought the fields and turned them into a trailer park."

"I can see why you're not crazy about development."

"Yeah." Luke put the truck in gear and started back down the road under an arching canopy of sugar maples. "Depends what they do with the land." He shifted gears. "Sometimes they don't care about it—just wreck it."

As they approached Luke's farmhouse, Sarah was shocked at how different the area looked in the daylight. Abandoned farm machinery and junked cars sat inside broken runs of rusty barbed wire fence, that hung loosely off cedar posts leaning at odd angles.

A rocky pasture was partially overgrown with bushes and young trees. A dilapidated barn leaned into a hillside behind the house, its wood so faded she could barely tell it was ever truly red. Beyond the small farmyard stood a row of aging house trailers, none of which appeared to be in good condition. Beside one trailer, a large woman in a blue housedress was hanging washing on an octagonal clothesline, a half-burned cigarette in the corner of her mouth. Several pieces of clothing lay in the tall grass beneath the clothesline.

As Luke downshifted and turned into his driveway, a couple of scruffy chickens clucked and scooted out of his way. Pulling to a stop, Sarah was startled by a trio of crows as they cawed and took flight from an old apple tree. Flapping their long, black wings so hard their tip feathers splayed, they swooped sideways and disappeared behind the barn.

"Well," Luke said, pulling on the parking brake, "here we are."

He seemed excited. Sarah forced a smile.

The screen door opened and a thin woman in an apron appeared on the porch.

"Come on," Luke said, opening his door.

Sarah stared at the sagging front porch, flashed back to Jed McCaffery's place. But this couldn't be as bad—could it?

CHAPTER NINE

Luke's mother looked frail as she stood holding the warped wooden railing at the top of the porch stairs.

Luke led Sarah across the muddy yard. "Mom, this is Sarah, the girl I told you about." His mother greeted Sarah with a warm smile and an unsteady hug.

"Nice to meet you," she said, looking Sarah over.

"Me, too, Mrs. Simms," Sarah said, feeling uncomfortable.

"Heavens, call me Mary." She motioned to the door. "Come in and we'll have some supper." She took Sarah's hand, more for support than anything else, Sarah thought, and they walked inside. A cobwebbed light hung inside the doorway, beyond which was a wooden stairway, its gray paint worn off in the middle of each stair. A faded pink and green floral wallpaper with innumerable scratches and tears ran alongside the staircase.

"Come along. We'll eat at the kitchen table."

Sarah followed Mary into the kitchen, in the center of which stood a wooden table, painted white long ago, and now covered with linoleum with plastic souvenir placemats stapled to it. Upon these sat three mismatched china plates, thin paper napkins, and tarnished silverware. In the center of the table a milk bottle held a bouquet of aromatic lilies-of-the-valley with three tall yellow tulips rising in the middle. The wooden floor was worn, especially in front of the stove and sink, where heads of square nails poked through. The enamel sink had a few chips out of it, and the back was streaked with a rusty water stain. In a bay window hung half-curtains and a yellowing Swedish ivy suspended from a coat hook. Mary's kitchen was the same vintage as Jeb's, but it had a whole different feel. It was pretty clean, and orderly in its own old-fashioned way.

Mary motioned to the table. "Sit down. Luke, get Sarah what she'd like to drink."

"Is there anything I can help you with, Mrs.—ah, Mary?"

"No, you just make yourself comfortable."

Sarah sat in a wooden chair that had been repaired, glue and screws holding the legs together. Luke held up a frosty pitcher from the fridge. "Lemonade?"

"Yes, please."

Sarah watched Mary lift a heavy pot from the stove and struggle to pour the contents into a serving bowl. Though her arms were clearly weak, her determination was strong. Luke brought a glass of lemonade for each of them then poured a cup of tea for his mother.

Mary brought a plate of fresh powder biscuits from the oven and set them next to Sarah. They smelled heavenly. Luke set the chicken and gravy on the table, then he and his mother sat on either side of Sarah. Mary needed a few moments to catch her breath then wiped her hands on her apron, pulled it over her head, and set it on the empty chair.

Luke immediately went for the biscuits.

"Luke—" his mother said. "Would you like to say grace for us?"

Luke grinned at Sarah and dropped the biscuit back on the plate. They joined hands and bowed their heads. "Thank you,

God, for the birds that sing, thank you, God, for everything."
After a short pause, they all said, "Amen."

Sarah couldn't help but let out a giggle.

Mary squeezed her hand. "He's not much on grace."

"I'll say."

The chicken and biscuits were delicious. Sarah even had a second helping. The dinner conversation was light, Mary inquiring about her father's building project and Sarah's music camp. By the time dessert arrived, Sarah was so full she had only a sliver of strawberry-rhubarb pie with a dab of vanilla ice cream.

As Sarah finished the last pie crumb, Mary turned to her. "Tell me about your mother. You haven't mentioned her."

"I'm stuffed," Luke said, throwing his napkin on the table.

"Luke, that's not polite."

"We've got to get over to Skinny's for the jam session."

Mary waited for a reply from Sarah, who was staring at her empty plate.

"Dear...?" Mary inquired.

Sarah glanced at her. "I'd rather not talk about my mother."

"Oh?" Mary said, seeming a bit confused.

Sarah looked at Mary, shook her head. "I can just tell you she's nothing like you."

CHAPTER TEN

RIDING TO SKINNY'S, LUKE WAS CONCERNED WITH HOW quiet Sarah was, and he wasn't completely clear what she'd meant saying her mother wasn't anything like his. Sarah seemed like she'd enjoyed dinner, but Luke was keenly aware that vastly different worlds had been mixing in that kitchen.

As they emerged from under a canopy of trees, a bright moon hung over the road ahead of them. "Beautiful night, huh?"

"Yes." Sarah put her hand on his arm. "I liked your mom. She seems like a good woman. It's just a lot to take in."

"What do you mean?"

"Her being sick but so determined and welcoming. She made a really nice dinner."

"Yeah, she's cool."

"And I couldn't help but be struck by the juxtaposition of her and my crazy, ambitious mother who is pretty cold unless you're *somebody* or she wants something from you."

Luke frowned. "Really? Your mother's like that?"

"Pretty much. It's why I love coming up here with my father—to get away from her." She glanced at Luke. "Or one of the reasons, at least."

Luke smiled.

"It's hard to be around her. She's self-centered and snobby, but my dad isn't, or he at least tries hard not to be. For a big wheel judge, he can be pretty cool."

Luke didn't say anything for a mile or so.

"Did you not like my father?" Sarah asked.

"No, he seems okay."

Sarah looked at him. "You're not good at hiding things."

Luke drove on in silence.

Sarah grasped his arm again. "Luke?"

Luke was not going to lie, but he didn't want to get into the whole relic situation or they'd be late for Skinny's and, more importantly, it could ruin things with Sarah. "I don't even know your dad. I'm just a little intimidated by a federal judge. Don't see many of those around here."

"Well, you'll probably get to know him."

Luke nodded. "'Spect so." He felt the uncomfortable need to come clean with her. He took the turn onto Shadow Lake Road and pulled onto the shoulder.

Sarah looked at him. "This going to be another roadside chat?"

"I guess." Luke stared through the windshield. "I don't like to accuse others of things, but I need to be honest. I think your father was involved in disturbing those Indian artifacts and not reporting them."

Sarah frowned. "Why would you think that?"

"Because, when I delivered more loads this week, I looked around where we saw those beads and arrowheads, and..." Luke hesitated.

"And what?"

"I found a tobacco pouch I'm sure belonged to Ritchie Morrill, the guy who did the excavating."

"So?" Sarah became impatient.

"And right near it was a cigarette butt, a Pall Mall. Nobody smokes them around here, don't even sell them at the store."

"That doesn't prove anything." Sarah crossed her arms against her chest. "Why are you attacking my father? He puts up with enough grief in Washington."

Luke put the truck in park. "I'm not, but I can't ignore what I saw. It's illegal to disturb an Indian site and not report it."

"It was just a few old relics. Besides, I'm pretty sure my father has supported Indian rights."

"Look," Luke said in a calm voice, "the site should be protected. It's part of the history of the area."

"So, now you're a history buff," Sarah said, sarcastically.

"Actually I am. I've got a little Indian blood in me, and important events went on around here, like over on the Bayley Hazen Road. As Dex said, that's where Indians attacked the old blockhouse in the late 1700s and killed two local soldiers."

"So why would you want to protect them?"

Luke frowned at Sarah. "Because it's part of our history—the right thing to do. Besides, the Indians weren't all bad."

They sat on the shoulder of the road for a few minutes. The tiny, shrill calls of thousands of peepers came through their open windows from a nearby swamp.

After a short while, Sarah spoke in a more sympathetic tone. "Why do you *really* care so much about the Indians?"

"There were so-called 'savages' around here, but I'm sure many were kind-hearted. One saved my great-grandfather from freezing to death."

"Oh, what happened?"

"He trapped along the Canadian border for beaver and lynx, whatever he could catch. Late one fall, he was up on Belvidere

Mountain and had a bear trap spring on him. Nailed his leg, and I guess he bled like crazy. There'd been an early snow and it was wicked cold. He was quite a ways from his camp and couldn't make it back. An Indian scout found him unconscious, got him out of the trap, and carried him to their village. They warmed him up and tended to his wounds. They saved his life."

"Okay, I can see why you have a soft spot for Indians."

"Though most people around here don't. Anyway, it's about having a clear conscience."

"I understand. So, what are you going to do?" Sarah asked.

"Not sure. It's complicated. I was going to ask your advice."

"Really?"

"Yeah, I respect you."

Sarah let her guard down some. "I respect you, too."

Luke looked at her. "Thing is, if your father's going to develop the rest of that land and build houses along the shoreline, it's going to have to be investigated first. And maybe they won't let him do it."

"But that's the only way he can afford to build the big house he wants. He's gotten the permits he needs."

"But they didn't know about the Indian relics."

Sarah fell silent for a few moments then looked at Luke. "Would you be able to talk to him?"

Luke looked at Sarah. "Do you think he'd listen to me?"

"I think so."

Luke nodded. "I'll think about it. I'm not too keen about arguing with a federal judge, *and* I don't want this to come between us. I just want to do the right thing."

"I get it."

"Thanks. Now, let's get to Skinny's. I don't want to be late."

"Okay. I want to show your friends how to properly play a violin."

Luke chuckled. "That'll be interesting."

They drove in silence, but Luke reached over and held her hand. When they arrived at the Bullpout, they heard the musicians tuning up inside. Luke grabbed his guitar case from the back, Sarah tucked her violin case under her arm, and they walked toward the door. She hesitated. "Maybe I shouldn't bring mine in."

Luke turned. "Why not?"

"Doesn't feel right. I'll just listen."

Sarah placed her case back in the truck, and she and Luke walked to the door, which had a weathered yellow and red "Salada Tea" push bar across the screen. Luke held the door for her, but she nudged him inside ahead of her. Sensing she was a bit nervous, he led Sarah to his usual table and pulled a chair out for her. Plates holding crumbs of Skinny's famous cornbread were scattered around the tables.

"Who ya' got with ya'?" Filly called loudly from her wheelchair, where she was snapping spoons on her thigh.

Ritchie Morrill spit a small wad into a coffee can on the floor. "That's the big judge's daughter, ain't it?" he said, out of the corner of his mouth.

"Give it a rest," Jed snarled at Ritchie.

Luke saw that everyone was staring at Sarah, who seemed to want to shrink into the floorboards. He gestured toward her. "Hey, this is my friend, Sarah. She's going to be around some this summer. She's a musician, too."

"What you goinna' play for us?" Filly asked.

Sarah sheepishly looked over at her. "I, uh, don't have my

instrument with me. I'd just like to listen. Luke's told me what great players you are."

"Have you now, Luke?" Mac, the Irish accordion player said with a sideward glance. "Let's hope we don't disappoint the little lady."

Jed adjusted his stumpy leg. "Enough, already. Let's wind'r up," he said with a wave of his hand.

Skinny struck a few keys on his piano. "Okay, hang on. 'Rock Around the Clock,' key of C."

Everyone raised their instruments and followed Skinny as he led them into the song. Feeling relieved that the spotlight was off of her, Sarah settled into a red-cushioned booth with historic black-and-white photographs of the area mounted on the wall. Above her, a colorful Old Milwaukee Beer lamp hung from the sloped wainscot ceiling. As music filled the café, the place felt cozier. Even though it was way different than the restaurants and pubs she was used to in Georgetown, Sarah felt unexpectedly at home. She listened intently to the musicians and was impressed how they came together as a tight, harmonious group. Though she didn't know all the songs they were playing, they had a good beat, held steady by Dexter and a grizzled old codger blowing into an earthenware jug.

After a while there was a beer break, and Sarah shared an awful-tasting Narragansett longneck with Luke. Thankfully, he soon drained it before speaking quietly to her. "Now we're going to practice our song for the barn dance at the summer festival. Check out Jed's solo."

After another round of cornbread and beer, everyone wiped off their hands, raised their instruments, and played spirited renditions of "Denver Belle," and "Black Mountain Rag." Though she suspected they didn't identify as such, there was definitely a pecking order of the players. She was quite sure Jed and Betty sparred for first violin, or *fiddle* that is.

All of a sudden, everyone quieted and turned to Jed, who rose on his good leg and leaned against a table. He steadied himself for a moment then raised his fiddle to his shoulder. Cradling his instrument against a weathered cheek, Jed closed his eyes, and drew his bow across the strings, making them sing. He conjured sounds from his instrument Sarah had never heard before. She was mesmerized by the beauty of his playing. Jed *had* gone to Berklee.

At the end of practice, Betty slid her chair closer to Jed and they exchanged riffs back and forth until they came to a shared, fever-pitched crescendo, after which they subtly nodded to each other. Delighted, Sarah shot up from the bench and began clapping.

Watching Sarah, Luke smiled, happy that she enjoyed their music.

Sarah approached Jed. "That was amazing. How do you make those layered, high-pitched sounds?"

Jed relaxed in his chair and slid a pinch of chaw into his lower cheek. "Practice," he said without looking up. "Even if you've got it in you, it takes years of practice to bring it out. It doesn't all come natural."

"You're so right," Sarah replied. "Most of the time I practice my violin three to four hours a day."

"Yup," Jed said. "I guess I practiced the same when I was a farm boy, even more when I was a student in Boston. 'Bout all I did 'cept working for a cobbler repairing shoes and handbags at night." He smiled. "Loved the smells in the leather shop." He carefully wiped his fiddle with a chamois cloth and secured it in its case. He pulled on an extra flannel shirt hanging on the back of his chair. "I'd like to hear you play sometime, missy." He got his legs under him, nodded to everyone, and limped out into the night.

CHAPTER ELEVEN

B ACK IN HIS PICKUP, LUKE TURNED THE KEY A COUPLE TIMES. The engine barely moaned.

"Sounds like it's dying." Sarah said, concerned.

"Yup." He tried it a few more times and realized he needed a jump. "Hoped this battery would make it through the summer and I'd find a good used one before winter."

"You may need one sooner."

Jed came up to Sarah's window. "You've got your instrument with you?"

"Yes."

"Fetch it out here, and I'll show you some things."

"Really?"

Jed nodded. "I saw how you were itching to join in with us."

"I was." Sarah looked at Luke.

"Go ahead. I'll find a jump."

Jed looked over at Luke. "Get your guitar and join us."

With her violin in hand, Sarah stepped onto the porch and sat on a wooden bench under a yellow lamp. As she and Jed took out their instruments, Skinny came outside. "I've got to get home to the missus. If you're still hungry, help yourselves to the rest of the cornbread. Won't keep." He tossed a key attached to a bottle opener onto the bench. "Just lock up and put the key in the usual place."

"Thanks, Skinny," Luke said. "We won't be long."

"I thought I heard your old beast moaning."

Luke nodded.

"If Jed's truck hasn't got enough juice to jump you, my old Power Wagon's 'round back. Touch the wires under the dash and she'll fire up. Just be patient raisin' the snowplow—piston's stiffer 'n hell."

Jed held his hand out toward Sarah. "Let's see…" She handed him her violin. He looked it over and plucked a couple strings. "Slender neck, good tone, high bridge, but that's okay. It's a violin after all." He handed it back to her.

"What do you mean, high bridge?"

He showed her his fiddle. "See here, we often sand off the bridge, make it a little flatter so we can play two strings t'once."

Sarah frowned. "Never heard of that."

"'Course not." Jed grinned. "Now, you hold the instrument a little differently when you fiddle, keep it straight out from your chin." He demonstrated. "And hold up higher on the bow than you usually would."

Sarah tried to mimic what he was doing, but it felt awkward.

"When we fiddle, you've got to feel free, looser with your instrument. Violinists tend to stranglehold the poor thing. And like I said, we play two strings t'once: one's the melody, the other's the ringing harmony."

Sarah was confused.

"Watch now." Jed held his bow up high and launched into a short riff.

Sarah loosened her grip a bit, trying to imitate the way Jed handled his instrument, but it didn't come off right. Stifling a laugh, Luke cracked a smile. Jed reached over and loosened

Sarah's wrist and elbow. She kept trying, and after a little practice her arm became freer.

"That's it," Jed said, joining her.

Luke began strumming, and the three of them found their way into a rendition of "Will the Circle Be Unbroken." Though Sarah struggled to follow Jed, she started to catch on. When they finished, Sarah relaxed against the bench and breathed in cool night air tinged with the fragrance of pine. "Thank you, Mr. McCaffery."

"It's Jed."

"Thank you, Jed. That was fun."

"Pleasure." He closed his fiddle case. "You know what they say..."

"What's that?" Sarah asked.

"A violin gets champagne spilled on it, a fiddle gets beer."

Sarah laughed.

"Never liked champagne." Jed stood and let his good leg get under him. "Taffy'll be hungrier 'n a horse. Won't know what's happened to me." He stepped toward his truck. "You've got good form but don't let fiddling ruin you. It's prob'ly driven my proper violin training clear out of me."

Sarah smiled. "I won't."

"Luke, you want me to jump you?"

"Thanks, we'll probably sit awhile. I'll bring Skinny's rig around to get her going."

"G'night, then. Don't forget to lock up."

"Got it. Night, Jed," Luke called after him.

Jed waved with one hand, climbed into his pickup, which looked to be in much worse shape than Luke's, and drove off.

Sarah just about jumped into Luke's lap. That was amazing!"

"He's something, isn't he?"

"So are you." Sarah wrapped her arms around Luke and kissed him on the lips.

Luke shut off the porch light and gave her a long kiss. The moon was low on the horizon, and as their eyes adjusted, the sky filled with stars.

Luke ran his fingers through Sarah's hair. "I feel like I'm in a dream."

"I know." Sarah held him tighter.

"Speaking of dreaming, I saw some bread pudding in Skinny's cooler that I know he won't miss. Come on."

Sarah followed him inside where he filled a bowl with pudding, on top of which he put a large dollop of whipped cream. "Let's eat it outside." They sat on the top of the stairs for a better view of the stars. "I can never see the sky like this in DC. There's way too much light."

"Can't imagine not seeing the stars every night. At least when there aren't clouds."

"It's beautiful. And that was way cool with Jed, though fiddling isn't as easy as I thought it would be." She made a motion as if raising her instrument. "You're right, he's not just a crazy old man."

Luke nodded, ate a big spoonful of pudding, getting whipped cream on his nose. Sarah laughed and quickly licked it off. She took a mouthful of cream and smiled, the cream oozing from the corner of her lips. Luke set his bowl down and slid his tongue into her sweet mouth. It was going to be a helluva summer!

CHAPTER TWELVE

WITH SARAH BACK AT HUNTER MOUNTAIN, LUKE worked like crazy during the week so he could spend time with her on the weekend. Though he was concerned about the artifacts and confronting her father, the war and impending draft scared him the most. It was difficult reconciling his desire to honorably serve his country with the tragic quagmire of Vietnam. Thinking about Sarah helped keep his mind off the atrocities in the news, which were hard to avoid. And then there was his boat—always a source of pleasure—which he worked on in the shed at Andy's late into the night. He not only wanted to win the race for his father, he wanted Sarah to see him beat Freddie McCormick.

After a few days of sunshine, the building site had dried up considerably. Luke knew Ritchie was anxious to dig holes for the heavy wooden pilings upon which the cabin would be built, so on Wednesday, Luke had to deliver the pilings. He also wanted to check on Ritchie's excavation work at the same time. With his being pretty frosty when they were both at Skinny's, Luke presumed Ritchie might still be unearthing and destroying more artifacts.

As Luke started descending toward the lake, he noticed a plume of smoke rising through the cedars down at the site. He figured they were burning slack from trees that had been cleared.

As Luke pulled into the parking area, he saw Ritchie on his old Caterpillar bulldozing over the area where they'd found the artifacts. Close to the road was a smoky fire of cedar boughs piled high over tree trunks, wood scraps, and other debris.

Luke parked and walked over to the burn pile, where he noticed more artifacts tossed in with the cedar. Pissed, Luke kicked some green boughs out of the way and pulled a couple of smoldering wood relics and a piece of broken pottery from the fire. He tried but couldn't get to anything else.

"What the hell are you doing?" Ritchie was off his dozer, charging across the lot.

"What the hell are *you* doing?" Luke yelled back.

"Burning a bunch of junk. We're clearing the lot."

Ritchie grabbed a couple of Indian pieces, and as he went to throw them back on the fire, Luke shoved him, causing him to drop them.

Ritchie's face reddened. "Back off, Luke. You got no damn business here."

"Oh, yeah? I've got plenty of reason to be here, most importantly to protect history from the likes of you." Luke glanced over at where Ritchie had been bulldozing. "You got no right covering all that up without letting the sheriff or the state university—somebody—look it over."

Ritchie snickered. "You think the sheriff gives two shits about this junk? You think I care about having those snobs from Burlington come poking around here?" He defiantly spit a wad of chaw on the ground. "None of their goddamn business."

Luke stepped toward him. "Don't you care about where we come from, about history? The Indians were here in Vermont long before we were."

"I don't give a shit about those goddamn savages. No injun blood in me."

Luke's pulse quickened. Heat rose in his throat. "Well, I do."

Ritchie turned away, snickered again. "Yeah, right. Who cares if you got a few drops in you? Don't mean nothing."

Luke shook his head, nudged the artifacts a little further away from the fire. "Listen, Ritchie, history matters to all of us."

Ritchie waved him off. "Progress the only thing that matters. Work like this from flatlanders that actually pays me something."

"Don't you get it? The world isn't just about you."

"Ah, shit, Luke, you sound more and more like one of them damn hippies. You've been reading too much radical trash." Ritchie threw another hemlock bough on the fire. It sizzled and burst into flames. "We gotta' take care of our own. Nobody else going to."

Feeling angry and conflicted, not wanting to acknowledge he somewhat understood where Ritchie was coming from, Luke fell silent.

"Screw all you radicals," Ritchie said dismissively, but with a twinge of fear.

As Ritchie walked back to his dozer, Luke scuffed out the smoldering ashes on the artifacts, and carried them to his truck. He shook his head. Despite not wanting to screw things up with Sarah, he knew her father was the real problem. Luke dropped the load of wooden pilings and left.

Back at the house, Luke wanted to talk to his mother, but she was sound asleep, so he decided to deal with the judge himself. He grabbed a cola from the fridge, his father's old ax from the shed, and went around back. He spent a couple hours splitting a half-cord of maple, beech, and birch into small pieces. Luke was certain the draft would take him away before what the *Farmer's Almanac* predicted would be a long, frigid winter. Luke wanted his mother to have plenty of dry wood to feed their woodstove. As his ax repeatedly arced through the air, he worried about his mother managing mostly alone.

By the time he was done, Luke's arms were tired, his T-shirt wet with sweat. He sat on the remaining stack, wiped his forehead with his arm, and finished his soda. He looked across the backyards of the trailers beyond their house and thought about Ritchie and the judge. It bugged Luke that he was so bothered by the Indian issue, when no one else seemed to care about it. But what had been tragically done to American Indians in the past disturbed him in a deep way. It also brought into stark focus that the American military was now sending boys off to Vietnam to kill thousands of native people. Was it creating another atrocity or a righteous fight to stop the communists? He wasn't sure about any of it.

Luke took a quick shower and went to bed. He didn't sleep well, disturbed by dreams of soldiers killing Indians and destroying their encampments, as well as TV images of Vietnam. He woke up early Thursday morning in a cold sweat, remembering Trace had said the judge would be at the building site midmorning overseeing things. It was time to confront him.

Since it was too early to see the judge, Luke drove to Andy's to work on his boat's outboard. That always settled him down. Besides, he needed to get out on the lake soon to start testing it. He'd already seen Freddie McCormick out there in his boat with the souped-up Mercury, though no one was supposed to run their boats at racing speeds until the official test dates. Luke knew the

$1,000 prize would be a huge help to him and his mom. And winning the race should impress Sarah, though she'd surely seen greater competitions in Washington.

Outside the shop, Luke found Andy in a J. Geils Band T-shirt untying a canvas cover on a boat that didn't look familiar. "Hey, Andy," Luke said, walking over to him.

Andy nodded as he pulled off the canvas, revealing a mahogany Chris Craft runabout that gleamed in the sunlight. "Wow," Luke said, admiringly. "Whose is that?"

"Mine," someone said from behind Luke. He turned. Judge Clements was approaching from his Cadillac.

"It's a beauty, sir," Luke said, feeling uncomfortable.

The judge ran his hand over the bow. "It sure is. It's going to be nice out there on the lake this summer."

Luke checked out the cockpit. "I'll bet it's fast."

The judge smiled, cupped his hand around a cigarette, and lit it. "They say, 'like lightning,' though I haven't driven it yet."

Andy opened the wooden doors revealing a spotlessly clean V-8 engine. Luke and the judge stepped closer.

"Wow," Luke said, "that's a Chevy 327 block with Holley four-barrel carbs. Don't see boats like this around here very often."

Andy chuckled. "Yeah, like never."

Luke peered into the engine compartment. "Look at those headers and that chrome air cleaner." He glanced at the judge. "Sweet boat. Where'd you get her?"

"A friend of mine in the judiciary used to race these classics down on the Chesapeake. He passed away, and his widow sold his collection at auction last summer. Mrs. Clements thought I was crazy to buy it, but I couldn't resist, especially knowing I'd be building up here."

The Indian issue hit Luke again, and for a few seconds, muted his enthusiasm for the beautiful boat.

The judge looked at Luke. "I hear you're quite the boatsman yourself."

"Been tinkering with them since I was a little kid. Nothing like being on the water."

"The truth be told, I've never driven a boat."

"*Really?*" Luke said with a quizzical look.

The judge nodded, motioned toward the lake. "Maybe you can show me the ropes."

Luke perked up. "That would be cool."

Andy put his hand on Luke's shoulder. "Luke's one of the best drivers around, probably going to win the race this summer."

"The big race over the Fourth of July?"

"Yup," Andy said, "folks come from all over. Only time the old geezers on the town council let us rip up the lake."

The judge smiled. "I'm familiar, try never to miss it. Lots of fun, as long as nobody gets hurt."

"It's a blast," Luke said. "I'm pretty sure I can win it this year if I get my motor running right."

"Ah, you'll get her tuned up in time," Andy said.

Luke thought about taking the judge aside to talk about the relics, but the timing wasn't right. "Real nice Chris Craft, sir." Luke turned toward the boat shed. "I gotta' get some work done on my own boat."

Luke threw the bolt on the doors, stepped inside the musty shed, and flipped a switch. Warm yellow light from several overhead bulbs illuminated the impressive collection of stored boats. He walked between the rich camp owners' boats to the corner where he'd talked with Sarah next to his rough-looking mahogany speedster. He brushed a layer of dust off the bow and frowned as blistered urethane came off in his hand. But then he looked at the steering wheel with the sewn leather cover his mother had made for him and smiled. "We'll show that fancy runabout a thing or two."

"Is that your boat?"

Luke turned, unaware Judge Clements had come into the shed behind him. Luke stood so as to cast a shadow over the worst of the peeling urethane. "Yeah, just an old motorboat."

The judge walked over. "These are great," he said, leaning against another boat. "When I was a kid growing up near Lake Charlevoix in northern Michigan, I always wanted a boat—any boat."

Luke was surprised the judge was talking to him like a regular guy. "Why couldn't you get one?"

"My folks barely had enough money to keep the household running, let alone get a pleasure boat. I used to ride my bike down to the lake and watch everyone go out on the water, especially on Saturdays after I got done working for my dad."

Luke relaxed. "I used to do the same thing over at our town ramp. We couldn't afford anything either, especially after my dad died."

"What happened to him?"

"He got killed felling a tree up in Maine."

"That must have been terribly hard."

"It was."

The judge looked at Luke's boat. "What do you have for a motor there?"

Luke put his palm on his black outboard, which had a metallic red stripe around the cowl. "'58 Mercury Thunderbolt. 65 stock horsepower—more like 70 when it's tuned right."

The judge examined the motor. "I find it amazing they can squeeze that many horsepower into such a small package."

"These Mercs are hot."

They were both quiet for a few long moments.

"It seems you and my daughter have an attraction."

Luke was surprised. "Yes."

"We expect she'll go to law school after college, clerk with one of the Supreme Court Justices," he said, proudly. "Sarah has a bright future."

Luke felt acid building in his stomach. "Yes, she sure does."

"Nothing wrong with a summer romance. We all just have to be realistic."

What the hell? Taking offense, Luke brushed dust off the Mercury. "Feels realistic."

"I think you know what I'm getting at."

Luke's jaw tightened. He restrained himself from letting the judge have it.

Judge Clements stepped back from Luke's boat. "I'll let you get back to work. Let me know when you have time to take my boat for a spin."

"I'll do that," Luke replied, without a hint of friendliness. When the judge walked out of the shed, Luke looked over his shoulder. "Asshole."

Luke thought for a few moments then quickly walked outside. The judge was about to get into his Cadillac. "Sir—"

Apparently not hearing Luke, the judge opened his car door.

Luke started across the yard. "Sir! I want to talk to you."

Judge Clements turned toward Luke, waited for him to approach.

Feeling nervous, Luke shoved his hands in his jean's pockets.

The judge became impatient. "What is it, boy?"

"I need to ask you something."

The judge waited. "Yes?" He seemed to snicker under his breath. "I hope it isn't to ask for my daughter's hand in marriage?"

Luke shook his head. "Nothing like that."

The judge shut his car door. "What then? Speak your mind."

Luke looked the judge in the eye. "It's about the Indians."

The judge looked confused. "What Indians?"

"You know…"

"No, I don't know."

Luke pulled a hand from his jeans, gestured toward the lake. "The relics down at your building site. Pottery and arrowheads and such."

The judge frowned.

"You had to have seen them."

The judge appeared uncomfortable. He pulled a pack of Pall Malls from his sport coat and slid one into his mouth. He flicked open a silver lighter and touched the flame to the end of the cigarette. After a long drag, he exhaled through his nose, like a steed readying to charge.

"What makes you think I know what you're talking about?"

"When you showed up that first day, you chased us away from where Ritchie had dug everything up. That's where we found the Indian relics."

"So? What's that got to do with me?"

"Later, when I delivered another load, I dug around and found one of your Pall Mall butts in the dirt where Ritchie covered things up."

"What does that prove?"

Luke was getting pissed again. "That you were probably

there when he buried the artifacts. Look, I don't mean to be disrespectful, I'm only interested in preserving our history. And I mean that personally, too."

"How so?"

"Way back, my family was part Abenaki."

"I see."

The judge took another drag then flicked the cigarette in the dirt and stamped it out. "You're quite the prosecutor, aren't you?"

Luke stood silent.

Judge Clements leaned against the side of the Caddy. "I was there, though I don't remember seeing much, maybe a pottery shard or something. Nothing important."

Luke was relieved the judge was being at least somewhat honest. "It's important because it shows that Indians were here. It must have been an encampment." Luke looked at the judge. "Did you find anything else?"

The judge shook his head. "No, that was all there was."

"Shouldn't you should tell the state about it? And I don't think the town would've given you a building permit if they'd known about it."

Judge Clements looked alarmed. "You spoke to the town clerk?"

"Not yet, I just looked up the regulations."

The judge thought about it for a few moments. He pulled out another cigarette but didn't light it. "I'm already building our house and getting the other lots ready for sale. I can't afford this project without bringing in money from the rest of the property. The permits are all in order; it's perfectly legal."

"Well, I hope you'll think about it. I've done what I should. I guess it's on you now."

CHAPTER THIRTEEN

GAIN, LUKE DIDN'T SLEEP WELL, DISTURBED BY HIS encounter with the judge. He was glad he'd said something and that Clements acknowledged he'd been there with Ritchie, but Luke figured the judge wouldn't do anything to protect the land. On the way to work Friday morning, Luke stopped at Willey's Store to check the paper for news from Vietnam. Around town, in one way or another, it seemed everyone felt the escalating stress of the war, as young men and their families waited anxiously for the next call-up. The whole situation seemed surreal.

Luke scanned the front page of the *Hardwick Gazette* and saw there'd be a funeral the next day in Newport for another Orleans County guy who'd been killed in Vietnam. Inside, there was another photograph of a dead college student recently shot by the National Guard on a college campus in Ohio. Nausea surged in the pit of Luke's stomach. He jammed the paper back in the rack. He'd have to check on the draft later. "Shit, don't even know what we're fighting for," he muttered, and climbed into his truck.

Driving to Trace's mill, Luke's thoughts turned to Sarah. He couldn't wait to see her, though he was a little nervous about his dustup with her father. Regardless, he knew he'd done the right thing. Sarah had hoped to get into town by late afternoon so she could take Luke to a summer kickoff party that evening at one of her father's friends. Maxwell Holmes was a New York banker who owned a big fancy house overlooking the lake. Sarah had said his parties were legendary in the eyes of the summer elite but disdained by most locals, particularly because he brought his own caterers and professional waitstaff with him from New York. Nobody in Greensboro was good enough for him. Luke wasn't too keen on going, but if it meant spending time with Sarah, he'd go.

Around four, Luke made his last delivery of shiplap pine to a sugarhouse being built at the base of Gordon's Hill. After quickly changing at home, he hurried to the inn to meet Sarah. Her car wasn't in the lot, but a bright red vehicle caught his eye across the road at Andy's. He pulled in and saw the Mustang was parked in front of the boat shed.

Luke slipped inside. The only dim light came from a couple of dusty windows off to the side.

"Hey, handsome."

His heart quickened at the sound of Sarah's voice. "You're back!" He slalomed around the boats and found her sitting on the bow of his in the back corner. Smiling, they kissed and slid their arms around each other in a long embrace. Warmth rose through Luke's body. "I missed you."

"Me, too." She kissed him again. "This boat is cool. I like that big outboard motor." She raised her eyebrows. "Looks powerful, like its owner."

Luke feigned a smile. "Well... I don't know if it's *that* powerful."

"Have you got it running?"

"Yeah, but the carburation's still off. Doesn't get up to full power." He ran his hand across Sarah's back. "But it will."

"I look forward to it," Sarah replied with a sexy look. She slid off the boat. "So, are you going to accompany me to this party?"

"Well…" Luke was hesitant. "I've never done high society."

"Don't worry, some of my father's friends are pretty cool. And most of them don't act like big shots, though I guess they are."

"What will they think of a local like me coming?"

Sarah smiled. "You're coming on the arm of Judge Clements' daughter, so they'll think you're just fine."

"You're crazy."

"I must be, dating a hick like you."

"*Dating?*" Luke was delighted.

She ran her hand down over the front of his jeans, instantly arousing him. "Isn't that what we're doing?"

"Absolutely."

They walked to the door of the shed. Luke looked to see if anyone—particularly her father—was around. All he heard was the sound of Andy pounding on something over at the repair shop. "I need to tell you something."

"Yes?"

"I saw your father here yesterday."

Sarah became excited. "Did you see his new boat?"

"Yeah, it's awesome. I'd love to have a boat like that someday." Luke felt nervous. "Look, I got into it with him about the artifacts."

Sarah looked surprised. "How'd that go?"

"He didn't tell you?"

"No. I haven't spoken with him since earlier in the week."

"Well, he seemed surprised I knew about the cigarette and all."

"Those darn Pall Malls."

"I think he's worried I'll report him to someone, but I told him it's up to him now, to do whatever he thinks is right."

Sarah nodded. "I'm impressed. That was the perfect way to handle it. He'll respect that." Sarah stepped outside the door, scuffed a stone out of the way. "He's in a tough spot, feeling desperate to have a peaceful place to escape Washington. I think he paid way too much for the land but it was the only big piece for sale. That's why he needs to sell off other lots."

"Yeah, well…"

Sarah didn't respond.

"Anyway, I've got a deal for you. I'll go to the party, if tomorrow morning you'll climb Mount Elmore with me to watch the sunrise over the Northeast Kingdom."

Sarah looked puzzled. "Now we're in a *kingdom?*"

Luke smiled. "Sort of, but not with castles and all."

Sarah shook her head. "*What* are you talking about?"

"It's my favorite place to watch the sun come up. There's an old fire tower on top of the mountain. You can see for miles. Once heard an old guy say it's as good a view as the Grand Canyon."

"I doubt that," Sarah said, skeptically. "You climb in the dark?"

"Yeah, but there's going to be a good moon tonight. It's no sweat, I've hiked that trail a hundred times since I was a little kid."

Sarah looked his face over. "You're crazy, but I trust you." She held out her hand. "Deal."

"Great." They shook on it. "And I'll figure out the thing with your dad," Luke said.

"I hope so."

Sarah sat close to Luke as they drove to the party in his pickup. He kept his arm around her, feeling about as peaceful as he ever had. He wanted to tell Sarah he was falling in love, that being with her was like nothing he'd ever experienced. But why chance screwing up a perfect ride?

"Turn here," Sarah said, pointing to a driveway framed with a stone arch on top of which sat a large lantern. Luke noticed a brass nameplate mounted on a stone that read "Holmes Estate" in large shiny letters. The gently curving cement driveway had flowery designs pressed into it and was lined with torches. Their dancing flames gave the twilight a yellow glow as Luke and Sarah ascended toward a huge, brightly-lit house set upon a hill overlooking the lake. Above the roof rose a tall cupola with a slowly rotating beacon, like that of a lighthouse.

"Wow," Luke said, trying to take it all in. "This place is something."

"Yes," Sarah agreed. "Maxwell Holmes is quite an ostentatious man."

"I'll say."

Sarah pointed to a lighted marble fountain of a Greek god in the center of the sloping lawn.

"Over the top," Luke said, shaking his head.

As they approached an ornate overhang in front of the house, Luke asked Sarah where they were supposed to park.

"They have a valet," she said, motioning to a man in a black jacket and white gloves, attending to a silver Mercedes roadster.

"Oh. Never done this before."

Sarah chuckled. "Just pull up there and leave your truck. They'll park it for you."

"For sure?"

"Yes. Wow, you really are a hick."

"You just figuring that out?"

Luke pulled up behind the Mercedes. When he took his foot

off the gas, the truck's engine sputtered, backfired, and fell silent. The parking attended looked at them and frowned.

"Oh, boy," Sarah said.

"We just get out?"

"Yes." Sarah's door squeaked as she pushed it open.

Luke grinned. "Leave the key in her?"

"Jesus, Luke. Yes!"

Luke got out and walked around back of his truck, keeping an eye on the guy with the white gloves. Sarah brushed something off Luke's shirt, took his arm, and they walked up a long set of graduated flagstone steps.

"Don't get her dirty!" Luke called over his shoulder.

"Luke—" Sarah yanked down on his arm. "You've got to behave."

Luke chuckled. "I couldn't resist."

As they approached the wide granite landing leading to the front door, Luke saw a pair of women in large, flowery hats chatting inside. Three men in light-colored suits and straw hats were smoking and laughing on the veranda. Luke became uneasy. "I don't know about this."

Sarah held his arm tighter. "I do." She pulled him straight over to the three men, then let go of his arm. "Hello, Mr. Watkins," Sarah said to the older of the three.

A gentleman with a pipe cupped in his hand, turned to her. "Miss Clements, what a pleasure." He bowed a bit then introduced her to the other men.

"This is my friend, Luke," Sarah said. Luke was too nervous to fully notice she had called him friend.

The men looked Luke over then extended their hands without introducing themselves.

"Are you one of the local boys working for Mr. Holmes?"

Sarah waited to see what Luke would say.

"No, sir," Luke stammered. "I'm here with…"

Sarah took his arm again. "He's here with me. Luke is my boyfriend."

Mr. Watkins' eyes opened wider. "Oh, well, I see," he said in a friendly tone.

One of the other men frowned. "Has his Honor met—Lucas, is it?" His voice was spiked with sarcasm.

"Luke," Sarah repeated. "Luke Simms."

The pompous fellow furrowed his brow. "You mean, Elijah's boy?"

"That's right," Luke said, fearing what might be coming next.

"I see." The man turned back to the others.

Sarah ignored him and nodded to Mr. Watkins. "It's nice to see you again." She subtly pulled Luke toward the front door.

"Thanks for getting me out of there," Luke said under his breath.

"You're welcome. Ignore that guy. He's a blowhard from Yale."

Another gentleman in a black jacket opened the large glass doors for them. Sarah and Luke stepped into a white marble foyer leading to a grand staircase over which hung a huge sparkling crystal chandelier. An ensemble was playing show tunes in the background.

As Luke took in the dazzling sights, a large man in a cream tuxedo rushed over from where he'd been conversing with someone next to a Greek statue. "Oh, Sarah Clements, how divine." The man swept Sarah's hand to his lips and kissed it. Luke recoiled.

"Mr. Holmes, thank you for inviting us," Sarah said politely. "This is my father's favorite summer party."

"Well, I should hope so. And yours, I pray."

Sarah forced a smile. "Of course." She turned to Luke. "This is—"

"Yes—" Mr. Holmes interrupted, looking over his rectangular bifocals at Luke.

"I presume you're that Simms boy. From that dreadful trailer park at the edge of town."

Luke bristled. "We live in the farmhouse before the trailers." Luke wanted to punch the asshole in the face and run out of there.

"Yes," Mr. Holmes replied. "Your father had to sell off the family land before he disappeared. Pity."

"He *died* logging over in Maine."

"Oh. Right," Mr. Holmes said, flatly. "Sympathies." He abruptly turned, swept his hand over the opulence surrounding them. "Welcome to my home. Please do enjoy yourselves." He spied someone in a bright, paisley jacket coming through the door. "Carlton!" he called out as he raced over to the new guest.

Luke shook his head. "Not sure I've met a bigger asshole."

"That was completely uncalled for." Sarah lowered her voice. "Do you want to just leave?"

"Are you kidding?" Luke motioned toward a large spread of food in an adjacent room. "Not till we fill up."

Sarah chuckled, went up on her toes, and gave him a kiss.

Luke headed into the next room where an impressive spread of food was displayed on a vast collection of raised glass serving dishes set on white linen-covered tables. The savory aromas made his mouth water. Though he could not identify all of the offerings, he knew barbequed teriyaki chicken when he saw it and had no trouble quickly eating a half dozen clean down to the wooden skewers. He watched a lady in a fancy yellow dress eat a couple of shrimp dipped in a red sauce. When she left, Luke grabbed his own shrimp, dipped them in the bowl of sauce, and ate them. The shrimp didn't have much taste, but the tangy sauce was delicious.

Luke was licking his fingers when Sarah came up beside him. "You look like you're making yourself right at home." She took a small glass plate and placed a few selections on it. "Though, you should put your food on these small plates. It's not polite to dip into the serving dishes."

"Oh," Luke said, grinning. "I just did it for your benefit."

Sarah shook her head and handed him a linen napkin. "You may need this."

"Thanks."

"And don't put any in your pocket."

He laughed.

After they'd had enough to eat, they each got a beer from a roving waiter and walked out onto the back veranda, where they enjoyed a sweeping view of Caspian Lake.

"Beautiful, isn't it?" It was Sarah's father, who had arrived late.

Luke nodded. "God's country, right there."

"I should say so." He turned to Sarah. "Are you enjoying yourself?"

"Yes. The food is excellent. Mr. Holmes, not so much."

"He's a rather eccentric fellow. Flamboyant and full of himself, but he means well."

Neither Sarah nor Luke responded.

The judge looked around. "Too bad your mother wouldn't come up with me. She would have enjoyed this."

"Yes," Sarah said flatly.

"I'll be leaving for the Green Mountain Law School in Manchester, shortly. I need to go down tonight because I'm leading a seminar in the morning."

"I hope it goes well," Sarah said. "Will you be coming back up tomorrow evening?"

"Yes, though I may stay for the faculty dinner." He rested his hands on Sarah's shoulders. "Will you be alright up here without me?"

"Of course."

Luke took a step forward. "I'll watch out for her, sir."

The judge nodded then looked at Sarah again. "I left the number for the law school with Victoria at the inn. Phone me if you need anything."

"I will." Sarah gave her father a hug. "Drive safely. I hope the seminar is successful."

"Yes, thank you. It's a brand-new law school with plenty of promise. I hope their inaugural event goes well. I've encouraged a few of my esteemed colleagues to attend."

"I'm sure it will."

The judge looked around. "I will say my goodbyes and be off."

"Good night," Luke said, not knowing what else to say.

The judge walked over to Mr. Holmes, spoke to him briefly, and left.

Once the judge disappeared, Luke slid his hands around Sarah's waist. She turned and smiled at him. "I'm glad you're going to watch out for me." She went up on her toes and spoke in his ear, her warm breath a powerful aphrodisiac. "You can start by getting me out of here."

"Happy to."

They left without saying a word to anyone. Luke could hear the valet having a hard time starting his pickup, which had been parked out of sight behind a row of cedars. When the fellow finally came back with the truck, Luke opened the door for Sarah before he walked around the rusted body, inspecting it.

"Looks good," he said to the valet, who Luke realized was waiting for a tip. Luke pulled a crumpled dollar from his pocket, gave it to the guy then jumped in. He and Sarah laughed as they drove off.

"Smooth escape." Sarah cuddled against him.

Luke put his arm around her. "Where do you want to go? It's pretty late."

"Take me to the inn so I can check-in with Vicky. I'll grab a blanket and sneak back out. Then we can go somewhere, maybe that old barn down by the lake."

Luke felt himself getting aroused. "Sounds good to me."

At the inn, Sarah told Luke to wait for her behind the boat shed. He drove across the road and parked out of sight. Wound with anticipation, Luke turned on his scratchy radio, reached out and jiggled the coat hanger antenna, and tuned to WPTR out of Schenectady, New York. He waited for Sarah, singing along to a new hit, "I Think I Love You."

Impatient, Luke got out and peered around the edge of the shed, from where he had a good view of the inn. All was quiet. Maybe Sarah had changed her mind or wasn't able to sneak out like she'd planned. But she was worth waiting for, so he leaned against the shed, tilted his head back, and tried to relax. It was a warm night without any breeze. Thin, moonlit clouds hung overhead.

After a while, feeling a mixture of disappointment and, perhaps, a bit of relief, Luke decided to head home. He was taking one last look at the inn and, to his surprise, saw Sarah coming out of an upper window onto a fire escape ladder. She was carrying a jacket and a blanket. Excited again, Luke ran across the road and greeted her at the bottom of the ladder. "You're crazy," he whispered.

"Vicky was still up, doing bookwork in the lobby. I had to escape another way." Sarah stuffed the blanket into his arms and gave him a quick kiss. "Come on, let's get out of here." They ran to the truck and held the creaky doors open as they took off.

Luke smiled. "You've got balls…"

"I think you mean, 'guts.' You're the one with balls, I hope."

Luke felt an erection harden beneath his jeans.

CHAPTER FOURTEEN

A HALF MILE DOWN THE ROAD, OUT OF EARSHOT FROM THE inn, they pulled their doors shut, and Sarah let out a joyful yelp. She pulled something from her jacket and held it up.

"Where'd you get that?" Luke said, admiring a gold-foil bottle of Michelob beer.

"Courtesy of Maxwell Holmes, my dear. And I've got a couple more."

"Awesome." Luke curled his arm around Sarah and she snuggled against him. She ran her hand across his waist, further exciting him.

"So glad my dad's away." She slid her warm tongue into his ear. "I've been wanting to get you alone."

Luke felt a little shy. He'd never had a girl come on to him like that. "Wait till we get to the barn, or you'll run us off the road."

"That would be too bad—we'd miss all the fun."

Luke hit the gas, the engine backfired, and they sped up, soon reaching the outskirts of town. Sarah held onto him tightly as they skidded around the corner at Jed's barn and headed down to the lake. In front of them, the moon broke through the clouds, illuminating an expanse of ink-blue water. Luke parked in a small meadow and dug a flashlight out of the glove compartment. They grabbed the blanket and Sarah's coat, which held the beers, and climbed the rock-strewn meadow to the horse barn.

Sarah stopped as they approached the deeply weathered building which leaned a bit toward the west. "Do you think it's okay to go in there? It looks creepy."

"Just an old barn with a bunch of hay in the loft."

"Sounds like you've been here before."

"Once." Luke felt a little embarrassed.

"You old Romeo, you."

"Not like that." Luke took her hand. "Come on."

Luke cleared a tangle of raspberry canes from in front of the door then pushed it open, its rusty hinges letting out an eerie squeak. He turned on his flashlight and wiped away cobwebs to make a clear passage for Sarah, who hesitantly followed him.

Luke shown the dim yellow light around the inside of the barn. On the wall hung a couple of cracked leather bridles and leads and a rusted horse comb that had sprung out of its wooden handle. Over a small window, a red Coleman Lantern hung on a square nail, its glass globe broken, its mantle desiccated to white dust. There were two empty stalls with old hay and small piles of dried manure on the dirt floor. Several of the side boards hung loose on their nails, the mark of horseshoes imprinted in the wood. In the corner, stood a set of rickety-looking stairs. "Over here," Luke said.

"Are you *sure?*" Sarah held tight to his arm.

"Yeah, the view from the loft is awesome." He led Sarah up the stairs, which creaked and moved slightly beneath their feet. A couple of birds fluttered out through a missing board as they came up into the hayloft. Luke looked around. "Good roof," he said, "still nice and dry up here."

They crossed a wide-planked floor to a mound of loose hay near the door. Luke pushed the door open as far as it would go, revealing a sweeping view of the lake. Through the tops of the cedars, moonlight reflected off the smooth surface, broken only by subtle ripples V-ing behind a white sailboat moving slowly along the far shore.

Sarah crouched in the open doorway. "This is beautiful."

Luke spread the blanket over a soft mound of hay then slid his hands over Sarah's shoulders. "So are you."

She turned and they began to kiss as they lay down on the blanket together. Sarah straddled him and started unbuttoning his shirt. His skin tingled as she ran her hand across his bare chest. "You like that?" Sarah asked between kisses.

"Yes." He slid his hands up over her breasts, her nipples firm beneath his fingers.

Sarah started unbuckling his jeans. Suddenly a bit scared, Luke touched her hand. "You sure?"

Sarah looked at him. "Don't you want to make love to me?"

"Yes, but... shouldn't you be married, or something before..."

Sarah smiled kindly, no hint of a smirk. "It's okay if you care about someone."

"Have you done it before?"

Sarah nodded. "Yes, with a boyfriend."

Luke was surprised, found it a little upsetting she was no longer a virgin. He also felt naïve. His erection softened.

Sarah took his hands in hers. He could see her full breasts inside her partially unbuttoned shirt. "Luke, I care about you. You're different than any guy I've ever met. I want to share my body with you, but if you want to wait—if you're not ready—that's fine." She pulled her shirt together. "You were getting me pretty hot and bothered. I assumed you wanted to—"

He sat up. "But I don't want to get you pregnant. Your father would kill me."

"Don't worry, I'm on the Pill."

"You sure it'll work?"

"Yes, hundred percent."

Feeling relieved, Luke looked into her eyes. "You're incredibly beautiful."

Sarah smiled seductively. Aroused again, Luke gently took hold of her arms and kissed her. He lay her back on the blanket, and unbuttoned the rest of her shirt. Sarah squirmed with pleasure as he kissed around her nipples down to her belly button.

Sarah unzipped his jeans. As he slid her shirt off, Sarah reached inside his boxers and fondled his penis. Crazy aroused, they tore off the rest of their clothes. Luke gazed at her naked body. "My god…" he said, almost out of breath.

She leaned up and kissed him. "Come inside of me, Luke," she whispered.

Feeling like his heart was racing out of his chest, Luke lowered himself over Sarah. She guided him into her warm, welcoming body. He felt totally home for the first time in his life. As he gently thrust inside of her, Sarah let out cries of enjoyment and arched toward him. She panted, her fingers deep into his back as she held him tight against her. He penetrated deeper and faster, and soon they shared a powerful pleasure. When the passionate surge was over, he gradually relaxed and gently slid off of her.

Their bodies smooth with sweat, Sarah's breathing slowly quieted.

Luke kissed her. "That was incredible…"

Sarah put her hand to his cheek. "That was wonderful—so intense, like you took over my whole body. So different when you love someone."

"I felt it, too."

Sarah snuggled against him, and Luke kissed her forehead. "I'm falling in love with you."

Sarah looked up at him. "Me, too."

Luke pulled the soft blanket over her shoulders and held her tight against him.

CHAPTER FIFTEEN

S OMETIME IN THE WEE HOURS OF MORNING LUKE WAS awakened by a bird chirping outside. His neck was stiff and his arm numb. It was still under Sarah, who was in a deep sleep. He looked out the hayloft door at a world losing its darkness to a subtle hue of pink lighting the tops of the trees. Realizing they'd slept till almost sunrise, he pushed himself up, gently arousing Sarah.

She slowly raised her head. "Hi," she said in a raspy whisper.

"Good morning," Luke said, smiling at her.

"*Morning*. What time is it?" She rubbed her eyes, trying to wake up.

"Almost daybreak, probably a little after five." Luke lifted hair away from her face.

Sarah's eyes snapped open. "Shit! I've got to get back before Vicky wakes up or she'll know I've been out all night. I'll be in so much trouble." She felt around for her clothes and started to pull on a shirt.

Luke smiled. "That might give you away."

"What?"

"The shirt—it's mine."

"Oh." Sarah pulled it off and pushed it toward him. "I wouldn't be so discombobulated if you hadn't brought me out in the wilds and—"

Luke chuckled. "You seemed to enjoyed it."

Buttoning her own shirt, Sarah smiled and kissed him on the lips. "It was awesome." She held his hand. "I feel honored to have been with you for your first time."

"You could tell?" Luke said, without any defensiveness.

She smiled. "Seriously, it means a lot." She glanced at his penis. "And you were great."

Luke nodded. "You, too. I was kind of nervous, but you made it wonderful."

"The way it's supposed to be."

They hugged each other for a few moments before pulling on the rest of their clothes. Sarah shook most of the hay off the blanket and grabbed her coat, out of which dropped a couple of beer bottles.

"Leave them for next time," she said, with a twinkle in her eye.

With Luke leading, they held onto a wooden beam and started down the stairs. Sarah touched Luke's shoulder. "Hey—"

He turned to her.

"I meant what I said last night, after we—"

Luke waited.

"What I mean is, that wasn't just sex. There's something deep here."

"I'll say."

She nudged him. "I'm being serious, Luke. I am falling in love with you."

Luke nodded. "So am I. It's crazy." Both smiling, they descended to the bottom of the stairs where he paused again, spoke without looking at her. "There's something I need to tell you."

Sarah looked concerned. "What?"

"As much as I want you to fall in love with me, you can't."

Sarah frowned. "Why not?"

"Because I'll be heading to 'Nam."

Sarah touched his arm. "How do you know?"

"My draft number is up—guaranteed to go. I'm just waiting to hear."

Sarah wrapped her arms around his neck and held him. "We've got to keep you out of that awful war."

Luke shook his head. "There's no way."

Sarah became emotional. "I want to be with you." She looked him in the eye. "You could go to Canada...you're, like, only 20 miles away. I could meet you there."

Luke leaned back against a beam. "I'm embarrassed to say I've thought about it, but serving my country's a duty I promised my Dad I'd do. Plus, a couple of guys I've known have gone over there to fight the communists. I can't just wimp out on them. Besides, we can't have another Simms flaming out on the military."

Sarah wiped her eyes with her sleeve. "This is hard, Luke. I respect you, but I sure don't like it."

After a few quiet moments, Luke took her hand. "Come on, let's not waste the time we've got." He led Sarah out of the barn and down the rocky meadow to the truck.

As they drove back up the road, the horizon behind Jed's farmhouse was lined with fire-red and orange. The sky above was a blend of peach and pink, against which his barn looked like a cutout from a movie set.

"Vermont is so beautiful," Sarah said. "I never want to leave."

Luke slowed. "What about law school and all that?"

"What about it?"

"You can't just give up your dreams."

"I'm not sure they're *my* dreams." Sarah pushed on his arm, changed the subject. "Come on, you've got to hurry it up! Can't this jalopy go any faster?"

"What about climbing Mount Elmore?" Luke glanced at her. "You promised."

Sarah gave him a look. "It'll have to wait."

"Okay." Luke floored the truck, which took off at an irregular gallop.

As the inn came into sight, Sarah became more nervous. "Just leave me off here, I'll walk the rest of the way. And please drive off quietly—no backfires."

"Okay, but can I see you later? Come down for the boat tune-ups on the lake this afternoon. The trial runs are tomorrow."

"If my father doesn't kill me first."

"He won't."

Sarah opened her door.

"I'll see you later, at the boat ramp below Andy's."

"I'll do my best." Sarah leaned over, kissed him on the cheek and got out, leaving the squeaky door ajar.

"Hey—thank you for last night."

Sarah smiled then hurried up the road toward the inn.

Luke turned around and headed slowly home, watching in his rearview mirror as Sarah disappeared into the inn. After showering and checking on his mother, asleep in her room, Luke grabbed his toolbox and headed to Andy's. If he was going to beat that damn Freddie McCormick, he needed to have his boat ready for the one day the town allowed full speed test runs, and that day was tomorrow.

At the shop, though his mind was on Sarah, Luke focused

enough to clean out his outboard's carburetors and check the magneto and wiring. He tightened and lubricated a steering cable that had loosened but looked strong enough to hold. After moving other boats around, he hooked his trailer onto his pickup, backed down to the ramp, and launched. He tied his boat off on the dock and waited. It was a beautiful clear day, the sky an ocean blue. Andy was supposed to meet Luke at ten. When Andy hadn't shown up by half past, Luke became concerned. The Select Board was allowing racers to use the lake only until noon. Luke wasn't sure what he could do—he had to have someone to drive while he adjusted the motor. From the north end of the lake, he heard McCormick repeatedly revving his engine. *Asshole.*

"Hey!" he heard behind him. He turned and saw Sarah running down the path. "I hope I didn't miss anything."

Luke smiled. "No, unfortunately I haven't even been out on the water."

"What's the problem?"

"Andy's supposed to be here to drive so I can tune the motor."

Sarah shrugged her shoulders. "Maybe I can drive."

Surprised, Luke frowned. "I wouldn't want you to get hurt."

"I wouldn't."

"You ever driven a boat?"

"Once."

"How big?"

"Little—at a kiddie fair."

Luke shook his head and chuckled. He pushed on the gunwale with his foot. "This baby's got a lot of power."

Sarah stepped onto the dock and leaned against him. "So's this baby." She pulled herself up by his T-shirt and kissed him.

"Show me how to run this thing. Don't you want to beat that Freddie guy?"

"You bet I do."

"So, let's do it." Sarah climbed into the cockpit.

Luke showed her the basics of running the shifter and the throttle, had her putt around just off the dock, and decided she'd be okay. He instructed her to drive the boat just outside the shallows at medium speed so he could make adjustments. "Watch out for the rocks near the shore; some of them just barely stick out of the water this time of year."

"Okay, I'll be careful." Sarah pushed on the throttle. The boat hesitated then lurched forward, knocking Luke off balance.

"Hey! Just give it, like, quarter gas. I want to stay in the boat."

"I didn't figure you for a sissy!" Sarah hit the throttle again. Luke yelled at her, causing her to slow down. "Alright, I'll be good. Half speed it is."

Luke shook his head. "Crazy girl—" He turned his attention to the motor, which was running pretty rough. He took a small screwdriver out of his pocket and tinkered with a needle valve to adjust the fuel blend. Sarah kept the boat on a good straight line. Luke turned the screw a quarter turn to a slightly richer blend and the engine smoothed out. "That sounds better."

"What?" Sarah yelled back to him.

"It sounds better!"

"Good!" She pushed the throttle forward and the bow of the boat came smoothly out of the water. Luke dropped into the seat beside her and hung on as they glided along the shore. "Seems to like you. Maybe *you* should race her."

Sarah glanced over. "Maybe I should."

Making a smooth arc through the water, they headed back.

As they approached the dock, another boat roared past, rocking them with its wake. Luke glanced up to see Freddie, who yelled at them. "Got a girlie drivin' your boat now!" He tore away, barely missing another boat.

"He *is* an asshole!" Sarah said.

Luke lassoed a line around a cleat on the dock. "Dangerous, too. Just like his old man."

When the boat was tied up, Luke helped Sarah onto the dock. "Thanks for your help."

"Sorry I almost threw you out of the boat." She smiled. "You know us women drivers."

"I'd say you did great."

"Hey, I wanted to tell you I understand about your serving in the military. I just don't want anything to happen to you."

Luke nodded. "I know. I try not to think about this crazy war, which the politicians won't even call a war. And the protesters rioting, burning American flags." He shook his head. "And worst of all, the unbelievable number of guys getting killed. It all scares the hell out of me."

Sarah held his arm tightly. "I've thought all those protesters were just radical hippie freaks—you know, draft dodgers—but thinking about you going over there makes me look at it differently. What the hell *are* we doing way over there?"

Luke sat on the bow, which tugged gently against its lines. "I saw the paper at Willey's, had pictures of those kids killed at Kent State. So sad."

Sarah shook her head. "The picture of that dead student laying in a pool of blood made me sick to my stomach. Even my conservative, stoic father got really upset about it."

"I can't believe soldiers shot those kids."

"I guess they were throwing rocks at them."

"So what? No reason to shoot them."

"I know."

They were both quiet for a few moments.

Luke stood and looked across the lake at the green hills beyond. "Until I got my draft notice, I just pretended the war didn't really affect us. Then, last winter, a kid I played basketball against got killed by Viet Cong in an ambush. Half the town turned out for his funeral. I should've gone but I just couldn't."

Sarah slid her hand over his shoulder. "I think we need to not let the war ruin everything. We've got to stop thinking about it, at least for a little while."

"I know, it just eats you up."

"Besides, you've got a race to get ready for."

"You're right, and trial runs are tomorrow, so I gotta' focus." He looked at Sarah. "And *I've* got to drive."

Sarah nudged him and smiled. "Maybe I'll let you."

CHAPTER SIXTEEN

S ARAH SAID GOODBYE TO LUKE AND HEADED ACROSS THE road to the inn. Knowing her father would be returning soon, she took a shower and waited for him in the upstairs sitting room. Soon, she heard him come in and say hi to Vicky downstairs. Sarah listened carefully. She was relieved Vicky didn't say anything about her being out all night, something Sarah was quite sure Vicky was aware of. She was cool.

Sarah stood as her father crested the staircase. "Welcome back."

Looking tired, he set his briefcase on the floor and smiled.

"How was the conference?"

The judge sat in a Victorian chair. "It was quite interesting. A colleague of mine from the New York circuit helped get the school off the ground. I must say they've done an impressive job. They're holding classes in a large renovated barn just outside of Manchester. The setting is really quite beautiful, like a Norman Rockwell painting."

Sarah was surprised. He was unusually animated about his visit. "I'll bet they were psyched to have a judge of your stature there."

"That's nice of you to say, and yes, I think they were pleased. I certainly enjoyed it."

"What was the conference about?"

"The usual judicial matters: Miranda, discovery, motions, appeals, those sorts of things. But the most interesting talk was on a new type of legislation Vermont is working on to protect the environment from uncontrolled development. It's called Act 250, and I think it is quite groundbreaking."

"Cool." Sarah sensed a bit of tenseness enter her father's voice. She became worried the topic of the relics might surface. "I had fun this afternoon at the lake with Luke. He was tuning up his motor for the boat race. I even got to drive."

"Really?"

"Yes, though there was this annoying guy, Freddie, out there, who Luke can't wait to beat." Sarah nodded. "Their test runs are tomorrow."

"That sounds interesting, but I hope you've been practicing your instrument; that music camp is quite expensive."

"Yes, Dad," Sarah replied, feeling disappointed. "That's what I'm going to do now." She turned away.

"Sarah…"

She paused.

"Let's keep this Luke thing in perspective."

Sarah didn't look at him. "I will." She smiled to herself and walked down the hallway to her room and shut the door quietly.

Sitting on the red-cushioned window seat, Sarah lifted her violin from its case. She checked the tuning of the instrument, and then, figuring her father might be listening, played a short sonata, one of his favorite pieces. When she heard him shut the door to his room, she quietly practiced a couple of fiddle riffs she had learned from Sis at camp. After playing classical violin for fifteen years, she found fiddling to be freeing and fun. It made Sarah feel her age. Sarah chuckled, looking forward to playing in the local contest she and Sis had decided to enter. Luke would be shocked, though Sarah hoped she wouldn't embarrass herself or Sis, or more importantly, Luke.

After dinner with her father and Vicky, Sarah went to bed early, dreaming of being back in the hayloft with Luke. He was an intoxicating combination of passion and gentleness. There was no question she was falling in love with this country boy.

The next morning, Sarah was up early practicing her violin before she joined her father downstairs while he had coffee and read the newspaper Vicky had picked up from Willey's. Though she didn't show it, Sarah was psyched her father had to leave for Washington by late morning. She had told Luke she'd meet him by one so they could go to the lake together.

Shortly after her father drove off, Sarah left the inn. On her way through town, she passed several people on ladders hanging colorful spinning streamers from telephone poles. Near Willey's Store, she slowed to watch others hanging a large red, white, and blue banner across the street announcing the "Annual Boat Race, Barn Dance, and Fiddle Contest." She felt a sense of small-town excitement as several women in front of the Community Church smiled and waved to her.

Approaching Luke's house, Sarah saw a couple guys at a trailer next door with their heads under the hood of a rusty car. Another pair of legs protruded from beneath the driver's door. As she pulled into the driveway, all three guys' heads emerged, staring at her and her Mustang as if in disbelief.

Sarah became nervous when she saw Luke's pickup wasn't around. She hurried onto the porch as the guys whistled after her. After Sarah knocked a few times, Mary appeared in the doorway. She explained Trace had Luke delivering a load of hemlock beams up on Stannard Mountain and he wouldn't be back for a while.

"But I thought he was doing his boat trials this afternoon."

"He's supposed to, but—" She paused to get in a couple of shallow breaths. "He has to work when Trace needs him. Only income we have."

Sarah nodded, glancing at the guys, who had resumed working on the car. "I understand, but I know he really wants to win."

"Sure does."

"Looks like quite a festival coming up. People were decorating downtown."

"Our big event of the year. People come from all around, lots of fun. Best fiddle contest anywhere."

Sarah stood on the porch, not sure what to do.

"Come in. I didn't mean to be rude."

"Oh, I don't want to bother you. I can wait in my car."

"Don't be silly." Mary slowly pushed the screen door open. "Nice to have company."

"Thank you." Sarah followed Mary into the house, which held a slight mustiness.

As she made her way to the kitchen, Mary steadied herself by holding onto the door casing. She nodded toward the kitchen table. "Make yourself at home."

"I shouldn't disturb you. I know you need your rest."

"Seems all I do is rest." Mary lit the stove and a bright blue flame burst to life under a tarnished teakettle. "No matter what the doctors try, my lungs keep getting worse."

"I'm sorry," Sarah said, sitting on a yellow padded chair.

While Mary made tea, Sarah looked around the kitchen, which seemed to have deteriorated since the first time she was there. A macraméd dreamcatcher hung in the window, its feathers dry and faded. The chipped gray linoleum floor hadn't been washed in a while, and tufts of dust were caught under the table legs. Over the stove, a square, red metal clock made a subtle squeaking noise as the second hand swept around its yellowed face. The off-white walls were streaked from years of cooking and steam, and a section of round metal pipe extended through the plaster ceiling above the cookstove. Sarah figured it was to allow heat to rise to a room upstairs. While dismayed by the condition of the kitchen, Sarah sensed this was a place of comfort, a *real* home, every bit of it.

When the teakettle sang, Mary asked Sarah to lift it from the stove for her and set it on an iron trivet on the table. They were enjoying a cup of aromatic spice tea when Mary suddenly looked alarmed. Staring out the kitchen window she frowned. "Those boys—"

Before Sarah realized what was going on, Mary grabbed a shotgun from behind a wooden hutch and, breathing rapidly, headed for the front door. Sarah glanced out the window and saw the guys from next door playing with her Mustang. With a surprising burst of energy, Mary pushed the screen door open and struggled to raise the shotgun in the direction of the car. "I'll give you ten seconds—to get—away—from that car—or you'll—wish you had."

The three guys jumped out of the car and took off running toward their trailers, one of them covering his backside with his hands as if that would save his butt from Mary's buckshot.

Sarah was amazed.

"Dear—" Mary said, leaning against the door casing. "Will you take this?"

Clearly, the gun was too heavy for her.

Sarah gingerly took the shotgun, and placed it behind the hutch before helping Mary back to her chair.

"Darn varmints," Mary said, as her breath returned. "Never shoulda' sold the land for a trailer park. Attracts riffraff like them."

"Luke said losing the land was tough."

"Yes. Been in his father's family for generations, but over the years they had to sell off most of it to keep going. After Luke's father died, I gave up trying to farm. I just keep a good garden out back. Have to be grateful for what we have, and Luke helps out a lot."

Sarah took a sip of tea and looked at Mary. "Luke adores you, and I see why."

Mary seemed surprised. Supporting her teacup with both hands, she set it on the table. "He's one special boy. Always has been. Though he sets the bar too high for himself."

"What do you mean?"

Mary hesitated. "Let's just say he carries a family burden that shouldn't be on his shoulders."

"I see."

"Best we let it be."

There was a silence.

"I admire how you keep your spirits up," Sarah said. "Where I live, the mood is dark. How do you do it?"

Mary's face broke into a knowing smile. "You just need some kind of faith and someone to love." She took in a breath. "That's the secret."

Sarah knew she was in the presence of a wise elder, someone who had figured it out. "Just in this short time, knowing Luke has changed me, shown me a different way to look at the world."

"Different than Washington, I guess."

"That is a treacherous place to be these days. The riots are so scary."

Mary looked at her. "So's the war."

"It's awful. Hard to comprehend it all." Sarah looked at her teacup. "I so hope Luke doesn't have to go over there."

Mary's face tightened. "Damn politicians. No idea what they're doing."

The wall clock methodically squeaked along. After a while, Mary spoke again. "You and Luke seem to make each other happy."

Sarah lit up. "Yes, he's such a cool guy."

Mary looked her in the eye. "Could you ever see yourself up here?"

Sarah smiled. "Maybe. I love it up here."

"Not a lot going on compared to Washington."

"But people seem pretty happy, and busy."

Mary chuckled, took in a good breath. "People from away think we're all bored and forlorn up here in the north country. But we've got everything we need; we don't want for anything. Don't need fanciness or a thousand people around us to be alright."

"I liked what you said about needing someone to love." Sarah looked into her teacup. "I think I'm falling in love with Luke."

Mary patted Sarah's forearm. "Good."

Sarah brightened. "Do you think he feels the same?"

Mary smiled and nodded.

Sarah saw how tired Mary was. "Do you think you should rest?"

"I am outta' gas. Would you be a dear and help me to the couch in the living room?"

Sarah pushed her chair back. "Of course."

After settling Mary on the couch, Sarah pulled a blanket up over her shoulders, and she soon fell fast asleep. Sarah set the kettle back on the stove and put the teacups in the sink. She noticed her tea leaves sort of formed the shape of a heart, which she thought was a good sign. She stood in the kitchen for a few minutes, trying to imagine herself living there. Not in that house, but in the area. Maybe she and Luke could build their own cabin on a plot of land overlooking the lake.

Back in the Mustang, Sarah slid on her sunglasses, backed out, and waved to the three guys still working on their beater. As she headed down the tree-lined road, she realized she had little idea what the future would bring. She just wanted to see Luke.

CHAPTER SEVENTEEN

BACK IN HER ROOM AT THE INN, SARAH SAT IN THE WINDOW seat that had a sweeping view of the lake, beyond which just a few soft clouds were making their way up the eastern flank of the Green Mountains. She took out her violin and wiped it down with a chamois cloth. She smiled, thinking of Sis showing her how to fiddle. She positioned her instrument and started playing a reel that Sis had shown her. It was a challenge to remember the whole piece, but Sarah kept practicing until she felt it come together.

"That was wonderful," a woman said, outside her door.

"Come in." Sarah set her violin in her lap.

Vicky stuck her head in the doorway. "Is that 'St. Anne's Reel'?"

"Yes. I love it."

Vicky stepped inside. "It's one of my favorites, written by David Mallett, a terrific folksinger from Maine. My uncle used to play it at kitchen tunks around here."

Sarah smiled to herself. "Sounds cool, but please don't tell my father I'm not practicing my classical violin. I don't think he would approve of this fiddle music."

Vicky chuckled. "No worries. He just doesn't know what he's missing."

Sarah wiped off her instrument and placed it back in its case.

"About last night, I…"

Vicky smiled. "Like I said, no worries. I was in love once."

Sarah breathed a sigh of relief. She closed her violin case. "What happened?"

"Oh, you don't want to hear my old story."

"I would. I've never really been in love before. I'm feeling a little off-balance."

Vicky sat in a wooden chair with a caned seat. "Hank was a stockcar race driver from over by Groton Pond. Handsome, strapping guy, kind of like your Luke fellow."

Sarah listened carefully.

"I met him at the races at Thunder Road, and we stuck to each other like a pair of magnets. We were only eighteen, but so in love we decided to get married—on the sly that is—after the summer racing season. He won the Milk Bowl, the last race of the season, and got to kiss the cow."

Sarah made a face. *"Eeww."*

"It's a local tradition. Anyway, the next weekend we all went to a post-season keg party out in the boondocks. We had a big bonfire, and a bunch of folks brought their guitars so we sang around the fire at the top of our lungs. It was the middle of the night by the time Hank was driving me home on a back road in his pickup." Vicky shook her head. "We were going fast—the only way he could drive. 'Hot-wired,' I used to say."

"I get it," Sarah said.

"Anyway, a couple of deer jumped out in front of us. Hank swerved hard and blew a front tire. It pulled us off the road, down a ravine, into a big oak tree." Vicky paused. "His side took the brunt of it, straight into the tree. I think he swerved that way so I wouldn't get hit so hard. Last thing I vaguely remember was his race trophy flying through the windshield like a missile. I think I've blocked out the rest, though it still seems like it happened yesterday."

Sarah felt her heart sink. "That's awful. I'm so sorry, Vicky."

"Thanks."

"How did you get out of there?"

"When I came to, there was an army of folks working around the car trying to get us out. There weren't any real rescue services back then, but a bunch of firemen and farmers somehow pulled the truck apart enough to get us out. They laid Hank on some hay in the back of a pickup and rushed him to the hospital. Doc Hanscom came right in and tried to bring him back, but it was no use."

Vicky looked out the curtained window. "Even though I was only half with it, I knew Hank was gone before he even left the scene." She pulled her hair back, revealing a jagged scar on her forehead. "This is pretty much all I got. Doesn't seem fair."

Sarah was shaken by Vicky's story, amazed she would tell her all that. After a short silence, Sarah spoke. "After such a terrible loss. Did you ever fall in love again?"

Vicky shook her head. "There were some other guys, minor flings, but nobody held a candle to Hank. He'd taken my heart." She put her hand to her chest. "Still has it. I was given one soulmate, that was enough. I'll catch up with him someday."

Moved by Vicky's story, Sarah was suddenly worried about Luke. Outside, the sun was descending over the lake. "I've got to find out what's going on with Luke. He was supposed to take a test run with his boat hours ago but had to work. Now it's going to be dark soon."

Before Vicky could say anything, Sarah heard a familiar horn blow outside. She looked out the window and broke into a smile. "Finally." She headed for the door then paused. "Thank you for telling me about Hank."

"I didn't mean to burden you with my stuff."

Sarah shook her head. "No, I appreciate it. You helped me."

Vicky nodded. "Me, too. Now, go have fun and be careful." Sarah ran down the hallway. "Ask Luke if he wants the smudge pots," Vicky called after her.

When Sarah reached the porch, Luke was coming up the stairs. He took her in his arms and swung her around.

"Where have you been? I've been worried."

"Trace sent me way up Stannard Mountain on a washed-out road with a heavy load of hemlock."

"I hope you didn't get stuck." She raised her eyebrows. "You know where that can lead."

Luke smiled. "Yeah, to wildly good things happening." He took her hand. "Come on, we gotta' get out on the lake before it gets dark."

Sarah pulled back on Luke's hand. "Wait, Vicky asked if you wanted her smudge-something…"

Luke thought for a moment. "Oh, her smudge pots."

"What are those?"

"Kerosene lantern pots. Good idea. I can use them to mark the tricky rocks in the shallows." Luke ran back up the stairs. "Hang on, I'll be right back."

Sarah waited on the flagstone walk in front of the inn, looking out over Caspian, the first golden tinges of the approaching sunset reflected off the water. Though she'd never had any interest in boats and motors and mechanical things, she loved sharing Luke's excitement about them.

Luke returned with a box of soot-covered lanterns, grabbed a full gas can he'd left by his truck, and he and Sarah crossed the road to Andy's ramp. Luke backed his boat into the lake and Sarah tied it off to the dock. He pointed to the shoreline. "If you drive her real slow along the edge, I'll lean out and put these pots on the rocks that stick out of the water. They don't look very big, but they're just the tops of bigger boulders under the surface. Hard to see as it gets darker."

"You want *me* to drive?" Sarah asked, smiling.

"Yes. I've seen your moves in that Mustang of yours. But just so I can put the pots out there."

"Hey Luke!" Andy yelled from up in the boatyard. "Be careful out there. Lake level's pretty high this year—barely see some of the rocks."

Luke waved.

"Lock up when you leave, will you?"

"Got it."

Luke sat with his legs dangling off the bow as they left the dock, guiding them along the eastern shore of the lake. As they approached the first boulder, he used an oar to keep them from hitting it, then set a smudge pot on top and lit it. The smoky yellow flame gained strength as the scent of kerosene drifted by. They placed lanterns on two other rocks then headed back to the dock.

Sarah smiled. "Those look cool with the flames reflecting off the water."

Luke dipped his hands in the lake and washed the soot off his fingers. "Yeah, my dad taught me to use them for markers." He topped off his motor's gas tank and set the half-full can back on the dock. "I can only take a few runs before it gets too dark."

"Can I ride with you?"

"Not now. I've got to see how the boat handles with me alone. I did some patchwork on the bottom last winter, and I had to move the battery box to one side. Actually..." he said, "it'd be great if you can watch from the dock and let me know if the boat is good and level in the water."

Sarah made a sad face. "I'd rather ride with you."

Luke ran his hand over her back and kissed her cheek. "Don't worry," he whispered in her ear. "You will later."

She perked up. "Promise?"

Luke nodded and started the Mercury.

Sarah stood on the end of the dock as Luke pulled away. He looked so handsome and happy at the wheel. She could tell how much he loved driving the old boat. She leaned against a wooden post and watched him motor down the shore, around a point of land, and out of sight. As she waited for him to reappear, darkening clouds crept toward the lake from the south and the air grew heavier, like it might rain. The rest of the lake was quiet, as everyone else had finished their trial runs and gone home.

Shortly, Sarah heard a motor rev, and Luke's boat came around the point. The whine of the motor rose as he headed toward her. Occasionally backfiring, Luke got up to a fairly good speed as he passed Sarah. He cut the throttle and came around. "How was that?" he yelled.

"The boat's good and level."

"Great," Luke yelled back, shutting off the motor. "I just gotta' adjust the carburetors again. That was nowhere near full speed."

The boat drifted slowly past Sarah. "For a minute there it sounded like your Mercury was farting." She laughed.

"Very funny." Luke lifted off the engine cover, made a couple of adjustments, and snapped it back on. "Now she should get up to full speed."

Sarah held onto a wooden post and swung out over the water, her blond hair spilling into the last of the golden light shimmering across the lake. "Let's hope so. It's getting pretty dark."

"Got to be patient with these temperamental old Mercs."

Luke started the motor and revved it up. It sounded smoother. "Get ready," he called out.

As Sarah watched him head back down the lake, a brisk wind whipped across the water ahead of the storm clouds, sending a chill down her back. She watched the boat again disappear around the point. A sharp gust caused the smudge pots' flames to dance. Soon, she heard Luke coming, his motor making a louder, high-pitched whine. Squinting against the wind, she watched him come into view just as the farthest smudge pot blew out. He was moving much faster, the distance between him and the rocks disappearing quickly. A jolt of fear went through Sarah as she realized he was angling awfully close to the extinguished pot. Scared, she began jumping up and down on the dock, waving her arms and yelling to warn him.

The boat's motor stayed at full throttle as Luke raced toward her. She screamed at him, but the gusty wind took her voice. As Luke bore down on the darkened rocks, Sarah watched in horror as his bow jolted violently upwards with a sickening crunch, sending pieces of wood across the water. Sarah screamed as the boat roared through the air, heading for the dock. Terrified, she ran for the water as the damaged boat crashed through the middle of the dock, splintering it to pieces. As if in slow motion, a blinding orange whoosh erupted from the exploding gas can.

Sarah fended off searing heat with her arms, as flames chased her off the end of the collapsing dock. As she hit the water, she caught a glimpse of Luke desperately bracing himself on the steering wheel as the boat careened toward boulders and cedar trees in the shallows.

CHAPTER EIGHTEEN

When Sarah surfaced, she searched for Luke but couldn't see him among the broken pieces of his boat in the shallows.

Gathering her breath, she struggled toward the wreck, avoiding patches of flames floating on the water. "Luke!" she yelled, "Luke!"

It was hard for Sarah to see in the dim, smoky light. Frantically looking for Luke, she slipped and fell on slick rocks under the surface. Righting herself, she kept looking, pulling burning pieces of wood out of the way.

"Luke!" she yelled, pushing into the tangle of cedars. "Luke, where are you?"

Sarah's foot caught on something soft that moved. She reached down—it was Luke's leg.

She dropped to her knees, dug her hands under Luke's shoulders and lifted his head out of the water. He looked dead.

She propped him up against a low-curving cedar as best she could and shook him. "Luke, you have to breathe!" She pushed on his chest then cupped her mouth over his and blew in as hard as she could. Hearing his lungs gurgle, she blew air in a couple more times.

Scared to death, Sarah jammed her fist into Luke's solar plexus. "Dammit, Luke, breathe!"

Just as she readied to give him another breath, Luke grunted and coughed up a weak trickle of water.

"Luke—" Sarah cried, wiping his face.

His body jerked. He gagged several times then coughed up a stream of water. Gradually coming to, he tried to shake his head. "Ouch," he said, grabbing his neck. Opening one eye, he looked around. "What the...?"

"My god, Luke, you're alive."

He reflexively wiped debris from his face. "I hope so."

She gave him a hug, causing him to wince. "Easy," he said, coughing again. "You'll have to wait till later."

"Jesus, Luke, be serious, I thought you were dead!"

In the sporadic light of lingering flames, she saw him manage a smile. "Me, too."

Sarah held his face in her hands then felt his arms and legs. "Are you alright? Is anything broken?" She shook her head. "That was a terrible crash."

Luke coughed up more water, gradually focusing on his destroyed boat, floating in pieces around him. "Oh, god..." he said, forlornly.

Sarah frowned. "Don't worry about the damn boat."

"The race...I promised my dad..." Luke tried to get up but winced when he put pressure on his arm.

"Let me help you," Sarah positioned herself in front of him. "Do you think you can stand?"

Luke tested his legs. "I think so."

"Then let's get you out of the water. You're starting to shiver."

Sarah slid an arm under Luke's good shoulder and helped him up. He was wobbly but managed to stand and lean against the tree.

Luke looked at the smashed dock. "Andy's goinna' be pissed."

"He'll be glad you're alive."

"I shoulda' counted the smudge pots."

"Come on." Sarah urged him toward the shore. Leaning on her, he limped through the water, frowning at the floating pieces of wood, his left arm hanging limp at his side. "This is bad..."

When they reached a place where they could climb up onto the bank, Luke stumbled back into the water. Exhausted, they both rested.

"Are you alright?" a woman yelled as she ran down the hill.

"Over here," Sarah called out.

Vicky came into view. "What happened?"

"Luke's hurt, crashed his boat, hit the dock where the gas can was."

Vicky hurried over. "My god, is he okay?"

"Barely." Sarah heard a siren approaching, saw a red light flashing along the road leading from town.

Vicky stepped into the water and crouched next to them.

"He was underwater for a short time before I could get him up. But he's been talking, and managed to walk this far."

Luke coughed a couple of times then threw up more lake water. "Hit that damn rock. Smudge pot musta' blown out."

"Never mind that," Vicky said. "Let's just get you out of here."

The town fire truck arrived up at Andy's shop. A couple of firemen jumped out and hurried down to them. "What the hell happened?" one of them asked, looking around.

Luke groaned as he struggled to his feet.

The fireman shined his flashlight on the wreckage of Luke's

boat. "Whoa…" He helped Vicky and Sarah get Luke up to drier land. "Better take him to the hospital."

"I don't need a hospital, just gotta' rest."

Sarah moved in front of Luke. "You can hardly breathe, and can't even move your shoulder. You need to get checked out."

Luke limped slowly up toward the boatyard.

"I'm not taking no for an answer," Sarah added.

"Alright, but I'm not staying."

Sarah and Vicky helped Luke into a fireman's car to head to the hospital twenty miles away. As Sarah tucked Luke's injured arm in beside him, he weakly grabbed her wrist with his good hand. "Glad you were here. Thought I was a goner."

Sarah smiled and kissed his blood-stained cheek. "Never happen."

CHAPTER NINETEEN

THOUGH LUKE WAS NOT HAPPY ABOUT IT, SARAH convinced him to stay in the hospital overnight for observation. Despite being in a lot of pain, his main concern was how he would find another boat to race. Feeling emotional, at one point, he took Sarah's hand in his and pulled her close. "Gotta' win the race. Might not be here next year."

Sarah frowned.

"You know, the war and all."

Sarah's spirits sank, though she tried to buoy his. Looking at his bruised face, she managed a smile. "If you survived that crazy crash, you'll make it through anything."

Luke held her close for a few seconds. "Let's hope so."

Exhausted, Luke relaxed back onto the bed, gradually letting go of Sarah's hand. Though he tried to talk, after the nurses gave him more medication, he conked out. While he slept, Sarah sat by his bedside, mostly holding his hand, still darkened by soot from the fire. It was a miracle that, despite crashing into a gas can, he'd suffered only flash burns to his face and arms. Sarah watched this country boy she'd fallen in love with, sleep, occasionally shaking her head in disbelief and gratitude he was still alive.

Around two in the morning there was a soft knock on the door to Luke's room. Sarah was shocked when the door opened. "Father, I thought you were on your way to Washington."

He let the door close quietly behind him. "I was, but when I got to Connecticut, I had a feeling something wasn't right."

Sarah sat up straighter in her chair.

"I found a pay phone and called Vicky. She told me what happened. I drove back as fast as I could. Are you alright?"

"I'm fine. Luke is the one who got hurt."

"Thank god. I was worried sick." He stepped closer to the bed. "How is he?"

Sarah looked at Luke. "He's been sleeping for a few hours. He's pretty banged up but is so lucky it wasn't worse. You should see his boat—totally destroyed."

The judge crossed his arms. "Sounds quite reckless to me."

Sarah frowned. "It wasn't his fault. One of the smudge pots blew out so he couldn't see where the rocks were. He hit one of them hard."

"Why in the world was he out there in the dark? And why were you with him? You could have been killed, for god's sake."

"He had to do a late lumber delivery before his test run. Luke's a very hard worker, Dad." Sarah touched Luke's hand. "I was there to help him. He's had trouble with his carburetors."

The judge shook his head. "He's going to have more trouble than that if he puts you in such danger again."

"I was fine," Sarah said, knowing she wasn't quite telling the truth. "Can we discuss this outside? I don't want to wake him."

The judge seemed a bit taken aback. "Of course." He looked at Luke, his face burned, one arm in a sling on top of a pillow. "There's no need to discuss this further. I just wanted to make sure you were alright."

"I am."

He stepped to the door. "Sarah," he said in a more compassionate tone.

"Yes."

"I'm sorry your friend got injured. I didn't mean to be insensitive. I was concerned for you."

Sarah glanced up at him. "Thank you." They were still for a few moments. "I won't be returning to Hunter Mountain this week."

Her father frowned, cleared his throat. "We will discuss that later."

Sarah stared at him. "No, we won't." She turned back to Luke and her father left the room, letting the door bang behind him.

Sarah's pulse quickened. She took in a deep breath. She had never spoken to her father like that. But perhaps it was time.

After half-napping next to Luke, around daybreak Sarah walked to the tiny cafeteria and got a cup of coffee. Standing in a window, she watched the peach and pink hues of dawn embrace the hills east of the hospital. A pair of robins pranced around the lawn outside, each attempting to pull the same earthworm from the ground. An orange and white striped tabby cat sat defiantly next to a fire hydrant as if guarding it from the neighborhood dogs. A Mansfield Dairy van pulled up in front of the hospital, and a deliveryman walked inside carrying two racks of white milk bottles.

Exhausted, Sarah decided to go back to the inn and rest. She retrieved her coat and stopped at the nurses' station. She asked a nurse in a pointed cap, named Mildred, to tell Luke she would be back in a few hours. "Do you know how long he will be here?"

"Should be a few days. Though knowing Luke, he's likely to spring himself sooner."

"You're probably right." Sarah started to leave.

"You his new girl?" Mildred asked in a kind voice.

"Yes, I guess so," Sarah replied, feeling unsure of herself.

"He's a great kid, one of the finest around here."

Sarah nodded. "I know." She stepped back to the counter. "Do you think he's going to be alright?"

Mildred smiled. "Oh, yes. It would take a lot more than a few bruises to keep him down, especially with the race coming up so soon."

Sarah was surprised. "There's no way he can race now."

"I wouldn't wager on it. I'll bet he's working on a new boat in a day or two. Nothing's going to keep him from trying to beat Freddie, or missing the barn dance over at Rowell's."

"Wow, you people are some serious about this Fourth of July festival."

Mildred straightened up. "It's tons of fun, and it brings a lot of needed cash into Greensboro." She made a motion as if playing an instrument. "Wait till you hear the fiddle-off after the dance. Take your breath away."

"Can't wait." Sarah smiled, thinking of she and Sis playing together. "Good night."

"I think it's day." Mildred smiled.

"You're right. I've lost track."

When Sarah approached the inn, she saw that Andy had pulled the boat wreckage from the water. Its burned-out skeleton sat at the side of the yard. *Amazing Luke lived through that.*

Back at the inn, Sarah found her father having coffee by himself in the breakfast nook. As she hesitantly approached him, he folded his newspaper into his lap and looked at her. "How is Luke doing?"

"He's still sleeping, but the nurse said he's going to be okay."

Sarah kept a safe distance. "I need to apolo—"

The judge held up his hand. "No need. I was insensitive, though I was genuinely concerned about you."

Sarah nodded. "I know. The truth is, I was pretty scared by the whole thing."

Her father gestured to a chair, and Sarah sat across from him. "Would you like some coffee?"

"No, thank you. I just need some sleep."

"Of course."

Sarah worked to get her courage up. "I would like to ask you something."

"Certainly."

"And this may sound really crazy under the circumstances..."

"Don't prejudice the judge before asking your question."

Sarah half-smiled. "Yes, sir."

He waited patiently.

"Luke has been getting ready for this race for a long time. It's very important for him to win it, in honor of his father. He died—indirectly—as a result of this jerky guy, Freddie, who sabotaged Luke's father's boat."

The judge looked confused.

"It's a long story. Anyway, the race is a big deal, and now the boat he's worked so hard to get in shape, is wrecked. He has nothing to race in."

The judge set his coffee mug down on the marble-topped table.

"So...I thought maybe...well, would you consider letting him use your boat?"

The judge's eyes opened wider. "The Chris Craft I just bought?"

Sarah looked at the floor. "Yes."

The judge grasped the arms of the chair, and leaned back. "You're correct, counselor, that sounds crazy."

Sarah felt embarrassed. "I know. It's just that he's such a good guy—honest, hard-working, takes care of his mom, who's quite ill." She looked at her father. "I'd so like to help him."

Pondering on it, her father slowly lifted his mug and took another swallow of coffee. Waiting for his articulate rejection, Sarah fiddled with her hair.

"I will give it some thought," he said. "This race sounds like a dangerous enterprise, but I know it's a big deal around here." He paused. "And I understand how you feel."

"You do?"

"Yes. I'm sure it's hard to believe, but I was young once." He pushed his chair back and stood. "With his injuries, do you think Luke will actually be able to drive a boat?"

Amazed her father would even consider it, Sarah stood. "Yes, for sure. He's determined."

The judge wiped his mouth with a white linen napkin and folded it onto the table. "Would he be able to have me visit? At the hospital, I mean."

"Yes, of course."

"Alright, then, I will take the matter under consideration and meet with Luke this morning before I return to Washington. Court is in session tomorrow."

As her father started to move away, Sarah gave him a brief hug. "Thank you, Daddy. I really appreciate this."

"You're welcome," he said and walked to the door. "We'll discuss the issue of music camp later."

CHAPTER TWENTY

D RIVING TO THE HOSPITAL IN MORRISVILLE, JUDGE
Clements worried about Sarah's summer romance derailing
her plans. He was also concerned about the Indian issue, which
had been nagging at him. Not wanting to back down, or change
his own development plans, he became increasingly resolute about
putting this Luke fellow in his place, in a way he wouldn't be able
to refuse.

As the judge walked toward the hospital entrance, he waited
as a couple of attendants unloaded an injured man on a stretcher
from the back of a white Cadillac ambulance. When he got to
Luke's room, the judge paused at the window and observed him
struggling to sit up in bed. As he watched Luke, Judge Clements
felt an unexpected wave of sympathy. Sarah's words took hold:
"honest, hard-working..."

Still, he needed to do this. He pushed open the door.

Luke looked surprised to see him. "Judge Clements—" He
pulled the sheet over him with his good arm.

"Do you feel like having a visitor?"

"Sure. Surprised to see you."

"May I?" The judge motioned to a chair.

"'Course."

He sat and crossed one leg over the other. "Sounds like you
had quite the crash."

167

Luke nodded. "Yes, hit a submerged rock. Stupid. I've known they were there all my life."

"We all make mistakes."

Feeling uncomfortable, Luke adjusted himself in the bed.

"Sarah says your boat is wrecked."

"Yes, and I'd just gotten it running right."

"Do you have another boat in mind?"

"Andy's got an old beater in the weeds out back with no motor on it. I don't know what shape my Merc's in, but if I can't fix it, I'll have to scarf up another outboard."

The judge motioned to Luke's sling. "How will you race with an injured arm?"

Luke shrugged his shoulders, causing him to flinch. "No problem. I'll be out of this in no time."

The judge cleared his throat, stood, and looked out the window. "Though I'm reluctant to do so, I have an idea that I would like to put forth."

"What's that?"

"Sarah told me a little bit about your father and why you want to win this race so badly."

Luke waited.

"She asked if I could help out." The judge turned back to Luke. "As you know, I have a new Chris Craft, at least new to me, and I'm told it runs quite fast."

"Yes."

"When I was growing up, I wanted to be free-spirited like you, but it was during the Great Depression. We spent most all our time finding some kind, *any* kind, of work so we could buy enough food for the family." The judge looked away. "My father and I hitchhiked out to the town dump to pick for copper or brass, anything we could sell. We didn't even dream of having something like a boat." He paused then looked back at Luke. "I take pleasure in seeing a young man like you excited about a race, so I would consider letting you borrow my Chris Craft."

"*Seriously?*"

"Yes, if we could come to an arrangement."

"What exactly does that mean?"

The judge looked at the floor. "A mutually beneficial understanding."

"Some kind of *deal?*"

"I suppose you could call it that."

Luke frowned. "So, what's the deal?"

Judge Clements cleared his throat. "I let you race the Chris Craft and you forget about the Indian relics. Let dead things lie."

Luke was hit with a wave of disappointment. He didn't say anything for a few moments.

"So, what do you say. Fair deal?"

"Sounds like a bribe to me."

The judge's body stiffened. "An arrangement, as I said."

Luke struggled to swing his legs over the side of the bed, causing the judge to move farther away. "My mother's taught me to be honest—about everything. And I try." He looked at the judge. "Sorry, sir, this isn't honest."

Judge Clements frowned. When was the last time he had been turned down? After an uncomfortable silence, he straightened his sport coat. "Well, then…" He walked to the door, hesitating before opening it. He turned back to Luke. "You're one tough young fellow, I'll give you that." He held tight to the door handle, paused for a few moments, then walked out.

He lingered outside Luke's room. When he looked in his

window, he saw Luke had closed his eyes. Something didn't feel right. The judge walked back in.

"Sir," Luke said.

"I have to say, I've come to respect you, Luke. And I'm not in the habit of changing my mind, but I've reconsidered. You may use my boat for the race. Seems like the right thing to do. No strings attached."

Luke was surprised, pleased, though he didn't entirely trust the judge. "You sure about that?"

"Yes. I would have loved to do something like that when I was your age."

"Judge Clements, if I use your boat, I can only race to win. Flat out."

"I understand. But if you wreck the Chris Craft, you're going to pay for it. And I'm not responsible if you get hurt. It's all on you."

Luke smiled. "That's pretty darn generous of you."

Luke held out his good hand and the judge awkwardly shook it. "Just don't put my daughter in danger again."

Luke nodded. "Deal."

CHAPTER TWENTY-ONE

W HEN LUKE AWAKENED FROM A DEEP SLEEP THAT afternoon, he wondered if he had dreamed about talking to the judge or if it was real. When a nurse came in, he asked her if he'd had any visitors.

"Oh, yes," she replied. "That man from downcountry came to see you."

"Thanks, I wasn't sure."

"Probably because of the pain medication."

Luke pushed up off the bed and steadied himself on the siderail. "So, when can I get out of here?"

The nurse gave him a look. "You don't exactly look like you're ready to roll."

"I will be, after some real food."

She chuckled. "Well, you'll *have* to get out of here for that."

The nurse brought Luke a tray of food. By the time he'd finished a bowl of watery chicken noodle soup and a couple of saltines, Sarah had arrived. She was psyched to see him sitting in a chair and gave him a careful hug. "I assume you've eaten everything on the hospital menu."

"I would if they'd let me." He pushed his table away. "All I got was a skimpy bowl of stringy soup. I'm ready to go."

"Home?"

"'Course."

Sarah helped him up. "Are you sure?"

"Yes, good as new." He grimaced trying to get out of his hospital robe.

"I see that." Sarah pulled some of his clothes from a paper bag. "I thought you might need these."

"Great, thanks."

Sarah laughed and held up a pair of sweatpants with little lumberjack designs on them. "Your mother, who's been very worried about you, said these were your favorites."

"Give me those." Luke tried to grab them but missed and fell back on the bed.

"Here, let me help you." Sarah got down on her knees and slid her hands up over his thighs. She untied his hospital johnny and pulled it off, revealing an erection. "My, you're recovering quickly..." She slid the sweatpants up over his legs, gently touching his penis. "You should save that for later."

"Don't worry, I will."

Sarah helped him button a red and green flannel shirt around his sling. When the nurse came in to get him ready for discharge, Sarah seemed to get a kick out of his still having an erection. "Anything else you need?" she asked, suggestively, in front of the nurse.

Luke gave her a sideward glance. "I'm good."

"I see that." Smiling, Sarah left to bring her car around.

On the way to Luke's house, Sarah drove the Mustang slowly, taking care to avoid as many potholes and bumps as possible. Three Dog Night's "Joy to the World" played on the radio.

"Can't this horse go any faster?" Luke had his good hand out the window keeping time with the music.

"I'm trying not to hurt you."

"Gotta' get home to practice for the jam session tomorrow night."

"I can't wait to hear you play with your gimpy arm." Sarah shot him a smile and sped up.

He chuckled then cringed. "Don't make me laugh. It makes everything hurt. Just drive."

In town, they passed under the colorful banner hung across the street. Nearby, in the park, a number of people were setting up brightly-colored booths. Sarah looked over at Luke. "I'm really glad you're alive."

He touched her arm with his sling. "Me, too. *And* I've got some awesome news."

"What's that?"

"Your old man came to see me. He's letting me use his Chris Craft for the race."

"What?" she said, feigning surprise. "Are you serious?"

Luke nodded. "Such a sweet boat. I'm going to beat Freddie's ass."

"Wow, how'd you get my father to do that?"

"Well, he wanted to work out a deal, an 'arrangement,' he called it."

"Let me guess. About the Indian situation?"

"Yes, but I didn't go for it. And to his credit, he still said I could use it."

"Amazing. You outmaneuvered a federal judge."

Luke smiled. "Cool, huh? But really, I just stuck to my guns."

"So, what are you going to do about reporting the relics?"

Luke looked down the road. "Not sure. Right now, I've got a

barn dance and a boat race to get ready for. Besides, seems it's up to him now."

Sarah left Luke at home where he rested for most of the day, though he did play his guitar a little. It was awkward and somewhat painful, but he managed to do it.

* * *

The next evening, Sarah picked him up and they met everyone at Skinny's for the jam session, probably the last one before the barn dance. Her Mustang drew some raised eyebrows and a few jealous looks, but folks seemed glad to see her, which made Luke happy. Inside the café, the sweet smell of Skinny's fresh cornbread was a balm for Luke's aching body.

Jed looked up from tuning his fiddle. "Good you brought that violin of yours," he said to Sarah. "Join in tonight."

"I'll try."

"Set right here next to me." Jed tapped the chair next to him.

Sarah glanced at Luke, who nodded. "You'll learn a lot," he whispered.

At Skinny's direction from the piano, the group joined in for a couple of slow songs, working into a rousing rendition of "The Saints Go Marching In." Toward the end, Jed motioned to Sarah to take a turn with her violin. She stood, hesitated, then cradled her instrument tight under her chin.

"Loosen that poor thing up," Jed said to her.

Sarah loosened her grip on her violin, then began to play, and pretty well at that, causing Jed to raise his eyebrows. However, she only played a few measures before she hit a sour note, and abruptly sat back down. Regardless, by the expression on Jed's face, Sarah suspected he knew she'd been doing some serious practicing, but neither said anything.

When the session was over, Skinny announced that Moosehead Amusements had arrived and invited everyone to head over to the town green to help them set up. When they got there, the fire department was using their ladder truck to erect a set of spotlights. As soon as the green was lit, lots of folks came out of their homes to help put the kiddie rides together. The big news was the company had a "new" Ferris wheel, bought and refurbished from a salvage company in Massachusetts. Even though the top of it was barely over the streetlights, for Greensboro, it was an exciting new attraction.

Sarah helped Vicky serve lemonade and beer, and the Community Church ladies put out a collection of fresh muffins, turnovers, and pies. The strawberry-rhubarb pies disappeared in a flash. It was late when the last ride, the carousel, was finally assembled. Luke and Sarah were exhausted. They sat on the edge of the bandstand, looking over the green. Sarah took hold of Luke's good arm and leaned into him. "I feel like I'm in a wonderful movie."

Luke chuckled. "Probably a 'B' movie." He kissed her on the head.

"Stop it, this town is wicked cool. Everyone knows each other, they help out with everything. It's like another planet compared with Washington."

"Geez, I'd hope so, that damn place."

"I could see myself living here."

Luke straightened a bit. "Really? A big city girl like you, with your whole life in front of you?"

"Yup," Sarah said, with a poorly-mimicked local accent.

"Well, I'll be darned." Luke smiled. "Sure glad I met you and your Mustang the day I delivered that load of beams."

"Me, too." Sarah looked him in the eye. "Which one do you like better?"

"That red horse sure is pretty…" He looked up as if thinking. "But it doesn't feel half as nice as you." He leaned in and they shared a long kiss.

CHAPTER TWENTY-TWO

B ECAUSE THE REGISTRATION PERIOD HAD PASSED, FREDDIE tried to get the race officials to disallow Luke's boat change, but they approved it due to "extenuating circumstances." Luke and Sarah spent the next couple of days preparing for the race, and Luke couldn't have been happier to be racing her father's Chris Craft.

When Luke wasn't around, Sarah found a secluded place and practiced her fiddling as much as possible. She didn't want anyone to know she and Sis would be competing in the contest.

On Friday, Vicky gave her an envelope that had come in the mail. Inside, was a postcard with a picture of a remote Appalachian cabin with locals playing music on the porch. On the other side was written: "Get ready to whomp 'em. See you Saturday, darlin'." It wasn't signed, but Sarah sure knew who it was from. She couldn't wait to see the look on everyone's faces when she and Sis took the stage.

In the days leading up to the festival, people came to town from all around. Lawns and fields sprouted dozens of tents, and, in a hayfield up the road from the town beach, a campground emerged where the farmer charged $3 a spot for the weekend. By Thursday afternoon, it was filled with travel trailers and pop-up campers, hooked together with a sprawling web of extension cords connected to a light pole. Scantily-clad children chased each other around the campsites, many of them with white daisies and red and yellow zinnias braided into their hair. The various dogs quickly found each other and roamed together in excited, tail-wagging packs. By suppertime, a campfire burned brightly in the central area where people cooked together, sharing their food at a long communal table made from rough-hewn planks supplied by Trace. In the evening, the sweet sounds of guitars, mandolins, banjos, and fiddles drifted into town on the cool night air.

Judge Clements arrived back Friday afternoon. He was excited to watch the race, and hoped Luke would win without killing himself or wrecking his new boat. Anxious to see the progress at their building site, he and Sarah drove down to the lake. As they approached, the wooden skeleton of the structure stood tall above the shore. After looking it over from the ground, they climbed a wooden ladder onto the first floor and admired the tight wooden pegs the carpenters had fashioned to securely join the posts and beams together. Standing on the wide pine floor, looking out over the lake, the judge put his arm around Sarah's shoulders. "Isn't this about the most beautiful view you ever saw? I can't wait to see this finished. I'm going to sit right here in my easy chair, drink coffee, and read the *Journal*. In time, I'll forget there ever was a war or a Washington, DC."

"I'm glad you found this beautiful spot. You've worked very hard for it." Sarah was uncomfortably aware of the relics bulldozed into the earth beneath them. As much as she respected Luke's feelings, she hoped he would let the native people and their belongings lie in peace.

Driving back to the inn, Sarah and her father saw two women in front of the library planting boxes of red and white petunias around a hand-painted sign that read: "Welcome to Greensboro."

"It's such a big event," Sarah said to her father.

"A great little festival, indeed. I tried to get you to come up for it a couple of years ago, but you weren't interested."

"I didn't know what I was missing. Besides, you never told me there was a handsome guy like Luke up here."

Her father scoffed. "How could I have overlooked that?"

On the corner by Willey's Store, a couple of scraggly-haired hippies in painted bell-bottoms held "Make Peace—Not War" signs. She glanced at her father. Thankfully, he didn't see them. Then, a short distance up the street, she saw a huge Uncle Sam puppet leaning against the front of a church. "That's the biggest puppet I've ever seen."

"Amazing, aren't they. From the famous Bread and Puppet Theater up in Glover."

They were headed out of town when her father asked, "This Luke fellow, what draws you to him?"

Sarah smiled. "He makes me happy."

He nodded subtly and looked out his window. "Can't remember the last time your mother and I made each other happy."

Sarah touched his sleeve. "It's not your fault. Mother has serious issues."

"Don't we all." He gave the Caddy the gas, and they left Greensboro behind them.

As they walked up onto the front porch of the inn, Sarah turned to her father. "Can I ask you something."

"Yes."

"Luke's mother is quite ill—actually, frail is a better description. I know she'd like to watch the race, but Luke won't be able to take her, and I don't want to leave him. If you didn't have other plans, would you consider giving her a ride into town?"

Her father pondered.

"She's a nice lady—tires easily, but has plenty of spunk."

He squinted. "I suppose I could."

"You could bring a couple of Vicky's lawn chairs and sit near the finish line."

He nodded. "Alright."

"Thank you, Daddy."

"Perhaps it's time I got to know a few of the regular locals."

Sarah couldn't help but chuckle. "You mean the people Maxwell doesn't associate with?"

Her father smiled. "Exactly, though he is a remarkable fellow."

"I guess, but he doesn't exactly fit in with the character of this place."

"Ah, but he adds spice to the town. Anyway, I suppose you'll be with Luke in the pit, or whatever they call it in boat racing."

"Yes. I want to stay close to him."

He looked her in the eye. "Not too close."

"Promise." She flashed the Girl Scout sign. "So, I'm heading over to Andy's to help Luke get your boat ready for the race tomorrow, then we'll be going to the festival in town tonight. I haven't had fried dough since you took me to Coney Island."

"Sounds good." He opened the front door.

"Would you like to meet us there?"

He smiled. "Kind of you to ask, but I'm quite tired from all this commuting. Besides, I bet the two of you would rather go on your own."

"Okay." Sarah hoped she was hiding her relief. "And if you're sleeping when I get back tonight, I'll see you in the morning before the race."

Her father waved his hand in acknowledgment as the door swung closed behind him.

Sarah immediately starting plotting how she could spend the night with Luke.

* * *

Over at Andy's boatyard, Luke had just taken the Chris Craft for a test-drive, and he was impressed with its power and how smoothly it cut through the water. Because his sore shoulder still bothered him, Sarah was a big help pulling the boat from the water. Then they took everything that wasn't absolutely necessary out of the Chris Craft, siphoned the gas tank and filled it half-full with fresh high-test, to which Luke added a bottle of octane booster for good measure. To finish up, Luke took a chamois cloth and proudly polished the brass lights, horn, and cleats that adorned the bow. By early evening, they had the sleek mahogany beauty ready for the race.

"This boat is really something. Hard to imagine ever owning one of these." He glanced at Sarah. "And I'm sure you had something to do with it."

"Maybe..." She ran her hand over the smooth wood. "Couldn't let my boyfriend sit out *this* race. Besides, a handsome dude like you should race in style."

Luke smiled. "Thank you. It means a lot." He slowly shook his head. "You have to be the most beautiful girl in the world."

She demurred. "Oh, there must be someone more beautiful."

"Nope." He slid his good arm around her and drew her lips to his. Leaning against the boat, kissing Sarah, he found it hard to let her go.

"Boy," Sarah said, taking in a breath, "for a hick, you are a really good kisser."

"Whoever said country boys don't know how to kiss?"

Sarah laughed.

"I love you, Sarah. I always will."

She broke into a big smile. "Ditto."

She helped him pull the heavy canvas cover back over the boat and fasten it to the trailer. The sun was setting on the western hills beyond the lake, bright streaks of orange reflected on the placid water. Luke held Sarah close. "So peaceful. Hard to believe the world's such a mess, and that this place is going to go nuts tomorrow."

"But there *is* tonight. My father was exhausted, has probably already gone to bed." Sarah looked up at him. "I know an old barn nearby where we could stay."

He shook his head again. "I love it, but I gotta' get some sleep and rest this arm for tomorrow."

She went up on her toes and whispered in his ear. "You won't need your arm."

He laughed and partially turned away. "No, seriously, as much as I'd like to sleep with you, I'm so beat, I gotta' go home and get some shut-eye."

She rubbed against his groin. "Okay, suit yourself."

He jerked away, grabbing his bad shoulder. "Shit, stop that. You're making me crazier than I already am."

"Alright. I'll go back to the inn all alone. It's a big creepy place, you know."

"No, it's not." Luke started to walk to her car. "Come on, I need a ride home." He patted the red hood of the Mustang. "Maybe you can show me what this sweet thing can do."

Sarah slid into the driver's seat. "Buckle up. And I don't want any whining."

She turned the key and the engine roared to life.

"Love the feel of what's under her hood."

Sarah gave him a sideward smirk, hit the gas, and fishtailed across Andy's gravel driveway, laying a screeching track of rubber when they hit the pavement.

Chapter Twenty-Three

WHEN THEY REACHED LUKE'S HOUSE, THEY KISSED AND played with each other in the car for a few minutes before Luke said he had to get to bed. Inside, he checked on his mom, already asleep in her small bedroom. He noticed a fly floating in her water, so he dumped it out in the kitchen and poured her a fresh glass. He placed it quietly on her bedside table, littered with used tissues, pill bottles, and *Reader's Digests*. "Good night, Mom," he whispered before leaving her door ajar so he could hear if she called out during the night.

Luke found an opened can of ravioli in the fridge, peeled off the paper label, and set it on the stove. Waiting for the yellow and orange goo to warm, he poured a glass of milk, sat at the table, and looked at the new Sears & Roebuck catalog. Too tired to read, he put the catalog down and noticed a letter standing between the salt and pepper shakers. Feeling uneasy, he slid the envelope toward him. The return address confirmed his fear: Selective Service System, with an official government seal. He tried to push the rush of visions of Vietnam from his mind: medics racing bloodied soldiers to helicopters, mud-caked GIs smoking cigarettes in the jungle, M16s laid across their laps. And the most terrifying image—the unloading of flag-draped caskets onto a tarmac stateside where a congregation of grieving loved ones were held back by a rope line.

"Shit," Luke said. No way he was opening it. Not going to ruin this weekend.

Smelling his dinner burning, Luke dropped the letter on the table and grabbed the can, singing his fingertips. He took a pair of pliers from a drawer, lifted the can to the sink, and blew over the top of the steaming ravioli until it cooled enough to be spooned out.

After he finished eating, Luke went to bed and soon fell into a restless sleep dreaming about leaving for boot camp and shipping out to the war. During the night, he was awakened by a noise from his mother's room. When he checked on her, he found she was just talking in her sleep, as she often did. On his way back to bed, he stopped in the kitchen and caught sight of the letter showing under the Sears catalog on the table. As much as he didn't want to see the bad news, he couldn't resist opening it. He slowly pulled out an official government letter. Across the top in bold letters was printed: "Order to Report for Induction."

Luke had a strong impulse to run—somewhere, anywhere, to get away from the damn war. But where could he go? What would people he cared about think? *Draft dodger? Traitor?* He'd probably end up in some brig, bringing more dishonor to his family. He stepped to the bay window where the first pink glow of the coming day illuminated his mother's dreamcatcher. He blew a layer of dust off it then looked out at the sleeping trailer next door. *What would even they think?*

Before going back to bed, Luke put the letter back in its envelope and slid it between the salt and pepper shakers like he'd never opened it. It took a while to get back to sleep, which was fitful at best. Later, awakened by pain in his injured shoulder, he sat up and was happy to see bright sunshine coming through his thin curtain. He heard his mother in the kitchen and smelled the aroma of bacon cooking on the stove. "Sweet," he said, knowing she must be having one of her rare good days.

On the kitchen table sat scrambled eggs and a small stack of buttermilk pancakes. "You didn't have to do all this," Luke said, giving his mother a kiss on the cheek.

"Need your strength for the race today. Then you'll be up half the night over to Rowell's barn, partying."

Luke plucked a piece of bacon from the pan, blew on it, and nibbled off the crusty end. "You're probably right. Plus..." He raised his eyebrows, "the awesome Sarah Clements will be with me this year."

His mother forked the other slices of bacon onto a plate and handed it to him. "Lovebirds."

"By the way," Luke said, licking drops of maple syrup from his fingers, "Sarah's father, the judge, said he'd give you a ride over to watch the race."

She looked surprised. "Really?"

"Yes. He'll bring a couple lawn chairs from the inn and set them up by the town launch near the finish line. You can watch the race together."

"That's nice of him." Mary poured the bacon grease off into an A&P coffee can. She felt her unkempt bun of thinning hair. "Heavens, I'll have to fix myself up."

"You look fine." Luke slid his plate into a pan of sudsy water in the sink. "Thanks for breakfast. I'm going to need it."

She took hold of his sleeve, looked him in the eye. "Now you be extra careful out there. You've a bum wing and a boat you're not familiar with." She took in a couple of quick breaths. "I know you want to beat Freddie, but you've already had one bad crash. It's not worth getting yourself killed."

"I'll be careful, promise."

Mary smiled at him. "Wouldn't your father be proud, to see you driving a nice Chris Craft? A judge's boat, no less."

Luke nodded. "Yeah, it's pretty cool. I'm psyched you'll be watching at the finish line."

Leaning against the sink, his mother gave him a thumbs-up.

Luke showered, said goodbye to his mother, and headed into town. Driving to Andy's, he was struck by a sick feeling that soon he'd be leaving home for boot camp. As he drove past familiar hayfields and long rows of corn, the thought of never coming back to Greensboro again overtook him. He slowed his pickup to a crawl. This was where he was supposed to spend his life, not off in some godforsaken foreign country fighting in a civil war. Feeling he was going to puke, Luke hung his head out the window. Taking in a few deep breaths, he steadied himself. He thought about his father. Despite being a disgraced vet, he still held military duty in high regard. But at the moment, he'd want Luke focused on the Great Race.

Luke looked at himself in his rearview mirror. "Get your shit together." He shifted into gear and hit the gas.

A traffic jam of pickups and boat trailers clogged the entrance to Andy's shop, so Luke drove cross-lots through an adjacent pasture to the boatsheds. He checked out the boats that were launching to size up the competition. The usuals were there: Clive Derby and his Feather Craft with a nice Scott-Atwater outboard, Cyrus Mitchell and his handsome wooden Thompson inboard, Lee McCarthy and his sleek Wolverine with a Johnson outboard, and old Darcy Beaulieu and her dented aluminum fishing boat pushed by a faded green Firestone outboard. Along the road, another line of boats, some of which he didn't recognize, waited for their turn to launch.

After parking, Luke saw Sarah waving to him, and hurried over to her. "This is so cool," she said, wrapping her arms around his neck. "Some of these outfits are great."

An old couple dressed as Uncle and Auntie Sam stood beside a birchbark canoe. A couple of kids were dressed up as Minnie and Mickey Mouse, and next to them someone looked something like Paul Bunyan.

Luke explained, "There's a little costume boat parade at the beginning for people who just want to have fun before the real race begins. When I was a little kid, my dad took me and some friends in a rowboat dressed up as Indians. We taped little chocolates onto a whole bunch of rubber-tipped arrows and shot them into the crowd. It was a wicked hot Fourth, and the chocolates made quite a mess, but it was a lot of fun."

Sarah smiled. "Wish I could have seen that."

"I'll bet. Even though I was only five or six, all I really wanted to do was race with the big guys."

"And now you're one of them."

"I guess." Luke waved to Skinny, who had just launched his boat, then frowned when he saw Freddie's boat tied up at a private dock down a ways from Andy's. He pointed. "You're going down this year."

"Yeah," Sarah said, also pointing. "You're going down!"

Luke chuckled. "Never had a cheerleader like you."

"Never had a crazy boyfriend that raced flaming boats."

"Easy, girl. I'm done with the flaming part."

Sarah helped Luke launch the Chris Craft and tie it up on

the end of the dock. Luke then pointed the racecourse out to Sarah. It ran north from Andy's past the outlet to Porter Brook before curving west around Burlington Point. It then swept the southern end of the lake before heading north past the town beach, around Birch Point back to Andy's. Each boat had to complete two clean circuits around the lake before crossing the finish line at the town dock. There were race monitors stationed at potentially treacherous points around the lake. If you hit a private mooring or got too close to a swim platform, sensitive wetlands, or a loon nesting area, you got a blast from a horn and could theoretically be disqualified, though that rarely happened. Years ago, Reggie Picard skidded over a big wave approaching Burlington Point, lost control, and tore the end off a dock close to where an unflappable woman sat reading a book. She was from a tough old lake family and allegedly turned toward the driver of the crashed boat, nodded at the dock, and simply said, "Better fix that."

Several more boats came down the lake toward the starting line as Luke envisioned the turns of the racecourse, carefully thinking through the most difficult parts in his mind.

He turned to Sarah. "So, the trickiest spots are coming around the points of land where the racecourse narrows. Freddie has a deep-V hull which is really good on those tight corners. Your dad's boat has less of a V, but tons of power. If I can get a good angle on the turns, I should be able to hang with Freddie then smoke him on the straightaways."

Sarah frowned. "Sounds dangerous."

"Can be, but believe me, I'm not going to wreck this beauty."

"I hope not, but you have that crazy look in your eye."

Luke grinned. "Gotta' race like it could be my last."

"Don't say that." Sarah hit his arm. "It won't be. And that's not even funny."

Someone spoke over a loudspeaker. "Attention all racers. You have ten minutes to make final preparations and get your boat to the starting line. You must line up and stay in your assigned lane. Chairman Jakes will give you a ten-count before he fires the starting pistol. Anyone who bangs another boat coming out of the starting gate will be immediately disqualified. I know there's stiff competition out here today, but we won't tolerate anything dangerous. We want a good, safe race."

Luke leaned close to Sarah. "What a bunch of bull. Most of us would damn near kill each other to win."

Sarah swatted him again. "You nearly killed *yourself* the other day."

"Nah," Luke said, grinning. "Gotta' go." He climbed into the boat and started the engine, its smooth rumbling keeping time with the bubbles coming from under the stern. "Doesn't she sound sweet?"

"Yes." Sarah stepped back. "Now get out there and win. And be careful!"

"You bet."

"I'll see you at the finish line."

Luke revved the engine slightly and motored toward the starting line. Sarah ran up to Andy's shop and climbed onto a hay wagon decorated with red, white, and blue streamers that was waiting to take people to the town beach.

As a shiny red Massey Ferguson tractor pulled the wagon onto the road heading to town, a woman in a dirty gray sweatshirt and barn boots, touched Sarah's arm. "You must be that new girlfriend of Luke's, from downcountry."

Sarah smiled. "Yes."

"Such a good guy."

"He is."

The woman shook her head. "Pity he's being sent over…and so soon."

Sarah felt a gut-punch. She frowned at the woman. "How do you know?"

"Letter came yesterday. Everybody knows he's heading to Fort Bragg like the rest of the poor lemmings."

Heart racing, Sarah choked with emotion. She turned away and leaned over the side of the wagon as they headed into town.

CHAPTER TWENTY-FOUR

T HE GREAT RACE HAD STARTED OUT AS AN ICEBOAT RACE in February of 1946, after the blessed end of World War II. Locals were still putting their lives back together, and in the middle of that long, frigid winter, they needed some sort of celebration. A number of locals had primitive iceboats, and Caspian had frozen over during a windless January, making the ice unusually smooth, perfect for a race. No one can seem to remember who won, but several old veterans remember the huge bonfire that was held afterwards at the town beach and the plentiful Canadian whiskey and hot mulled cider that kept everyone warm. By the late '50s, however, the novelty of racing and partying in the cold had worn off. The event was moved to the Fourth of July weekend, and the Summer Festival was born.

When the hay wagon arrived in town, Sarah jumped off and headed toward the beach, wanting to get away from the woman who had upset her. From the top of the knoll, she watched the last entries in the costume parade, led by a rendition of General George Washington crossing the Potomac in a refrigerator with the door taken off and two steel beer kegs lashed to the sides for flotation. An American flag painted on a T-shirt flew from the top of a fishing pole mounted on the fridge. George looked very precarious in his Revolutionary vessel, which rocked back and forth with the slightest movement.

Five lavishly decorated duckboats followed, tied together to look like a train. Up front in the locomotive, a jovial Santa waved to everyone, dressed in blue swim trunks and a Johnson Woolen Mills red-and-black plaid hunting coat. Santa and his elves fired bags of candy from potato guns at gaggles of kids waiting expectantly on the shore.

Sarah smiled at all the hoopla, which helped put the news of Luke's call-up out of her mind. As soon as the parade ended, the race was set to begin. She flinched as the sharp crack of the starting gun echoed across the water. "They're off!" came over a loudspeaker from a podium mounted on the back of a farm truck near the finish line. She was happy to see her father and Mary among the sea of people in folding lawn chairs that covered a gentle slope above the podium. When Sarah reached them, she heard a couple of women talking to "His Honor." Her father seemed to enjoy being a bit of a local celebrity.

Sarah sat on the ground between Mary and her father, but soon they were all on their feet, straining to see the boats as they rounded Burlington Point in the distance. As the racers got closer, the whine of their engines grew louder. Four boats were tightly packed in the lead, Luke on the outside, running right next to Freddie. As they approached the south end of the lake, it appeared there couldn't be more than a foot between them, both men hunkered down behind their windshields, eyes covered with ski goggles against the heavy spray. Even from a distance, Sarah could see their fierce determination.

As the racers approached the beach area, one boat let out a loud backfire followed by a puff of black smoke. Luke's speed dropped, as he must have been distracted. Freddie took advantage and gained a boat-length on Luke as the damaged boat puttered toward shore, smoke and flames erupting from beneath its engine cover. Two firemen with extinguishers ran toward the stricken craft.

Mary's arm shot into the air. "Come on, Luke!"

Sarah held her arms tight to her chest, nervous for so many reasons.

Sarah's father waved at Luke. "Give her the gas!" Sarah smiled at his seeming more interested in Luke winning than the safety of his boat.

"Final lap!" the man on the loudspeaker yelled.

With the boats roaring north, the waters were so choppy, it was impossible to tell who was in the lead. As the racers approached the shallows before rounding Birch Point, Sarah willed Luke to stay on the inside, away from the rocks. She squeezed her eyes shut, pushing the vision of his boat crashing out of her mind.

When the leaders abruptly turned west, Luke and Freddie were again neck and neck. Behind them, another boat must have hit something because it jumped in the air and veered off the course.

"Hang in there, Luke," she said to herself.

Once around Birch Point, the boats disappeared from view and continued north. A collective sigh of relief rippled across the crowd. The racers had made it past that treacherous area. Down in front, a lanky farmer in overalls with a big smile clapped his hands together. "Yes, sir," he said loudly, "we got ourselves a dandy of a race. Hope Luke gives that Freddie a good shellacking, but he can't let up for a second." A woman in a blue sundress and a straw hat agreed. "His daddy would be so happy."

"Yeah!" Sarah spontaneously yelled, causing the couple to look back and give her a smile.

* * *

Trailing just behind Freddie, so much spray came off his boat, Luke could hardly see through his goggles. He gripped the steering wheel so tight, a hard charley horse hit his injured arm. He tore the sling off and leaned against the throttle, adjusting it with his elbow. It was almost scary how much power the Chris Craft had, and he loved it.

Freddie glanced back at Luke, who took advantage of Freddie's momentary lapse to cut a diagonal off his stern. Luke got enough of a boost riding Freddie's wake that he was able to pull parallel to him. Luke crouched low and struck a perfectly straight line across the northern expanse of the lake. As they headed for a large rock outcropping on the northwest shore, Luke realized Freddie was forcing him toward the boulders that stretched a hundred feet into the lake. If he hit them, it would be a disaster.

As the outcropping got closer, Luke tried to squeeze Freddie so he'd back off, but he didn't budge. They had to veer soon or they would both crash. Luke glanced at the throttle, which offered a little more horsepower. With only 50 yards between them and the boulders, Luke turned his bow into Freddie's. His arm searing with pain, and the two boats bumping each other, Luke held the wheel steady and forced Freddie toward the broad lake.

Freddie yelled something and turned hard into the Chris Craft. This was the do-or-die moment Luke had waited years for. He floored it, edging past Freddie, whose bow hit Luke's boat, tearing off the red port light. Luke snuck by him just in time to turn sharply east away from the rocks. He flinched when he heard Freddie's lower unit paint one of the boulders with its prop, but he stayed right on Luke's tail. *Bastard!*

The pain in Luke's shoulder kept him from maneuvering like he wanted to, but he managed to curve a smooth arc just inside the race markers heading toward Burlington Point. The other boats had been left behind, making it a two-man race.

As they entered the south sweep of the racecourse, Luke kept his elbow hard against the throttle. Approaching the final, tight turn, a shot of fear went through him. They had never raced that fast. If they didn't ease off, they could both lose it before the finish line and crash into the crowd.

* * *

Sarah was on her tiptoes as Luke and Freddie entered the final turn. The boats were so close together she was scared they would crash into each other.

The loudspeaker blared. "And here they come, out of the final turn, Luke and Freddie neck and neck!"

Freddie turned his boat into Luke, trying to force him toward the shallows near the beach. Sarah's heart jumped as Luke grimaced and grabbed his injured arm, momentarily losing control of his steering wheel. With his bow pointing straight at the crowd, she heard Luke pull back on the throttle. Freddie snuck past him. "You sonofabitch!" Luke yelled.

"You cheater!" the judge and Mary both yelled. They looked at the race officials, who didn't do anything.

Freddie caught Luke's wake, which slowed him a bit. Luke

regained control of the Chris Craft and headed straight for the finish line. Silence came over the crowd as the two men raced toward the finish, running dangerously close to the beach.

"Get back!" the announcer yelled, waving his arms. The people closest to the shore struggled out of their lawn chairs and ran to safety. As the two boats thundered past, a heavy spray of water drenched the first few rows of chairs and blankets, and those who couldn't get away fast enough.

Sarah realized she was squeezing both her father's and Mary's hands as the boats zeroed in on the finish line. Fearing Luke and Freddie would crash, she sensed they were all holding their breath. With both bows pointed straight at the banner, Luke suddenly veered away from Freddie. A disappointed groan rose from the crowd. But the vacuum created by Luke's maneuver caused Freddie's boat to lurch toward Luke's stern. Luke floored the throttle and roared through the finish line as Freddie tried to regain control. Instead, he crashed through one of the marker buoys, throwing him from the boat and bringing the red banner down on him.

Luke's good arm shot up as the crowd went crazy. Sun hats, towels, streamers, and beer cans flew through the air. Sarah, her father, and Mary, all hugged each other. "Thank the Lord," Mary said, collapsing, out of breath, into her chair.

"He did it!" Sarah yelled, running down the lawn to greet her champion.

Luke quickly brought the Chris Craft around to where Freddie had crashed. "You alright?" he yelled to him.

Freddie tore the banner from around his neck. "Yeah."

"You suck, Freddie!" "You dirty bastard!" "Cheater!" people yelled from onshore.

Luke, who appreciated the all-out nature of the competition, frowned at the spectators.

"You ran a helluva race," Luke said, extending his hand.

Freddie threw the banner into the water. "So'd you." He reached up and reluctantly shook Luke's hand before climbing back into his boat, and taking off down the lake.

Luke motored over to the dock next to the judges' stand.

"Luke!" Sarah yelled, as she caught the slightly damaged bow. "That was great!"

He beamed at her, quickly tied off, and took her in his arms. He twirled her around, and when they kissed, the crowd roared with pleasure. "That was a close one," he whispered to Sarah.

She looked at him. "That last move was brilliant."

"You caught that?"

"I sure did. Freddie thought you were losing it, but your wake veered him off course."

"Pretty cool it worked. It was my last trick."

"Well, the crowd loved it—and you."

Luke waved to the many folks cheering for him. "Good people."

Sarah chuckled. "And it was quite a sight watching the finish line collapse on Freddie."

"Perfect ending."

They walked over to the judges and other dignitaries who were waiting for Luke. He shook all of their hands. "Thank you, gentlemen." Then he saw Judge Clements helping his mother down the lawn, and quickly headed over to her.

"You did it," Mary said, weakly. "Your dad would be so proud you beat him."

Luke hugged her. "I hope so. Freddie threw everything he

had at me. Nearly did me in when he pushed me toward those big rocks on the north end."

Sarah squeezed his arm. "Glad I couldn't see that from here."

"Seriously."

Chairman Jakes came over the loudspeaker. "Let's get our winner up here to the awards podium."

"Come on." Luke took Sarah's hand and led her to the farm truck decorated with patriotic streamers. She let go as he started to climb the makeshift stairs. Luke stopped and looked at her. "You gotta' come up with me."

Sarah hesitated. "But *you* won the race."

Luke waited, nodded to the podium.

"Okay." Sarah smiled and joined him.

Luke and Sarah stepped onto the podium, his good arm holding her tightly. "Thank you for being here for me."

She gave him a quick kiss on the cheek. "Wouldn't miss it."

The crowd cheered as they gathered around the truck. Nothing better than a hometown favorite winning a race, and an unlikely love story to boot. Mr. Jakes stepped to the microphone. "That was a whale of a race. Everybody got their money's worth!"

"Hell," said a drunk guy down front. "I didn't pay nothin' to watch."

Mr. Jakes frowned. "Go back to sleep, Henry."

"Today we witnessed the toughest competition ever." Mr. Jakes gave Luke a sideward look. "For a few seconds, there, I thought you both were going to drive right through the crowd."

Luke looked sheepishly at the floor then out at the people. "But we didn't!" he yelled, and the crowd roared in approval.

"Before we make the trophy presentation, I'd like to ask Luke's mom to join us. She's been waiting for this win for a long time."

Luke was pleased, though his mom looked awfully tired. He stepped to the stairs to help her, but Judge Clements was right there supporting her. When she reached the top of the stairs, Luke took her hand and helped her to a folding chair. "Thank you," Mary said in a whisper.

Mr. Jakes turned to the roof of the truck's cab and retrieved a wooden plaque with a shiny brass propeller mounted on it. He held it up so all could see the inscription, which read:

GREENSBORO'S ANNUAL GREAT RACE
1970 CHAMPION

"Luke Simms, it is with great pleasure that I declare you our race champion for 1970!" He handed the plaque to Luke and they both held it while the photographer from the *Hardwick Gazette* snapped a few photos. Then Luke and Sarah moved toward his mom, and the three of them held the plaque up to the crowd.

"Would you like to say a few words?" Mr. Jakes handed the mic to Luke.

Luke looked at the crowd for a few moments then spoke into the microphone. "Thank you, all, for cheering me on, especially my mom and my girlfriend, Sarah. And to Judge Clements for letting me use his beautiful boat. I couldn't have won without it." Luke looked at the judge and lowered his voice. "There's a little ding in the bow we'll discuss later." The crowd laughed.

"No problem," the judge called back to him.

Luke became serious. "As most of you probably know, my father was robbed of a win years ago by some cheating, which makes this victory even more special." Luke lifted the plaque toward the bright blue sky. "This one's for you, Dad."

The crowd gave Luke resounding applause, and then with considerable fanfare, Mr. Jakes made a much-anticipated announcement. "And now it is time for our annual Independence Day barbeque, once again sponsored by our good neighbor, Maxwell Holmes."

"Let's eat!" someone yelled.

A cheer went up, and the crowd moved in unison from the lake toward the town green, where an elaborate barbeque had been set up. In the middle, Maxwell stood in a tall French chef's hat and starched white apron, that made him look like the Pillsbury Doughboy.

"This ought to be good," Sarah said, as they helped his mother off the podium.

"Oh, it will be."

Sarah held Luke for a moment and looked into his eyes. "I love you, Luke. Everything about you."

He smiled and kissed her. "Can't be half as much as I love you."

CHAPTER TWENTY-FIVE

THE JUDGE WENT TO GET HIS CAR TO TAKE LUKE'S exhausted mother home. Luke and Sarah said goodbye then followed the crowd to the town green. Lots of people congratulated Luke, but many disparaged Freddie.

"I almost feel bad for Freddie," Luke said.

"I don't," Sarah replied. "He cheated, crashing into you like that."

Sarah was concerned Luke didn't seem as excited as she'd expected he'd be. There was a tinge of sadness about him, and she figured she knew why.

The green was decked out in patriotic bunting from one end to the other. The carnival rides were all running, music was playing, and kids were chasing each other around with fluffs of cotton candy as big as their heads. Several had pieces of red candied apples stuck on their cheeks. Flags of every variety waved in the slight breeze, and hundreds of spinning foil streamers hung from branches of trees lining the streets. Greensboro was ready to party.

Maxwell, self-proclaimed "maestro" of the barbeque, waved a long wooden spoon through the air like a conductor's baton. "Step right up and fill your tummies," he called out in every direction.

Even by Washington standards, Sarah thought Maxwell's

spread was impressive. There were honey-glazed barbequed chicken skewers, racks of spareribs, a platter of pulled pork, and large silver trays piled high with hotdogs, hamburgers, and links of smoked sausage. One table held two large bowls of potato salad, as well as steaming pots of homemade chili and maple pork and beans. There were fresh loaves of bread, and a huge tossed salad, beside which sat fancy cut glass decanters of Italian, French, and creamy ranch dressings.

"Look!" Sarah said, pointing at an aging Tilt-a-Whirl, twisting and turning just beyond the smoking barbeques. "We used to ride those when my father would take us to Coney Island." She pulled on Luke's good arm. "Let's take a ride."

Luke motioned to the food tables. "But, look at this food."

"Just one ride, *please*. Besides, you'll probably throw up if you eat first."

"You calling me a wuss?"

"Never. Come on, it's about to empty out."

Luke looked like he'd never ridden a Tilt-a-Whirl, and appeared dizzy when the ride ended and they staggered off right into the line for the Ferris wheel.

"We gotta' go eat," Luke said, turning back toward the food.

Sarah held onto his shirt. "Just one more ride. You'll be able to see all the selections better from up there."

Luke shook his head, seemed a little irritable. "That's like a kiddie ride."

Ignoring him, Sarah kept tugging him toward a carnie loading people into the chairs. Without another word, they got on and soon started to rise. The first couple of times around, Luke just sat there looking over the crowd.

"Hey," Sarah said, grasping his arm as they rose above the

church roof. "You don't seem very happy for a guy who just won the big race."

Luke squinted against the sun. "Got things on my mind."

Sarah looked at him. "What's up?"

Luke shrugged his shoulders. "I guess I need to get something off my chest."

"Okay, you can tell me anything."

Luke slowly shook his head, gazed out toward the lake. "I don't want to hurt anyone."

Sarah waited while their chair descended past the carnie running the ride.

"Got the letter," Luke said, as they started rising again.

"*The* letter?"

"'Report for Induction,' it said. Two weeks, Fort Bragg."

"*Two weeks?*" Sarah said, alarm in her voice.

"Seems pretty quick."

They passed a maple tree decorated with silvery spinners reflecting in the sun. "Feels like my whole life is coming down to a moment that takes me away from everything I've ever known. Doesn't seem natural. I wonder if all these protests aren't trying to tell us something." They started heading up again. "Can't be all these people are so upset for nothing."

Sarah adjusted herself on the seat as they came down over the smoking barbeques. "Maybe we can get you some kind of deferment. My father could help."

Luke sort of smiled. "He already let me use his Chris Craft. I can't ask for more than that."

Sarah tugged on his sleeve. "Seriously, Luke, I'll talk to him."

He shook his head.

"Then, listen, there are other ways."

"Like what?"

"I read in the newspaper that guys are fleeing to Canada, pretending they're homosexual, or even—and I know this sounds gross—punching holes in their eardrums so they'll flunk their physicals and be deemed unfit for combat." She looked straight at him. "It would be worth it if it saved you."

Luke shook his head and grinned. "Do I look like a homosexual? And how am I going to play you songs on my guitar if I've wrecked my ears?"

"Oh, Luke."

"Seriously, why should I be treated special? Other guys from around here are going."

Sarah looked at him quizzically. "Jesus, Luke, you could get *killed*."

Luke paused as the ride slowed and the carnie started unloading chairs below them. "Don't get me wrong, I'm scared about fighting in that jungle—and I sure don't wanna' die."

Sarah felt tears form in her eyes.

"But the worst of it is, I don't want to leave you and Mom, and have you worrying about me."

"How could we not worry about you?"

"I'll take care of myself," he replied as their chair stopped at the platform. The carnie raised the safety bar and motioned for them to get out.

Avoiding a couple of old ladies who waved to them, Luke and Sarah darted behind the ticket booth. "Look," Luke said, "I shouldn't have said anything. It's just been on my mind. Pisses me off the letter came in the middle of festival."

"Listen, Luke, this is a very special weekend. You just won an awesome race, and we've got a fun dance and fiddle contest tonight. *I'll* be pissed if you're all mopey." She looked Luke in the eye. "I've got plans for you tonight."

Luke perked up. "You're right. The Army can wait."

"To hell with them." Sarah kissed him. "We'll make it two weeks we'll never forget."

Luke looked at her. "Like I could ever forget you."

"You'd better not." She pointed to a small photobooth. "Let's get a picture, so you can't forget me."

Luke followed Sarah into the booth and pulled the curtain closed. She dropped a quarter in the slot, and they looked at the camera. Seeing that Luke had a glum look on his face, Sarah nudged him. "Smile!" He still didn't look very happy. She tickled his ribs.

"Ouw, my shoulder."

"If you don't smile, I'll twist it for you."

"You're a brute."

"You remember, I'm from DC."

She tickled him again. He smiled, she hit the button, and the flash went off. They got three more shots as Luke turned and tickled her. They waited a couple minutes for the black-and-white print to come out. Sarah laughed. "You look like I just beat you up."

Luke pointed. "I want the one on the end. Great picture of your smile."

Sarah gave him the one he wanted. "There you go. Yours forever."

Luke looked at it for a few moments and put it in his shirt pocket. "Thanks, I love it."

"Can you hurry up in there?" someone said outside the booth.

"Ooops." Sarah pulled back the curtain to find a line waiting. "Sorry."

Luke took her hand. "Come with me, I want to show you something. Then we'll eat."

He led her through the crowd to a granite military monument at the far end of the green. Luke pointed at the names of the World War II vets inscribed into the stone. "You see what's missing?"

Sarah looked puzzled.

Luke pointed to the men's names starting with "S."

Sarah quickly read the names and nodded. "Your father—he's not here."

"Exactly. And he should be. I know he screwed up, but he still fought like hell for his country. It's not right." Luke touched the stone with his fingers. "I'm going to make up for it someday."

"What happened to him isn't your fault."

"I know, but it's my family, and by serving honorably I'll help make it right."

Sarah looked admiringly at Luke for a few moments. "I'm sure you will."

Luke turned back to the festival. "I'm starved, let's eat."

Sarah took his arm and they made their way along the bountiful barbeque. With heaping plates of food, they sat in the shade of a weeping willow on the lawn in front of the church. Before long, Skinny came by to say hi. Behind him Dexter carried a plate overflowing with hotdogs and baked beans.

"Hey, guys," Luke said, wiping barbeque sauce off his cheek.

Skinny nodded to Sarah. "Miss Clements."

"Please call me Sarah."

Skinny smiled. "Alright, Sarah."

"This chicken is awesome." Luke took another bite from a

drumstick. "Maxwell's a strange dude, but he sure does put on a good spread."

"Yes, nice of him, too," Skinny replied. "He pays for everything himself and donates money to support the festival to boot."

Dexter wiped his fingers on his dungarees. "Hey, did you guys hear that Sis is going to be in the contest tonight?"

Skinny's eyes widened. "You don't say…"

Luke stopped chewing. "*Sis?* From the Carolinas?"

"Yessir," Dexter said with a wry smile. "I saw Jed this morning before the race, and doesn't he have his shorts up in a knot!"

Luke looked at Skinny. "And I'll bet Betty's just 'a rippin'.'"

Dexter nodded as he shoveled in another mouthful of baked beans, talking as he chewed. "They tried to get Sis disqualified but she'd entered just under the deadline."

Sarah wiped her mouth with a napkin, feigned ignorance. "Who is Sis?"

Skinny looked at her. "One of the best fiddle players anywhere. From the Appalachian Mountains, been in our contest a couple times. Gave Jed and Betty a real run for their money, but she couldn't quite beat them. To tell the truth, I thought she was the best, but Jed got the hometown nod."

"Why would she come way up here?" Sarah asked, with a straight face.

"Well," replied Skinny, "we just so happen to have one of the premier contests in the whole northeast. You'll see tonight. They'll be fiddlers from all over."

Sarah smiled. "I can't wait."

CHAPTER TWENTY-SIX

S IS HAD BEEN IN GREENSBORO FOR A COUPLE OF DAYS, camping on the outskirts of town. She and Sarah had met several times to practice, and were both excited by how well Sarah had picked up fiddling. Sis thought they even had a shot at winning.

The annual barn dance topped off the Fourth of July festivities, including a children's parade with decorated wagons, carts, and bicycles. Kids clothespinned baseball cards to the spokes of their bicycle wheels, creating a rhythmic rat-a-tat-tat as they made their way down the main street. Some children had dogs, goats, calves, or sheep in tow, dressed up as Uncle Sam, Abraham Lincoln, and other patriotic characters. Jed's wife, Mabel, once marched Claws in the parade, but after she nearly ripped the face off Eleanor Stacy's bewildered St. Bernard, Mabel had to drag her from the procession as onlookers backed away from the ferocious feline.

After Maxwell's barbeque and a brilliant fireworks display launched over the lake, most everyone got ready for the dance at Rowell's barn in neighboring East Craftsbury. Sylvester Rowell built his stately dairy barn over the summer of 1906 with hand-hewn hemlock timbers harvested from his land. The first dance was held in the late 1940s, and was such a success, the family had to build another barn for storing hay so they could keep the big barn open for dances.

When people arrived at the enormous yellow barn, they parked in adjacent fields and on the road for at least a quarter mile in both directions. By nine, the barn was packed, save for the dance floor up front by the stage. The evening commenced with Skinny's Bullpout Band performing several country hits, including Dick Curless's "Tombstone Every Mile," which featured solos by Luke on guitar and Lester Patenaude on mandolin. The Asbestos Boys from nearby Eden did a couple of Elvis tunes including "Jailhouse Rock," which raised the already warm temperature in the barn considerably. Vermont's famed Rick and the Ramblers threw down a couple of tight Western Swing tunes, which drove even more people to the dance floor. The Aroostook Cousins from Maine followed with a pair of blazing bluegrass numbers, and finally, The White Mountain Grenadiers from Jackson, New Hampshire, brought the house down with a rambunctious medley of "The Orange Blossom Special" and "Dueling Banjos."

The only interruption in the music and dancing came when a drunken fight broke out near the stage. Delano Meacham accused Reggie Miller of cheating with his wife, which, as everyone knew, was true. Their sordid affair had gone on for years. The band cleared the stage to jump into the fight, except for Danny, the drummer, who kept the beat until some brawny loggers helped a deputy sheriff throw the brawlers through the milk room door, so they could finish each other off outside.

When he wasn't playing, Luke swung Sarah around the dance floor, shafts of dry hay scooting across the smooth boards beneath their feet. Strings of lights leading to a mirror ball swung overhead, as the bands played on into the evening. After midnight, things slowed down and Violet Dwinell sang a moving version of the

Beatles' new hit, "Let it Be." Lester played a beautiful mandolin solo as Luke and Sarah slow-danced together. When she curled into the nape of his neck, he knew he wanted to hold her forever. Sadly, in his heart of hearts, he knew he probably couldn't.

It was late at night when the dancing ended and most people went outside to cool off. Meanwhile, rows of folding chairs were set up, and the stage was readied for the much-anticipated fiddle contest. A "WELCOME—BIENVENUE" banner was strung from the beams, and some of the church ladies decorated the stage with large sprays of flowers. A green carpet was rolled across the center, then stools and microphones were put in place and a wooden lectern was set on the side. Several old-fashioned popcorn machines were pulled up the tractor ramp into the barn, and dozens of people took paper bagsful of the fluffy white kernels to their seats.

When spotlights lit the stage, a pair of acrobatic barn swallows could be seen arcing among the rafters overhead. Several fiddlers were warming up in the back of the barn, which seemed to have gotten Sarah's attention.

"What's going on?" Luke asked. "You seem worried about something."

Sarah shook her head. "No, just tired, and surprised at how many people are here. It's almost one in the morning."

"Morning chores will be rugged, but this is the best night of the year, along with Christmas Eve, when Santa comes."

Sarah gave him a look. "Don't tell me you believe in Santa."

Luke frowned. "Don't *you?*" He laughed. "Anyway, besides the good music, most of the people are here to see who'll win— Jed or Betty. As big a competition as the boat race."

"Doesn't anyone else ever win?"

"Probably way back, but not that I can remember. Sometimes it's razor close."

"Who judges?"

"The crowd, by how loud and long they cheer." He smiled at her. "And how much popcorn flies."

Sarah frowned. "That doesn't sound very scientific."

Luke laughed. "Nothing scientific about it. You'll see." Luke pointed to his ears. "Gets awful rowdy. You may need to stuff some cotton in before the night's over."

When Luke wasn't looking, Sarah kept sneaking peeks around the room. She couldn't imagine Sis wouldn't show up, unless something had happened to her.

The crowd quieted as Chairman Jakes stepped to the lectern and cleared his throat. "I want to welcome you all to the famous Annual Greensboro Fiddle Contest. We have ten of the best fiddlers anywhere for you tonight, and judging by this crowd—which is bursting the barn at its seams—you are ready for some great music."

The crowd started yelling and clapping.

Mr. Jakes motioned for them to settle down. "As you know, each contestant will play their competition number, accompanied by one other instrument, either a guitar or a mandolin. No noisy banjoes." He chuckled into the mic. "Each contestant will be introduced at the time of their performance, so none of you will know the order in which they play." He leaned into the mic and whispered, "That's so we can keep you here all night.

"Per tradition, judging is done by the reaction of the audience, which will be recorded by Miss Haverford." He nodded to an elderly, bespectacled woman with white hair drawn back into a tight bun. She was hunched over a leather journal at an old wooden school desk, pencil held firmly in arthritic fingers. "If Miss Haverford can't determine a clear winner, I have been entrusted to make the final decision." He leaned back into the mic. "And remember, this is a volunteer position. No rotten vegetables will be thrown!"

The crowd laughed. "Just bring on the fiddlers!" a fellow yelled, who'd clearly drunk plenty of beer.

Mr. Jakes pointed at the fellow. "Good idea!" He quickly turned to the side of the stage, in front of which hung a heavy canvas tarp hiding the contestants from the crowd. "And first off, returning again from Bedford, Quebec, is our oldest fiddler, Malcom LaFontaine, accompanied on guitar by his wife, Genevieve."

"Malcom's a good fellow," Luke said to Sarah. "Been coming to this thing for many years."

"Great."

"Though he's not the best fiddler," Luke whispered, "especially since he lost a finger to a baler a few years back."

Sarah cringed. "Way too much information."

Malcom limped onto the stage followed by his wife, who sat in a folding chair while he plopped onto a stool.

"Evening, folks," Malcom said, with a Quebecois accent. "Merci for having me and the missus again."

Without further ado, he settled his instrument low under his chin, lifted his bow and began a plodding version of the traditional Civil War song, "Sally Goodin." Genevieve joined in with one of her guitar strings slightly out of tune, and though the song was meant to be played fast, they enjoyed playing their slow version, swaying along to the music together. When they finished, they pushed themselves up, held hands, and bowed. The audience clapped politely as they left the stage. A couple of people tossed a few kernels of popcorn toward the front.

Sarah clapped a few times and spoke quietly to Luke. "I thought you said there would be great fiddlers here tonight."

Luke grinned. "Hang on, they're just part of the tradition. It's nice they let them play first, sort of an honor. Plus, it gets them out of the way for the really good ones."

"I hope so." Sarah glanced around again. There, in the back corner, stood Sis in a yellow summer dress, a fiddle case tight under her arm. She had on the same straw hat she'd worn at music camp. She glanced at Sarah, but neither acknowledged the other.

Sarah noticed her father heading outside, probably for a cigarette, and hoped he'd come back in time to hear her play, even if he had no idea she was going to. Maybe he'd appreciate this new fiddle music she'd discovered.

Mr. Jakes stepped back into the light. "Thank you very much, Malcom and Genevieve. Our next contestant is Felix Montcalm, who hails from right over here on the Wheelock Mountain Road. Been fiddling in kitchen tunks since he was just a small fry. He's goinna' play a great foot-stompin' tune, 'Fourteen Days in Georgia.' Please welcome back, Felix."

The audience clapped and several hooted and hollered. Felix was a big, tall fellow in faded overalls with a striped engineer's cap holding down a rim of gray hair. He stepped shyly into the spotlight, which illuminated a weathered face capped by thick, sprawling eyebrows. He adjusted the mic up to his level and, without saying a word, launched into a high-spirited bluegrass classic that quickly had much of the crowd stomping their feet. As he deftly sawed the bow back and forth, Felix never took his eyes off his instrument, its sweet sounds filling the barn. When he finished, the crowd broke into enthusiastic applause and several handfuls of popcorn arced through the air. Sarah looked up at Luke. "Now, *that* was good."

"Told you. And you ain't seen nothing, yet."

Mr. Jakes fumbled with the silver microphone then tapped on it to make sure it was still working. "Thank you, Felix." He looked at his sheet. "Now we're going to hear from a couple from Earth Peoples Park, the new hippie commune up to Norton." He squinted at his list. "Here's Dian-thus and her partner, Harmony, playing a good Texas tune, 'Lone Star Rag.'"

A barefoot, obviously braless woman in a flowing patchwork dress stepped onto the stage and waved to the crowd, who didn't react. She had long sandy hair with flowers braided into it, and dangly earrings that appeared to be little dreamcatchers. Behind her trailed a wiry fellow in sandals, a tie-dyed T-shirt, and frayed bell-bottom jeans. His black hair was unkempt, and colorful beaded necklaces hung about his bony neck. "This ought to be good…" Mr. Jakes was heard to say as he walked off stage away from the mic.

Dianthus appeared both nervous and excited as she gyrated up to the microphone with a huge smile. "Look at all you beautiful people!" She pulled a daisy out of her hair and awkwardly flung it toward the front row. Disapproving murmurs spread around the barn.

"She must be stoned," Luke whispered to Sarah.

"You *think?*"

"Play some music or get off the stage!" some guy yelled.

"That's why we're here," Dianthus said seductively into the mic. She turned to Harmony, who had a banged-up guitar with him. "Ready, love?"

He nodded.

Dianthus tossed her hair out of the way and shouldered her fiddle, which had a colorful peace sign painted on the body. She broke into a smooth as silk performance of "Lone Star Rag," which caused people to look at each other in surprise. By the time she finished, Dianthus had delighted the audience, though when she swept her bow through the air and bowed, the crowd offered up less applause and popcorn than she deserved. Harmony slunk off the stage behind her.

Sarah looked at Luke. "Imagine what she'd sound like if she wasn't stoned."

Luke chuckled. "She might not be half as good."

CHAPTER TWENTY-SEVEN

THE AUDIENCE ENJOYED SEVERAL OTHER GOOD performances and then, as expected, Mr. Jakes announced they were "saving the best for last," which Sarah thought was unfair to the other contestants. Betty was to play before Jed, then this out-of-towner, Sis, would perform with accompaniment, but didn't reveal with whom.

The crowd quieted. Betty took the stage in a light blue dress and black shoes, followed by Lester wearing a western shirt and carrying his shiny Gibson guitar. She stood with perfect posture in front of the microphone. Though she had only been a couple years ahead of Luke in high school, she appeared much older.

"Good evening, everyone," she said, cradling her fiddle. "This is an old-time jig, 'I Don't Love Nobody.'" She closed her eyes and hummed a note so she and Lester could get in tune. They nodded to each other and Betty launched into a high-pitched reel, tapping her foot in time as several people got up and danced in front of the stage. They performed the number beautifully, and when Betty brought the song to a close, enthusiastic applause broke out. Quite a few handfuls of popcorn flew through the air. Betty and Lester stiffly bowed. She waved awkwardly to the crowd and followed him off the stage.

Mr. Jakes returned to the lectern. "Thank you, folks, that was great."

Luke curled his arm around Sarah. "I've heard Betty play better."

"I thought she was good."

"Just seemed a little off." Luke pointed at the stage. "Now, get ready for this."

Mr. Jakes leaned to the mic. "And now, ladies and gentlemen, I present to you Greensboro's 'Father of the Fiddle,' all the way from the East Craftsbury Road on the other side of town, Mr. Jed McCaffery!"

Loud clapping and cheers broke out as some in the audience rose to their feet. "Jed'll be playing an all-time crowd favorite, 'Dusty Miller.'"

"About time he come on!" a woman in the front corner called out.

"I'll say," yelled a farmer in the back. "Let 'er rip, Jed. Gotta' git up and milk soon!"

Jed limped onto the stage, his artificial leg dragging behind him, and settled onto a stool in front of the mic. Sarah smiled when she saw he was going to play his beautiful Jean-Baptiste Vuillaume. It almost felt like a sacrilege to compete against such a rare and treasured instrument.

The audience fell silent as Jed plucked the strings of his beautiful instrument. He spoke into the mic. "Gettin' old, might be my last competition, so go easy on me."

Luke chuckled out loud, and Sarah elbowed him.

"He says that every year, looking for the sympathy vote."

Sarah shook her head. "He's a sly old fellow, isn't he?"

"You have no idea."

As Jed prepared to play, the only sounds in the barn were the creaking of the roof timbers, moved by the gathering wind outside. Jed lifted his instrument to his collarbone. "Here she is, 'Dusty Miller,' Orleans County-style." A satisfied smile crossed his face as he pulled his bow smoothly across the strings and commenced playing. With his arthritic fingers dancing on the neck, Jed swung back and forth with the rhythm of the music. He got so into the tune, at one point, he looked as if he might slide right off the stool. His playing was remarkably energetic, smooth and sweet, and, as he led up to the song's crescendo, he rose to his feet, almost dancing as he played, intermittently balancing on his artificial leg.

"Wow," Luke said as he and the rest of the crowd could no longer hold back their applause.

Sarah appeared spellbound by Jed's total mastery. As cheers rang out and popcorn flew through the air, she shot to her feet, yelling with joy, clapping her hands in the air. "That was *amazing!*"

"He's something else," Luke said, shaking his head. "The old rascal's won it again."

As the audience started to settle, Sarah looked at Luke. "I thought there was one more contestant."

Luke kept clapping. "Yeah, some old lady from down south. But nobody can beat that."

Sarah tugged on Luke's sleeve. "I need to go to the bathroom. I'll be right back."

"Hurry up, you don't want to miss Jed getting the trophy."

"Oh, I won't." Sarah felt both excited and nervous after hearing Jed play.

Sarah quickly made her way back through the crowd, a few of whom were calling out Betty's name, though the majority were yelling for Jed. She found Sis waiting at their pre-arranged spot by the old hay wagon ramp. "Hi, darlin'." Sis handed Sarah her violin. "You ready to smoke 'em?"

"I don't know, Jed was awesome."

Sis took her fiddle out of its case. "'Course he was. He's a great fiddler." She looked Sarah in the eye. "And so are we. I never seen a girl pick up fiddlin' fast as you have." She motioned toward the front. "Come on. We're going on."

Feeling apprehensive, Sarah grabbed hold of Sis' dress and followed close behind her, as they made their way along the sides of the barn to the performers' area.

"Ladies and gentlemen," Mr. Jakes boomed into the mic. "I know it's late, but we've finally come to our last contestant of the evening. She comes all the way from the Appalachian Mountains of Carolina, a self-taught fiddle virtuoso, who you'll remember placed second a few years back. Please welcome Sis and her surprise accompaniment."

As the crowd politely applauded, Sis squeezed Sarah's hand. "Jed got 'em all revved up for us. Now, let's bring the house down."

Sarah felt a surge of excitement. "Okay. Let's do it!"

When Sis hit the stage, more people clapped, but when Sarah emerged from behind the canvas and stepped into the spotlights, a hush fell over the crowd. Mr. Jakes stared at her and frowned.

"What in the hell?" someone said from the front row.

"What's *she* doing up there?" Freddie McCormick called out.

Undeterred, Sis spoke into the mic. "I'd like to introduce my partner, the lovely Sarah Clements." Sarah stayed partially hidden behind Sis.

Luke stared in disbelief. "What the...how can...?"

Skinny elbowed Luke. "You know about this?"

Unable to speak, Luke just shook his head.

Some woman in a leather cowgirl vest pointed at Mr. Jakes, who was moving off to the side. "You can't have two fiddlers, one helpin' the other."

Mr. Jakes glanced at the crowd, seeming confused at what to do. "Well, I don't believe we've ever had another fiddle accompany the official contestant."

"T'ain't fair!" a woman yelled out.

"Besides," the cowgirl said, "ain't that a violin, not a fiddle?"

Sis kept her composure, giving the crowd a subtle but knowing smile. "No difference in the instrument, just how you play it."

"Nonsense," the woman retorted. "Cain't be the same thing."

Commotion built around the barn until finally Jed pushed himself up off his chair and waved his arm, quieting people. "Nothin' in the rules against it. Not normal, but there's nothin' normal about these times." He gave Sarah a quick supportive nod. "Now, just let the poor girl play."

Outside of a few lingering grumbles, everyone sat back down. "Here we go with 'Red Apple Rag,'" Mr. Jakes announced and quickly left the stage.

Excited, Skinny leaned into Luke. "Dandy tune. This oughtta' be good."

Sis turned to Sarah, motioned for her to get closer to the mics. "Come on, darlin', we're doing this here tune together."

Sarah glanced at the crowd. Luke was still standing, a broad smile across his face. After staring at him for a moment, she slid her violin under her chin, and she and Sis got in tune.

Skinny whispered to Luke. "Need a guitar to accompany this tune."

Luke kept his attention on Sarah, who looked beautiful standing there in the spotlights. For a moment, he flashed back to when he first saw her sitting on the hood of the Mustang. Then the barn fell silent. Tension held the air, as if everyone was waiting for a rocket launch.

Sis tapped her foot on the stage twice, raised her bow high, and drew it sharply across the instrument. She broke into a fast fiddle tune, her fingers literally flying over the strings. Sarah followed along in the background until Sis stepped back and Sarah seamlessly took over the parts a guitar would normally play. Sis came back in, and soon they furiously climbed up and down the scales together, in perfect harmony. Luke could barely believe his ears. Sarah and Sis were amazing together. He glanced around, saw the crowd was spellbound, in as much disbelief as he was. This was something special.

As the women built to a crescendo, the marvelous sound of their instruments completely filled the barn. In the audience, Betty stood and started clapping, followed by a dozen others. She suddenly grabbed her fiddle and marched toward the front, shouldering her instrument as she stepped onto the stage. The rest of the crowd rose to their feet, clapping, as whole bags of popcorn shot into the air. Lester and Skinny made their way to the front and joined in. Sis and Sarah kept the song going, as surprised at what was happening as everyone else. Soon the rest of the Bullpout Band came out of the woodwork with their instruments and crowded onto the stage. Amazed, and not knowing what else to do, Mr. Jakes pushed haybales out of the way to make more room.

Finally, Jed rose from his chair. Grinning, he limped onto the stage, and proudly stood between Sis and Sarah and joined in. They both stepped back, giving him the honor of center stage. Luke had never seen anything like it. *Never* had other musicians joined a contestant before. What a night!

Sarah motioned for Luke to join them. He grabbed his guitar, raced up, and gave her a huge, one-arm hug. "You're amazing!" he said, slipping his guitar strap over his shoulder. He joined in playing rhythm as Jed led the group into a rousing rendition of "Will the Circle Be Unbroken." The entire barn seemed to lock arms, swaying back and forth, singing with voices so powerful the upper rafters shook. Seemingly overwhelmed by the unprecedented spectacle, Mr. Jakes threw his arms in the air and started singing along with everyone else.

Sarah and Luke shared huge smiles, surrounded by ebullient townspeople celebrating the joy of just being alive and having an excuse to forget all the tragic things going on in the world.

As the musicians brought the joyful song to a close, an uproarious celebration filled the barn. Mr. Jakes tried to get people's attention but the PA system was no match for the crowd. Finally everyone seemed to run out of steam and the musicians, except for Sis and Sarah, left the stage.

"Well," Mr. Jakes said, still catching his breath, "that was something! In all my days, I never seen such a reaction. Took my breath away."

Sis gave Sarah a hug. "I knew you could do it."

Mr. Jakes turned to Miss. Haverford, the official scorekeeper, who was showing more emotion than she had in her 40 years of officiating. "What say you as to this year's winner?"

Markedly hunched over, she stood from her small desk and stepped slowly across the stage. She handed the open leather journal to Mr. Jakes, who looked it over.

"It's official," he said, raising his hand in the air. "There's no question, Carolina Sis and Sarah Clements are the 1970 Greensboro Fiddle Champions!"

From high above the stage, a shiny brass trophy descended on a hay lift into Mr. Jakes's hands. The trophy was made from a discarded hockey tournament trophy to which a shellacked fiddle had been added. It gleamed like gold in the spotlights. Mr. Jakes ceremoniously presented the trophy to Sis, who smiled and handed it to Sarah. They both thanked the crowd then Sarah gave the award back to Sis and jumped for joy into Luke's arms. She wrapped her arms around his neck, which held the sweet scent of hemlock and pine. He spun her around under the spotlights as the crowd continued to cheer. "I love you so much, Luke," Sarah said into his ear.

Luke kissed her. "I know. I love you, too, Sarah."

When there was no more popcorn to throw and the spotlights went out, the exhausted crowd made their way out through the barn doors. Folding chairs were haphazardly knocked over, and the wide-planked floor was so littered with popcorn it looked like it had snowed inside.

Dave Rowell unplugged the PA system and came over to Luke and Sarah. "This is a night to remember. Just what we all needed." He looked at Sarah. "You were amazing. I appreciate good music, and that performance was *great*." He smiled. "When you and Sis brought that song to a crescendo, I thought old Jed was going to lose his load right there in his chair. And to his credit, he knew you two had done it and didn't hesitate to join in the congratulations." Dave shook his head. "Never thought I'd see the day that every musician in the competition would get up and honor the winners like that. Something else, it was."

"Thanks, Dave," Luke said, curling his arm around Sarah as he looked around the barn. "And thanks for letting us all enjoy this great place."

"You're welcome, I'm sure." He chuckled. "Wonder what my grandfather would think of all these goings on in his haybarn."

"He'd probably love it," Sarah said.

Dave nodded. "Well, it's far past my bedtime." He started for the door. "Stay and savor as long as you like. Good night." He walked out, leaving Luke and Sarah alone in the cavernous barn. They both looked around the remarkable structure, a bright moon shining through cracks in the upper woodwork as a trio of barn swallows swooped and arced between the posts and beams. They held onto each other tightly.

"I don't want this moment to end," she said, tears forming in her eyes.

Deep emotion welled inside of Luke. "I know."

"Luke, you've touched me somewhere I never knew existed."

"Being with you like this, I feel my life is complete, that I'll never need anything else."

They stared at each other, framing each other's beauty in their minds and hearts.

Chapter Twenty-Eight

LUKE TURNED OFF THE LIGHT OVER THE BARN DOOR, CURLED his arm around Sarah, and they left. It had already been quite a night, and he looked forward to spending the rest of it together in the hayloft.

As they walked down the tractor ramp heading to Luke's truck, someone spoke. "I must say, Sarah Clements, that was most impressive."

Startled, Sarah and Luke stopped in their tracks. As their eyes adjusted to the darkness, they saw her father standing beside his Cadillac.

"Father, what are you doing here? I thought you left hours ago."

"I just went out to get some good night air, but came back to hear Jed." He stepped closer to Sarah, a serious look on his face. "But then, to my utter amazement, I heard my classically trained daughter play old-time fiddle music, of all things."

In the hazy moonlight, she wasn't sure whether she was about to be reprimanded or congratulated.

Her father crossed his arms. "I don't think your mother would approve of such use of your expensive instrument..."

Luke's arm tightened around her waist. She felt deflated, that old feeling of never being good enough.

"However," her father continued, "I thought it was marvelous! Transformational, somehow."

It took Sarah a few seconds to process what he had said. Seeing a big smile on his face, she handed her violin case to Luke and embraced her father. "Oh, Daddy," she said, choking up. "That makes me so happy."

"Wasn't she amazing?" Luke chimed in.

"Yes, totally." He looked at Luke. "Did you know about this?"

Luke shook his head. "No idea."

"Well, Sarah, you surprised us all."

She wiped away a tear. "That was the idea. But keeping it a secret wasn't easy."

"I assume you met this Sis lady at violin camp?"

"Yes. She offered fiddle lessons on the side. First time I'd ever seen her at camp."

"I see."

"When I told her I'd spent time at Caspian Lake, she became all excited, said she'd played in this contest before. After listening to Jed and Betty fiddle at the Bullpout, I wanted to learn how to play. Meeting Sis was fortuitous. I couldn't resist taking a few lessons, and loved it."

Judge Clements nodded. "I thought I heard you playing fiddle music at the inn one day, but I guess I couldn't truly believe it."

Sarah stepped back beside Luke. "I didn't know you liked fiddle music."

"Shhh. Don't tell your mother, but I've been coming to this contest for years."

"I knew you were a hick at heart," Luke said, surprising himself.

"Perhaps, a bit. My grandfather was an old-time mandolin player in vaudeville."

Sarah cocked her head. "I didn't know that."

"He used to tour up and down the East Coast with other musicians and minstrels. He even played with a big band in the Roseland Ballroom in New York once, and that was a very big deal."

"That's cool," Luke said, admiringly. "Jed used to talk about some of those great musicians."

"Well," her father said, stepping back toward his car, "I just wanted to give you my congratulations."

"Thank you, that means a lot."

"And by the way," he called over, "the two of you look good together."

Sarah ran over, gave him another hug, and spoke softly. "Daddy, I need to talk to you tomorrow, if you have time. It's important."

"Of course. Come down for a late brunch, say eleven?"

"Yes, thank you." She walked back toward Luke.

"Don't stay out too late. Actually, never mind, it's already three in the morning." Her father waved and drove off.

Sarah was amazed at her father's reaction. As the red taillights of the Caddy disappeared around a bend, they looked at each other and laughed.

"Come on," Luke said, smiling, "I know a cozy place we can have for the night."

"You made us a reservation?" Sarah said, jokingly.

"Yes, we got the only hayloft available."

Sarah followed Luke's pickup to the horse barn where they raced up the stairs to the haymow. Filled with emotions, they spent the rest of the night lying on the soft trapper blanket making sweet love with each other.

Chapter Twenty-Nine

WITH LUKE'S BEAUTIFUL NAKED BODY WRAPPED AROUND her, Sarah awoke slowly, the sweet, sweaty scent of lovemaking surrounding them. She smiled at him sleeping, his sinewy arm still draped over her hip. She couldn't remember how many times they'd made love, just that it was delicious, a sensuous blur she wished could go on forever. She squinted as she looked out the barn door at the lush green woodlands surrounding the lake, a thin mist hovering over its placid surface.

She slowly slid from under his arm and pulled on her shirt.

Luke aroused. "Morning." He pushed himself up from the blanket, tangled with hay, and stretched his arms.

"Hi, sleepyhead," she said, tussling his hair.

He slid his hand over the soft skin of her belly. "Where're you off to?"

"I have to meet my father at the inn."

Luke pulled her toward him, kissing her neck. "Are you sure? It's so nice here."

She cupped her hand around his cheek. "Last night was amazing."

Luke smiled. "I thought I'd gone to heaven."

"Pretty close." Rolling away from Luke, she slid her legs into her jeans.

"Don't go," he pleaded, holding onto the tail of her shirt.

"It's important I meet with him." She gently pulled away. "You know my father is punctual, and I desperately need a shower before I see him."

Luke looked into her eyes and shook his head. "God, I love every inch of you."

"Ditto." Sarah tucked in her shirt and made a vain attempt at straightening her hair. "I'll see you later. Maybe we can have dinner with my father before he goes back to Washington."

"That'd be cool, *if* I can spend another night with his daughter."

"You are one horny hayseed!"

"You bet."

As Sarah put on her sneakers, she assumed his Army induction was on both of their minds, but was relieved neither of them spoke of it. On the way to the inn, she thought about how she would approach her father. She hoped he'd still be in a good mood, though he might not be pleased she'd spent the night with Luke. But what did it matter? She was madly in love and her father knew it.

At the inn, Sarah parked out back and quietly snuck upstairs. She stepped into a hot shower, breathing in deeply as steam mingled with Luke's scent. Being with him felt *so* good: the way he talked to her, looked at her, touched her…it was like being in a wonderful dream.

Sarah dried off, put on a summer dress, and brushed her hair out. When she came down the main staircase, her father was seated at his usual spot, a marble-topped table in front of a sunny, south-facing window, a white linen napkin carefully spread across his lap. When he saw Sarah, he folded his newspaper and motioned to the other chair.

"Good morning," Sarah said, sitting down.

"Almost afternoon. Coffee or tea? Vicky has both."

"Tea would be great."

He motioned toward the kitchen then smiled at Sarah. "That was quite a night. You must be exhausted."

"I'm still pretty wound up. I cannot believe we won. I actually feel a little bad for Jed."

"Oh, don't give it another thought. He's won the contest so many times. Besides..." He leaned closer. "He had a big smile on his face when you won, paid you a huge compliment by joining you and Sis on stage. Never seen anything like it."

"Well, your congratulations meant a lot to me. I didn't even realize you were still there."

"Right in the back with Maxwell, who was so excited I thought he'd have a stroke."

Sarah chuckled.

Her father took a swallow of coffee. "So, what did you want to talk about?"

Sarah adjusted herself in her seat, wasn't sure how to begin. "I want, I need..."

Looking at the floor, she stumbled over her thoughts and words, trying to keep her emotions in check.

Her father lowered his coffee cup. "Yes?"

"It's about Luke. He received his Army induction letter to go to Fort Bragg." With tears in her eyes, she managed to raise her head and look at her father. "I don't want him to die over there. He's such a wonderful guy, I just can't lose him."

The judge sat back in his chair and pondered. "Go on."

"Well, I thought...I was hoping you might do something to help him."

"How?"

"You're a powerful judge. I know you have ways of influencing things."

He leaned forward. "I understand your fears, Sarah, but military service is the law. It's every man's civic duty to serve, to safeguard our precious freedom."

"But what has Vietnam, halfway around the world, have to do with that?"

"If we don't defeat the communists over there, they'll be invading our own shores next. I'd much rather fight them in Southeast Asia."

"You really believe that?"

He looked her in the eye. "I do."

"I don't know." She slowly shook her head. "It seems like thousands of our guys are dying for nothing."

"Don't ever say that," he said, getting irritated. "They are fighting for our country."

Sarah looked straight at him. "Respectfully, Father, I'm not so sure. It seems they're fighting in bloody rice paddies that have nothing to do with the United States. That's what all the protests and riots are about."

They fell silent, both staring at an untouched plate of croissants. Sarah began to cry.

"I love him so much, Daddy."

The judge wiped his mouth with his napkin and folded it beside his plate. He appeared to soften. "I understand more than you may think. I have my own concerns about this conflict. And I was in love once, before, you know, your mother went off the deep end."

Sarah was surprised, wiped her eyes. "I don't remember. It

must have been before I was old enough to know."

"It was." Her father looked out past the window's lace curtains toward the lake, shimmering in the sunlight. "It was a wonderful time, before she became so uppity and full of herself." He shook his head. "I don't know what happened. Washington dramatically changed her." He looked at Sarah. "Then, when you came along, it didn't matter. My whole world brightened like the sun had finally come out. I'm grateful you're not full of yourself."

"Thank you. That's one of the things I love about Luke. He doesn't think he's better than anyone else."

"That's certainly a good thing."

"He's been through some tough times, mostly with his family. But he has a real humility about him."

"I see he's a fine young man, but I have to be honest, he's hardly someone for you to be with long-term." He looked at her. "As I've told you before, you need to be realistic about your life plans and your dreams of becoming a lawyer."

Sarah started to interrupt, but he held up his hand. "You'd never be happy making a life up here in this backwater, beautiful as it is."

Sarah shook her head. "You don't know that."

"I think I do." Her father remained calm but firm. "Perhaps you are the one who doesn't yet realize it." There was a long silence during which he buttered a croissant, spread homemade strawberry preserves over its golden surface, and ate it. Sarah sat quietly while he finished his coffee.

"So, I'm still interested in why you requested we meet."

"It doesn't matter now. Your mind is made up."

He grinned. "Counselor, assuming you know what the judge is thinking is usually fraught with peril."

Sarah jammed her napkin under the edge of her china plate. "I would like you to get Luke some sort of deferment. At least so he doesn't have to go to Vietnam. I know he wants to serve, it's just that…going over there is such a death sentence."

The judge's expression didn't change as he subtly nodded. "I suspected that was what you were going to ask." As tears trickled down Sarah's cheeks, her father thought for a few moments. "At times like this we have to steel ourselves against emotions."

Sarah wiped her cheek. "I can't do that."

Her father shifted in his chair. "Let's be clear, he would *have* to serve, but there are circumstances where he could avoid the infantry, which is the most dangerous because they fight on the front lines."

Sarah felt a bit of hope.

"Does he have any physical or medical problems? Some of the crazy hippies are even puncturing their own eardrums to get rejected."

Sarah shook her head. "Luke's in perfect shape."

"That's unfortunate as there are conditions that can qualify someone for a deferment."

Sarah's spirit sunk. "Maybe he has all sorts of diseases I don't know about."

Her father frowned, looked over his glasses at her. "Is he not interested in entering college?"

"I think he wants to but not until after his military service. He's determined to make up for failings of his father, who was dishonorably discharged after World War II. It's been a big embarrassment."

"Sounds difficult."

She looked down and shook her head. "I know, but still…"

Her father leaned on the table. "If it's that important to him, perhaps you shouldn't interfere." He put his hand to his chin. "Regardless, if he wants a deferment, he's not doing much to help himself."

Sarah felt a bit sheepish. "It's me that wants the deferment."

"I see." He straightened his silverware and pushed his chair back. "I will give it consideration. There may be a way I could help him, but I will have to speak to Luke directly about the matter."

Sarah stood when her father did. "I would so appreciate it."

"I want to do what's best for you, Sarah."

"Keeping Luke out of Vietnam would be for the best."

"I'm flying back to Washington this afternoon but will be back in a few days. I will try to figure something out. I have a friend who may be able to help." He straightened his chair. "Do you know when he is to report?"

"In like a week and a half."

"That doesn't give us much time."

"I know."

The judge thought a little more. "One thing…"

"Yes."

"I will meet with Luke alone about this, man-to-man."

"Okay," Sarah said, feeling a little confused. "Whatever you want, if you can just help him."

The judge nodded. "Alright, then." He stepped inside the doorway to the kitchen and thanked Vicky for breakfast. Walking to the front door, he turned back to Sarah. "I'll see you in a few days. Congratulations again. Last night was something I'll not forget, nor will this town. I loved the look on your face when you won."

As the door closed behind her father, Sarah stood in the middle of the foyer feeling some hope Luke could get help from her father, and the unsettling sense of not totally trusting him.

CHAPTER THIRTY

WHEN LUKE GOT HOME, HIS MOTHER WAS STILL sleeping, exhausted after her major outing to the race. He wished she could have stayed for the fiddle contest, but it would have been way too much for her. At least she'd planned to watch the fireworks from their porch.

Despite the excitement of Sis and Sarah winning, and the wonderful night in the hayloft, when Luke entered the kitchen, he felt a sense of dread. He set the kettle on the stove and turned to the table. The letter was out of its envelope, open on a plastic placemat. Across the top of the official letterhead, written in his mother's shaky handwriting were the words: "My dear Luke, God will watch over you."

Luke touched his mother's words with his fingertips, felt a bit of comfort from the strength of her abiding faith. He pondered for a few moments. Maybe it would be okay, fighting the commies with a good bunch of guys.

He turned the paper over and read the list of things he needed to bring to boot camp. It said most essentials were provided by the Army but a few personal items were allowed including a hygiene kit, a watch, small pocket notebook and pen, a wallet, copy of his birth certificate, and his bank account info. The final item allowed was a pocket Bible or a small religious book. Luke felt a little funny having not had any interest in religion. It probably didn't help that his father had been an atheist and his mother's condition had made it so she could no longer attend her Methodist services. He decided he'd bring the *Tao de Ching* and the picture he and Sarah took in the photobooth. That was spiritual enough for him.

In his reverie, Luke didn't know his mother had gotten up until he heard the familiar squeak of the hinges on her bedroom door. "G'morning, Mom."

"Morning. Looks like a dandy." She walked slowly toward the stove, holding onto the counter. "You kids have fun last night?"

"Did we ever." Luke folded the letter and slipped it back into the envelope. "The contest didn't end till well after two. And you won't believe it, but Sarah and a lady from down south won."

His mother's face lit up with a mixture of surprise and delight. "*Sarah* won? No foolin'?"

"Telling you straight. It was awesome."

"Land sakes, didn't know Sarah even fiddled."

"Well, this woman, Sis, taught her at her music camp in New York."

His mother turned back to the stove. "My, Sarah must be an awful quick study."

"She sure is. And somehow, she's been practicing like crazy on the sly. I had no idea, was as surprised as everyone else."

"Isn't that something," she said, fumbling with the coffeepot. "Come to think of it, I've heard Sis play up here over the years. She's terrific."

Luke got up and offered a hand. "Here, you sit down. Let me get your coffee." He helped her to a chair at the table.

"Must have surprised the dickens out of Jed."

"You aren't kidding—and Betty, too."

Luke made her a cup of coffee and sat next to her. "And you won't believe what happened…"

His mother lifted her cup with both hands, blew weakly across the surface, and took a sip. "What's that?"

"Sis and Sarah played 'Red Apple Rag.'"

His mother's eyes lit up. "That's a good one."

"They were awesome, and when they got close to the end of the song, the whole place was on their feet. I mean *everybody* was caught up in it. Even Betty and Jed went up and joined them."

His mother looked puzzled. "On *stage?*"

"Yes. The whole Bullpout gang got up there."

"Land sakes, I've never heard of such a thing."

"I was so surprised at first, I couldn't move, but I finally went up when Sarah and Jed got everybody singing 'The Circle Be Unbroken.'" Luke shook his head. "Sarah just lit the place up. Beautiful. I'll never forget it." He looked at his mom. "I wish you coulda' been there."

She touched his hand and smiled. "Your telling me makes me feel like I was."

Luke pushed the letter aside, reached over, put his hand on hers. "I love you, Mom."

"I know you do." She looked at him and nodded. "I'm proud of you, Son." She took in a couple breaths and glanced at the letter. "You'll do us proud over there."

Luke made a face. "Not sure how much of a fighting man I am, but I'll try."

"You've got plenty of fight in you, just don't get carried away trying to make up for your father's failures."

"I do want to make up for it somehow."

She looked him in the eye. "That's on him, not you."

"I guess."

She studied her son's face, put her tremulous hand to his cheek. "You've got a special soul, Luke. Just don't let them change who you are."

"I won't, Mom."

Luke was touched by his mother's words but by the time they were finished talking, he was dying to see Sarah. By noon, the heat and humidity were getting oppressive, so Luke called the inn and asked Sarah to go for a swim. Driving through town, after the strong wind overnight, all that was left of the festival was trampled grass on the green and a few decorations dangling from lampposts and trees. The big festival banner suspended across the street was twisted so the words were upside down. He slowed his pickup, looked over the empty common, and felt that strange emptiness that remains after an event is over and everyone has gone home.

At the inn, before Luke could get out of his truck, Sarah came racing down the front stairs, a beach towel under her arm. Her blond hair flew behind her, her mirrored sunglasses reflecting the blue sky over the lake. He jumped out, took her up in his arms, and swung her around. "I missed you."

She gave him a look. "I believe I was naked in a hayloft with you a few hours ago."

Luke smiled. "Hmmm. That was sweet, but it seems like ages ago."

They kissed.

"I missed you, too," Sarah whispered in his ear. "But don't tell anyone."

"I won't."

They climbed into the truck and headed to the lake.

They pushed his raft from under the cedars out onto the lake. When they dove in, the water was wonderfully refreshing. They laughed and kidded with each other as they swam. After cooling off, they climbed back on the raft, and Sarah lay against him. They relaxed, admiring the majestic beauty of Caspian and the vibrant green hills beyond.

"I wonder if they have places like this to swim over in 'Nam," Luke said, knowing what was on both of their minds.

"They have steep mountains and beautiful green terraces that stretch down to the lowland rice paddies."

Luke was surprised. "How'd you know that?"

"I read it in the *Encyclopedia Britannica.*"

"Oh." Luke splashed water over his face. "I'm glad some of it's beautiful, 'cause the pictures on the news sure aren't."

Sarah became uncomfortable. "Luke, I need to tell you something."

"Yeah."

"I spoke with my father, about somehow getting you out of going over there."

Luke interrupted. "I told you—"

Sarah held her hand up and continued. "Not about not serving, just not on the front lines."

Luke frowned. "How'd that be possible?"

"He has powerful friends in Washington."

Relief and guilt collided inside of Luke. "But like I said before, what about the other guys from around here?"

Sarah shook her head. "You're such an altruist, Luke. You're always thinking of others. Even after Freddie tried to run you into the rocks, you were concerned about him." She smiled and shook her head. "I've never met anyone like you."

"Same here. I mean, *you*, of course."

"Oh, there are lots of me around."

He shook his head. "No, there're not."

She slid her hand over his bare chest and looked him in the eye. "So, if my father comes up with something, you'll consider it?"

"Sure, if it's legit." Luke scoffed. "I'm sure as hell not looking forward to the war. But I've got to be able to face people when I come home."

They stared at each other, pondering his optimistic assumption he would make it back.

"Alright. He'll be back in a couple of days and said he would talk to you."

"Roger that." Luke pointed to a boulder sticking out of the water 50 yards away. "Last one to that rock is a rotten egg."

Luke dove in.

Sarah pushed off the raft and they both swam hard toward the large, black boulder that looked like an old man's face. They tried to slow each other down, but ended up reaching the rock together.

"I think I won," Sarah said, swishing water from her hair as she caught her breath.

Luke took hold of a fissure in the rock. "I think my fingers touched it first."

"No way."

They pulled themselves up onto the boulder, which was warm from the sun. As strongly as he was attracted to her, looking into Sarah's eyes, Luke felt more deep emotion than he did hormones.

She wrapped her arms around his neck and they held each other as gentle waves lapped against the rock. He felt something warm on his shoulder, then heard Sarah softly crying.

"I don't want to lose you."

Luke held her tightly. "You never will." Fighting to hold back his own tears, he kissed Sarah on the forehead. "I think we'll be soulmates forever."

CHAPTER THIRTY-ONE

LUKE SPENT THE NEXT COUPLE OF DAYS WORKING HARD, making deliveries for the mill. Anxious about getting ready for boot camp, he was glad for the diversion. He also avoided the news after he heard a football star from nearby St. Johnsbury Academy had been killed by the Viet Cong. Luke wished Sarah's father could help him out, but it was too hard to get his hopes up knowing there was really no way it would happen.

On Wednesday, Trace sent Luke to deliver a load of white oak to Judge Clements' cabin, the flooring for his great room. As he approached the turn at McCaffery's barn, he yelled to Taffy, who lifted his head and let out a muffled howl. Descending to the lake, Luke smiled as he drove past the horse barn to the cabin. It was impressive with its pointed prow facing the lake, though it was out of character compared to the other small family camps.

When Luke pulled to a stop, he saw the judge's Caddy parked off to the side. "Shit." He'd be bummed if the judge couldn't help him out and feel beholden to him if he did.

A couple of carpenters came out and helped Luke unload. It wasn't until they finished that the judge walked over, taking a last drag on a cigarette. "How are you doing, Luke?" he asked, flicking the butt into a patch of milkweed.

"Good, sir," Luke replied, taking off his gloves.

There was an awkward silence.

The judge stood in front of Luke's truck. He seemed uneasy. "Sarah spoke to me about your draft situation, asked if I could do something to keep you from the front lines."

Luke straightened. "I heard."

"I spoke to a friend with Army connections. As you probably know, normally you get to pick your service only if you enlist, not if you wait to get drafted."

"I know. I probably should've enlisted, but with my mother… it's complicated."

The judge looked at the lake. "This man owes me a favor, so I think he could get you assigned to a supply or training company, possibly even stateside. At least you wouldn't be in the trenches."

Luke liked the sound of that.

The judge took another Pall Mall from a pack in his pocket. "There would be one condition…"

Luke's pulse sped up. "What's that?"

Judge Clements tapped the end of the cigarette on the hot hood of the truck. "I love my daughter very much, and you two obviously have affection for each other." He paused. "I think you are a fine young man, but let's face it, this is not the life she is meant to lead." He looked over his glasses. "I think you know that."

Luke steeled himself for what was coming.

"Bottom line: I'll get you this assignment if, once you say goodbye, you agree to leave Sarah alone—to never see her again." He stepped on a spider and ground it into the gravel. "I don't mean you any disrespect. She just needs to be free of all this so she can return to her normal college life in in the fall."

A wave of anger and frustration, sadness and love, rose like a volcano. Luke had a hard time looking at the judge. "Don't worry. I'll let her go." He stared at Judge Clements. "But it's not because of you and your damn deals. It's because I appreciate what's best for her. I love her that much."

Feeling like he might explode, Luke climbed into the cab and hit the starter. As the judge stepped from in front of the truck, he fumbled with his cigarette, which fell to the ground. Gripping the steering wheel so hard his fingers burned, Luke revved the engine and backed the truck around. As he headed off, he glanced in the rearview mirror. The judge was still standing there.

Luke shifted into neutral, and yanked up on the parking brake. He got out, and, hands on hips, looked straight at the judge. "I hope you know what an amazing person Sarah is. She's kind, and real, and wicked smart. She doesn't need you to tell her what to do."

Judge Clements bristled, pointed at Luke. "Now you listen here—"

Luke pointed right back at him. "And I don't need you, either. Keep your damn deals." He spit on the ground, got back in the truck, and slammed the door. Grinding into first gear, Luke hit the gas and headed up the road.

As he left the judge behind, Luke started to feel a little better, like he'd been freed from something. Maybe from several things.

* * *

Luke's last week at home started off with an article on the

front page of the *Gazette*, with disturbing details of what had happened to the guy from St. Johnsbury. His platoon was ambushed, called in airstrikes to support them, and gunfire from one of his own Hueys killed him. "Friendly fire," they called it, about the dumbest term Luke had ever heard. The paper said his body would be coming home by train at the end of the week, about when Luke was to leave.

Over the next couple of days, Luke had a hard time getting images of the war out of his mind, but he did his best to focus on what needed to be done in the next few days. The time went by all too quickly, finishing work for Trace, packing for boot camp, and setting his mother up with ladies from the church to help her out while he was away. Sarah had gone against her father's wishes, and didn't return to her music camp, which allowed Luke to spend as much time with her as possible, and that was the hardest. As much as he loved being with her, the terrifying dangers of the war constantly hung over them. He started to get emotional several times but was able to pull himself back from that edge. Luke knew he and Sarah shared a strong sense of fear and anxiety, but that they also shared a deep, unspoken need to be strong for each other.

As Luke finished things up, only a couple of local vets made a point of wishing him well. He assumed the others were soldiers who had shunned his father.

* * *

Luke's last day before leaving for Fort Bragg was sunny and warm with wisps of cirrus clouds gently drifting over Caspian from the west. Sarah knew they were going to spend the night together, but during the day he was at home repairing a few loose stairs, replacing a cracked pane of glass in his mother's bedroom, and installing bathroom grabrails for her.

Feeling restless, Sarah took a drive to a beautiful patch of wild flowers she'd admired along the road outside of town. She wandered into an old pasture of fieldstones, interspersed with white daisies, red clover, and bright yellow buttercups. A few tall milkweeds were covered with monarch butterflies. She picked a handful of flowers, then came upon an abandoned, horse-drawn farm implement, its long arm of rusty teeth intertwined with tall grass. She brushed flakes of rust off the metal revealing the words: John Deere No. 4 Sickle Mower. There was a cast-iron seat atop a thin, graceful strip of metal, with a couple of levers to the side.

Intrigued, Sarah set her flowers on the ground and climbed up onto the seat, which gently bowed beneath her. She imagined the sweltering job of cutting hay behind a smelly, laboring horse. Taking hold of one of the long, rusty levers, she tried to pull on it, but it wouldn't budge. Feeling comfortable, Sarah looked out over the rolling hills toward the shimmering lake in the distance. She thought about how her life had changed so unexpectedly, how a part of her was now rooted in this majestic land. Luke had settled deep into her heart, but she felt so much sadness around their impending separation. She was also unsure if she could actually live her life in northern Vermont, despite its charm and beauty. She tried to tamp down a building sense she was about to lose so much.

Sarah slid off the mower and was gathering up her flowers when a familiar pickup stopped on the road. Jed was behind the wheel, his truck running rough as usual. When he shut off the engine, it backfired, sending a burst of smoke from the exhaust pipe that dangled on a wire beneath the rear bumper.

"Hi Jed," Sarah called out, waving with her free hand.

"Nice bunch." He motioned for her to come over.

Sarah stepped back onto the road and lay the flowers on the front seat of her Mustang. She kept a few out for Jed, walked over to his window, and presented them to him.

He looked surprised.

"Lovely, aren't they?"

He smiled. "Been a dog's age since anyone give me flowers." He showed them to Taffy. "Right, old boy?"

"I picked them just for you."

"I'm sure you did." He nodded. "Well, I thank you." Taffy opened his jowls and let out a wide yawn as Jed set the flowers on the dusty dashboard. "Just so happens, I've something for you." He retrieved a long slender package wrapped in newspaper from a pile of debris on the floor. He slid the package through the window, presenting it to Sarah as though it was something sacred. "Something special for you."

She looked it over. "What can this be?"

"Open it, you'll find out."

Sarah untied a piece of twine and unraveled the newspaper, revealing a silk cloth surrounding a beautiful wooden violin bow. She lifted the polished bow from the cloth. "Wow," she said, running her fingers along the length of the bow. "This is Pernambuco, the best wood there is." She closed her eyes and drew it over her shoulder. Sarah looked at Jed. "It's beautiful."

He nodded. "Thought you'd cotton to it. Given to me by Maestro Benetti, one of my professors at Berklee back in the

'40s. I guess he took a likin' to me, left it to me in his will."

"I'm honored, but I don't know if I can accept such a great gift."

"'Course you can. You earned it with the performance you and Sis put on. Something to behold."

"Thank you, but—"

Jed started his pickup. "No buts about it." He ground the transmission into gear. "Enjoy it. Slides over the strings like warm butter."

"I'm sure." Sarah looked at the bow admiringly.

Jed revved the engine, popped the clutch, and lurched forward a few feet before screeching to a stop.

"Sarah—" he called out the window.

Holding the bow tight against her, she hurried over to him.

"Tough watchin' a loved one go off to war."

Sarah felt herself choke up. "Thank you. It's been hard, thinking about what might happen."

"Well, I've seen your strength. You'll get through. And I hope Luke will lay his ghosts of the past to rest."

Sarah nodded. "I hope so, too."

Jed reached out the window and gently squeezed her forearm with his leathery hand. "Kid's got a good head on him. He'll be back." Jed took hold of the wheel, gave the truck some gas, and let off the clutch. Sarah watched as he took off down the road, trails of dust following after him.

CHAPTER THIRTY-TWO

Back at the inn, Vicky helped Sarah pack a picnic dinner for her and Luke. Luke picked up Sarah, and when they got to the lake, she spread a red-and-black checkered tablecloth over his raft and laid out celery sticks with cream cheese, slices of apples and cheddar cheese, curried chicken salad sandwiches on homemade bread, and a couple of granola bars. Sarah knew they were both hungry, but with so much on their minds, it was hard to truly relax and eat. She looked out over the lake, as gentle waves lapped against the raft, darkening the edges of the tablecloth.

After a while, Sarah slipped her hand over Luke's. "Did you get to talk to my father?"

She felt Luke's muscles tighten.

"Yes."

Sarah waited a few moments. "And?"

"He, uh, offered something I couldn't agree to."

"Oh. Can you tell me what?"

Luke withdrew his hand. "I'd rather not. It doesn't matter now."

"Okay." Sarah stifled her curiosity. "Let's eat, then."

"Sounds good."

After they ate, Sarah slid closer to Luke. "This was the first place you kissed me—in that freezing water."

"Yeah, but I think it was you that kissed me. And it *was* cold, but you warmed me up."

She ran her hand up his muscular arm. "Same here."

For a few moments, Sarah felt an unfamiliar awkwardness between them, but looking into each other's eyes, their love rose and softened into sadness. She cuddled against him and they held each other for a long time. In the distance, the longing calls of a pair of loons drifted across the water.

As the sun started to descend toward the Green Mountains, Luke took Sarah's hand. "So, what's going to happen to us?"

"I wish I knew, but I don't."

Luke shook his head. "This is way too powerful to be just a summer fling."

"That I know."

They leaned back against a sloping cedar and watched as the sun descended over the lake, its bright golden glow illuminating ripples from the occasional fishing boat passing by. After watching a stunning sunset light up the sky in fire red, pink, and orange, they drove to the horse barn and made a bed out of soft blankets in the haymow. They shared a couple of beers and lay down together. Planning to make love, they instead found themselves comforted by just holding each other long after the sky was dark and speckled with flickering stars. Finding it hard to talk, they both cried, wiping away each other's salty tears.

Sarah whispered in Luke's ear. "You're going to be alright. I know it."

He smiled and kissed her. "I hope so. I have the love of my life to live for." With his arm around her, Sarah cuddled under Luke's chin, and they soon fell asleep.

Luke was suddenly awakened by the loud cawing of crows squabbling with each other in the branches of trees outside the barn. He sat up abruptly.

Sarah slid off him. "What's the matter?"

"I've gotta' get up."

"What time is it?"

Luke looked outside. "Must be around 5:30."

Sarah slid her hand around his thigh. "That's too early."

"No, it isn't. I've got to be at the train station in Greensboro Bend by 7:30. If I'm late, they court-martial me or something."

"They wouldn't dare," she said, sliding her hand over his penis, which immediately hardened. "I'll help you get ready." She rolled him on his back and got on top of him. She kissed him and then slid him inside of her. He fondled her breasts as she rose and fell on him. They were soon moist with sweat as they climaxed together. As Sarah's breathing calmed, she laid against his chest. He held her as they both broke into tears. "I'm going to miss you so much."

"Me, too," Luke said, wiping wet hair from her face. "It's like you've taken over my heart."

For a short while they lay there as if their bodies were one.

Finally, Luke got up. "I gotta'—"

"I know, or you'll get court-martialed." She smiled. "I'll always remember what it feels like to make love with you."

"I hope so." Luke bent over and kissed her. "Don't worry, I'll refresh your memory someday."

* * *

Luke left Sarah off at the inn and drove home where his

mother had his favorite buttermilk pancakes waiting for him. He could tell she had struggled to make them as batter had dripped over the rimmers and down the front of the stove. Coffee had been splashed on the table.

Luke gave her a gentle hug and sat down. He lathered butter on the pancakes then drenched them in warm maple syrup. His mother sat next to him and laid her hand on his arm as he ate.

"So good," he said, licking syrup off his cheek. "Perfect breakfast."

"I figured you needed a good send off, something to hold you on the train. The Army isn't known for their cooking."

"I'm sure they're not." He kissed her on the cheek. "Thank you, Mom." He looked at her lovingly. "You've always been there for me, been my cheerleader, my rock."

Mary smiled. "We've had our challenges. Life's not always easy, but we've done alright." She pushed herself out of her chair, steadied for a few moments, then moved to the sink. "Now, you best get ready. Army won't wait."

Luke went into his bedroom and quietly shut the door. He stood silently in the place he had always called home. He looked at the collage pinned over his bed. His varsity letter in football, though he couldn't afford to buy the sweater to sew it on. A ticket stub from a bluegrass festival up at Burke Mountain, and a faded Hawaiian lei a girl brought back for him from a family trip. There were album covers pinned to the wall—Dylan's *The Times They Are A-Changin'*, the Beatles' *Abbey Road*, and Credence Clearwater Revival's *Bayou Country*. He'd played "Proud Mary" so many times the needle had worn deep into the vinyl causing it to skip.

He patted the stuffed rabbit on top of his bureau his mother had given him as a child. Next to it was a small black-and-white photo of his dad waving while fishing over on Long Pond. Behind the photo sat his father's dog tags, their chain curled like a tiny snake. Luke held the tags up to his neck in front of the mirror. "Soon I'll have my own, Dad. I'll try and make you proud."

In the corner was a partially deflated football. He picked it up and thought of throwing it out the window, one last touchdown pass, but let it fall back to the floor where it had been. He looked around the room one final time, and as he put Mr. Hensley's book in his duffle bag, noticed there was a small envelope taped to the outside. "Open when you get there" was written in his mother's handwriting. He started to tear up, then took a deep breath and slipped it inside. He hooked his arm through the strap of the bag, lifted it from the bed, and left his room.

Back in the kitchen, his mother had taken off her apron, revealing she was wearing her best blue flowered dress, the one with a bit of frill on the bottom. "You look nice, Mom," Luke said, touching her thin shoulder.

"Thanks. Didn't want to embarrass you in my usual rags."

He frowned. "You never embarrass me."

Through the kitchen window, Luke saw the red Mustang pulled up out front.

"Nice of Sarah to drive us," Mary said, grabbing a sun hat off a nail.

"Nice to have you both see me off."

"'Course."

He put on his pack then carried his duffle bag in one hand and helped his mom with the other as they walked out onto the porch. Sarah was out of her car, at the foot of the newly-repaired stairs. "Hi there," she said, obviously working to hold her emotions in.

"Hey," Luke said, as he helped his mom to the passenger's door. "Thanks for coming."

Sarah smiled and put her hand on his waist as he settled Mary in the seat.

"I'll get in the back." Luke put his pack and his duffle bag on the back seat.

"No way. You're driving—right next to your mom." Sarah hopped into the back seat behind Luke.

Luke smiled. "Thanks."

He got in and started the engine. With Sarah running her fingers through his hair, he took one last look at his house and drove off.

"Now, don't drive this hot rod too fast," his mother said, touching his arm.

Luke held his mother's hand while they drove in silence the few miles to Greensboro Bend. There was just too much to say and nowhere near enough words to say it. As they approached the Bend, the wooden train station with its high, overhanging eaves, came into view. On the gravel walkway in front of the single track, Luke saw several young men with duffle bags similar to his saying goodbye to their families. He parked the Mustang, and watched a mother burst into tears as she held her son. A lump formed in Luke's throat, but he was not going to fall apart, at least not until he was on the train rolling down the track. Three World War II veterans stood by the ticket entrance, wishing the young draftees well as they stepped into the darkness of the station. A black station wagon with a silver cross on the window idled off to the side.

"Now, Luke," his mother said, "I'm going to say goodbye, for now, right here. You and Sarah go over together."

Luke took both of his mother's thin hands and gave them a gentle squeeze. "I love you, Mom, and I'll write to you, let you know what's going on."

"Please do, I'll love getting letters from you."

He leaned over and held her.

"Remember what I told you," she whispered.

"Don't worry, I will."

They kissed each other on the cheek. He got out and joined Sarah, who was standing behind the car holding his duffle bag. He put his arm around her and they walked slowly toward the station.

An officer in uniform called out from the small porch. "Hurry it up, men. All draftees on the train in five minutes."

"Asshole," Sarah said.

Luke stopped. "Don't let him hear you, I'm in the Army now."

She looked up at Luke. "Don't take any shit from them."

Luke chuckled. "From what I've heard, I'll have to take a ration of it on a regular basis."

Sarah wrapped her arms around his neck. "Oh, Luke, I'm—"

"I know," he said softly as they held each other.

"You better write," she said, tears trickling down her cheeks.

"I will. The Army must have some pens." He grinned. "And you, too."

"I promise." Sarah looked at him and managed a smile. "You're something else."

He held his hand up to her warm cheek. "I love you, Sarah. I always will."

She put her hand over his and began to cry. "Soulmates forever."

"All aboard!" a conductor called from the train platform.

Sarah squeezed his hand. "Please be careful."

"I'll do my best." Luke kissed her on the head. "I better go."

Their arms outstretched, holding hands till the last second as he moved away.

"Hey, Luke! Did you forget something?" Sarah held up his duffle bag. He ran back and grabbed it, and gave her a kiss on the lips. "You just wanted another kiss."

"Darn right." He turned and ran for the train, and hesitated.

The three old vets stood at attention beside the last car as a flag-draped coffin was taken from the train to the waiting hearse. The guy from St. Johnsbury.

Luke put his head down and climbed aboard. Behind him, the conductor pulled up the metal stair and closed the door.

Luke stuffed his pack and duffle bag overhead and slumped into a saggy leather seat. He sat quietly, working to keep his emotions in check. Then he heard familiar music coming from the platform. He slid the window open, and to his amazement, saw the Bullpout Band, including Jed, Skinny, Betty, and Sarah with their fiddles, playing "When the Saints Go Marching In." Next to them, stood Judge Clements, who waved when he saw Luke.

The train's bell rang, and a sharp hiss came from beneath the car. As it began to move, Luke hung out the window like most of the guys. He waved to his mother and to Sarah and the others. And to—of all people—Maxwell Holmes, who, in a royal blue suit, stood at attention with tears in his eyes, saluting as the train passed.

At the end of the platform, a group of older vets lined the track, standing at attention and saluting. As the train gained speed and pulled away from the station, the sound of the music faded away. Approaching the bend that would take them out of sight, Luke tried but couldn't bring himself to look back. He had to look forward.

CHAPTER THIRTY-THREE

O N THE LONG, TIRING TRAIN RIDE SOUTH, LUKE SPENT hours staring out the window, watching the familiar landscape of New England, the crazy congestion of huge East Coast cities, and the majestic Blue Ridge Mountains of Virginia pass him by. Interspersed with a few card games, he slept off and on, the clack-clacking of the rails sounding like the cadence of marching formations he'd seen on TV. When he arrived at Fort Bragg, he was taken aback by the enormity of the sprawling base, where, he was told, thousands of soldiers and airmen were being trained. As a draftee in the Regular Army, Luke was assigned to a platoon of 80 men living in one of many large barracks, each man assigned a metal bed and a footlocker to call home. He was able to quickly adjust to the tightly regimented life, which helped to keep his mind off missing home and Sarah, even if reporting for KP duty at three in the morning was pretty annoying.

Luke's days were filled with military instruction, and miles of marching in formation, grueling runs, and struggling through increasingly difficult obstacle courses. His least favorite was the 50-foot "low crawl" under barbed wire hung about a foot off the ground. Unfortunately, it was his drill sergeant's favorite, and when anyone in his platoon screwed up, everyone had to do an extra crawl or two. Luke was the culprit only once, when he missed polishing a tiny spot on the heel of one of his boots. He didn't do that again. By and large, he stayed under the radar and gave training his all, answered the drill sergeant's questions in a strong, confident voice, and didn't make trouble. They seemed to respect his efforts, but he didn't take anything for granted.

In addition to an occasional game of hoops, Luke looked forward to mail call, where soldiers lined up in front of their barracks and letters and packages were passed out. He had written several letters home, and though it took a couple of weeks, he was psyched when he finally received a letter from his mother, whose handwriting looked shakier than ever. A couple days later he was relieved to hear from Sarah, though he was disappointed she didn't seem as affectionate as she'd been in person. It probably seemed that way because he was cooped up in boot camp, desperate for his girl back home. When he got the chance, he'd lay on his bunk and read her letter over several times, and hope he'd receive another soon. If he could stay awake long enough, he liked to end the day with a passage from the *Tao de Ching*, though sometimes he'd wake up during the night with the book still open on his chest.

Luke felt bad for the soldiers who hadn't gotten any mail, including the guy in the bunk next to him. Jimmy Baker was a smart, skinny kid who hailed from the mountains of Kentucky. He had also lost his father at a young age, and unlike many of the other guys, he loved to read. He'd even read *Bury My Heart at Wounded Knee*. Luke enjoyed talking about the book and the tragic plight of American Indians with Jimmy, and shared with him what had happened to Mr. Hensley. One night they sat up unusually late, engrossed in a discussion of Melville's *Moby Dick*, another favorite book, both impressed by the sheer maniacal determination of Captain Ahab. They paid for it the next day during a ten-mile run in the oppressive Carolina heat.

Noticing Jimmy lacked street smarts and wasn't the strongest physically, Luke helped him out when he could during training sessions. One day, Luke saved Jimmy's butt—literally—giving him a much-needed push to make it over a tall wooden wall on an obstacle course. At the end of basic training Luke was psyched he and Jimmy were assigned to the same unit before shipping out.

Bummed not to hear from Sarah again before the end of his time at Fort Bragg, Luke focused on getting ready to leave for Vietnam. Both he and Jimmy were excited to be flying for the first time, on a Flying Tiger Line *jet*, no less. Sitting next to Jimmy, Luke was fascinated watching the patchwork quilt of farms, ranches, and golden wheat fields pass far beneath them as they soared over the American heartland. As they made their way west, the Rocky Mountains were particularly spectacular, their snow-capped peaks reaching skyward like the tufts of frosting on a cake. Before this experience, Luke had had no idea how enormous the United States was. Flying across it gave him a patriotic chill.

After refueling at Edwards Air Force Base outside of Los Angeles, the long haul across the Pacific to Japan made both Luke and Jimmy nervous. Luke couldn't imagine being rescued if they went down over that vast expanse of water. To distract themselves, he and Jimmy did some reading and played many games of gin rummy on the tiny tray table between them.

On the last leg of the trip, Luke felt a mixture of excitement and dread, anticipating what combat would really be like.

Looking out the window as they finally approached Saigon, he saw jagged mountaintops and miles of terraced rice paddies, just like Sarah had described. Sadly, the rich green landscape was marred by plumes of smoke rising from areas blackened by fighting.

Once on the ground, Luke heard distant gunfire and explosions, and the beating of the acrid air by swarms of helicopter gunships.

During his first week in-country, Luke was moved by the small children who waved to him and the other GIs as they drove by in their Jeeps. It disturbed him, though, that older locals looked terrified and ran when they saw Americans approaching. And then he remembered the slaughter at My Lai a couple of years before. When he could, Luke slowed his Jeep and tossed Vietnamese children a few pieces of candy. But that soon stopped when he was reprimanded by an officer who told him they could be a decoy for the 'Cong or a lure toward a landmine at the side of the road. "Treat everyone like they're the enemy," he had said, which went against Luke's nature.

The weekend before Luke's first mission, his platoon was given a few hours off. He and Jimmy visited a local market outside their compound, and Luke was psyched to find a man under a tarp selling cheap musical instruments. Luke paid him $5 for an old guitar and Jimmy bought a slightly dented harmonica. Luke missed his jam sessions at Skinny's, so he was psyched to have someone to play with. That night they sat outside on a bench and worked on a few tunes, including a respectable rendition of "Oh! Susanna."

"We sound like we're on an Old West wagon train," Jimmy said when they hit the sack that night.

Chuckling, Luke agreed. "Maybe they'll put us on *Hee Haw* when we get back."

Luke realized the other men in the barracks enjoyed hearing him and Jimmy play. Soon they started making requests for songs like Kristofferson's "Me and Bobby McGee," and Dylan's "Mr. Tambourine Man." Even the sergeant seemed to enjoy having a little live music in the platoon. Until the morning Jimmy left his harmonica laying on his bed during inspection. That cost the barracks 50 pushups, but the men said being able to listen to the music was worth it.

One morning, Luke was unexpectedly called into the commander's office. Lieutenant Coldwell told him he was being transferred to help out Task Force 116, a shorthanded "River Rats" company operating down south in the Mekong Delta. The Brown River Navy patrolled the many waterways, trying to keep the Viet Cong from using them to launch attacks or to move supplies and munitions. For this operation, the Army was working in consort with the Navy.

Luke figured he was chosen because of his experience with boats. He welcomed getting back on the water, and joked, "I probably won't be working on mahogany runabouts like I'm used to."

The lieutenant just shook his head. "After you survive a monsoon or two, you'll be glad you're not on a fancy runabout."

"Lieutenant Coldwell, sir," Luke said before leaving the office. "I'd like to request that one of the other men in my platoon be transferred with me."

"Who's that?"

"Private Jimmy Baker."

The lieutenant thought for a few moments. "The kid from Kentucky?"

"Yes, sir."

"And why would I send him to the 'River Rats'?"

"Sir, we work very well together, he's wicked smart, and has, um, a lot of astronomy knowledge which will make him a cracker-jack nighttime navigator."

The lieutenant looked over his glasses at Luke, who stood at rigid attention. "Are you serious?"

"Yes, sir."

"Can Baker handle a gun? Is he combat-ready?"

"I believe so, sir."

Lt. Coldwell perused the file in front of him. "Simms, you received high marks in basic training: honest, good common sense, felt to be officer material." He looked up at Luke. "Let's hope they were right." He closed the file. "Private Baker will be transferred with you."

"Thank you. Appreciate it, sir." Luke saluted.

"And Private—"

"Yes, sir."

The lieutenant removed his glasses. "Sometimes a natural soldier like yourself can take on watching out for someone who isn't. I get that. But remember, Baker has to learn to take care of himself. It's survival out there—every day."

Luke felt himself blush. "Understood, sir."

"That will be all."

Luke saluted again then quickly turned on his heel and marched out of the office. He was psyched.

Back at their barracks, Luke told Jimmy what he'd arranged, and he was excited to be staying with Luke.

"You must have bullshitted them about me," Jimmy said.

"Just a little."

"I don't know a thing about boats. Or nighttime navigation, even if I'm into astronomy."

"You're a fast learner," Luke replied with a smile.

On the trip to their new basecamp in the back of an Army truck, Luke gave Jimmy a quick primer about working with boats, accentuated with fun stories about life on Caspian. He left the story of his fiery accident before the Great Race for another time.

Bouncing on bumpy roads for the last ten miles, they were tired and sore when they arrived at a camp along the Bassac River. As darkness fell, they were given a tour of the docks, maintenance shed, small mess hall, the couple of tents with the men's bunks, and a pair of wooden latrines with crescent moons shot out of the door. That night, when they finally crashed on their cots, Jimmy gave Luke a fearful look. "I don't know about this."

Luke chuckled. "Wait till we get on the boats. You'll love it."

The next morning, Luke and Jimmy were given a brief introduction to their small fleet. The rugged, heavily equipped rivercraft, were propelled by a jet-drive system to operate in the delta's shallow waters. In addition to a small arsenal of hand weapons, the boats were armed with two .50 caliber machine guns mounted in the bow, and another in the stern. The boats were operated by a crew of four men, including a petty officer, who served as the captain. Luke was assigned to be an engineman, and Jimmy, a gunner's mate. Seeing how uneasy Jimmy was on the boat, Luke was concerned he'd requested to bring him along, but figured he'd get used to it. He'd have to. Besides, Luke wanted Jimmy close so he could keep an eye on him.

Their first patrol mission was to strafe a 'Cong hideout a couple miles downriver. As they approached the target area, the captain swerved toward shore bringing the boat in hot. He yelled at Jimmy to fire as they cruised past enemy positions hidden amongst the thick mangroves. Jimmy began firing but had a hard time handling the big gun. "Shoot the goddamned thing!" the captain yelled, which made Jimmy even more nervous, causing him to fire several rounds over the trees.

When the enemy returned small-weapons fire, the captain took evasive action, sharply angling the boat away from the shore, impressing Luke, but causing Jimmy to throw up. They made it back to camp uninjured, but Jimmy's future on the water was in doubt. A week later, more Navy reinforcements arrived, and Luke and Jimmy were reassigned to river-based ground assaults, which minimized their time on the boats. In between missions, Luke worked with Jimmy to improve his firearm and combat skills, which seemed to make quite a difference.

After a chaotic month in 'Nam, Luke was increasingly disappointed he hadn't heard from Sarah, even though he realized, with his new squad constantly on the move, mail delivery was erratic at best. Despite working crazy hours in blistering heat and torrential downpours, he missed her terribly. He kept their picture in the shirt pocket over his heart for good luck, and when he could clear his head, loved thinking about their time together that summer. When he did get a chance to call Sarah at the number she'd given him at her college, it had been disconnected. All he could do was investigate the damn mail situation as soon as possible.

One afternoon, Luke and Jimmy were called in to back up another squad which was pinned down under relentless fire from the Viet Cong. As their boat approached the shore near the area of fighting, a sniper wounded one of Luke's comrades, who grabbed his leg and fell to the deck. Luke saw the sniper perched in a thicket of trees and reflexively fired at him with his M16. The soldier fell, and Luke knew from the way he splashed into the murky water the guy was dead. It was unnerving to have just killed another human being, but glancing at his wounded friend made him feel better. He knew he'd do it again.

Back on their camp's dock, Luke helped carry his friend from the boat to waiting medics who started an IV line, splinted his leg then took him to a field hospital. After some chow and another empty mail call, he and Jimmy got their orders for the next day. They'd join men from another platoon to recapture a critical hill the 'Cong had recently taken by overpowering South Vietnamese forces.

Before crashing for the night, Luke lay on his bed, surrounded by the now-familiar smell of the canvas tent, moistened by all the rain.

"Hey, Luke," Jimmy said, pulling out his harmonica. "Let's play a couple songs."

"I gotta' get some sleep, man."

"Come on."

"Alright." Luke took his guitar from under his bed. "But just one, and I can guess what it'll be."

"'Mr. Tambourine Man,' of course," Jimmy said. "I've been practicing, think I've gotten it down."

When they finished playing the song, the sergeant stuck his head in the door. "You guys better get some sleep. Tomorrow's going to be a bitch."

Sitting on the edge of his bed, seeming more nervous than usual, Jimmy turned to Luke. "What do you think the sergeant meant?"

Luke looked at Jimmy. "Not sure, but it didn't sound good."

"Hmm," Jimmy said then laid down and pulled a pillow over his head.

CHAPTER THIRTY-FOUR

EARLY THE NEXT MORNING, LUKE, JIMMY, AND OTHER soldiers boarded a patrol boat to take them to recapture the strategic hill. With a fine mist in the air, it was unusually quiet as they motored down the river, but as soon as they hit land, they came under fire from a sniper. One of the gunners quickly took out the 'Cong with the .50 caliber machine gun. The hill was only a mile away but Luke knew it was going to be a hard slog through swampy terrain.

Joining another squad, Luke's group trudged through the bug-infested lowland toward the hill. Soon, Lt. Leary split the men up so they could approach the target from two flanks. When Luke's group made it to the foot of the hill they stopped to rest.

Almost immediately, they came under intense fire from enemy entrenched at the top. Knowing they were in trouble, Luke told a couple of guys to cover him and Jimmy while they dug a shallow foxhole for protection. While the men hunkered down, the Americans on the other flank seemed to be in a better position to attack and were able to take out a few of the North Vietnamese.

Soon, the lieutenant ordered Luke's group to advance. Luke crept out of the muddy foxhole. With Jimmy right behind him, he crouched low and started up the slope. About halfway up the hill, a machine gunner opened up over to their left.

"Shit!" Luke dropped into the mud.

Still too exposed, they got up and made a run for it. There wasn't any good cover nearby, so they zigzagged back down the hill to the foxhole. Machine gun rounds riddled the ground around them as they dove for cover.

As soon as Luke caught his breath, he checked on Jimmy.

His buddy lay next to him, helmet off, glasses cockeyed, shaking so badly he could hardly hold his rifle.

"I can't see, Luke…" Jimmy's voice was strangled with fear.

Luke straightened Jimmy's glasses, then peered over the lip of the hole. Two other guys from his platoon were 50 yards away, hunkered down in a thick, swampy area. Luke checked to see if they were being pursued. Seeing no one, he turned back to Jimmy, who seemed shell-shocked.

"Luke, I can't see."

"Your glasses are covered with mud. Hang on, let me—"

"Help me, Luke," Jimmy pleaded.

"Jesus, Jimmy, let me get the shit off your lenses." Luke leaned his M16 against his leg and pulled a red bandana from his pocket. "Give me your glasses."

Jimmy didn't respond.

"Hey, we haven't got all day." Luke checked the perimeter again.

Jimmy slumped over, making a gurgling sound, his eyes barely open.

"Jimmy. Jimmy!" Luke slapped his cheek. "You alright?" Luke put his arm around his friend to help him sit up. His hand slid across something warm and wet. When he pulled his hand back, it was covered with blood.

"Shit." Luke's heart sank. He reached over his shoulder and pulled his radio from his pack. "Medic—I need a medic here!" he yelled into the mic. "Man shot— bleeding bad."

"I'm not going to make it, am I?"

"You hang on, buddy, medics are coming. They'll fix you up."

"Luke…" Jimmy said in a weak whisper.

Luke put his ear down. "Yeah, Jimmy?"

"Lorraine…tell her…"

"Jimmy, stay with me."

Jimmy's hand grasped at Luke's shirt. "Tell Lorraine I…" He fell silent. His body lurched and went limp.

"No, Jimmy! You gotta' hang in there. Medics are coming."

Luke felt Jimmy's neck. No pulse. He started pushing on Jimmy's chest.

More gunfire erupted from the top of the hill.

Luke grabbed his gun. Continuing to work on Jimmy's chest with one hand, he reached up and fired several shots in the direction of the machine gunner.

Luke thought he heard Jimmy speak so he stopped and leaned down to his mouth.

Nothing.

Luke restarted his revival efforts. That's when he saw the pool of blood under Jimmy, spreading wider with each compression.

"Oh, god…" Luke fell back against the side of the foxhole, dislodging clumps of dirt onto both of them.

Jimmy's last request resurfaced. Lorraine.

"I will, Jimmy," Luke said to Jimmy's face. "I'll tell her you love her. I promise." A powerful wave of nausea churned in his gut. He looked at his friend with the funky Southern accent. "I didn't know you were hit." Choked with emotion, Luke tried to cradle Jimmy's expressionless face in his hands. "Jesus Christ, Jimmy, I'm sorry."

Gunfire again erupted a short distance away. Overcome as he was with grief, Luke knew his only chance was to push Jimmy's death out of his mind. He touched his chest pocket. "Please, God, help us."

Fear and rage rising within him, Luke grabbed his gun and peered out of the foxhole again. He saw the 'Cong advancing along the edge of the swamp toward his other comrades, who were blind to the enemy. Silently, Luke slid over the top, partially protected by a large rock. He swiped mud off his gunsight, zeroed in on the commies, and squeezed the trigger. In a violent burst of fire, he took out the two men before they even saw him.

Several others emerged from the dense vegetation. Luke continued shooting as they returned fire. From where his buddies were, they had no shot; all they could do was stay hunkered down. It was up to Luke. He'd be damned if he was going to let anyone else die.

Bullets ricocheted off the rock next to him. Stone fragments hit his cheek and shoulder. Luke emptied his rifle, and then fired another clip in the direction of the 'Cong. He reached down and pulled Jimmy's rifle from under his arm. When the intense fire let up for a few seconds, Luke shimmied a few feet sideways along the foxhole, and blasted across the enemy's position. He hoped they'd think they were outgunned. Two other Americans had made their way to the edge of the swamp. Now they opened fire. Several North Vietnamese were hit and fell. It was hard to tell, but it looked like others were retreating back into the jungle. Luke just kept firing, hoping he'd take out a couple more. For Jimmy.

When things quieted, several other Americans advanced up the slope spraying the top of the hill with gunfire until all was silent except for the intense ringing in Luke's ears. He crawled out of the foxhole and, with his rifle at the ready, slunk up the hill. He approached the machine gunner who had ambushed them. He was splayed on his back across ammunition boxes and spent shell casings. He was the bastard who shot Jimmy. Raging inside, Luke pulled out his pistol and jammed it into the guy's forehead. Grinding his teeth, Luke held the gun so hard his hand shook. He tightened his finger around the trigger. *"Don't let them change you,"* his mother had said.

After a few moments, he pulled his gun back. The guy was dead.

Gunfire echoed across rice paddies a short distance away. Soon, Lt. Leary came up behind Luke. "These guys are all dead. The rest took off." He looked around. "Where's Jimmy?"

Luke's heart stopped. He kicked the leg of the dead machine gunner. "This bastard got him—in the back." Luke motioned toward the foxhole. "He's gone."

Lt. Leary angrily shook his head. "Sonofabitch." He glared at the machine gunner. "Fucking 'Cong." He pulled his pistol out, and before Luke could turn away, shot the guy in the head three times. "Take that, you gook cocksucker."

Luke was repulsed at the sight of what Lt. Leary did. He shouldered his rifle and shook his head. "Never should have let a kid like Jimmy in the damn Army."

Lt. Leary nodded. "Yup. Bound to happen. They'll send anyone over here. Fucking wasteland." He spit out a brown wad of chaw. "Come on. We gotta' get Jimmy out of there. You call for medevac?"

"I started to, then Jimmy…"

"Call 'em now!" Lt. Leary snapped. "Flyboys' gunships are about to paint this area orange."

"Yes, sir." Luke called it in. He felt sick about Jimmy, and knew they couldn't carry his body all the way back to their boat, left hidden along the riverbank. The delta was so infested with 'Cong, moving slowly with a body, they'd be sitting ducks. But there was no way they were going to leave Jimmy behind.

The Huey with a red cross on it arrived within ten minutes. Luke helped lay Jimmy's body on the floor alongside a litter where a corpsman was caring for a guy shot in the abdomen.

Luke choked up as he watched the chopper lift off. He appreciated the few moments Lt. Leary gave the men before leading them along a rice paddy, through a thick stretch of jungle, to the river. Holding their rifles over their heads, they struggled through another couple hundred yards of swamp before making it back to their boat.

As soon as they started the engine, they came under fire again. Luke ducked down and fired his M16 in the direction of the attackers. Another soldier scrambled to the stern, grabbed the mounted machine gun, and began firing. Shell casings flew by Luke. He hung on as Lt. Leary gunned the engine and they headed downriver. The sound of bullets ricocheting off the boat's ceramic armament reminded him of when he and his friends used to plink cans in the town dump with their .22s.

Though exhausted, Luke kept watching for more 'Cong as they raced through the murky water. Once they were well away from the most intense area of fighting, he leaned back against the side of the boat. With its powerful diesel roaring beneath him, he scratched at the red welts covering his arm. Sonofabitch. So, this was Brown Water Navy.

Luke closed his eyes for a few seconds, a peaceful image of the calm, blue waters of Caspian floating across his mind.

It was almost dark when they arrived back at their base. After securing the boat, he and another man pulled off their muddy clothes and took a bath in the river. The water was disgusting, but it was wet.

Luke sat in the shallows mourning Jimmy, thinking about what a trooper he'd been. He was pissed with himself for bringing Jimmy with him to this watery hellhole. Luke shut his eyes, saw Jimmy's cockeyed glasses and the desperation on his face as he was dying. Luke hung his head on his knees. "I should have saved you, Jimmy. That's what a real buddy would've done."

"Come on out of there Simms," Lt. Leary called to him from the bank. "That water'll poison you."

Luke waved his hand in acknowledgment. When he stepped on the shore, Lt. Leary was still there. "Tough day. And though we're a unit, we all gotta' deal with this shit our own way." He put his hand on Luke's shoulder. "This war will kill you if you let it." He looked Luke in the eye. "Don't let it."

Luke sat outside the barracks and cleaned his rifle, then hit the mess for a little greasy meatloaf, soggy mashed potatoes, and tasteless green beans. The meal fit the way he felt. Having missed mail call, he checked to see if any had come for him. Seeing a letter, his heart momentarily cheered up, but sank when he saw it was from the damn Army. They could wait.

Bummed out and sad, he sat on his cot and pulled out his picture of Sarah. Even though he'd covered it with plastic, it was getting pretty beat up. He stared at that amazing smile of hers.

Though he could barely keep his eyes open, he had promised himself he would write to her, as he hadn't been able to for several days. He pulled out a small notebook, licked the end of a pen, and began to write. "Hey, Sarah, I thought boot camp was tough, but this place is hell. Wicked tough day. Lost my best friend, the geeky guy from Kentucky. Crazy he ended up on the front lines."

A lump of guilt formed as he wrote. He tried to think of something upbeat to say, but couldn't. "Sorry, but everything about this place sucks. If I didn't have you to think about at night, I'd never get any shut-eye. I love you. Luke." He wanted to write more, but was too wrecked. He tore off the paper, folded it, and slid it into an envelope. He was upset he hadn't heard from Sarah again, but that was probably the mail system messing up, especially since he'd already been transferred from one company to another and his new squad was constantly on the move. She *had* to be thinking about him.

That night, Luke avoided looking at Jimmy's bed for quite a while, but finally did. There was Jimmy's harmonica, left in the middle of the blanket again. Luke reached over, picked it up, and held it against his chest. There was no use trying to hold back the tears.

Tommy, one of the other guys, came over, sat down, and put his arm around Luke's shoulder. "Real sorry, man. Jimmy was a cool little dude."

Luke wiped his eyes with his sleeve. "Yeah."

"You were a damn good friend to him. He told me he'd never made it over here without you."

Luke scoffed. "A lot of good that did him."

Tommy slapped Luke on the thigh. "Come on, it's nobody's

fault except the fucking 'Cong. Tomorrow we'll pay those bastards back." Tommy stood. "But tonight, we should sing one of those songs you two were practicing, you know, for Jimmy."

"I don't know."

"Come on. You know he'd like that."

"Yeah," chimed in another guy. "That's what Jimmy'd want us to do."

Luke thought for a few moments, then nodded his head. "Alright. We'll do it."

Tommy bent toward Luke. "How about that Bob Dylan song 'Mr. Tambourine Man'?"

Luke felt a well of emotion again. "That was the song we were going to do for you guys tonight."

"Alright, then." Tommy turned and waved the other guys in the barracks over. "Come on. We're going to sing for Jimmy."

The guys gathered around, several visibly upset at losing one of their own. Luke placed Jimmy's harmonica on his pillow, then pulled his guitar from under his bed. He tuned a couple of strings then looked up. Lt. Leary stood silently in the shadows by the door.

"This song was Jimmy's favorite. It won't sound very good without his harmonica, but here goes." Straining to hold back his emotions, Luke started strumming and led the guys in a slightly off-key, though stirring rendition of "Mr. Tambourine Man."

Jimmy would've been proud.

CHAPTER THIRTY-FIVE

L UKE HAD A HARD TIME PUSHING THE IMAGES FROM THE foxhole out of his mind. Devastated by losing Jimmy, he struggled with intensifying internal conflict. His stomach bothered him a lot, and nagging headaches kept him awake at night. He still wanted to believe the US was in South Vietnam for legitimate reasons, but it was hard to convince himself the bloodbath around him was warranted or worth it. At the same time, he knew he had to keep believing in the mission to some degree lest he completely lose his mind.

Mercifully, after two months of arduous fighting, Luke and his unit got a much-needed short pass for a couple days in Saigon. Luke was excited for a change of scenery but before they left the miserable jungle, he searched out Ziggy, their grouchy quartermaster, to find out where the hell his mail was. He found Ziggy sitting behind a Quonset hut smoking a joint, reading a magazine.

"Hey, can I ask you something?"

"Can't you see I'm on break?" Ziggy said, without looking up from a tattered *Playboy*.

"A quick question—"

Ziggy impatiently shut the magazine and glanced at Luke. "What d'you want?"

"My mail. I haven't gotten any from my girlfriend since

YOU WERE ALWAYS THERE

I transferred over here, and I know she's writing to me."

Ziggy scoffed. "That's what they all say. If I had a nickel..." He took a drag. "Outta' sight, outta' mind. That's what I say." Smoke blew out of both nostrils.

"I'm telling you, I'm sure she's been writing me. Where the hell is all my mail?"

As Luke got pissed, Ziggy stood up. "Look, your unit's been all over the place—up and down the river, sleeping on the boats. How the hell are we supposed to get mail to you?"

"We're back in camp now, and I still haven't seen any."

Ziggy squeezed off the end of the roach and slid it into his shirt pocket. "Give me a second." He disappeared into the hut, the flimsy aluminum door slamming behind him. Through the window, Luke saw him rifling through two large mailbags, watched several letters fall to the floor. After a couple minutes Ziggy threw up his hands and came back outside. "I don't see anything for you."

"That's it?"

"Yeah, that's it," he snapped. "You guys always want something. What do I look like? Santa Claus?"

"You *are* the quartermaster." Luke shook his head. "Useless damn Army." He turned and took off. Even though the only letter he'd received from Sarah came when he was in boot camp, he wasn't ready to give up on her.

Luke piled into the back of an Army truck with the other guys, and shared a few beers on a backbreaking ride to Saigon. When they finally got there, Lt. Leary climbed out of the cab, reminded them they had 48 hours to blow off steam, and told them to not get in any trouble. Rolling his eyes along with the other men, Luke promised he'd behave. Like the rest of them, he wasted no time getting to it.

The streets bustled with throngs of bicycles, motorcycles, scooters, and pedestrians darting back and forth between them. The side streets were jammed with dive bars, walk-up food shacks, and more loose women than Luke could comprehend. The plentiful beer, cheap shots, and easy marijuana surrounded the GIs, and before long many of them were stumbling drunk. At first, Luke tried to pace himself, but the booze caught up with him, and soon he was toasting to any and everything, singing at the top of his lungs with the rest of them.

At some point, Lt. Leary showed up at one of the bars, and took Luke and Roger, another reliable man, up a dark set of stairs into a dimly lit hallway. Even drunk, the stale smell of alcohol, sweat, and cigarette smoke repulsed Luke.

Lt. Leary banged on the wall, and a couple of doors opened, from which seductive, scantily-clad women emerged.

"Here, give the boys a good time." Lt. Leary jammed a couple greenbacks into the black threadbare bikini of a skinny woman whose cheeks were bright with thick red makeup.

Roger lunged, and the woman darted out of the way. He lost his balance and landed on a bed with a stained mattress. Ignoring Roger, the woman approached Luke and ran her hands down over his chest to his groin. She said something he didn't understand then pushed up his shirt. He felt her warm breasts against his skin. Suddenly, he was kissing her, her smoky tongue doing wild things with his. Her hand grabbed his erection and she pulled him onto the bed with her. Rolling a passed out Roger out of the way, she spread her legs. A vision of Sarah lying next to him in the hayloft flashed across his mind.

As horny as Luke was, he was revolted. "No," he said in a haze of booze and confusion. He pushed away from the woman and steadied himself against a sticky wall. Staggering out of the room, he made his way along a hallway and fumbled down a set of back stairs that led outside into the humid, acrid air.

Luke threw up near a mangy dog, which quickly licked up his puke. "Fuuckk..." he moaned, trying to wipe his mouth with his arm. Too drunk to go very far, he slid into a narrow alley next to a cluster of garbage cans. His head spinning, he pulled his knees up to his chin and held them. Feeling like he was cracking in two, Luke started to cry. Harder than he ever had. He'd landed in hell, and neither Sarah nor his mom were there to save him.

When Luke came to, the sky over the city had darkened. Someone dropped a bag of trash on top of a garbage can but they didn't notice Luke. He was still drunk but was at least able to stand without feeling like he'd fall over. For a moment he wondered if he'd had sex with the woman upstairs but was pretty sure he hadn't.

He was taking a badly-needed leak when he first smelled smoke, different than the bitter haze that hung in the street. He looked around. Gray smoke poured from a broken window above him. The building was on fire! Fear rifled through him—the guys were probably still up there.

He stuck his head in the staircase and started yelling. "Hey! Get out of there! The place is on fire!"

People on the street were gathering, pointing, and yelling at the fire. He heard a weird siren approaching in the distance.

Luke knew that anyone inside might not survive by the time help arrived. He thought of Jimmy laying in his arms. He took in a deep breath and raced up the stairs. When he opened the hallway door, a hot cloud of smoke blew over his head. He could see the flicker of flames down the hallway, near the room he had been in. Crawling on the floor as fast as he could, he yelled into one room and then another. No response.

The intensifying smoke choked him. Coughing, he called into the next room just as bright flames flared from a sofa by the window. Eyes burning, he caught a glimpse of two people on the bed, one of whom had on Army boots. Struggling to breathe, Luke crawled to the window, hung his head out, and gulped in some air. He yelled down to the street for help, then grabbed the soldier, and shook him. He was next to a naked woman.

Luke took hold of the soldier's legs and dragged him off the bed into the hallway where the smoke was a little less intense. For a split-second, he thought about leaving the girl behind, but couldn't. He had to try and help her. Back in the room, he lifted her scrawny body over his shoulder and crawled back into the hallway as flames erupted along the ceiling overhead. His lungs on fire, feeling like he might pass out, Luke grabbed one of the soldier's ankles with one hand and pulled himself along the floor with the other. Balancing the woman on his back, he struggled down the short hallway.

As Luke made it to the stairway, a stream of water from a firehose shot over him. As someone came up to help him, he laid the woman on the stairs. He struggled to lift the soldier, then carried him down the stairs. Luke collapsed on the ground. Violently coughing and wheezing, he tried desperately to get in enough oxygen.

From somewhere, a couple of his buddies appeared. They started working on the other soldier, whom Luke feared was dead.

"Oh, my god, it's the lieutenant!" one of them said.

Just then, a rescuer crouched beside Luke, loosened his shirt and put an oxygen mask over his face. "Simms, you're crazy, man! You saved Leary."

A Vietnamese fireman started yelling, frantically motioning for the crowd to get back. The rescuer helped Luke to his feet and they moved with the others away from the burning building, just before the wooden structure collapsed onto the street, hot embers scattering all around them.

CHAPTER THIRTY-SIX

LUKE WAS ONLY ABLE TO OPEN ONE EYE, REVEALING THE vague image of a dark-haired nurse in a white uniform. His stomach felt like it was full of sour lemon juice, his back and arms hurt like he'd been beat up. It was hard to get in a good breath. He managed to push himself up on one elbow. "Where am I?"

"Saigon," the woman replied, as she checked bandages on his hands. "US 3rd Field Hospital."

"Shit—the fire. Did Lt. Leary make it?"

"Yes, he's in intensive care, about to be transferred to a burn hospital in England." The nurse encouraged him to lay back. "They say you're the guy that saved him."

"Really?"

"Yes, a nasty fire over a bar. Bad neighborhood down there."

"I'll say."

"And you also saved one of the workers."

"That woman—" Luke said, his memory clearing.

"Yes, she's only 17. Her family came by. They are very grateful."

"She shouldn't be in that place."

The nurse didn't respond, just adjusted Luke's IV and carefully covered him with a sheet.

"When can I get out of here?"

"When your doctor says so. Captain Hogan will be making rounds later this afternoon. He's concerned about the amount of smoke you inhaled."

Luke held his head. "My eyes are burning, and I've got a wicked headache."

"Probably from the smoke." She paused. "And other things."

"Yeah. We drank a lot."

"Imagine that," the nurse said, flatly. "Thankfully you were sober enough to get them out or they'd be dead."

"I'm glad."

"Why don't you get some rest, and I'll get you something for your eyes. And by the way, I'm Isabella."

She smilled, then left, pulling the curtain closed behind her.

Luke heard several people moaning in the background, including what sounded like children. With some effort he got up and peered out from behind the curtain. At the end of the room two children lay on a stretcher, their clothes tattered and partially burned. Luke spoke to a man he presumed was an orderly. "What happened to those kids?"

"Napalm. Collateral damage," the man replied matter-of-factly.

Luke frowned. "From us?"

"Yeah. Happens all the time."

When a medic touched one of the kids, he screamed out in pain.

Luke looked away. "It's not right."

"Nothing's right about this war," the orderly said before he disappeared behind another curtain.

Luke shook his head, which made it hurt more. He lay back

on the bed and looked at the cracked cement ceiling. A squeaky fan mounted on the wall oscillated back and forth, the only breath of relief from the oppressive heat. He was relieved that Lt. Leary was alive, but otherwise, felt as low as he ever had.

Soon Isabella came back in and applied eyedrops that cooled the pain. "Where are you from, soldier?"

"Vermont. Up near Canada. God's country."

She wiped the moisture streaking down his cheek. "Anywhere is god's country compared to here."

"Yeah." Luke blinked a few times. "And you? Where're you from?"

"Erie, Pennsylvania." She put the drops back in a white metal cabinet on the wall. "You got a girl back home?"

"Sure do."

"You real sweet on her?"

"Yeah."

"Lucky her."

"Haven't heard from her in quite a while."

"Mail's a mess over here."

"I guess." Luke looked at her. Isabella was tall and beautiful, with searching blue eyes. But it didn't matter.

Isabella checked the dressings on Luke's burns then gently squeezed his foot. "I'm going off shift, now. Good luck to you."

Luke was disappointed. "Thanks. You've been very kind."

Isabella smiled at him. "I like real gentlemen." She started to part the curtain. "By the way, what's your girl's name?"

"Sarah."

"Well, Sarah's a lucky girl. If things don't work out with you two, look me up after the war."

"But I don't even know your name."

"Not too many Isabellas over here." She smiled and disappeared behind the curtain.

Tantalizing as she was, Luke knew he'd never see her again. At least she'd made him feel some better.

Luke must have fallen asleep. The next thing he knew, a chaplain was standing at the foot of his bed, a rosary hanging from his hand. Luke managed to open both eyes and squint at the padre. "Did I die or something?"

The chaplain shook his head.

"Did Lt. Leary make it?"

"Yes. He'll hopefully recover." The chaplain stepped closer to the bed. "I'm Father Melville. How are you feeling?"

"Okay. I've had better days."

"You performed God's work in that fire."

Luke just nodded.

Fr. Melville touched Luke's arm. "I do have some sad news for you, though."

Luke's pulse quickened. "Something happen to Sarah?"

"Don't know anything about a Sarah, but I'm sorry to tell you your mother has passed on. She's with the Lord now."

It took a few seconds to sink in, even if it had only been a matter of time.

"I don't know many details. The chaplaincy service said she passed peacefully at home with a couple of her church friends with her."

The wave of sadness that hit was too much to bear at the moment. "She'd been sick for a long time. Problems from a farm injury when she was a girl."

"So sorry," Fr. Melville said.

"She was tough, a real good woman."

"I'm sure she was."

"I'm grateful she went peacefully."

"Yes. The Lord is merciful." Fr. Melville reached for Luke's hand. "Would you like me to pray the rosary with you?"

Luke slid his hand under the sheet. "No, thanks, that's okay. I'm not really into that religious stuff. No offense."

"None taken, my son." He stepped back. "I wasn't told of any plans for a service, that sort of thing. Do you have siblings, or other family?"

Luke shook his head. "No, just me, the last of the Simms."

"You would be able to go back stateside if there is a funeral."

Luke nodded. "I don't think there'd be hardly anyone to attend." Luke pulled the sheet up over him. "I'm good right here for now."

"Alright." Fr. Melville put on his black hat. "Feel free to let me know if you need anything. That's why I'm here."

"I will. Thanks for coming by."

He opened the curtains.

"Father—"

"Yes."

"Could you have my nurse, Isabella, come back in?"

"I would but she just left. She was here filling in, and has gone back to her regular unit."

Luke's heart sank lower. "Oh..."

"Take good care, my son."

The curtain swung closed behind the chaplain. All Luke could hear was silence. He closed his eyes and saw his mother struggling to serve him his last meal the day he left home. He could still smell the warm buttermilk pancakes lathered with butter and maple syrup. He saw her tending her garden, and thought about her amazing strength and determination, felt this hole inside that she had always filled. Though Luke had tears in his eyes, he mostly just felt numb. With Sarah gone, and now his mother, the world as he had known it had changed forever. He was alone in the middle of an awful war.

Physically and emotionally exhausted, Luke fell asleep, and soon began dreaming of life back home in Vermont: the sweet smell of fresh pine logs at the mill, jam sessions at the Bullpout, and watching sunsets over the placid waters of Caspian. He dreamt about a conversation with Mr. Hensley, the fall of his senior year. They were sitting on a bench outside the school discussing *Bury My Heart at Wounded Knee*, as brilliant red and yellow maple leaves fell gently to the ground around them. Mr. Hensley explained why it was so important to "teach the truth." In his dream, Luke told him about the Vietnamese who'd been burned in a napalm attack, and the thousands of villagers killed or driven from their homes by the intense fighting.

Luke sat in his filthy Army uniform, hanging his head, not sure what to say.

Mr. Hensley leaned down and looked Luke in the eye. "What can *you* do about it? What is in your power?"

Uncomfortable, Luke stood and paced around in front of the bench, wanting all the ugliness to all go away, to shrug it off, like a constricting snake's skin.

Mr. Hensley looked at Luke with his wise, encouraging expression.

"I could...teach the truth," Luke said.

"Yes, that's it. When you come back, you can teach the truth, just like those who were at Wounded Knee, Little Big Horn, or at Iwo Jima."

Luke watched his own face brighten. "You're right," he said to Mr. Hensley. "I could teach what war is *really* like."

Then Mr. Hensley was gone. Luke was alone, standing by the bench, looking at his school.

Someone put their hand on his arm.

Luke slowly opened his eyes and saw an older nurse next to his bed. "You were talking in your sleep. About teaching or something. Are you alright?"

Remembering pieces of his dream, Luke nodded. "Yes. I think I'll be okay now."

CHAPTER THIRTY-SEVEN

AFTER LOSING JIMMY AND HIS MOM, LUKE PRETTY MUCH gave up on ever hearing from Sarah again. His heart hardening against the world, he lived the next year in a blur of battles, blood, and deepening discouragement. The only heartening thing he could do was focus on trying to protect his fellow soldiers. When a comrade was killed, it was devastating, until the next one, and the next. Many in his platoon drank and drugged themselves into oblivion every chance they got, but Luke knew, for him, that would just make things worse. He wanted to keep his mind intact as best he could, and took some solace in keeping a journal of things he hoped to eventually teach others, like being truly grateful for each new day we have.

By December of 1971, Luke was war-weary, and when again no Christmas card arrived from Sarah, the last hope drained from his soul. He wrote her one last letter. In it, he told her he couldn't understand why she had just abandoned him after what they'd shared.

Offered a chance to go to Da Nang for one of Bob Hope's legendary Christmas shows, he passed, feeling too depressed to go. With no one to go home to, he decided to re-up for another tour. He knew the dangers but the constant chaos of war was a routine he'd become used to. It helped keep his mind off his aching heart.

Luke managed to keep most of his wits about him and advanced through the lower ranks to quartermaster sergeant, largely on his strong work ethic and organizational skills he learned working for Trace. That rank got him off the front lines into a support unit outside Saigon.

By the spring of 1973, the US was rapidly withdrawing its forces, and most of Luke's company had either gone home or been reassigned. The only soldiers left were support staff like Luke, who were busy packing up and closing their facilities.

One sweltering afternoon, Luke was outside his Quonset hut burning a pile of folders when the phone rang. Expecting it to be command telling him of his departure plans, he ran inside and snatched up the receiver. It was Joe, a friend who was the quartermaster of another unit. "Hey, Woodchuck, got a surprise for you."

Luke pulled a rag from his pocket and wiped the sweat dripping from his face. "I can only imagine."

"No, seriously. I finished with my unit's work, so headquarters assigned me to sort through a shitload of lost mail collecting in a warehouse outside Saigon."

"And?" Joe had Luke's interest.

"Hang on." Joe yelled to someone else.

Luke waited impatiently, buried hope racing to the surface.

"So," Joe continued, "there was a sack of mail for your unit. Mostly the usual Army stuff and USO care packages, but there was also a bundle of letters that hadn't been delivered. Wrong unit address or something. Some of them looked like they'd been through a grinder."

"And?" Luke's heart surged with anticipation.

There was a pause. "Nothing for you."

"You sonofabitch!" Luke spit into the wastebasket. "You think that's funny?"

He was about to slam the receiver down when Joe yelled, "No, Luke, I'm just fucking with you!"

Steaming, Luke waited.

"I found your letters—a whole bunch of them."

Luke's breath caught before he was able to speak. "Who're they from?"

"Well, some of them smell pretty nice, even after being in a mailbag."

"Give me the names."

"Looks like a Miss. Haverford."

"A lady from my mom's church. Who else? Sarah Clements?"

"Yup, most of them, and a few, I guess, from your mom."

"How many—from Sarah?"

He muttered as he counted. "Couple dozen, at least."

Stunned, Luke fell back into a chair. "You must be kidding me."

"Scout's honor."

Luke couldn't believe it. "Shit, Joe, that's great. You're amazing!"

"I thought I was a sonofabitch."

Luke broke into a genuine smile for the first time in ages. "An amazing sonofabitch."

"I gotta' bring some materials over there in a few days. I can drop them off."

"Bullshit on that. You're only an hour away. I know a jeep that's itching for a drive."

"Can you sneak out of there?"

"Yeah, there are some 'very important materials' here I know have to get returned to you—pronto. Plus, the major's over in Bien Hoa till tomorrow, so nobody'll care." Luke looked out the window at the burning drum. "Let me put this fire out, and I'll be over."

"You're crazy burning on a scorcher like today."

"Major's orders, wants these files destroyed."

"Alright. Catch you this afternoon. Let's get a couple beers and you can read your letters to me. I mean the ones I haven't already read."

"Asshole."

"See you then."

"Hey, Joe."

"Yeah?"

"This means a lot."

"Thank god I won't have to listen to you whine about the postal service anymore."

"Never again!" Luke held the receiver for a few moments, before he set it back on its cradle. He shook his head. "I can't believe it."

He wanted to get his hands on those letters more than anything—except Sarah herself. He quickly smothered the fire, then got Frank, one of his men, to cover for him, and jumped in a Jeep. With a gallon of water on the seat next to him, he took off.

An hour later, just as he reached Joe's unit, he got a call on his radio. He pulled up and answered it. Frank was nerved up. The major was coming back earlier than expected. He'd be there in a few hours.

Luke told Frank he'd somehow make it back in time, and hung up.

Joe came out and greeted Luke. "Good to see you," he said, shaking Luke's hand. "You got here fast."

"Yeah, and now I've gotta' leave fast 'cause the major is already on his way back."

"Don't you hate it when the brass change plans?"

Joe led Luke inside and motioned to a metal desk. "They're in the bottom drawer."

Luke opened the drawer like he expected to find a cache of gold. He smiled as he lifted the bundle of letters and held them to his nose.

"Sweet, huh?" Joe said.

"You have no idea."

"You're right, I don't. You're a lucky guy, Luke."

"I hope so," he replied, heading to the door. "Thanks again. We'll catch those beers another time."

"Yeah, hopefully stateside."

Luke secured the letters in an ammo can, and tore off in his Jeep. Racing over the bumpy road back to his camp, all he could think about was what Sarah had written. His heart feeling full, he couldn't wait to read the letters, but the rest of the files had to be burned before the major returned. As soon as he arrived, he stashed the ammo can under his bed and got back to work. Both drums had flames leaping into the air when the major arrived.

"Sergeant Simms," he called over, climbing out of his Jeep.

"Yes, sir."

"I've received your orders. You're going home."

"That's great news, sir. Can't wait."

"Forty-eight hours and this place is history."

"What?" Luke motioned to the stockyard of trucks, Jeeps,

artillery, and helicopters still parked at the camp. "How are they going to move all this equipment in 48 hours?"

The major shook his head. "They're not. Only the Hueys are going to fly out, with us on them. They're leaving the rest behind."

Luke frowned. "But it's worth a ton of money."

"Get back to work, Sergeant. Forty-seven hours and 59 minutes left."

"And the papers you wanted saved?"

The major thought for a moment. "Burn all of them except the brown file box on my desk chair. That's personal, goes with me."

"You got it, sir." He gave him half a salute and headed into the hut.

With 20 more boxes to burn, Luke got another man to help him set up a couple more empty oil drums and fill them with files. With a good soaking of kerosene, they lit up like a jet engine pointing skyward. The heat from the fires seared the men's chests and foreheads as they fed handful after handful of files into the drums. No one seemed to care how hot it was. They were going home.

It was long after dark by the time Luke put the last of the files on the fires. When they had burned down, he washed his face with cold water and hit his bunk. He reached under his bed and pulled a letter from the ammo can. Exhausted, with his eyes burning, he could barely keep them open as he started to read. Hours later, he awakened at sunrise still holding the letter.

"Up and at 'em, men!" the major called from the door. "Logistics needs help pulling the radios and antennas from all these vehicles so the 'Cong can't ever get them."

Luke sat up on the side of his cot and rubbed his stiff neck. His watch said 6:08.

"Get some grub. They'll show you what to do."

Luke stretched his aching arms, his back sore from driving on a lousy road so fast the day before. Determined to read Sarah's letter, he took it to the latrine, locked the door, and stared at the personalized embossed stationary.

My Dear Luke,

I guess this will be the last time I write as you have not written again since your very confusing letter accusing me of abandoning you. Nothing could be further from the truth. I cherished every one of your letters and always wrote you back. I have hung onto hope of being together again, but clearly that isn't something you share.

Luke's eyes were wide. "Oh, my god, Sarah, I can't believe..." He kept reading.

Everyone tells me war changes people, and I can sort of understand that, but to be honest, I didn't think it would change you, at least not this much. We shared something so special I thought it would always be there, though I can understand if you've found comfort with someone else during these years apart.

"No, Sarah!" Luke's heart pounded. "I never heard from you. I gave up because I thought you had."

Anyway, I graduated from college last year and have been living back in Washington. I got an interesting job with the State Department, so I've put off going to graduate school. I just wanted you to know I am okay and will always care about you. Walter Cronkite said on the news last night that the US will be withdrawing most of its troops over the next year, so I hope you make it back to beautiful Vermont safe and sound.

I will always hold the memories of our special summer close to my heart.

Fondly,
Sarah

Luke stared at the signature, a torrent of emotions surging through him. How could the fucking military postal service ruin his life, steal the most beautiful thing he'd ever had, and what could have been.

"Simms, let's get moving!" the major yelled from outside.

"I'm coming!" Feeling half-paralyzed, he shook his head in disbelief. Luke was completely overcome by Sarah's words and the love she had held for him. He couldn't look at the letter anymore.

He finished in the latrine then stuffed the letter back in the ammo can under his bunk. Not the least bit hungry, he walked straight to a row of trucks and got instructions on how to strip out perfectly good radios, switches, and other gear. Throwing them into trash cans seemed weird but actually felt good. Somehow a fitting end to the war.

It was noon and stiflingly hot by the time the major came by. "Hey, Simms, you alright?" he asked, a tinge of concern in his voice.

Luke stopped what he was doing. "I think so, sir."

"You look like you've been shot and left for the jackals. Get out of the sun and have lunch."

"Alright. It is pretty hot."

Luke walked to the mess and gulped a couple glasses of cool

water. After eating half a sandwich, he got back to work with the other men, but Sarah was all he could think about. By the time they were done, Luke was spent. Too tired to eat, he crashed on his cot. Too upset to read any more of Sarah's letters, he soon started to fall asleep. Then it hit him. He sat straight up in bed. He had to find her!

CHAPTER THIRTY-EIGHT

L UKE JUMPED OFF HIS COT AND CHECKED THE CLOCK ON HIS desk which read just past eleven. He picked up the phone and rang Larry Miller, a friend in communications over at HQ. If an officer needed to speak to anyone, anywhere, Larry was the guy who could connect them. It was a long shot that he'd answer at that late hour, but Luke let it ring a dozen times anyway. He was about to hang up when a sleepy voice came on the line. "What-d-ya' want?"

"Larry, it's Luke, over at the 51st."

"Yeah? So what?"

"I need your help."

"'Course you do. Why else would you wake a hibernating bear?"

"I promise I'll owe you one."

"Yup, you will."

"I need to get in touch with a federal judge in Washington."

"What'd you do now?"

"Nothing like that. I need to talk to him to find his daughter."

"Huh?"

"Look, never mind. It's complicated, but real important."

"Finding a judge—federal type—will cost you. What's your cigarette situation, quartermaster?"

"Shit, Larry, most everything's been shipped out of here."

"What'd you say your cig situation is?"

"Alright, I'll find them. Luckies and Winstons, right?"

"Case of each."

"I'll try."

"You better. We don't want to leave this hellhole on bad terms now, do we?"

"Okay. Okay."

"So, what's his name? It's getting late. I'm falling asleep *again*."

"Clements, John Clements, Circuit Court, I think. He's a bigwig."

"Hang on." Luke heard Larry fumbling through his big, carefully-guarded phone books. "Not in that one." A book hit the desk. Larry mumbled to himself as he searched. "Let's see... Federal courts, DC jurisdiction..."

"Did you find it?" Luke asked, excitedly.

"Keep it in your pants, I'm looking."

Luke waited.

"Yup," Larry said, with an air of satisfaction. "Don't get many calls for a federal judge."

"You got it?"

"Right here."

"So, what's his number?"

"Goinna' cost you."

"I'm already getting you cigarettes."

"I have to add on an after-hours service charge."

"What is it?" Luke said, frustrated.

"Box of White Owl cigars—Invincibles."

"Alright! For god's sake, what's his number?"

"Do you want me to ring it for you, sir?"

"Jumpin' Jesus, just give it to me!"

Luke got the number and rang off. He figured out what time it was in Washington and decided to wait another hour and try the judge when he should be at work. Way too wound up to sleep, Luke pulled another couple of letters from the can and read them carefully. He just couldn't believe she had been hanging in there with him for months.

He looked at the addresses on several envelopes. They had the wrong unit number, the one he'd been in for just a week or so before his first transfer. The envelopes were stamped with "Addressee not found," and "Return to sender," but clearly were never returned. Luke shook his head. "No wonder she thought I abandoned her."

Luke went outside, leaned against the bumper of a Jeep, and looked around the barren place he had lived in for the last year. It seemed strange for it not to be full of activity. It was still hot, having cooled down to 90 degrees overnight, and at least there was less heat radiating from the pavement. He was happy they were headed home. How he missed the lush green hills of Vermont. The only pieces of green in camp were an artificial palm someone had nailed to the side of a maintenance shed and a ratty piece of discarded carpet a couple guys used for putting practice.

By midnight, Luke couldn't wait any longer. It took a couple of tries before he got on a long-distance line and dialed the judge's office number. After several rings, a serious-sounding woman answered. Luke cleared his throat. "Is the judge in?"

"Who might be calling?"

"Luke, Luke Simms."

"Mr. Simms, I don't see where you have a telephone appointment with the judge."

Luke became nervous. "No, ma'am, I don't, but I know the judge. We're friends, sort of."

"Your name isn't familiar to me, sir."

"I'm from Vermont, where Judge Clements summers. I know him from there."

"Then this is a personal call?"

"Yes, ma'am. I'd appreciate it if you let me speak to him."

"I'm afraid the judge is very busy in his chambers. He has a tight schedule."

"It's very important—"

"You can leave a message I will give to his Honor."

"No, please, it's very important I talk to him."

"I heard you, sir. Now would you like to leave—"

"It's about his daughter, Sarah."

"Is she in trouble?" the woman asked, concern taking over her voice.

"Not really, but there's been a huge misunderstanding. It's serious."

The woman raised her voice. "Is Sarah in any danger?"

"Not physically. But please, I have to talk to him."

There was a pause on the other end. "This is highly irregular, but I will see if the judge might have a few moments to speak to you. If this is a crank call, the authorities will have their way with you."

"I promise you this is very real."

Luke was put on hold, during which an Army recruiting tape played, of all things. It seemed an eternity before the line clicked and the judge came on. "Yes."

"Judge Clements, it's Luke, from Greensboro."

"What's this about Sarah being in trouble? I just spoke to her last evening."

"She's not in trouble, sir, it's just that I need to speak to her. We've been writing these last few years, but her letters got held up in 'Nam. I never got them till today. She doesn't know I didn't receive them."

"I see." There was a pause. "That's too bad, Luke, but I think Sarah moved on from your relationship after you stopped writing."

"She told you?"

"Yes, you know we're very close."

"But, sir, it was all a mistake, her letters had the wrong address. Right after I got over here, I was trans—"

"Luke," the judge interrupted. "I'm sorry about this, but there's nothing I can do."

"Yes, there is. You can give me her phone number so I can explain."

"Sarah is working very hard here in Washington. She has a good, new life, I don't—"

"*Please*," Luke pleaded. "I just need to talk to her once. If she doesn't want to talk to me, I'll never bother her again. I promise." Luke choked up. "You know how much I love her."

There was silence, then Judge Clements cleared his throat. "If I give her your message, is there somewhere she can call you back?"

"Not at the moment. I'll be in transit back to the states. I'm leaving Saigon tomorrow, I hope."

Silence.

"I feel like I'm dying not being able to explain this to her. It's worse than the damn war."

"Luke, you can't mean that."

Luke worked at composing himself. "I mean it, sir."

There was a lengthy exhale on the judge's end. "Alright, but I take no responsibility for anything that happens. And don't you hurt her."

"I won't."

He gave Luke Sarah's number. "Now, I have to get back to my chambers. Goodbye, Luke. And thank you for serving your country."

"That will be all, then," the stern lady said, in a friendlier voice than before. Apparently, she had been listening.

"Thank you so much, ma'am."

"You're welcome. By the way, I remember Sarah talking about you after that summer they were building the cabin."

"Really?" Luke felt a bit hopeful.

"Yes." The woman's voice dropped to a whisper. "It's not my place to say, but I'd never seen her so smitten."

"Wow, thanks for telling me."

"My pleasure," she said. "Good day, Mr. Simms."

The line went dead.

CHAPTER THIRTY-NINE

L UKE STARED AT THE PHONE, POWERFUL EMOTIONS RUSHING through him. He'd gone from giving up on Sarah because he was sure she'd given up on him to reading letters in which she professed her love for him. Then she said goodbye because she thought he'd stopped writing. And most likely found somebody else!

With the rest of the troop clearing out in the morning, he didn't know when he'd have access to a long-distance line again. He paced around the desk before he went back to the phone. He had to call.

Luke pulled the worn photo of Sarah from his wallet and propped it against the clock on the desk. He took in a deep breath, tried to relax, and dialed the number. After a few clicks, it started ringing, but it sounded distant and scratchy. He didn't want it to be a bad connection, so he hung up. "Shit. That was stupid."

He quickly dialed the number again. This time, it connected, the sound was clearer. It rang five or six times before an unfamiliar girl answered. "Is Sarah there?" Luke said, his hand shaking.

"Hang on—" The woman set the receiver down. In a few seconds, she came back on. "Who's calling?"

"Luke," he said in a weak voice.

"*The* Luke?"

"Yes."

"He says it's Luke," the girl called out, putting the phone down again.

Someone gasped in the background. Soon the receiver was lifted. "Hello?"

"Oh, my god, Sarah, it's you."

There were a few moments of silence.

"Luke...Luke Simms, is that you?"

At the sound of Sarah's voice, Luke was overwhelmed with love for her. "I...have..." It was hard getting his words out.

"Luke, are you okay? Have you been injured?"

"No, nothing like that. I just got all your letters," Luke blurted out.

"What do you mean?"

"They were lost in military mail. It sounds crazy—"

"You didn't get *any* of my letters? I wrote you a ton."

"I know. I didn't get them, just one way back in boot camp. I've been so upset you forgot about me."

"Oh, my god."

"You got mine, though, right?"

"Yes, but you stopped writing. I didn't know what happened."

"I never heard from you. I gave up."

"But I... This is crazy!" There was a silence on Sarah's end of the line. "I can't believe this, Luke. It's been three years. I've checked so many times to see if you'd been killed. And when I heard you'd re-enlisted, I thought you didn't—" She took in a breath. "So much has happened."

"Sarah, hearing your voice is the best thing that's happened to me in three years. I've missed you so much."

"I missed you, too."

"I'm coming home, leaving 'Nam tomorrow. I can't wait to see you."

"Oh, Luke, this is so much to absorb all at once. It's like you've come back from the dead."

Feeling hesitation in Sarah's voice, Luke paused. "Do you still go to the cabin?"

"Yes, in fact I'm going there for vacation next week."

"Well, I should be home by Friday. Probably on the train."

Sarah chuckled. "I doubt that. The train to the Bend stopped running a year ago."

"Really? Well, then they'll probably send me on a bus."

There was an awkward silence.

"Luke, I'm really sorry, but I have to go back to work. My team is on a tight deadline, and our supervisor is all over us."

"Oh..."

"Look, what if I find out when you'll arrive and meet you at the bus stop?"

Luke smiled. "That would be great."

"Unless you have someone else picking you up."

"There's no one else."

"I'm sorry about your mom."

"Thanks. It sounded like she was in really tough shape at the end. A blessing in disguise, I guess."

"That's exactly what she would say." Sarah paused. "She was a good woman."

"Thanks. She was."

"Alright, then."

"I love you, Sarah."

"I love you, too, Luke. I'll see you soon," she said, with less emotion than he'd hoped to hear.

Slowly, Luke hung up the phone. He looked out the dirty window at an empty Army truck rolling by, dust and sand swirling behind it. It was so powerful hearing Sarah's voice, but even after all that time, he detected something fundamentally different.

"What do you expect after three years?" he said, standing. He slid the photo back into his wallet.

He was startled by the door swinging open. The major stuck his head in. "Simms, it's late, and we're hauling out of here 0630 tomorrow. Be ready."

"Yes, sir. Almost packed."

"Good." The door closed behind him.

* * *

Two days later, heading home from the empty base didn't hold quite the enthusiasm it had. After 48 hours of shitty travel, it was ten at night when the long flight from London finally landed at Andrews Air Force Base. He and the other soldiers filed off the plane like a string of zombies, and hauled their packs and duffle bags across the tarmac to a group of waiting busses.

Luke stepped through a cloud of blue diesel smoke and climbed onto a Greyhound. He settled into a tired seat and pulled his baseball cap over his eyes. He must have fallen asleep because the next thing he knew, the driver was announcing their arrival at Port Authority in New York. Luke stretched his back, slung the strap of his bag over his shoulder, and climbed off. He figured it would be easy to find his bus to Vermont, but the place was a gigantic maze of gates, tunnels, and ramps that all looked the same to him. After 45 minutes of trying to find his bus, during which his uniform got the evil eye from some anti-war protesters, he was so tired he finally dropped his bag on a bench, sat down, and let his pack fall against the tile wall.

Soon, a lady in a USO shirt came over and sat next to him. "You look like a lost soul," she said in a friendly voice.

"I feel like it. This place is nuts."

"Craziest station in the country. Where are you going?"

"Northern Vermont. Supposed to be catching a Vermont Transit bus about now."

"Well," she said, "we'd better hurry. You're where all the trains are, busses are on another whole level." She gave Luke a pull up off the bench, grabbed his duffle bag, and they headed up a ramp.

"Let me carry that," Luke said, straining to keep up with her.

"Nonsense, you've carried it a plenty."

Ten minutes later, she'd led him to a bus gate. She set his pack on the ground. "Now you get home and get some much-needed rest. Vermont is a beautiful state."

"Sure is." Luke hesitated.

"Go on, now," the lady said, motioning to the bus door.

"I can't thank you enough."

The woman smiled. "Your service is plenty thanks."

Luke stepped to the doorway and turned back to her. "My mom believed in angels, but I didn't till now."

The lady blew him a kiss. He waved and climbed up into the bus.

As the rattly old bus made its way up through Connecticut, Massachusetts, and finally into Vermont, passengers filed off at the many small-town stops. Only a few people were left onboard after the stop for gas and coffee in White River Junction. As they continued north on the interstate, the bus driver invited Luke to sit up front with him. He had an anchor tattoo on his arm and a navy-blue USS Iowa cap on his head. Around the brim, the ship's moto was stitched: "Our Liberties We Prize, Our Rights We Will Maintain." He extended his hand. "Charlie McDougal, US Navy, retired."

Luke moved up front and shook his hand. "Glad to meet you. Name's Luke, 51st Infantry."

He sat in a seat kitty-corner to the driver.

"Just getting back?"

"Yeah. Three years in 'Nam."

"Whoa. You must have re-uped."

"I did."

Charlie glanced at Luke's uniform. "Quartermaster sergeant. Better than the front lines."

"You can say that again."

"Where're you heading?"

"Greensboro."

"Beautiful country up there around Caspian. About the greenest spot on God's earth."

Luke nodded. "Yes. It'll seem like heaven compared to 'Nam."

The driver smiled. "Love that sweeping view driving up over the hill from Hardwick."

"You know the area well."

"Used to go to my uncle's camp on the lake. Even remember some movie star that used to sunbathe skinny on the rocks. We'd all sneak around trying to get a view, but she was too smart for us."

Luke laughed. "I heard about her, but wasn't sure it happened."

Charlie glanced at him. "You can take my word for it."

"Cool."

As they followed along the eastern foothills of the Green

Mountains, many miles passed before they spoke again. "You boys should get the same welcome home we got after World War II. All these anti-war protesters with their demonstrations and flag-burnings get me in a rage. The wife won't even let me watch Cronkite if he's got 'em on. Ingrates. Oughtt'a be illegal."

Luke stared out the window as the bus's yellow lights raced along the shoulder of the road. "I'm not sure what I think about what's going on. It was different back then. You guys fought a war to save the world from the Nazis. Not sure what all we were doing."

Charlie frowned at Luke. "Your *duty*, that's what. Doing what your country asked you to do."

Yeah, right, Luke thought.

The bus made it down the long winding hill past South Royalton and up through Bethel before they spoke again.

"Anyway," Charlie said, "not right you fellas' don't have a good homecoming waiting for you."

Luke scoffed. "All I care about is seeing my girl."

"Ah, I remember I couldn't wait to see Margaret, wondered if she'd still be there for me."

Luke nodded. "Same here."

Charlie shifted into a higher gear. "Thing that surprised me was she'd changed, just like I had. I don't know why I thought things would be just the same. Folks on the home front went through a whole lot, too. We worked it out, been married 26 years this October. As she likes to say, 'things are working out *so far.*'" He chuckled.

Charlie glanced over at Luke. "Don't worry, your girl will be there for you."

"I hope..."

As they climbed toward Barre, the sun rose over the White Mountains to the east, illuminating the hills with a bright rose-colored wash. After stops in the capital of Montpelier, and then Waterbury, they headed further north to the ski town of Stowe, arriving just after eight. Luke combed his hair in the reflection of his window and tried to straighten his wrinkled uniform.

"You look plenty good," Charlie said, glancing at Luke in his rearview mirror.

"Thanks." As they made their way into town past the Green Mountain Inn, Luke searched the sidewalks for Sarah. When the bus pulled up to the bus stop, he was crestfallen there was only one old couple sitting on a wooden bench, a dog on a leash next to them. He gathered his bag as he continued to look out the windows. No Sarah.

Charlie shook his hand. "Good luck to you, son."

"Thanks," Luke said, feeling disappointed. "I'd say you're a pretty darn good welcoming committee."

CHAPTER FORTY

ONELY AND DEJECTED, LUKE STEPPED OFF THE BUS. He was turning toward Shaw's General Store, when he saw her. Sarah stood beneath the limb of a maple with the morning light shining through her blond hair. His heart swelled.

When she saw him, a smile broke across her face and his fears melted away. She ran toward him. Luke dropped his duffle bag on the sidewalk, swept her up in his arms, and twirled her around. When he let her land back on earth, they stared at each other, and kissed for just a few seconds before Sarah pulled back.

"My god, is it good to see you," Luke said, looking her over. "You look great, though you cut some of your beautiful hair."

Sarah took hold of the ends of her shoulder-length locks. "For work. It's the city style."

Luke led her to a park bench. "How are you? I mean, I read your letters, but there's a whole year or more since."

"I'm well, Luke, working for the EPA."

"That's great. And that you still come up here."

"I love it up here. The cabin is beautiful. I don't think you ever saw it finished."

"No, I had to ship out."

"You look pretty sharp in that uniform, and I see you're a sergeant. Congrats."

"Just a quartermaster."

"Still a sergeant." Sarah stood. "Come on, let's head to Greensboro. It's going to be a beautiful day." She walked toward her car, which was parked across the street in front of Lackey's Drug Store.

Luke felt a distinct distance coming from Sarah as they talked—awkwardly—in the same red Mustang on the way to Greensboro. She slowed as they approached the house, where his pickup sat along the side, rusting in a tangle of blackberry bushes.

When Sarah pulled up in front of the house, they both just stared. The lawn was overgrown with tall weeds and bushes. Screens were torn on the front porch, and the steps he'd repaired had separated from the house. An upstairs window over the porch was broken, its tattered curtain blown out and caught on a nail. Shiny shards of glass were scattered among curling shingles and pieces of crumbled brick dislodged from the chimney above.

"Did you know what the house would look like?" Sarah asked in a kind voice.

"Not really. I think Trace tried to take care of it after Mom died, but gave up. I heard the bank's taking it back. Sad, but they'll probably demolish it." Luke shook his head. "I'll have to get my things out of there."

Sarah looked at him sympathetically. "Do you really want to stay here? It looks sort of grim."

"It's home, or it used to be." Luke stared at the lifeless house. "I guess I can go to Jed's place."

Sarah touched his arm. "You could stay with me at the cabin for a couple of days, until you get your feet under you."

Luke looked at her. "That'd be alright?"

Sarah nodded, a loving but conflicted look on her face.

"Yes, of course." She withdrew her hand. "It'll give us a chance to talk."

"Okay. This place is sort of depressing."

Sarah started the Mustang, and they drove to the lake in silence.

Inside the cabin, Luke was amazed by the sweeping cathedral ceiling finished in smooth pine boards. A deer antler chandelier hung in the middle of the great room and a long couch covered with Hudson Bay blankets faced the lake. "Wow, this place is beautiful. Hard to believe it started with those rough-hewn post and beams I delivered."

Sarah opened the refrigerator and took out a couple of beers. "It's great, though it doesn't get as much use as it should."

She motioned to the couch and sat a few feet away from Luke. She handed him a beer and they tapped the longnecks together. After a couple of swallows, Luke leaned toward her, but Sarah tried to avoid eye contact. Soon, they ended up staring at each other, and Luke felt the stiffness between them melting. They slid closer on the couch.

"My god, you're beautiful," Luke said, touching her cheek.

"You've been in the Army too long."

Luke shook his head.

Sarah blushed and looked at the floor. Luke gently lifted her chin and she looked into his eyes again. She touched the scars on his forehead and cheek.

"Just some little shrapnel wounds."

Sarah looked concerned. "What happened?"

The memory of Jimmy dying in his arms reared up, but Luke pushed it back down. "Tough day—one of many."

"I'm sorry."

"It was hell over there. But now I'm here with you." He leaned in to kiss her, but Sarah turned away. "I can't…"

He waited, sliding his hand onto her thigh.

"Oh, Luke…" She paused then leaned forward.

Her lips met his and their breathing quickened. They kissed deeply then relaxed and looked at each other.

Luke smiled. "Wow, have I ever missed that."

Sarah nodded. "Me, too. Nobody's ever kissed me like you do. Makes me crazy."

"Good."

Luke wrapped his arms around her, and they kissed again, her hands on his abdomen. "I am so in love with you, Sarah," he said after catching his breath. "I want to—"

"Wait—" Sarah put her fingertips to his mouth.

"I've *been* waiting—way too long."

Sarah seemed to gasp for air as she gently held him away from her.

Luke frowned. "What's the matter?" He searched her face. "Are you alright?"

It took Sarah a few seconds to get control of herself. She laid both palms on his chest. "I love you, too, Luke, have from the moment I met you. But I was so hurt when I stopped hearing from you. You didn't call or anything. I thought you'd forgotten about me."

"But I've told you what happened, and we were on the move all the time. It was crazy."

"I'm sure it was, but I was still devastated. I've never felt so lonely."

Luke felt like he was floundering. "I tried to call you at college but your phone was disconnected."

"We changed apartments several times."

Luke slid his hand over hers. "But we're together now."

Tears formed in Sarah's eyes. She took in a deep breath. "There's something I have to tell you."

Anticipating the worst, Luke's heart sank. Sarah looked at him, her face full of yearning, sadness, and love. "Luke, this is so hard..." She looked away for a few moments, then back at him. "I wasn't looking, but I met someone else after I graduated from college, and we clicked. He fell in love with me fast. It was a little overwhelming because I was still in love with you. He asked me to marry him, and I said 'no' many times. Until you stopped writing." She looked at the floor. "He's not you, but Richard's a decent guy. I finally said 'yes.'"

The sound of the guy's name shot through Luke's chest. "Jesus Christ, Sarah!"

"Luke, I thought you were gone forever." She started crying. "What was I supposed to do?"

"Have faith. Wait for me. I never gave up on you."

"Yes, you did. You stopped writing."

Luke shook his head. "But I told you why."

There was a long silence before Sarah spoke again. "I think the world of you, Luke. You're the coolest, most authentic guy I've ever met, but—"

Luke dropped back against the cushions, putting more space between them. The last of his energy left him.

"Marrying Richard is the right thing to do. I'm sorry to spring this on you, but I didn't have the heart to tell you when you were at war."

"But this is so much harder. My heart full of expectations and all."

Sarah looked Luke in the eye. "Loving you forever is a fact of *my* heart that I will not deny. I had to tell you this in person. To tell the truth, I figured you'd moved on."

Luke looked at her incredulously. *"Moved on?* You were all I could think about over there. Night and day. I crouched in shitty foxholes with bullets and mortars going off all around me, brothers dying, scared shitless I would die any second. The only thing that kept me going was my love for you."

Sarah's face seemed to break into a thousand pieces.

Luke struggled to unbutton the pocket of his shirt. He pulled out the tattered photo of them and dropped it on the blanket. *"That's* how much I thought about you."

Sarah gently lifted the photo and cradled it in her palm. She bent forward, tears dropping on the picture. "I'm sor…" Her voice caught. She tried to wipe the tears away but only smeared the photo.

"I'm sorry, too, but I guess it doesn't matter now."

Sarah fell into him. Fighting back his own tears, Luke took her in his arms and held her for a long time.

When they finally sat back, Sarah wiped her swollen face with her hands. "Seeing you, holding you, I feel so confused. None of this makes sense."

"I know." Luke said, sympathetically. He stood. "Look, I'm going back to the house, see if I can wrap my head around all this."

Sarah got up. "Luke, I truly never meant to hurt you like this. I'm so sorry."

"Me, too." He put on his pack, shouldered his duffle bag, and walked to the door. "I came home to propose to you, and you tell me you're getting married." He shook his head. "The whole thing is so screwed up. It's worse than the damn war." Luke opened the door, the cool scent of cedar wafting into the cabin.

"Wait, I'll give you ride."

He shook his head. "I need to walk." He paused in the doorway. "I'm sorry you were in pain, too. I just know this can't be the end of us."

He let the door close behind him.

.

CHAPTER FORTY-ONE

W ALKING HOME, THE FIRST LICKS OF FALL WERE IN THE air as clouds gathered over the lake from the southwest. When Luke reached Jed's place, he thought of stopping, but he was in no shape to talk to anyone, even Jed. He noticed Taffy wasn't in the yard and saw that only one orchid plant remained in a rusty Quaker State oilcan on the windowsill.

Trudging down the road with his heavy gear felt familiar. Just one more march, but at least this time it was back home in Vermont. He hiked cross-lots through town, avoiding anyone who might be outside Willey's Store. An hour later, he climbed over the broken stairs onto his own porch. The smell of oil drum fires from the trailer park next door reminded him of his last days in 'Nam, and, strangely, gave him some comfort.

Luke couldn't help but notice a yellow posting stapled to the clapboards beside the door, "REPOSESSED" printed in large letters across the top. He looked in the window as if he was checking to see if his mother was up. Pushing the door open, he stepped into the silent house. The air was stale, a mixture of mustiness from roof leaks, dried urine, and the faint hint of cigarettes. His mother must have started smoking again before she died. Why not?

From the kitchen doorway, he could see his mother's favorite coffee mug sitting on the edge of the otherwise bare linoleum-covered table. As he walked toward the sink, he was startled by an equally surprised mouse that raced across the counter and disappeared into a small hole in the wall beside the wooden breadbox. He dropped his duffle bag and slid off his pack. Time for some grub.

With the electricity shut off long ago, he thought he'd warm a can of beans on the gas stove, but it wouldn't light. He turned the burner up all the way and sniffed. Nothing. He wasn't sure he was hungry enough for cold beans.

Luke pulled a clean T-shirt from his bag and wet it with cold water that ran slowly from the tap. He scrubbed his face and ears and neck. Thank goodness their water was gravity fed from the shallow spring up back in the pasture.

Luke couldn't bear to see his mother's bedroom, so he walked past its closed door down the hall to his. The bed was made, and his few dusty sports trophies stood on the bureau right where he'd left them. At the window, he looked out through the cracked pane at the overgrown yard where his mother had grown vegetables for so many years.

Feeling like the world had collapsed around him, Luke sat on his bed. It sagged worse than his Army cot. He felt something under the blanket, and pulled out an envelope. His name was on it in his mother's writing. The card had a bluebird gripping a branch on the front. Inside, in shaky but determined writing, was written: *"You were the best son any mother could ask for. You brought me so much joy. I know you will be alright. My love is with you always. Mom."* Her handwriting trailed off at the end, witness to her failing strength.

Luke laid back against a musty pillow, hugged the letter against his chest, and stared at the mildewed ceiling. Crushed by a loneliness heavier than he'd ever felt, he closed his eyes. "You will be alright," he whispered. *You will be alright.*

CHAPTER FORTY-TWO

URING THE NIGHT, THE YAHOOS NEXT DOOR IN THE trailer park set off a couple strings of firecrackers, which startled Luke so badly that he hit the floor, searching for his gun. Images of firefights raced through his head: hundreds of red tracer bullets zipping through the dark.

After he realized he was home, he caught his breath, got up, and stood in the window watching the guys next door. They were still the same numbskulls he'd grown up next to. He particularly didn't like Savage, the oldest brother, who drove around with a Confederate flag flying off the back of his pickup. Didn't he have a clue what the Civil War, or any war, was like? The carnage? The indescribable loss? Luke stared at the yellow flames licking the rim of their oil drum. The answer was, "no," he didn't have a clue. And it wasn't because he was stupid, or just a thoughtless asshole. It was because no one had taught him the truth about war. Or at the least, he hadn't paid attention.

Luke thought back to that long ago conversation with Mr. Hensley, and to the quote that had rung true for him in the *Tao*:

> *"Do you have the patience to wait till your mud settles and the water is clear? Can you remain unmoving until the right action arises by itself?"*

337

Standing in his bedroom window, after all the loss and carnage he'd experienced, Luke wondered if his water would ever clear. He lay back down, and with a weak flashlight, read his mother's letter again, closed his eyes, and fell back to sleep.

The next morning Luke awoke weighted with a deep loneliness. It was especially painful knowing Sarah was at the cabin just across town. As badly as he wanted to see her, he mustered enough dignity—for him and for her—to stay away. Fate had dealt them a tough hand, and he knew when they had kissed that she was suffering, too.

Though exhausted and drained, Luke made himself get up. He blew dust off his favorite baseball then rolled it in his hand as he walked slowly around the farmhouse. Despite its deteriorating condition, he felt a familiar comfort exploring the only place he'd ever called home. On the way back to the kitchen, he passed his mother's bedroom door without opening it; he still wasn't ready to see the place she took her last breath while he was half a world away.

The kitchen was a mess so he began half-heartedly cleaning things up. It was difficult without electricity or hot water, and he soon gave up, hitched into town on a milk truck, and stopped at the tiny electric company office. Mrs. Haywood, his retired third grade teacher, was delighted to see that Luke had made it home safely. He explained the situation with the house, and she said she'd be happy to turn his power back on. As long as he kept current with his bill going forward, she'd write off whatever arrears were left when his mother died. Luke thanked her then crossed the green, avoiding the spot where he and Sarah had taken their photo at the summer festival. His heart felt like it weighed a thousand pounds, but the soldier in him kept moving.

Circumventing a couple of hippie protesters in front of the post office, Luke walked up the granite steps into the Craftsbury Bank and Trust.

Mr. Sherman, who'd been president of the bank for what seemed like 100 years, was, as always, in his small, glassed-in office off the lobby. When he saw Luke, he pushed himself up from his desk. "Luke Simms, so good to see you. Welcome, back." Mr. Sherman patted Luke on the forearm. "That Vietnam must have been something else."

"Sure was." Luke shook his bony hand. "Good to be home."

"Please ignore those filthy hippies from Earth Peoples Park out there demonstrating. You courageous soldiers deserve better." Mr. Sherman motioned to a wooden captain's chair. "Please, have a seat."

Sitting across the oak desk from Luke, Mr. Sherman leaned forward on his elbows. "I assume you're here about the house."

"Yes, the sign on the front door says it's been repossessed."

"Well," Mr. Sherman said, sounding apologetic, "that was a formality we had to go through with for the underwriters. I would have had the sign taken down if I'd known you were coming home. The bank hasn't done anything with the place, hoping you'd come back and be interested in it. Skinny, who's on the bank board, was pretty sure you'd return and want to fix it up."

"That's awful nice of you. I do have some money saved up from the Army, but not a whole lot."

Mr. Sherman waved his hand. "Not to worry." He lowered his voice. "Let's say we float you a loan, and we'll hold the interest for six months so you can get your feet under you and make some repairs. Then you can get on a regular payment plan."

Luke nodded and managed a smile. "Thanks, Mr.

Sherman." They shook hands. "Are there papers I need to sign?"

"Just a few, but not to worry, we'll get that done soon enough. Your word is better than any fancy document." He walked Luke to the front door. "I'm glad you stopped by. Pleasure to see you."

Luke gently shook his hand again. "You know, Mr. Sherman, it's because of people like you that I wanted to come back."

Mr. Sherman looked pleased. "Why, thank you. That means a lot. We need young fellows like you keeping their roots here. Now you have a good day."

As Luke descended the granite steps, Mr. Sherman called to him from the door. "One other thing, Luke." He came down to the sidewalk. "I didn't know if you were aware that Mr. Martin, from the funeral parlor, has your mother's ashes."

"Oh, thank you." Luke felt a wave of sadness.

Mr. Sherman spoke in a low voice. "As you know, Mary was a very private individual. She didn't want a service or anything."

"Sounds like her. I'll have to decide what to do with her ashes."

"Certainly. I'm sure you'll do something fitting."

"Thanks again, Mr. Sherman."

By the time Luke got home, an electric company lineman was already up on the pole in front of the house, and Jed was waiting in the driveway in his decrepit pickup. Luke noticed how much he had aged and that Taffy wasn't on the seat next to him. "Hey, there."

"Good to see ya'." Jed looked Luke over, pausing for a second at his forehead. "Not too bad. Just a few scratches."

"That's right."

"Glad you made it back in one piece." Jed watched Luke's face for a few moments then touched his chest with his crooked fingers. "Just take care of the inside, my friend. We old warhorses know all too well it's the wounds that don't show that heal the hardest."

Luke was touched by Jed's empathy. "I hear you, Jed."

Jed looked him in the eye. "And you add romance problems to it...well, it can about do us in."

Luke nodded, cleared his throat. "How are you?"

"Gettin' along. I miss old Taffy awful, but it was time. His legs were bad, lotta' pain. Doc offered to put him down but I couldn't do it. Selfish, I guess. Maybe the car hitting him was meant to be."

"Sorry, I didn't know."

"Last fall, when the leaves were just passing peak. Some downcountry peepers gawking at that maple hillside 'cross from the house."

"Did they stop at least?"

"Yup, felt bad. Not your usual flatlander assholes. Even offered to pay me."

"Really?"

"Can you imagine figurin' a price for old dilapidated Taffy?"

"Ah, he was priceless. I'll miss him, too." Luke looked at Jed. "And how are you, otherwise?"

"Like I said, getting' along. Arthritis set in my back pretty bad, and my heart started skippin' a lotta' beats last year. They stuck one of them pacemakers in my chest." He motioned to his shirt. "Sticks out like a sore thumb, but who cares? I'm no spring chicken."

"Well, I want you to take care of yourself."

Jed smiled. "You're a good fella', Luke. Always thinking of others." Jed patted his arm. "You going to stay around, fix up the old place? Could use a few licks of paint."

"Could use a lot more 'n that."

"Good. See you Sat'd night. Usual time. Hope Skinny don't burn the cornbread."

Luke was surprised. "He's been burning his cornbread?"

"Yup. Twice. Think his eyes are goin'."

"Too bad, but everybody's getting older."

"Not to worry, he still plays the ivories just as well." Jed caught Luke's gaze. "So, you'll be there?"

Luke looked at the ground. "I'll try. Not sure I want to see everybody yet. Kind of feel like shit."

"To be expected."

A noisy Chevy Nova with Filly behind the wheel and its bumper duct-taped to the fender, pulled up behind Jed. Hearing it, Jed pushed his creaky door open and climbed out. He motioned toward Luke's pickup out back in the brambles. "She's not looking so good."

"Nope."

Jed nodded at his pickup. "Truck's yours 'till you get some wheels that roll." He limped over to the rusty Nova, elbowed the roof as he lowered himself in. Filly tooted, waved, and drove off, revving the engine, though the car barely crawled.

Luke was glad some things never change.

After they were gone, Luke looked over Jed's nearly hopeless pickup. Taffy's bag of dog biscuits still lay on the floor of the passenger's side. Luke turned and climbed up onto his sagging porch, loneliness again descending over him.

"Power should be back on," the lineman called as he descended the pole. "I'd just check the fuse box to make sure everything's okay."

Luke gave him a lackluster wave and walked inside to smell dust burning from a lone lightbulb in the hallway. In the kitchen, the refrigerator had come to life and was making a familiar whirring noise. Luke looked around and thought about cleaning up but was overwhelmed by the mess. In his bedroom, he pulled the rest of his belongings from his pack, including the batch of Sarah's letters. Unable to look at them, he tucked them away in the bottom drawer of his bureau, and laid down for a nap.

The next few weeks were a solemn blur. Mostly staying in the house, Luke felt he was living in slow-motion. Barely functioning, he probably wouldn't have eaten much of anything if his mother's church friends hadn't brought over homemade dishes, including a spicy Shepard's pie, hot cross buns, cheddar mac and cheese, and a bean and hotdog casserole. The small amounts he ate tasted good, but he had hardly any appetite, so some of it went to waste. Spending a lot of time sitting quietly at the kitchen table, he got a little enjoyment from watching mice scavenge scraps from dirty plates he'd left on the counter.

Though he thought about it, Luke didn't show up at the Bullpout on Saturday nights, and he figured that's why Jed and Filly had driven slowly by the house a couple times. Luke had stayed hidden inside still overwhelmed at losing Sarah. He didn't want to talk to anyone.

When the weather was nice, Luke would sometimes venture outside and check on his abandoned pickup, its cab snarled with long blackberry canes. Behind the house, he'd lean against the cedar posts holding up the old chicken wire fence, and survey the grown-over remnants of his mother's once-bountiful gardens. Sitting for hours on an old tree stump, Luke would look over the pasture that sloped sharply up to the hardwoods that crowned the ridge. He watched a red fox and her grown litter hunting near a fallen stone wall that bordered the east side of the field. Luke knew the mature pups would soon be off on their own, leaving their mother alone.

It was strange to be living in a sort of suspended animation, but it didn't matter much. The two beautiful women in his life were gone, he'd left the strange comfort of the military behind, and his boyhood home was threatening to collapse around him. Maybe that was how it all ended.

One morning Luke was awakened early by a noise but couldn't identify it. His shoulder was sore, so he got up and rubbed liniment on it. Standing on the cold floor in the bathroom, he took a leak in the stained toilet then caught sight of himself in the cabinet mirror. Beneath a scraggly beard, his face had become so thin his cheekbones protruded. "Jesus..." he said, turning away.

He heard the noise again—a dog yipping, but not the usual growling mongrels from the trailer park. He walked into the kitchen and listened. Something was scratching on the front door. Opening it, he saw a cute golden retriever puppy looking up at him with expectant eyes.

"Where did you come from?" Luke pushed the screen door open and the puppy immediately came to him. Luke patted his head and soft ears as he looked around outside. No one was there. "What are you doing out here alone?"

The dog wagged its tail and pranced around inside the house.

"Come back here," Luke said as the dog took off toward the kitchen. "All I need is you shitting up the place."

Luke caught up with the puppy by the refrigerator. He sat and stared at Luke.

"I suppose you're hungry. Well, you've come to the wrong place. I don't have any dog food."

The dog cocked its head at Luke and let out a pitiful whine.

Luke tried to stare him down but the dog won. "Alright. You want some Shepard's pie?" He pulled the pan from the fridge. "It's not exactly fresh, but you *are* a dog."

As soon as Luke put the plate on the floor, the puppy started eating.

"Guess you were hungry. Eat up, but you're not staying."

Luke put on his clothes and went outside to see if anyone was around that might have seen where the dog came from. The only person up was Savage, who looked hungover as he relieved himself off his trailer's stoop. He said he didn't know anything about the dog.

The puppy took to Luke right away, following him everywhere he went. He curled up on his bed at night, which Luke found both annoying and comforting. While the dog distracted Luke, he still couldn't shake the pall that had descended over him. After a few days, Luke tired of calling him "Dog," so he named the affectionate little fellow Jimmy. It seemed fitting. It also reminded Luke to keep the solemn promise he'd made to Jimmy as he was dying. Before he did anything else, he sat at the kitchen table and wrote Jimmy's girlfriend, Lorraine, a letter. He told her how much Jimmy cared about her, and that he professed his love for her with his dying breath.

One afternoon, Luke sat daydreaming in the cab of his marooned pickup. Jimmy was beside him on the seat, looking like he expected to go somewhere. Luke heard a car pull into the driveway and turned to see Jed climb out of Filly's Nova. Thankfully, he was alone. Luke ducked down in the cab as Jed limped up onto the porch and rapped on the screen door. With no answer, he descended the rickety stairs and looked around the yard. Just then, Jimmy let out a couple of sharp yaps, which drew Jed's attention. Walking over to the truck, Jed peered inside, as Luke, embarrassed, sat back up in the seat.

"Takin' the old girl for a spin?" Jed asked.

"No. Just thinking."

Jed leaned against the passenger door. "Suspect you've been doing a lot of that lately." Jimmy stood on his hind legs and licked Jed's fingers. "Where'd you get this little fella'?"

"He just showed up the other morning."

"You don't say. He good company?"

"I guess," Luke replied flatly.

Jed pulled a corncob pipe from his shirt pocket, pushed a pinch of tobacco into the bowl with the head of a nail, and lit it. Soon, a couple of perfect smoke rings floated past Luke's windshield. "After Mabel died," Jed said, cupping his pipe in his palm, "I don't think I talked to another soul for a couple months or more. Almost let her orchids die, but she would've been cross with me if I had."

Luke pretended to not be paying attention, but he was listening carefully.

"I've grudgingly accepted that losing people and animals, and even parts of our bodies, seems to be the natural order of things. Don't like it, but it's a fact. And though it seems natural at the time, isolating for too long t'isn't good for us. Feeds on itself, till we really do end up all alone."

There was a long silence, during which Jimmy curled up on the seat.

"I just can't make sense of it all," Luke said, staring out the windshield. "It's like my whole life has disappeared."

Jed looked in the window again. "Well, not your *whole* life. They's plenty of good folks who care about you. And I know you care about them."

Luke shook his head. "I don't know…"

"It's your choice, Luke. As my mother used to say, 'When life runs you hard, you can get bitter, or you can get better. It's our choice.'" Jed gave Jimmy a pat on the head then got his cane under him. "Hope you get better."

Jed limped back to the Nova and drove off.

CHAPTER FORTY-THREE

L UKE SAT IN THE TRUCK FOR A LONG TIME, LETTING JED'S words set in. Appreciating the fatherly advice, Luke felt something shift inside. He committed to himself to get his life back on track, regardless of what he might feel like. And he thought about the passage from the *Tao*. Maybe his mud was finally settling.

A noise came from next door. He looked over. Savage was starting another fire in their oil drum, a gas can in one hand, a beer in the other. Feeling bad for him, Luke experienced a spark of energy for the first time since he'd left Sarah at the cabin. Guys like Savage needed someone to enlighten them about the world beyond the trailer park. It was suddenly clear to Luke—he'd go back to school and become a teacher.

Luke let Jimmy out of the truck, then stood in the driveway looking at the house. His mother wouldn't have wanted him to let the place go to ruin. He had to find the motivation to fix it up, though the magnitude of the project was overwhelming. But before he did anything else, he decided to drive to Morrisville and check out the new Community College of Vermont, where he'd heard you could earn a teaching degree on the GI Bill. He wasn't sure Jed's truck would make the eighteen-mile trip, but with a quart of Motor Honey to smooth the cylinders and Jimmy riding shotgun, it did.

The lady in the small CCV office was very encouraging and helped Luke enroll in a veterans' benefits program that would pay for most of his courses. He was psyched he was able to sign up for both education and American Literature courses that started a week later. "In two years, you could be a part-time teacher," the lady said with a big smile. "The schools are looking for subs. And think of how valuable your own experience will be for your students."

"That's what I'm hoping for," Luke said and wished her a good day.

Back home, Luke ate the leftover hotdog casserole and shaved his gnarly beard. Feeling newfound energy, he left Jimmy in the house and drove to the mill. Trace seemed glad to see him. He told Luke he needed a new manager and he could start that afternoon. Luke hesitated, but figured it would be good to jump right back in. Besides, he could use the money. He also told Trace he'd be going to college part-time, to which Trace just nodded.

Working back at the old mill seemed to lift Luke's spirits, but he refused to make deliveries anywhere near the Clements' cabin. In addition to his academic books, he read Whitman's poetic *Leaves of Grass* for the literature course. He thought it was terrific. When he could, he did work on the house, but it was hard to make any substantial progress. He did, however, buy a colored TV and mounted an antenna on a solid part of the roof that brought in three good channels. He made many trips to Gilson's Feed and Supply, buying gutters, window glass, clapboards, roof patch, as well as primer and paint. He brought home lumber and a new metal pipe so he could repair the porch and front steps, and replace the broken railing.

One Sunday morning, Luke was having coffee in the kitchen with Jimmy, looking out at the imposing pile of building materials on the front lawn, most of which he hadn't touched. He ruffled Jimmy's ears. "What do you think, should I just let the bank have the place and find my own trailer somewhere?"

Jimmy looked at Luke curiously and whined.

It was a nice day, so Luke decided he'd at least put up the new railing by the front steps and replace a few rotting porch boards. Outside, the autumn air was cool and crisp, a perfect day for working. While the maples on the surrounding hillsides had lost most of their vibrant reds, they still held a golden hue that was quite beautiful.

Luke started by replacing the cracked board on the top step, then pulled off the old railing with a crowbar. He was struggling to hold the new pipe while screwing it in, when someone drove up the road, tooting their horn. Figuring it was a friend of the yahoos next door, he ignored them. But then three vehicles pulled into his driveway, led by Jed and Filly in her Nova. Skinny pulled in beside her, and he and Lester got out, both in carpenter overalls. Dexter, Betty, and even Ritchie Morrill, the excavator, climbed out of another pickup, the bed of which was loaded with tools and a few more guys.

Surprised, Luke dropped the railing and stood up. Snapping to attention on the porch, Jimmy let out a couple of excited barks. "What the—" Luke said, as Jed pulled a toolbelt from the car.

"You look like you could use a little help," Jed said, "and we happened to be in the neighborhood."

Luke was totally blown away by the small platoon of carpenters. "You folks don't need to spend your Sunday working on this old house."

Betty walked straight up to Luke. "Oh, yes, we do, and you've got nothing to say about it."

Luke laughed.

Skinny walked over with a skill saw in his hand. "We're here to help, Luke. Just tell us what to do."

Luke gestured. "Well, just rebuild the whole house, I guess."

They all laughed, causing Jimmy to bark.

Jed pointed to the partially repaired porch. "I'll get to work on that. You younger folks can tend to the roof and chimney."

Luke went over the projects needing the most urgent attention. Ritchie helped him bring a couple of ladders around from the back, and everyone set to work. Luke was amazed at all the work they got done. By noontime, the two broken windows upstairs had new glass, about half the bad shingles and clapboards had been replaced, someone was mortaring new bricks into the chimney, and the front porch was well on its way to being rebuilt.

Jed sat down on the edge of the new porch floor and gave Jimmy a pat. They both looked tired after a busy morning. "'Bout time we had something to eat, don't you think?" he said to the dog.

Luke came over, looking a bit sheepish. "Geez, I don't have much food in the house, but I'll run over to Willey's and get some cold cuts."

"No need," Jed said, lifting his bushy eyebrows toward the road.

A station wagon pulled in behind the other vehicles. Two of his mother's church ladies, as well as Mrs. Haywood from the electric company, got out and opened the back. They set up a couple of card tables and filled them with sandwiches, containers of potato and macaroni salads, and a huge bowl of potato chips.

"You've got to be kidding me," Luke said, walking over to the ladies. "How did you even know?"

"Word gets around," Mrs. Haywood said. She lowered her voice. "And we all know what loss feels like. Can't imagine it after coming home from a war."

Luke was touched by her kindness. "Well, it's awful nice of you."

She smiled at him. "Wait till you see dessert."

"Dessert?"

"Oh, boy," Skinny said as he headed for the food.

Everyone piled their paper plates high with the fixings then sat around the yard eating and chatting. Luke noticed Savage and his brothers were eyeing the food, but they kept their distance.

As people finished their lunch, Luke climbed up on the tailgate of Skinny's pickup. "Hey, everybody, I just want to thank you from the bottom of my heart. I never dreamed of something like this." He paused as a wave of emotion hit him. He looked at his friends. "I've really missed you guys."

"Same here," Skinny said.

"It's been tough settling in after the war, and losing Mom, and…"

Everyone stayed silent as his voice caught.

"I just want you to know how much this means to me. To have the whole Bullpout gang over here working…it's a little overwhelming."

Jed chuckled. "You ain't seen nothing yet." He lifted his cane and pointed toward a shiny gold Lincoln Continental coming up the road. From under its enormous hood, a showtune played from a speaker in its grill.

Luke squinted against the sunlight. "What in the hell…"

The Lincoln pulled up in front of the house and a white tuxedo-clad Maxwell Holmes waved from the driver's window. The trunk popped open and an assistant appeared from the backseat, who pulled a three-tiered cake from the trunk. "Welcome Home" was written in icing along the side. He carefully set it on one of the lunch tables as Maxwell emerged triumphantly from the car. With his usual flare, he pulled a gold lighter from his jacket pocket and lit a fuse on the top of the cake. In a few seconds, flaming balls shot straight into the sky, their sharp reports causing Jimmy to race around the lawn, barking. This time, Luke didn't flinch; he just smiled at the amazing spectacle.

Maxwell doffed his tall, white chef's hat, pulled a silver serving knife from an inner pocket, and waved it through the air. "Dessert, anyone?"

Luke stood there, shaking his head in disbelief. He looked over at Jed, who grinned and nodded in his knowing way. Luke was finally home.

CHAPTER FORTY-FOUR

AS THE DARKER DAYS OF NOVEMBER ARRIVED, LUKE began to feel somewhat better, but was still awakened by recurring nightmares from the war. Either he was jumping into the foxhole with Jimmy, or taking heavy ground fire and about to crash in a Huey. It helped to get up and read, and take notes on his experiences, until he could go back to sleep. Though the nightmares exhausted him, over time they became less frequent and the terror associated with them lessened.

By the time deer season came along, the cold weather bothered the shoulder Luke had injured in the boat crash many years before. Since much of the work at the mill was outside, he thought an indoor job would be better. Harold, the owner of Gilson's, was looking for a new manager, and he said he'd be happy to hire Luke. Not wanting to leave Trace in a lurch, Luke gave him a month's notice, and moved on after New Year's.

Luke loved working in the store with Jimmy at his side. Gilson's had an old-fashioned potbelly stove, beside which was a big brass kettle that one of the boys always kept full of firewood. There was a very busy popcorn maker, and a pickle barrel with a checkerboard mounted on it. Luke had always enjoyed the smell of the grain bins and the fresh bread Mrs. Haywood brought in to sell three mornings a week. He got a kick out of kids that came in with their parents to buy penny candy out of the collection of jars along the front counter. He usually looked the other way if they slid a complimentary piece into their mouths.

When the store was quiet, Luke sat by the stove and read *Huckleberry Finn* or a textbook on educational methods his professor had assigned. Though the writing assignments were difficult, he worked hard and was proud to bring home a B+ on his first paper. After three years of living in a war zone, it was great being in the store interacting with normal people. He also enjoyed delivering bags of horse feed, grain, dewormer, or gardening supplies to older customers on his way home. Life back in Greensboro was good, and peaceful. Over time, the recurring horrors of Vietnam began to fade, unlike his need to tell the truth about the war, which only grew.

When Luke returned to the Bullpout, he noticed a new whitetail buck mount on the wall by the piano. A nice eight-pointer hung over a framed photograph of the now-famous fiddle contest. The stage in the barn was filled with celebrating musicians, and in the middle stood Sarah and Luke, one arm around each other, the other thrust into the air in celebration. What a night that was! And how long ago it now seemed.

Betty often tried to catch Luke's eye during their Saturday night jam sessions, but as nice as she was, spending time with her only reinforced that Sarah was the only one for him. Rarely a day went by he didn't think of her. He did his best to just accept things the way they were, and to convince himself she never would have been truly happy living a country life.

Though Luke was unable to push Sarah completely from his mind, he knew if he got through the emotional hurdle of Christmas, he would start to feel better. A customer mentioned Sarah's family was at the cabin for the holidays, but Luke kept his distance, knowing even a glance of her would've been more bitter than sweet.

By the time the spring snowmelt had swollen the brooks and rivers of the Northeast Kingdom, Luke was in a much better place. Working through his second semester, he was feeling comfortable at night school, and excited he'd eventually be a substitute teacher. He enjoyed the seasonal uptick in business at the store as both locals and returning summer folks stocked up on flower and vegetable seeds, fertilizer, lime, and fresh cedar mulch.

As the strengthening sun warmed the hillsides, Luke planted a garden out back, blending his mother's ashes into the rich earth she loved to work with her bare hands. When he was done, he said a few words of gratitude for her life then pounded a white wooden cross into the ground at the edge of the garden. When he'd finished planting, he worked to revive a small orchard of apple trees behind the house his dad had planted the year before he died.

The first week of May dawned warm and sunny, and Luke felt the hope that spring always brings. Nixon was getting the last of the US forces out of Southeast Asia, and even though the whole Watergate mess was gaining steam, somehow the world seemed more peaceful than it had in a long time. One Friday evening, Luke finally said good night to the last of his customers and flipped the sign that hung in the store's front window to "Closed."

On the way home, he picked up a barbequed chicken at Willey's and made it to the farmhouse a little after seven. He was about to turn on the *CBS Evening News,* when he noticed a fancy pink envelope sticking out of a Western Auto ad he'd grabbed from the mailbox. His heart quickened, knowing it had to be

357

from Sarah. It was postmarked two weeks before, but it wasn't unusual for mail to take a long time to get to his house. For a split second, he thought of just discarding it, but instead, dropped it on the kitchen table.

Luke took his box of chicken, settled into the new recliner he'd bought from Buck's Furniture, and leaned back. He watched the rest of the news, then tuned in to his favorite show, *All in the Family*. He liked to catch the beginning of the show and always got a kick out of listening to Archie and Edith singing, "Those Were the Days."

Tired from work, by the second commercial break, he was struggling to keep his eyes open. He got up and went to the kitchen to make a cup of coffee. While he waited for the water to boil, Sarah's letter called to him.

As Luke opened the envelope, a subtle essence of Sarah entered the room. He unfolded the embossed paper.

Dear Luke,

I hope this letter finds you well and that you don't mind my getting in touch.

As you may know, I am getting married in a few weeks and will be coming up to the cabin with girlfriends for my bachelorette party over a long weekend on May 18th. I would love to see you while I'm up there. I know this may seem strange, but I still care a lot about you and feel sad at how we left things last summer.

Please let me know if you'd like to get together. If I don't hear from you, I'll certainly understand.

Fondly,

Sarah

When he finished reading, Luke slowly shook his head. "You gotta' to be kidding me." He tossed the letter on the table. "So you can break my heart again?" Crossing his arms tightly, he leaned against the cold porcelain sink. They could have had so much.

He pushed himself off the sink. Was she crazy? She was getting married, for god's sake! He abandoned the idea of coffee, took a cool shower, and went to bed.

Exhausted, Luke soon fell asleep. The vague nightmares of the war thankfully passed into dreams of Sarah that summer: swimming in the clear blue waters of Caspian, kissing her under the stars on his raft surrounded by the sweet smell of cedars leaning over the lake. His shoulder bothering him, he half awakened, rolled over, and squinted at the clock: 1:30 in the morning. He bunched a pillow under his head, hugged another, and fell back to sleep.

Sometime later, he was startled awake by the telephone ringing out in the hall.

"What the...?" Hardly anyone ever called the house. Still half asleep, he got up and answered it. On the other end of the line, Credence was playing in the background. "Hello? Who's this?"

"Luke—Luke! I've got to see you."

Sarah. She was drunk.

His mind took off. It was one of *those* moments, a critical crossroad in his heart. Which road would he take? He held the phone so tightly it was as if he was using it to steady himself.

"Sarah—"

"Yes, Luke, it's me. Did you get my letter?"

"I just got it."

"I sent it a while ago."

"Who'll stop the rain..." Credence sang, with girls chattering in the background.

"I know."

She laughed. "The post office doesn't like us."

"I guess not." He paused. "What do you want, Sarah?"

"You, silly."

"Aren't you at your bachelorette party? Like, before your *wedding.*"

"Yes, but I miss you so much."

Love, and lust, and guilt collided inside him. Even drunk, her voice was intoxicating. "I miss you," he said, without thinking. "But..."

"Then meet me at the old horse barn."

At the mention of their special place, Luke's groin tightened. "I can't."

"Come on. You said you missed me."

Another girl came on the phone. "Come on, Luke! You're all she talks about!"

"Sorry—" Sarah said, taking back the phone. "Please come see me, just for a few minutes."

Luke winced at the ache, the awful longing that had lived in his heart for so long. "Sarah, it's not right. You know how we were together."

"That's why I want to see you. One last time. *Please.*"

"It's not right."

"Please come." Her voice suddenly sounded more serious, not drunk at all. "I have something I want to tell you."

Luke's resolve weakened. He'd been unable to resist her from the moment they met. *Screw it. It's my last chance.* "Alright, but just a quick visit."

"Thank you. I know I'm a little drunk, but I mean it."
"I'll meet you there in half an hour."
"I'll be waiting."

CHAPTER FORTY-FIVE

LUKE DIDN'T REMEMBER HANGING UP THE PHONE. HE STOOD in the hallway frowning and smiling at the same time, not sure what he was doing. Without thinking, he pulled on a pair of jeans and a flannel shirt. In the bathroom, he splashed cold water on his face and ran wet fingers through his hair. For a few moments, he stared at himself in the mirror. He'd waited for this moment through a damn war and what already seemed like a lifetime. He couldn't miss it.

Jimmy followed him to the door, expecting to go somewhere, but Luke shut him in the house and climbed into the new pickup he'd bought through the store. As he sped into town, the moon played hide-and-seek behind patches of gray and white clouds. All was quiet as he rounded the corner at Willey's and headed north. Approaching the horse barn, he felt some trepidation. Was this the right thing to do? But he didn't stop. Parking at the edge of the pasture, he quietly shut the door and listened. Over in the cabin, the music had stopped. He assumed her friends had finally run out of steam and gone to bed.

Luke walked silently up to the barn and stepped inside. A dim light flickered at the top of the stairs. He climbed them to the hayloft, and there, exactly where they had first made love, sat Sarah, on an opened sleeping bag, her face illuminated by a kerosene lantern. She broke into a smile when she saw Luke, and motioned for him to come to her.

"Pretty dangerous to have a kerosene lantern burning up here."

"That's not the only dangerous thing," she said.

They came together, and without saying a word, wrapped their arms tightly around each other.

"Oh, Luke," Sarah whispered, "I have missed you so."

When they relaxed, their lips met, and they shared a long-overdue kiss.

Feeling himself losing control, Luke finally leaned back. "Sarah, you taste so good, but we have to stop. It's not right."

Sarah got up on her knees and looked him in the eye, her breasts full beneath a Georgetown T-shirt. "Nothing could be more right..."

"But you're getting—"

"I know, but it doesn't mean I don't still love you. I can't bear to not have you in my life—somehow. It's a fact my heart cannot deny. That's what I had to tell you."

"But I can't be a second fiddle the rest of my life."

Sarah looked into his eyes. "You and Richard are different fiddles—no one's second."

Luke shook his head, sat back on his heels. "I love you too much to do this, Sarah. You're my soulmate."

Sarah kept staring at him, her eyes deep with love. She put her fingers to his lips. "There's too much to say, Luke. Tonight, let's just *be*." She pulled her T-shirt over her head.

"Jesus, Sarah," he said, an erection bulging in his jeans.

She unbuttoned his shirt, ignoring his meager efforts to stop her. As she pushed it over his shoulders, Luke kissed her, drawing her tongue deep into his mouth. There was nothing in the world beside her and him.

Pulling each other's clothes off, they laid down, sliding their hands and legs over each other's anxious bodies.

"Make love to me," she said, pulling him onto her. He kissed her again, then gently entered her. Thrusting inside of her, Sarah's arms holding him tight against her, her cum cries soon surrounded him as they joyfully climaxed together.

As their sweaty bodies relaxed and their breathing settled, they lay entangled with each other for a long time.

"That was wonderful," she said, her head resting on his chest. "Like the first time."

Luke stroked her hair. "I could stay here with you like this forever."

"Sounds so nice." Sarah cuddled against him, and they lay holding each other. After a while, Sarah lifted herself on one elbow. "Hey, you want to go for a swim? Your raft isn't far from here."

Luke smiled. "Sounds great. You sweated all over me."

"Really?"

"Yeah," he said, pointing to his shiny abdomen.

Sarah leaned over and licked his belly button.

Luke stiffened. "If you do that anymore we won't be going swimming."

Sarah's head popped up and she kissed him. "Come on, lover boy, get your clothes on. You're with a judge's daughter, for heaven's sake."

Luke grabbed her around the waist and tickled her, then they got dressed. He blew out the kerosene lantern, took Sarah's hand, and they ran down to the trail that encircled the lake. They made their way in the waning moonlight to Luke's old raft. Tossing their clothes on the raft, they untied it, pulled it from the underbrush, and pushed it a short way out. They slipped into the cool, silvery water and swam around in a circle before meeting back at the raft. Pulling Sarah up next to him, Luke felt he had been dropped in the middle of an amazing dream.

They paddled back to shore, dried off in the cool air, and got dressed. Sitting on the raft, Luke leaned back against a curving cedar and held Sarah. "So, how can this work?"

"We'll have to find a way to stay connected." She touched her heart. "In here, I mean, even if we can't be together that much."

"My heart will always be connected to you."

"That's good."

Gentle waves rippled under the raft. "Do you love him?"

Sarah nodded. "In ways." She cradled Luke's arm around her waist. "Not like this, but it's enough, most of the time."

"What does he do for you?"

"He gives me that life I like: the beehive of activity in the city, the great restaurants, exciting politics. It's an important part of my reality." She looked up at Luke. "And so are you. A very special part."

"Is he good to you?"

She nodded. "Yes, in his way. He's not the most thoughtful guy, but he's supportive and gives me the space to do my own things."

Luke smiled. "And we know you're just a bit strong-willed."

She held his arm tight against her. "Ya' think?"

"Will you come up here often?"

"That's the plan. For part of every summer, and in the fall to see the leaves, and in the spring to watch all the green return. And probably for Christmas."

"That sounds great." Luke chuckled. "You should just move up and save the commute."

"Can't. Richard is a real city guy. He'll come up off and on for a long weekend, but that's about it. Believe it or not, he misses all the noise of the city, says the 'eerie quiet' makes him nervous."

Luke chuckled. "That's pretty funny."

"Even though I like the buzz of the city, I *love* the peace and quiet here. And I love you." She looked at him. "Speaking of whom, how are you? What are you doing these days?"

"Well, I'm going to community college, part-time to earn my degree."

Sarah's eyes lit up. "That's excellent, Luke."

"Yes, I'm going to be a substitute teacher. I want to share my experiences in the military. Not the bloody war part as much as what I learned about people and aggression, how the world's got to find better ways to deal with each other."

"That's so great. I'm proud of you." She looked at him. "And I heard something really cool about you from my dad."

"What's that?"

"You saved some people's lives in Saigon, from a fire. One of his military buddies told him."

"Yeah, that was a while back. Sketchy situation."

"They should give you a medal."

"No. Anyone would have done it."

"Doubt it. Only my hero."

"You've been drinking."

"Yup, but my mind's clear as a bell." They shared another kiss then Sarah said she had to get back to the cabin before everyone woke up. "Like my girlfriends don't know what's going on," she said, sarcastically. "They couldn't wait for me to see you."

Luke nodded. "To be honest, I couldn't either, though I'd pretty much given up ever seeing you again."

Luke didn't care about how it all looked. He was surprised he didn't feel the least bit guilty. He and Sarah belonged to each other in whatever ways they could figure out. He walked her back to the cabin and waited at the foot of the stairs as she slid inside. As he turned to leave, he saw one of her friends appear from behind a curtain in an upstairs window. A broad smile broke across her face. Luke nodded, walked to his truck, and drove off.

Chapter Forty-Six

THE SWEET ESSENCE OF SARAH LINGERED WITH LUKE FOR days. He found himself staring out the window at work, joyful from the feeling of making love to her, of even just holding her. Though part of him was conflicted, there was a certain peace about having been with her, especially knowing it was probably the last time they would be together like that. He accepted and appreciated that they would always be a part of one another. He was also grateful the usually active rumor mill was silent and no one had said anything about her bachelorette weekend. And with her wedding being held in Washington, he figured he was out of the woods as far as anyone finding out about their tryst.

By the end of the summer, Harold told Luke he was too old and tired to keep working and was going to sell the store. He asked Luke to take it over and offered to help finance it. Though Luke hadn't thought about owning a business, the idea appealed to him. With the help of Mr. Sherman at the bank, by Thanksgiving, the deal was done. After a very busy Black Friday sale, Luke closed up for the first time as the store's proud owner. He went out front and brought in the snow shovels, scrapers, and flying saucers, and pulled a tarp over the bags of salt and sand. He flipped the sign in the front door window then stood looking out at his little town and smiled. There was no question this was where he was supposed to be.

Luke worked long hours building up the business. By the next spring he had hired a couple of part-time helpers and had expanded several of their hardware and gardening lines. Jed helped him install a small machine shop in the back, and Luke even started a tool rental business on the side. The locals strongly supported the changes, appreciating not having to drive to bigger stores in Hardwick or Morrisville so often.

Luke spent most evenings attending to his college studies, enjoying works by great American authors, like Faulkner's *The Sound and the Fury*, Steinbeck's *Cannery Row*, and Jack London's *The Call of the Wild*. He loved being able to step into other peoples' worlds and read about how they dealt with their struggles, which helped him deal with his own. He was less enthralled with the education textbooks, but understood they were important, too.

As an indulgence, even though he was a bit embarrassed about it, Luke bought a copy of *Love Story*, the silly novel Sarah was reading when they first met. He read it before going to sleep at night, and actually felt it wasn't silly at all. Resonating with his own love story, it brought him some comfort.

On Saturday nights, Luke always made it to the Bullpout for a few hours of playing with the crew. He felt a strong déjà vu when they started practicing for the upcoming summer festival. Everyone said there'd never been another contest like the one Sis and Sarah won. And there never would be.

When he could find time, Luke got over to Andy's to work on a classic Chris Craft runabout he bought from one of the summer people. But he was so busy studying and working at the store, and with his shoulder issues, he decided not to enter the Great Race. And besides, he'd seen enough competition and combat in 'Nam to last a lifetime. Predictably, Freddie McCormick had won every year since Luke left for the Army, but that didn't matter.

He and Betty saw each other off and on, but for Luke it was mostly to have someone to do things with. Over the Fourth of July weekend, he left the store in the hands of his young clerks and met her at the festival. After the race, they were sitting on a bench eating candied apples when he was shocked to see Sarah and, he assumed, Richard, appear from the crowd pushing a baby stroller!

Unfazed, Betty stood and said hi, and before Sarah could say anything, introduced herself to Richard. He had a short, preppy haircut, and was wearing a tailored sport coat over a polo shirt. His tan slacks held a pressed pleat which fell just over his shiny brown penny loafers.

Luke sat there speechless, trying not to stare at the baby in its fancy stroller.

"Luke—" Sarah said, "and Betty. How nice to see you both." Her sociable voice sounded sort of fake, like she was a character on a soap opera. Sarah turned to Richard, who gripped the handle of the stroller tightly. He looked quite uncomfortable. "This is my husband, Richard Worthington. We came up for the festival." She motioned to the stroller. "And to show our baby, Jason, what Vermont looks like."

Betty peered into the stroller. "Cute little fellow. How old is he?"

"Almost five months," Sarah said with a twinge of awkward pride. "Our beautiful honeymoon baby."

Luke collected himself enough to set his sticky apple on a napkin and stand. He held his hand out to Richard, who seemed reluctant to shake it. "Nice to meet you, Luke. Sarah speaks highly of you and her time up here."

"It's a beautiful place," Luke replied, "as you can see."

"It's certainly different than what we're used to. Charming, though."

Luke looked at Sarah, who gave him a weakened smile. "Good to see you, Sarah. Hadn't heard you had a baby. Congrats."

"He's wonderful."

Luke nodded, flicked his eyes at Betty, signaling it was time to move on.

"Nice to see you folks," Betty said. "Enjoy the festival." She turned to Luke. "Shall we?"

As Richard started to move away, for a split second, Sarah glanced at Luke. "Good to see you."

Luke nodded. "Yes." Then he caught up with Betty, who was heading toward the tables holding the floral competition. As they walked together, Betty spoke. "That was awkward. Richard looks about as comfy here as a cat on a hot tin roof. Sarah's always nice, though."

"He sure doesn't look like a country boy." Luke took Betty's hand and led her away from the flower arrangements. "Let's take a turn on the Tilt-a-Whirl." After a dizzying ride, they played a couple of games of chance, then said goodbye. Luke went home to try and shake meeting Sarah's family from his system.

* * *

The next few years flew by, the displays at the store changing with the seasons and with the endless cool gadgets people were inventing. Though running the business demanded a huge amount of his time, for the most part Luke enjoyed it. When the only plumber in town developed Parkinson's, Luke even started making minor repair calls to people in need. It was good to keep busy.

Luke completed his associate degree and was called upon as an occasional substitute teacher at the high school. He hoped to someday complete his full degree and have a class of his own, but even the part-time teaching meant a lot to him.

One summer, out of the blue, Luke received notice the Army was going to give him the Soldier's Medal for distinguished heroism, for saving those people from the fire in Saigon. The commander of the local American Legion helped set up the ceremony, which was a bit awkward as Luke had never even set foot inside their post. Though he missed a couple of his comrades in the Army, and meant them no disrespect, he had no interest in hanging out at the Legion or attending military get-togethers. When he left Vietnam, he was done. He did, however, appreciate the recognition for saving Lt. Leary and the Vietnamese girl. He hoped she was in a much better place.

The day of the ceremony, Luke was surprised and delighted that both Sarah and her father were there. Attended by a couple dozen men in uniform, it was a brief affair held on the town green, during which a retired colonel spoke—somewhat inaccurately— of Luke's actions that day. Though, Luke had to admit, having been drunk, and with the passage of time, his own recollections had become rather cloudy.

After the ceremony, Luke exchanged congratulatory pleasantries with the locals, and with the judge, who was clearly proud of him. As the group dispersed, Sarah hung back and told him how cool it was that he was given the well-deserved honor.

Luke took Sarah aside. "Do you have a minute?"

"Of course."

"I want to show you something that's really cool."

Luke took her over to the granite memorial at the head of the green. Sarah read the names in the section for those serving in Vietnam, and lovingly ran her finger along Luke's.

"But that's not the cool part," he said, smiling.

Sarah looked puzzled.

"Look here." With a twinkle in his eye, Luke pointed to the World War II section.

At the bottom of the list of names, Sarah saw that "Elijah Simms" had been freshly engraved. She reached out and touched his name then looked at Luke. "Oh, Luke, that is so cool. He's in his rightful place now."

Luke felt a twinge of emotion. "Yes."

"How did they end up doing it?"

"It was time."

Sarah looked at him. "You had a hand in it."

"Maybe."

"I'll bet you wouldn't receive the medal unless they put his name up there."

"You know me well." Luke grinned. "The Legion couldn't bear to miss out on a local hero's ceremony."

Sarah gave him a hug. "Good for you." She nodded to his father's name. "And for him."

"It was the right thing to do. Despite his failings, he served his country well."

Sarah looked at him with admiration, and kissed him on the cheek. "You're the coolest dude I've ever known."

CHAPTER FORTY-SEVEN

THAT MOMENT IN FRONT OF THE MONUMENT BECAME A bittersweet memory for Luke as it was years before he heard from or saw Sarah again. Occasionally, he would pick up a bit of news from customers talking in the store, but rarely did anyone mention Sarah to him. The townsfolk seemed to appreciate and respect his love for her and the difficulty of the situation. Despite how much he missed her, Luke was committed to not interfering with her family's life.

Over time, Luke made enough money to renovate the rest of the farmhouse. He'd installed a butcher block countertop and replaced the wobbly linoleum-covered table with a refinished antique oak one. He even built a deck off the back with a wood-fired hot tub that he regularly enjoyed after work. Though Luke left his mother's room intact, he eventually gave it a good cleaning, a new coat of paint, and a nice set of linen curtains he ordered through the Sears & Roebuck catalog. She would've liked it.

Luke was aware Sarah continued to visit Greensboro every summer, and she and her family spent most Christmases at the cabin. A couple times, on cold winter nights, Luke had snuck down the road and admired how they'd decorated snow-laden boughs of pine trees with red bows and sparkling white lights. He would watch her family's holiday gathering from the edge of the woods. Once, he saw Sarah stand for a long time in the front windows under the cabin's prow facing the lake. He wondered if she was thinking of him. When she disappeared behind a beautifully decorated Christmas tree, Luke snuck back through the snowy woods to his truck and drove home.

The next summer, Luke was in the lumberyard behind the store assembling a wooden swing set when one of his clerks yelled to him that he had a phone call. "Can I call them back?"

"Said it was urgent. You better take it."

Luke dropped his wrench, dusted off his overalls, and grabbed the phone by the back door. "Can I help you?"

Silence.

"Hello?"

"Luke, it's me, Sarah. I'm sorry to bother you, but I need help at the cabin."

"What kind of help?" he replied, keeping his voice business-like.

"There's a leak from the upstairs bathroom. It's going to flood the kitchen. I'm here with Jason and didn't know who else to call. The plumber's number in the yellow pages is disconnected."

"He's sick, but there's a couple plumbers down in Hardwick."

"I called one. He can't come up until tomorrow afternoon. The place will be ruined by then."

Luke frowned. He hadn't heard from her in years, and a leaky toilet got him a call. Nice as it was to hear her voice, it sounded weaker than he remembered.

"Look, Sarah, get some buckets under the drip and put towels around them. I'll come out soon as I can. I'm in the middle of something at the store so it'll be at least an hour. What's in that bathroom?"

"A sink, stand-in shower, a toilet, and a tub."

"What kind of tub?"

"Like a jet tub. Whirlpool type."

"Those damn things always leak."

"Thank you so much, Luke. I really do appreciate it."

"You're welcome. See you in a bit."

Luke hung up, and for a few moments stared at the wall above the phone where numbers and penciled messages written for decades gave a microhistory of Greensboro. At least he didn't feel as off-balance hearing from her as he had in the past.

He finished putting the swing set together, grabbed a bag of plumbing tools, and headed over. As he drove through town, he was glad to see the Community Church Auxiliary was having their annual pie sale. At the last minute, he pulled over and bought a scrumptious-looking strawberry-rhubarb with a crust so flaky he could've eaten the whole thing on the way to the cabin. But he'd let Sarah and Jason enjoy it.

As he drove down the hill toward the lake, Luke felt good. After all these years, it would be nice to see Sarah and her son, of whom he'd only occasionally caught glimpses when they came into town. When Luke knocked on the door, a handsome boy answered it. His eyes were bright and alive, and he had a friendly smile. "Come in, I'm Jason." He shook Luke's hand, his grip strong and sure for whom Luke guessed was a teenage boy.

"Nice to meet you—again. I mean, you were in a stroller the last time we met."

Jason motioned to his long legs. "I don't think I would fit anymore."

Luke stepped inside and handed Jason the pie."

"That looks awesome. Thank you."

"You're welcome." Luke saw Sarah on the couch in front of the windows that faced the lake. On a side table sat a violin case covered with dust. "Hi Sarah," he said.

She had put on weight, her hair was turning gray, and her color seemed pale. The beautiful blond girl had aged more than he would have expected.

Sarah sat up. "Oh, Luke," she said, looking sleepy. "Thank you for coming. I don't know what we would have done otherwise. I'm not feeling particularly well, and the leak seems to be getting worse. I know it's stupid, but we have hardly any tools."

Jason nudged Luke's elbow. "If we did, I could've fixed it."

Luke smiled. "I bet." He motioned to the stairs. "Let's have a look."

Jason headed upstairs. Before following, Luke turned to Sarah. "Sorry you're not feeling well."

"I'm sure it will pass. Would you like some coffee?"

"Thanks, I'm good."

Upstairs, the bathroom was paneled in beautiful knotty pine, the fancy gold fixtures like nothing Luke sold in the store. Jason showed him a wet spot at the base of the wall near the whirlpool tub. "Looks like it's leaking behind the wall."

Luke took a look. "You're right. We'll have to take some of the wood off to get at the supply lines." Luke made a face. "Your mom won't be happy with us, but it's the only way."

Jason grinned. "Better than the downstairs flooding out. I unscrewed the fuses to the kitchen so nothing would blow up."

"Smart. It would take the fire department a long time to get out here."

Jason helped Luke carefully remove a few boards with a

prybar, then Luke used his new cordless drill to unscrew the pipe attachments.

"That's cool," Jason said, "runs on batteries?"

"Yes. Just got them in. They don't hold a charge very long, but they're real handy."

He passed it to Jason, who gave it a try. "It's a little off-balance, but nice."

"Observant fellow, aren't you? I told the tool rep the same thing. He said they're working on improving the weight distribution."

Jason was smart and polite and a pleasure to be around, not surprising given his mother. They found leaks in two copper elbows inside the wall. "Not enough solder on those joints," Luke said, pointing. "We'll redo them." He pulled a propane torch out of his bag along with a roll of solder and a small container of tinning flux. "You ever soldered?"

"No."

Sarah appeared in the doorway. "I'm sure he'd love to."

Jason's eyes lit up. "Sure would."

Luke looked at Sarah.

She was smiling. "You boys, just don't burn the cabin down. It would take the fire department a long time to get here."

Jason looked up. "That's what Luke just said."

She chuckled. "I've heard him say it a dozen times. Must be the slowest moving fire department in Vermont."

Luke shook his head, looked at Jason. "We've got a good department. Trucks are hard starting, is all. Sit in the station most of the time."

Luke repaired the first elbow, showing Jason how to sweat and resolder the pipe joint. "Now, you give it a try on the other one."

Jason wiped the copper with flux then lit the torch, which whooshed to life. With Luke gently guiding his hand, he heated the golden pipe and watched the end of the solder melt over the joint. Only a few silver drops landed on the beige tile. "Now blow on it to cool it off."

Jason blew hard on the joint then looked at Luke and smiled. "That is so cool."

"Good job, you're a natural. You want to be a plumber?"

"No, sir. I'm going to be a mechanical engineer."

Luke nodded. "Well, good for you. You'll be great at it."

Sarah had lingered in the doorway. "We've always had to buy Jason toys above his age to keep him stimulated. He's had a talent for making things since he was a toddler."

"I can see that." Luke started putting his tools back in his bag. "If you're interested, I could use more help around the store. Gets crazy busy in the summer." He glanced at Sarah. "If it's okay with your mom, of course."

"Isn't he a little young?"

Luke looked at Jason and winked. "What are you, thirteen or fourteen?"

Jason smiled. "Something like that."

"Jason," Sarah said, "you're only twelve."

"Almost thirteen."

Luke stood up and rubbed his shoulder. "Well, you're too young to employ, but we've had kids your age help out back, you know, as an educational experience." He looked at Sarah. "*And I could use him over at Andy's to help me get work done on my boat. I just can't find enough time."

Jason's face lit up. "*Boat?*"

Looking tired, Sarah sat on the toilet seat. "Remember, I

told you Luke won the Great Race the summer he went into the Army."

"That's right. That sounded amazing."

"It was some race. Lucky we all survived with Freddie up to his old shenanigans."

"I would *love* to help you out, as long as you're okay here, Mom."

"I'll be fine. But you would have to be very careful."

"I would be."

"Then we'll do it." Luke turned back to their plumbing repair. "I'd let this set overnight, make sure everything's working and there's no leaks. We'll fix the wall up in a couple days."

"Cool," Jason said, playing with the drill again.

With his tools packed up, Luke followed Jason and Sarah back down to the great room. She seemed unsteady on the stairs. At first Luke was concerned she'd been drinking, but he couldn't smell any alcohol or see any bottles around.

"I'm going to meet a friend to go fishing," Jason said to Luke. "It was really nice meeting you." They shook hands.

"Likewise. I'll let your mom know about a time when you can come work at the store."

"That'd be great, and I'd love to see your boat." He waved and headed out, catching the screen door so it didn't slam behind him.

"Nice kid," Luke said, looking at Sarah, who was back on the couch.

"He's a sweetheart. Going to go places."

Luke stepped closer. "You seem awfully tired. You okay?"

"It's not been a great year. I have some muscular thing going on. Makes me weak and very tired."

Luke sat on an ottoman in front of Sarah. "Have you gotten it looked into?"

"Yes. I saw a neurologist and had a battery of tests at George Washington. They have a pretty good idea of what's going on. It's not good."

"I'm sorry about that."

Sarah looked chilly. Reflexively, Luke pulled a blanket over the bare skin of her legs—beautiful legs that had intertwined with his when they made love. "I hope they can get you some help."

Sarah looked up at Luke with sleepy eyes. "Thanks. Me, too. I don't like being so exhausted all the time."

"Really. I used to barely be able to keep up with you."

As Luke started to get up, Sarah put her hand on his arm. "Do you have to run? I would love for you to stay a while."

Luke relaxed. "I suppose I have a little time before I get back to the store. Don't dare leave it too long."

Sarah pulled her legs up and motioned for him to sit on the couch. Luke hesitated before he got up and slid next to her.

"Will you just hold me?" Tears were forming in her eyes.

"Of course." He slid his arm around her back and she leaned against him. He felt their bodies becoming as one, like in the old days.

"This feels so good," Sarah said, softly. "Like being home after a long, hard trip."

He wrapped both arms around her and held her tightly. Years of emotions came rushing in. "I've tried not to, but I've missed you, Sarah. Like I could hardly breathe sometimes. I've worn out that picture of us."

Sarah raised her head. "You still have it?"

"Of course. Right here." Luke fished his leather wallet from the back pocket of his jeans. He pulled the photo from behind some business cards and gave it to Sarah.

She held it like a priceless treasure. The edges were worn off as was most of the glossy coating, but there they were, cheek to cheek smiling, so obviously in love. She smiled and shook her head. "I can't believe you still have it after all these years. All these miles."

"I'll never part with it."

"That was the best summer of my life. Magical, like you and I were the only two people on the planet." She looked up and kissed Luke, a loving but much weaker kiss than in the past.

"I know exactly what you mean. I don't think I've ever recovered from it."

Sarah chuckled. "That's a good way to put it."

Luke felt Sarah's body tremble for a second. He saw her wince. "Are you alright?"

"I will be, in a minute. I get these intense burning feelings and sometimes get dizzy. Even my vision gets blurry. Weird stuff."

It took Sarah a couple minutes to settle. When she had, she pushed herself up and looked at Luke. "I want to tell you something that I haven't told hardly anyone."

"What is it?"

"The doctors don't know exactly what type, but they're sure it's multiple sclerosis."

Luke frowned.

"It destroys the sheaths around your nerves, which makes them go all haywire. Over time, your body stops working right, sort of shuts down, even your brain and memory. The specialist I saw is concerned I have the type that progresses rapidly. I can already tell my walking is off, and my speech isn't right at times."

Luke held both her hands. "Sarah, I'm so sorry. I had no idea."

"I know. When I come up to the lake, I pretty much stay here in the cabin. When I can, I still love swimming, but it's a challenge. Thank goodness Jason is here. He's such a joy, but I worry I'm becoming too much of a burden."

"What about your husband?"

"My disease makes Richard nervous, or embarrasses him, or something."

"Asshole."

Sarah smiled. "Regardless, he's never liked being in the country."

"Sorry, I shouldn't have said that. It's just…"

"It's okay. No one's ever cared for me like you, Luke."

"What can I do for you now?"

Sarah looked into his eyes. "Spend time with Jason. He loves it up here. He isn't a city boy, and he and his father don't mesh well. I saw the way he lit up working with you upstairs. He's never like that with Richard. And he's always wanted a boat. Unfortunately, my father won't let him drive his, says he's too young."

"Nonsense. I was driving a boat on my father's lap when I could barely turn the wheel." Luke looked out the window. "Where *is* your father's boat? I don't see it on the dock."

"He hasn't gotten it out this year. He's been up here only once, just to open up."

"He used to love it up here."

"I know, but his health isn't the greatest. And to be honest, I think he hates to see me deteriorating and knows I get a lot of comfort being here, so he mostly stays away."

"Geez. How could anyone stay away from you?"

Sarah smiled. "Still the country charmer, aren't you?"

"Anyway," Luke said, "I'd love to spend time with Jason whenever he's up here. I have a little machine shop in the back of the store, and folks bring in parts that need repairing. He might like that. And we'll get him out on my boat for sure."

"That would be wonderful." Sarah softly touched Luke's face. "You're the kindest person I've ever met." She touched her heart. "Luckily, I get to keep you right in here."

"I'm glad. Me, too."

Sarah closed her eyes. "I think I need to rest now. So glad you came." She motioned to the kitchen. "And you need to have a slice of that pie."

Luke patted her hair, pulled the blanket over her again, and stood. "I'll get a piece next time."

"Oh, it won't keep."

"So, I'll have to see you soon."

Sarah smiled. "I hope so."

Feeling a swell of emotion, Luke picked up his tool bag and walked to the door. "By the way, the high school lost one of its teachers, so I'm going to teach my first full class this fall. They're even letting me pick the books."

Sarah brightened. "I bet I know what the first book will be."

Luke smiled. "Yes. *Bury My Heart.*"

"You'll be so good for those students."

"Thanks, I hope so." He pushed the door open. "Get some rest, now."

He quietly closed the door behind him then looked back in at the couch, where Sarah's head had fallen against the blanket. "I love you, Sarah Clements."

CHAPTER FORTY-EIGHT

W HEN LUKE RETURNED TO PUT THE BATHROOM WALL back together, there was a renewed softness between he and Sarah. He was moved and saddened by the news about her disease and wanted to be supportive in any way he could. They made plans for Jason to come by the store that weekend, which he was excited about.

Luke taught him how to do minor repairs in the shop out back. Luke was impressed at what a quick study Jason was and, more importantly, thoroughly enjoyed having him around. They seemed a natural fit, often sitting out on the loading dock having a soda and talking, with Jimmy sitting between them. Though their struggles had been different, they shared challenges regarding their fathers. Their discussions seemed to comfort each other, and Jason loved having a dog to play with. On Saturdays, Jason helped Luke with his runabout, and was thrilled when Luke let him drive it.

The next summer, Luke taught Jason how to play guitar, and one Saturday night took both him and Sarah to the Bullpout for a jam session. Having lost much of her lower body strength, Sarah struggled to walk with her canes, but was happy to be there. Neither Sarah nor Jed were able to play anymore, but they sat together in a booth and kept time with the music. Sarah smiled watching Luke and Jason playing together, proud that her son seemed to have loads of natural ability.

* * *

Sarah's father retired from the bench after he was diagnosed with advanced colon cancer. Luke hadn't had much to do with him over the years, but was happy to know he ended up selling only two small lots out of his remaining shoreline, leaving the rest undeveloped. Until he passed away, no one in town knew what the judge was going to do with the rest of his lakefront property. When his will was read, however, it was revealed he had left the unspoiled land to the town of Greensboro for a nature preserve. He'd had papers drawn up which dictated it was to be left undeveloped in perpetuity.

The following summer, Sarah arrived in a handicap van because she could no longer walk and was confined to a wheelchair. One day, she asked Luke if he would take her to the new nature preserve, which neither of them had seen. Luke was delighted she felt up to it, and when they got there, he rolled her wheelchair over to a wooden path that led to the shoreline. A brass plaque was mounted on a boulder by the entrance. Luke was shocked at what the inscription said. He read it to Sarah:

"Welcome to

The Luke and Mary Simms Caspian Lake Wildlife Preserve

'The ground on which we stand is sacred ground.
It is the blood of our ancestors.'

- Chief Plenty Coups, Crow Nation"

They both stared at the plaque. "Wow," Sarah said in her weak voice.

"You didn't know?"

She shook her head. "No, but I love it."

Luke ran his fingers over the raised letters. "I'd heard about this new wildlife sanctuary, but had no idea what your father had done."

Sarah touched his leg. "My father respected you."

Luke was glad he had stood his ground on the relics they had discovered so long ago. It felt good his unwavering beliefs had made a lasting impression on the judge. "I wish I'd been able to thank him."

Sarah smiled. "As always, he did it his way. He knew you'd appreciate it."

The judge left the cabin property to Sarah. Most of the rest of the estate went to supporting her mother, who by then had been in a psychiatric nursing home for years. Dementia had taken over her mind, and Sarah, who had never meaningfully reconnected with her, had stopped visiting her years before.

In the last section of the will, Judge Clements left his law library to the Green Mountain Law School. Two valuable Persian rugs went to Vicky to replace the worn-out braided rugs in the lobby of the Greensboro Inn. Finally, he bequeathed his beloved Chris Craft runabout to Jason, who had cared for it the last year of the judge's life. The final time the judge was out on the lake, Jason took him, Sarah, and Luke for a tour around the entire shoreline, following the course of the Great Race. Luke grinned when they passed Burlington Point. Even after all those years, one of the shallow rocks still sported paint from Freddie McCormick's propeller.

Jason attended Middlebury College and graduated with honors in Environmental Studies. He took a job with the Nature Conservancy in Washington, but spent part of each summer in Greensboro, which was the highlight of both Luke and Sarah's year. She had full-time care, and Luke saw her as often as he could, except when Richard was in town. Luke and Jason built a wooden wheelchair ramp from the camp down to their dock. Often, when Sarah and Luke were alone, he would sit beside her in an Adirondack chair with Jimmy at their feet, enjoying the peace and beauty of the lake. Luke always brought a blanket, which he would carefully tuck around Sarah's legs and hips to keep her warm.

Soon, speech became more of a challenge for Sarah. She and Luke could no longer converse much, but their enduring affection for each other never waned. Sarah loved hearing about Luke's substituting at the high school, his discussions in class, and what his students were up to. Luke would often read to Sarah from *Leaves of Grass*, one of their favorite books. Whitman's beautiful, rhythmic poetry always brought a smile to her face. Often, as the sun descended behind the western shore, and he could no longer see to read, Luke would slide his hand over Sarah's and hold it while twilight emerged. If it was a warm evening, she'd want him to keep reading to her, so he would bring along a flashlight to illuminate the pages.

By the summer of 2000, Sarah had failed dramatically, both physically and mentally. Luke realized it was the last time she would be able to come up to the cabin. Even though Richard had arranged the full-time nursing care, Luke took much of the summer off so he and Sarah could spend it together. Sometimes, he would take the night shifts for the nurses, which allowed him and Sarah to enjoy being alone together.

That Labor Day weekend, Richard was sending a transport ambulance to bring Sarah back to Washington. The night before, Luke slept on Sarah's bed with her. Though she seemed only vaguely aware of his presence, he played his guitar, softly singing songs, including her favorite, "Mr. Bojangles."

The next morning, Luke gave Sarah a sponge bath and dressed her in a fresh set of soft sweats. When the ambulance arrived, he held Sarah for several minutes, feeling her heart beating strong against his chest. If only the rest of her were as strong. After the attendants carefully loaded Sarah into the ambulance, Luke crouched next to her and tucked one of her favorite blankets in around her. He took her hand in his and she tried to speak. Unable to form words, Sarah's eyes filled with tears. She tried to raise her hand to his face but was too weak.

Luke gently hugged her. "I will always love you, Sarah." He kissed her forehead. "Soulmates, forever." The corner of her lips managed a meager smile.

Standing in the driveway, Luke watched an attendant close the ambulance door, and he could no longer see Sarah. After they drove away, Luke stood silent, looking at the spot in the clearing where he had first seen Sarah sitting on the hood of her Mustang. Somehow, his heart was full, and breaking into pieces at the same time. After a while, he walked down the path to the edge of the lake. He sat in his usual Adirondack chair, watching the morning mist rise from the water. Soon, he slid his hand over the arm of his chair as if Sarah were still sitting there. Despite the pain and sorrow, he felt grateful for having been blessed with life's greatest gift.

During the fall, with Sarah no longer able to speak on the phone, it became difficult for Luke to keep in touch. He was grateful Jason gave him a call every few weeks, but as his mother failed, it became longer between updates. Luke understood it was hard for Jason to keep reporting on her worsening condition. That winter, no one came to the cabin over the deep-snowed Christmas, but Luke made sure the place was plowed, nobody broke in, and the pipes didn't freeze.

One Sunday afternoon, he was shoveling off the steps when the sun broke through the clouds, illuminating the cabin with a beautiful yellow light. He stopped working and leaned on his shovel, thinking back to when he left Sarah on those same stairs the weekend of her bachelorette party, with her girlfriend smiling in the upstairs window. In a funny sort of way, he took solace in everyone knowing how in love they were, despite their not having been able to spend their whole lives together. Ironically, through her illness, they were graced with precious time together, and Luke had cherished every moment.

Though Sarah was always on Luke's mind, there was no further communication until a letter arrived during the middle of mud season in April. It was from Richard on his law firm's official stationery. Luke sat at his antique kitchen table to read it, in the same place he had read his draft induction letter so many years before. Knowing what the letter heralded, he wished his mother was still there. Despite her physical weakness, she had a spiritual strength that always held him up when life's burdens seemed too heavy.

SMITH, BLANKENSHIP, WORTHINGTON, AND BENNETT
ATTORNEYS AT LAW

Mr. Luke Simms
39 Old County Road
Greensboro, Vermont 05841

Dear Mr. Simms, the letter began.

"Stiff old Richard," Luke said, shaking his head.

It saddens me to inform you that my wife, Sarah, passed away peacefully at home on Tuesday April 12th. Our son, Jason, was by her side until the end. The family will have a small, private service, and then her ashes will be interned at the Highland Park Mausoleum in the Georgetown Section of Washington.

Luke could feel a pause in Richard's thoughts.

I know you and Sarah meant a great deal to each other. Accepting that was the only way for us to be together, and it was more than worth it. I tried to be a responsive husband, but am not good at showing emotion, something that was discouraged in my family. However, I know Sarah needed that, and the fact that you were able to give it to her—particularly these last difficult years—is something for which I am sincerely grateful.

I wish you the best for the future.

Richard.

Richard L. Worthington, Esquire

Luke read the letter several times, carefully absorbing Richard's sentiments. It must have been as hard to write as it was to read. Though the news of Sarah's passing was deeply sad, it was not unexpected and, perhaps, a blessing in disguise.

Part of him was disappointed there was no invitation to attend Sarah's service, but Luke understood. He cringed, then chuckled about what she would think of being stuck in a cold mausoleum for eternity. Richard still didn't get her even after all these years.

For the next few days, Luke tried to go about work at the store as usual, but there was nothing usual about it. A light that he'd carried through most of his life had gone out, like the last embers of a dying campfire. The emptiness was profound. Luke didn't mention Sarah's passing to anyone, though it wasn't long before word got around. Betty came by the store late one afternoon, ostensibly to buy a new rake, but she waited around until she had Luke to herself. Standing beside a display of Vesey's Seeds, she simply said, "I'm sorry, Luke," and gave him a compassionate hug. Emotions welled as they held each other for a few moments. "Thank you for understanding, Betty," he said. She left with the rake still leaning against the counter.

* * *

Jason would be devastated by his mom's death. Luke wasn't sure where he was but hoped he'd get in touch when the time was right.

One Saturday in early May, Luke was in the garden behind the farmhouse hoeing composted manure into rich black hills for planting, when he sensed someone watching him. He looked around. Jason stood at the corner of the clapboard house. Luke dropped his hoe, and they ran toward each other, embracing at the garden gate.

"*So* good to see you," Luke said, standing back and looking at the strapping young man before him.

"Likewise," Jason said. "It's taken me a while to get myself back together. The last few months were tough."

Luke nodded. "I'm sure they were. I'm so sorry for your loss, Jason. I've been thinking about you ever since I heard."

"Thank you." Jason looked at Luke. "Mom wanted you to know how much comfort you gave her. She talked about you all the time." He pulled a greeting card out of his pocket. "Do you have a little time? I want to show you something."

"Of course, let's go inside. This garden isn't going anywhere."

They sat at the kitchen table and Luke served coffee and raspberry turnovers he'd bought at Willey's on the way home the night before.

Jason pulled a card from a familiar-looking pink envelope. "My Mom gave me this a few weeks before she died, said it was the most important letter she'd ever written. She made me promise not to read it until after she passed. Then she wanted me to share it with you in person." Jason smiled. "You'll see why."

Luke waited patiently.

"May I read it to you?"

"By all means."

Jason opened the card and cleared his voice.

Dear Son,

I guess you could call this my last will and testament, at least the only one that matters. I'm sure Richard will have me cremated and he's bound and determined to inter me in that sterile vault in Georgetown, where the rest of his stiff-upper-lip family 'rests' in cold marble squares. You know that's the farthest thing from what I want. So, I have a favor to ask. Before I get entombed in stone, I'd like you to switch out my ashes with some from our fireplace at home so you can bring the real me up to Greensboro.

Jason's voice broke, but he mustered the strength to keep going.

Please read this letter together with Luke and, if possible, on May 12th, take Luke's raft out and scatter my ashes across the surface of my beloved Caspian. It will be the time and place Luke and I first kissed on a beautiful moonlit night in 1970. I will take great pleasure and solace knowing the three of us are together again in that sacred place. You two are the true loves of my life, the beloved family of my dreams. I pray you will always keep your hearts close, as Luke and I managed to do all these years. My undying love (so to speak) to you both.

Forever more,

Mom

When Jason finished, they were silent for a time, tears trickling down their cheeks. "Wow," Luke said after a while, "that was powerful. Thank you for following through with her wishes."

"She was a beautiful spirit." Jason lay the card on the table then looked at Luke. "She loved you deeply. I hope you know that."

Luke smiled and nodded. "I do know, and it was entirely mutual."

"So, today's the day—May 12th."

"Amazing. Thirty years ago today we met. She was the most beautiful person I'd ever seen, sitting on the hood of her red Mustang."

Jason shook his head. "I wish she'd hung onto that car."

"Me, too, it was a honey. She drove it like a banshee, and boy, did your mother look hot in it."

"Alright," Jason said, chuckling, "let's not get too carried away. She was my *mother*, you know. Anyway, do you still have that old raft of yours? I remember Mom showing it to me."

"I haven't been down there in a long time. It might have floated away, or sunk, but let's go see. I'll grab a couple towels just in case."

With Sarah's ashes in a wooden box on the seat between them, they drove to the lake in Luke's pickup and fought their way through thick brambles that had overtaken the path to his special swimming place. When they made their way to the water's edge, they found the old raft wedged beneath overhanging cedars. "Will it still float?" Jason asked, looking concerned. "I'm sure Mom wanted us out on the water. She so loved it here."

"Yes. Absolutely." Luke untied a decaying rope holding the raft to a tree.

They took off their shoes, rolled up their jeans, and got in the shallow water so they could wrestle the raft from under the trees, which had grown over it. "Still pretty solid," Jason said.

"Built it when I was eleven, after my father died. It was my secret getaway."

Luke steadied the somewhat wobbly raft while Jason climbed on, and then got on himself. Though the wood was waterlogged, the raft floated enough they were able to hand-paddle a ways out from shore. "This was the spot," Luke said, as they drifted to a stop. "That day, I thought my heart was going to come clear out of my chest."

"Boy, you two had it bad for each other."

Luke looked across the placid surface. "We sure did."

For a few moments they didn't seem to know quite what to do.

"Before we do this," Jason said, "I need to share a secret Mom told me a few months ago, before she lost all speech."

"Oh? What's that?"

Jason hesitated. His chin began to quiver. He looked at Luke. "You are my *real* dad. That's why we have such a strong connection."

Luke's heart swelled. A huge smile broke across his face. "My god, that makes me so happy." He and Jason hugged each other. "I love you, Son."

They held each other tightly until the raft started to list.

"I guess it's time," Jason said, catching his balance. "We'll do this together."

Luke nodded.

Standing next to each other, they turned to the golden horizon in the west. Together, they lifted the box and opened the lid. Within a few seconds, a delicate cloud of gray and white ash swirled up into the warm summer air. Supporting each other, they watched as a soft breeze carried Sarah across the peaceful blue surface of the lake.

ACKNOWLEDGMENTS

I gratefully acknowledge the terrific first readers who toiled over the manuscript and made this a much better story: Marietta Scholten, Toby Sadkin, Phillis Mosher, Bill Schubart, and Jonathan Edwards. Thank you to my friend and consummate bass player, David Rowell, of East Craftsbury, Vermont. He not only helped me appreciate the history of the Caspian Lake region, he also gave me permission to use him and his amazing *Brassknocker* barn in the story. I also learned a great deal studying *The History of Greensboro—The First 200 Years*, published by the Greensboro, Vermont Historical Society in 1990, Susan Bartlett Weber, editor.

Appreciation goes to legendary folk singer, David Mallet, of Sebec, Maine, who allowed me to use lines from, "Somewhere in Time," for the epigraph. I must have listened to that beautiful song a hundred times during the writing of this book. I also benefited from, and used brief quotations from, Stephen Mitchell's splendid translation of Lao Tzu's *Tao te Ching*.

It takes a talented and dedicated team to bring a book to publication. I want to thank Kathy Quimby Johnson for her excellent copyediting, Carrie Cook for her lovely interior design and beautiful cover, Natalie Stultz for the author photo, and Lara Bessette for her meticulous proofreading. Also, a special thank you to my longtime editor, Lesley Kellas Payne, of Fresno, California, who read and edited an early draft of the manuscript.

Finally, very special thanks to my wife, Marietta, who has not only invested her heart and soul into multiple readings and edits of this and many other manuscripts, she also gracefully puts up with the exigencies of having a writer for a husband.

CPSIA information can be obtained
at www.ICGtesting.com
Printed in the USA
BVHW051941200623
666169BV00002B/29